After Twilight

AMANDA ASHLEY
2000 Lifetime Achievement Award Nominee
"Masquerade"

"Sensuous! Mesmerizing! Electrifying! . . . Amanda Ashley makes a dazzling debut."

—*Romantic Times* on *Embrace the Night*

"Amanda Ashley proves herself a true master of her craft."

—*NewAge Bookshelf*

CHRISTINE FEEHAN
2001 RITA Award Nominee
"Dark Dream"

"Ms. Feehan does not disappoint!"

—*Under the Covers Book Reviews*

"The exciting and multi-faceted world that impressive author Christine Feehan has created continues to improve with age."

—*Romantic Times* on *Dark Challenge*

RONDA THOMPSON
"Midnight Serenade"

"Ronda Thompson is one of those authors that you should have on your authors list."

—*Romance Communications*

"Ms. Thompson has proven herself to be a writer of distinction and power."

—*Under the Covers Book Reviews*

After Twilight

Amanda Ashley
Christine Feehan
Ronda Thompson

LOVE SPELL NEW YORK CITY

A LOVE SPELL BOOK®

September 2001

Published by

Dorchester Publishing Co., Inc.
276 Fifth Avenue
New York, NY 10001

ISBN 0-505-52450-3

Printed in the United States of America.

To Chris and Ronda for being there when I need them, and to all the sweet people on my eGroup list for their continued love and support.

For Sara . . . I love how you love your children.
Madeline . . . you know the meaning of friendship.
Ronda . . . you said yes when we asked.

A special thank you to Linda Kruger, my agent,
for being so supportive of me and my work,
and to Mandy and Christine for being wonderful
authors, nice people and great friends.

Masquerade

Amanda Ashley

MASQUERADE

See me
the man I was
before the darkness
fell upon my soul

Know me
the monster
who hides his ugliness
in the shadows
of the night

Release me
from my lonely prison
let your light drive the bitterness
from my tortured heart

Love me
free me
from this endless
masquerade

—A. Ashley

Chapter One

Los Angeles, 1993

He was a very old vampire, weary of living, weary of coming alive only in the darkness of the night.

For three hundred years he had wandered the unending road of his life alone, his existence maintained at the expense of others, until the advent of blood banks made it possible to satisfy his ever-present hunger without preying on the lives of the innocent and unsuspecting.

And yet there were times, as now, when the need to savor fresh blood taken from a living, breathing soul was overwhelming.

He stood in the dim shadows outside the Ahmanson, watching groups of happy, well-dressed people exit the theater. He listened to snatches of their conversation as they discussed the play. He had seen the show numerous times; perhaps, he thought wryly, because he could so easily sympathize with the Phantom of the Opera. Like Sir Andrew Lloyd Webber's tragic hero, he, too, was forced to live in the shadows, never to walk in the light and warmth of the sun, never able to disclose his true identity.

And so he stood on the outskirts of mortality, breathing in the fragrance of the warm-blooded creatures who passed him by. They hurried along, laughing and talking, blissfully unaware that a monster was watching. It took no effort at all to drink in the myriad smells of their humanity—a blend of perfume and sweat, shampoo and toothpaste, face powder and deodorant. He sensed their happiness, their sorrows, their deepest fears.

He waited until the crowds had thinned, and then he began to follow one of the numerous street beggars who had been hustling the theater patrons for money and cigarettes. There were hundreds, perhaps thousands, of homeless men roaming the streets of Los Angeles. On any given night, you could find a dozen or so panhandlers lingering outside the Ahmanson, hoping to score a couple of dollars that would enable them to buy a bottle of cheap booze and a few hours of forgetfulness.

A faint grimace played over his lips as he moved up behind his prey.

After tonight, there would be one less beggar haunting Hope Street.

Chapter Two

He was there again, standing on the corner of Temple and Grand, his long, angular face bathed in the hazy glow of the streetlight.

Leanne felt his hooded gaze move over her as she left the side entrance of the theater and made her way toward the parking lot across the street. Behind her, she could hear the excitement of the waiting crowd build as Davis Gaines, who many considered to be L.A.'s best Phantom, appeared at the stage door. She agreed with them. Davis had the most incredibly beautiful voice. And he was always generous with his time, signing programs, answering questions, posing for pictures. It was her dream to one day be cast in a leading role, to make her mark upon the world. To have people clamoring for her autograph.

She was unlocking her car door when she felt a hand on her shoulder. Startled, she whirled around.

It was the tall, dark man she had seen on the corner. Up close, he was taller and more handsome than she had thought. His face was made up of sharp planes and angles, totally masculine, totally mesmerizing. His hair was black and straight and fell well past his shoulders. His eyes were an intense shade of blue, deep, dark. Fathomless. She stared into his eyes and had the ridiculous yet inescapable feeling that she had been waiting her whole lifetime for this moment. For this man.

"I did not mean to frighten you," he said in a deep, resonant voice. He held out a theater program. "I was hoping you might sign this for me."

"Why on earth would you want my autograph?" she exclaimed. "I'm only in the chorus."

"Ah, but you have such a lovely voice."

She laughed softly. "You must have excellent hearing, to be able to pick my voice out of all the others."

His smile was devastating. "My hearing is quite good for a man my age."

Leanne's gaze moved over him curiously. She didn't know how old he was, of course, but he didn't appear to be much more than twenty-five or twenty-six, thirty at the most.

He offered her a Sharpie, one brow raised in question.

"Who should I make it out to?"

"Jason Blackthorne."

"Blackthorne." She gazed up at him intently. "Why does that name sound so familiar to me?"

"Does it?"

She nodded, then took the pen from his hand. "This is my first autograph, you know."

Looking over her shoulder, he read the words as she

wrote them. "To Jason, may you always have someone to love, and someone to love you. Leanne."

He felt a catch at his heart. Someone to love . . . Jolene. Leanne's resemblance to his first and only love was uncanny.

He smiled his thanks as she handed him the program, his gaze moving over her face, lingering on her mouth before moving to the pulse that beat in her throat. She was small, petite, with skin that looked as though it rarely saw the sun. Her hair was the color of sun-kissed earth; she had deep, luminous green eyes fringed with thick, dark lashes. She wore a black T-shirt with a Phantom logo, a pair of black tights that clung to her shapely legs like a second skin, and sneakers.

Jason clenched his hands at his sides as he fought the urge to draw her into his arms, to touch her lips with his own, to sip the sweet crimson nectar that flowed in her veins.

She frowned up at him as she capped the pen and handed it to him. "Is something wrong?"

"No. I was just wondering if we might go somewhere for a drink."

She knew she should say no. There were a lot of crazy people running around these days—obsessive fans, serial killers—and yet there was something in Jason Blackthorne's eyes that made her trust him implicitly.

"I know a little place not far from here," she suggested with a tentative smile.

"I'll follow you in my car," Jason said, somewhat surprised by her ready acceptance of his invitation. Didn't she read the papers? Muggings and rapes and murders were rampant in the city.

A faint smile tugged at his lips as he crossed the parking lot to his own car. Indeed, he mused as he slid behind the steering wheel, she would be far safer with one of the city's lowlifes than she was with him.

The bar was located on a narrow side street. He knew a moment's hesitation as he followed her inside, and then sighed with relief. There were no mirrors in sight.

They took a booth in the rear. She ordered a glass of red wine, as did he.

"So," Jason said, leaning back in his seat. "Tell me about yourself."

"What would you like to know?"

She felt his gaze move over her face, soft as candlelight. "Everything."

"I'm twenty-three," Leanne said, mesmerized by his gaze. "I'm an only child. My parents live in Burbank, but I have a small apartment not far from the theater." She smiled at him, a shy, intimate smile. "Someday I hope to make it to Broadway."

"Have you a boyfriend?"

"No."

You have now.

Did he speak the words aloud, or was her mind playing tricks on her, supplying the words she wished to hear?

"How long have you been with the play?"

"Two years."

"I hear it will be closing soon. What will you do then?"

"I'm not sure."

"How long have you been acting?"

"This is my first role." Leanne smiled. "I always wanted to be on stage and I decided, what the heck, why not go for it? So I tried out and they hired me." She put her elbows on the table and rested her chin on her folded hands. "What do you do?"

"I'm a cop." The lie rolled easily off his lips.

"You're kidding!" He didn't look like any police officer she had ever seen. Dressed in a loose-fitting white sweater, a pair of black jeans, and cowboy boots, he looked more like a movie star than a policeman.

One black brow lifted slightly. "I take it you don't care for the police."

"No, no, it's just that . . ." She made a dismissive gesture with her hand. "It's just that you don't look like a policeman."

"How's that?"

"No mustache." Leaning forward, she ran the tip of one finger over his upper lip. "Every cop I know has a mustache."

Jason grunted softly. "And do you know a lot of cops?"

"Not really. Where do you work?"

"Hollenbeck."

"That's a rough area."

Jason shrugged. "I like it." Their drinks had arrived during their conversation, but neither had paid much attention. Now Jason picked up his glass. "What shall we drink to?"

Leanne lifted her glass. "Long life and happiness?" she suggested.

"Happiness," he repeated softly. "I'll drink to that."

"And long life?"

His gaze was drawn to her throat, to where her pulse beat strong and steady. "Long life is not always a blessing," he said quietly, almost as though he were speaking to himself. "Sometimes it can be a curse."

"A curse! What do you mean?"

He dragged his gaze from her neck. "Just what I said. I've seen too many people who have lived past their prime, people with nothing left to live for, with nothing to hope for but a quick death, an end to pain."

"I don't agree. Life is always precious."

He leaned forward, his gaze burning into hers. "And do you think you would like to live forever?"

"I know I would." She laughed softly. "This conversation is getting too morbid for my taste. Tell me about yourself. What do you do when you aren't making the streets safe for the rest of us?"

"Nothing very exciting. Read. Watch TV. Ride my horse."

Her eyes lit up with interest. "You have a horse? Where do you keep it?"

"I have a small place up in the hills, nothing elaborate."

"Oh, I've always loved horses. Do you think . . . do you think I might be able to ride your horse sometime?"

Jason frowned. "I sleep days, so I usually ride at night."

"How romantic," she remarked, her voice suddenly low and husky. "Perhaps we could go riding together some evening."

Jason swallowed hard. Was he imagining things, or was she suggesting more than she was saying? The thought of holding her close, of having his arms around her waist, of burying his face in the wealth of her thick, dark hair, flooded him with desire. His gaze moved to the pulse throbbing in her throat once again and he glanced away lest she see the sudden heat, the hunger, that he knew was burning in his eyes.

"It's getting late," he said, tossing a handful of bills on the table. "I'd better let you go home and get some sleep."

"We don't have to go," Leanne replied, reluctant to see him leave. "I'm a bit of a night person myself."

"Then we have more in common than a love of horses," Jason replied dryly. "Perhaps we could go to a late movie tomorrow night?"

"Sounds good to me."

"I'll pick you up at the stage door."

Leanne gazed into the depths of his eyes, felt the attraction that flowed between them, an almost tangible bond, as if their souls had found each other after traveling through years of darkness.

She had been born for this man.

The thought entered her mind, quiet and unshakable, like the answer to a prayer.

Chapter Three

He fed early the next night, his eyes closing in something akin to ecstasy as he emptied a bag of whole blood into a glass, warmed it with his gaze, and slowly drained the contents, enjoying the rich, coppery, slightly salty taste of it on his tongue.

Only yesterday he had contemplated putting an end to his life. It would be so easy to terminate his existence, so easy to stand out on the terrace and watch the sun come up one last time.

So easy, but oh, so painful. He had felt the sting of the sun on his skin, known the agony of its touch on preternatural flesh. Now, as he dressed, he wondered, as he often had in the past, if he truly possessed the courage he would need to face such an excruciating death.

But it was a moot point now. He no longer wished for death. Life was new again, filled with excitement and anticipation, and all because of Leanne. Lovely Leanne. During the long hours of the day, as he slept the sleep of the dead in the basement of his house, her image had drifted across his mind. That, in itself, was strange, he thought. Never before had his rest been disturbed by images of anyone, living or dead. But even during the heat of the day, when he usually slept the deepest, he had seen her face in fragmented dreams, heard the sound of her voice, yearned for the touch of her hand.

Restless, he wandered through his house, trying to see it through her eyes. She would no doubt find it strange that there was no food in the kitchen, that there were no mirrors to be found, not even in the bathrooms. He could easily explain the security bars on the doors and windows. After all, crime was prevalent in the area. The old paintings, the ancient books and scrolls, would not be so easy to account for, not on a cop's salary.

He had collected quite a few masterpieces in the last three hundred years. Paintings thought destroyed in the wars that had ravaged France and Spain resided in the bedroom; sculptures believed to have been lost centuries ago graced his library. He had one of Shakespeare's original plays, signed by the Bard himself. His basement was crowded with ancient scrolls, with furniture and clothing from ages long past.

Perhaps he should have told her he was a retired antiques dealer. But it was far easier to tell the few people he interacted with that he was a cop, to say that he worked the graveyard shift and slept days, that he worked weekends and holidays and was therefore unable to attend the picnics and parties to which he was occasionally invited.

He paced the floor for an hour and then, unable to wait a moment longer to see her, he drove to the theater. He could have willed himself there with a thought, but he enjoyed driving, enjoyed being in control of a powerful machine.

The performance was sold out, but it was an easy task to slip past the usher, to find a place in the shadows at the back of the theater.

The play mesmerized him, as always. He had lost count of how many times he had seen it, had long ago stopped wondering what there was about the production that he found so endlessly fascinating.

Lost in the dark, he became one with the Opera Ghost, lusting after the fair Christine, knowing in the depths of his aching heart that she would never be his.

He heard the anguish in the Phantom's voice as the Phantom watched Christine find comfort in the arms of the handsome Vicomte de Chagny, felt the deformed man's pain as he cursed her.

But he had eyes only for Leanne. Her presence called to him until he was blind to everyone else on stage, until his pulse beat in time with hers. He felt her excitement as she sang her lines during "Don Juan Triumphant," felt her pleasure when the crowd applauded.

As soon as the final curtain came down, he left the theater, eager to see her again, to discover if she was truly as beautiful, as desirable, as he remembered. Surely her eyes could not be as green as those he had seen in his dreams, her skin could not be as creamy and unblemished. No lips could be so pink and well shaped; her hair could not be as long, as thick, as he recalled.

And then she was there, walking toward him, a smile

of welcome lighting her face as if they had known each other for years instead of a few hours.

She was breathtakingly beautiful in a pair of slinky black pants and a green blouse made of some soft material that clung to her, emphasizing the deep green of her eyes, outlining every delectable curve.

He felt his mouth water just looking at her.

"Shall we go?" she asked, tucking her arm through his.

"My car's in the lot," he said, and for the first time since the dark curse had been bequeathed to him, he felt young and alive.

They ran across the street.

"Is this yours?" Leanne asked when he stopped beside his car. She hadn't noticed what he was driving the night before.

Jason nodded. "Like it?"

Her gaze swept over the sleek curves of the black Porsche. "What's not to like?" She slid into the seat when he opened the car door, her hand stroking the soft leather. "You're not a cop on the take, are you?"

Jason shrugged as he slid behind the wheel and turned the key in the ignition. "No," he said, thinking quickly. "My grandfather left me quite well off."

"Then why do you work?"

"A man has to do something with his time."

They made small talk on the way to Hollywood. She told him about some of the funny things that had happened on stage, like the time the Phantom's boat went the wrong way, and the time the apple fell out of the pig's mouth, and the night the manager dropped the Phantom's opera score, and he told her about the case he was supposedly working on.

After parking the car, they walked hand in hand toward the movie theater.

Inside, they sat in the last row. Of its own volition, his hand found hers again. The touch of her fingers entwining with his sent a warm ripple of awareness surging through him, a jolt of such force that it almost took his breath away.

In the darkness, his gaze sought hers. She had felt it, too—he could see it in the slightly surprised expression in her eyes, hear it in the sudden intake of her breath. The attraction that hummed between them was electric, palpable.

Time and place were momentarily forgotten as his hand slid up her arm, across her shoulder. Cupping the back of her head, he drew her slowly toward him. She didn't resist, but came readily, her eyelids fluttering down as his mouth slanted over hers.

It was a kiss unlike any he had ever known—sweetly potent, volatile, explosive. His body's reaction to her nearness, to the scent of her perfume and the taste of her lips, to her life's essence, was instantaneous, almost painful in its intensity.

With the rise of his desire came another hunger, one that was more painful than unfulfilled passion, and far more deadly for the woman in his arms. Unable to help himself, he pressed a kiss to her throat, let his tongue caress the pulse beating there. Her skin was warm, the sweetness beneath tempting, so tempting . . .

With a low groan, he drew away.

"Jason, what's wrong?" Her voice was husky, drugged with desire.

"Nothing." He raked a hand through his hair, conscious of the people around them. "This isn't the time, or the place."

He could see her smiling at him through the darkness, her green eyes smoky with passion.

"Any time," she murmured in a breathy whisper. "Any place."

"Leanne . . ."

"I'm shameless, I know, but I can't help myself. I've never felt this way before. It's as though I've known you all my life." Her hand slid over his chest. "Waited for you all my life."

For a moment, he closed his eyes. Her words fell like sunshine on his soul. And then he smiled at her through the darkness.

"We have time, Leanne," he whispered hoarsely "All the time in the world."

He didn't remember what the movie was about as he drove her home, but it didn't matter. Nothing mattered but the connection between them, and the knowledge that he would see her again the following night. And every night after that for as long as she lived.

Chapter Four

He sat on the sofa in the living room, his feet resting on a leather hassock, his gaze fixed on the dancing flames in the raised hearth. The fire served no purpose save that he found it pleasing to look upon. He had no need of its warmth; he felt neither the heat nor the cold, but sitting in front of a fire on a cool autumn night seemed a very human thing to do. And tonight, tormented by vivid memories of his past, he had a strong desire to feel mortal again.

He had been born in a time of great superstition, when a young woman with the gift to heal might be judged a witch and burned at the stake, when country folk believed that werewolves prowled the forests in the dead of night, when restless ghosts were thought to wander the rooms of castle and hovel alike.

He had never seen a ghost and he had never put much stock in werewolves, but he had come to believe in vampires. Oh, yes, he would never forget the night he had learned about vampires.

It had been a warm summer evening, just after supper. He'd had an argument with his wife, Jolene. He could not now remember what they had quarreled about, but he had stormed out of the cottage and headed for the tavern, determined to drown his troubles in a mug of ale. He had been working his way through his third tankard when Marguerite approached him. There had been something about the way she looked at him, the way her dark eyes caressed him, that chilled him to the very marrow of his bones, and yet the look in her hell-black eyes had drawn him to her side.

Mesmerized by her dark beauty, by the husky tremor in her voice, by the come-hither look in her deep brown eyes, he had followed her upstairs. Never before had be been unfaithful to Jolene, but that night it was as if he'd had no control over his passion. And so he had followed Marguerite up the narrow wooden stairway and into a life of eternal darkness.

She had drugged him with kisses, aroused him until he had been mindless with need, and then, in the midst of their lovemaking, she had taken his blood and returned it to him. She had left him just before dawn, warning him that he would need to find a place to hide himself from the sun unless he wished that night to be his last.

He had not believed her. Until he stepped out into the light of a new day. The pain of the sun on his face had been excruciating. With a cry, he had run into the woods and taken refuge in a cave.

Trembling with pain and fear, he had lain there, unable to move, only vaguely aware of the ghastly changes taking place in his body as Marguerite's accursed blood wrought the hideous transformation.

Weak, helpless to resist, he had died that day, his body convulsing as it purged itself of useless fluids. And as the sun climbed higher in the sky, he had lain as one dead until the setting of the sun. When he awoke the following night, he had known his old life was gone.

He had sought Marguerite when he left the cave, begging her to undo the evil she had wrought upon him, but she had only laughed softly as her hand caressed his cheek.

"There is no going back, *mon amour.*"

"There must be a way!"

"None that I know, except . . ."

He had grabbed her by the arms, his fingers biting deep into her cool white flesh. "Except?"

"It is rumored among the ancient ones that there is a bloodline that has the power to transform a vampire into a mortal again, but I have no idea as to how it is done. I know only that the power is not in the blood." She shrugged, as if the whole conversation were unimportant. "That is all I know."

"Whose bloodline? Where do I find it?"

"I know not. I care not. I am happy as I am, and have no wish to be mortal again."

She had pried his fingers from her arm, then patted his cheek, much as a mother might comfort a weeping child.

"Give it time, *chéri*. One day you will bless me for what I have done."

Bless her! He would have killed her had he known how. That night, he had gone home to find Jolene frantic with worry, her beautiful face ravaged by tears.

She had been disbelieving when he told her what had happened, disbelieving until the sun came up and she had seen for herself the deathlike lethargy that held him captive in its grip.

To Jolene's credit, she hadn't turned her back on him. Although she had been repulsed by his lust for blood, by the corpselike figure that slept in the cellar by day, she had never stopped loving him. Blessed woman that she was, she had kept his secret until the day she died.

And that had been the hardest thing of all to bear, watching his beloved wife grow old and feeble while he stayed forever young and strong. Her unblemished skin had wrinkled with the passing years; her hair, once as fine as black silk, had turned white; the joy of living had gone out of her eyes, those beautiful green eyes that had ever looked on him with love. It had been torment of the worst kind, watching her body weaken and wither, watching her sicken and die. In desperation, he had offered to save her, to transform her into the horror he had become, but she had refused, and in the end, she had died in his arms, whispering his name.

In his youth, he had been zealously religious. Always, he had believed in a just and loving God. He had been faithful in his prayers, certain they were heard. But now, monster and murderer that he had become, he was cut off from the powers of heaven, unable to offer a prayer in behalf of his wife.

That night, for the first time since Marguerite had turned him into a monster, he had contemplated putting an end to his existence. Considered it and found he lacked the courage, for far worse than the thought of dying was the knowledge that, in death, he would come face to face with the Almighty and have to confess his sins.

In all the years since Jolene's death, he had kept a tight rein on his emotions, never letting anyone get close to him. He made no close friends, mortal or otherwise. Trusting one of the undead could be as dangerous to his existence as trusting the living, and so he had trusted no one, loved no one.

Until now.

He thought of Leanne, and her memory engulfed him with a warm, sustaining glow. She had brought light to his existence, given him a reason to live, pierced the protective wall he had erected around his heart, and forced him to accept the fact that he had fallen in love again.

Fallen in love with a woman who looked enough like his beloved Jolene to be her sister.

A long, slow sigh escaped his lips. He could not endure the agony of watching another woman he loved grow old and die, nor could he be responsible for giving her the Dark Gift. Leanne was a creature of sunshine. He could not condemn her to a life spent in the shadows.

And yet he could not think of facing the future without her, not now, when he had glimpsed her goodness, felt the sweet magic that had flowed between them the moment their eyes met for the first time.

He soon grew tired of meeting her after the theater and spending the evening in a darkened movie house or a smoke-filled bar, and since he dared not go to her house, which no doubt contained several mirrors, he brought her home.

Never before had he brought a woman into his

house. He bade her wait in the entry hall while he went inside and lit the candles. No doubt she would think it strange that he eschewed electric lights, but he much preferred the soft glow of candlelight to the glare of modern electricity.

Returning to the entry hall, he bowed over her hand. "Welcome to my humble home," he said, and kissed her hand in courtly fashion.

"Do you mind if I look around?" Leanne asked.

"Please," he said. "Make my home yours."

Leanne wandered through the house, enchanted by the works of art, the sculptures. Several of the paintings were signed J. Blackthorne. The signature was bold and distinctive.

"Blackthorne," she exclaimed softly. "Now I know why the name sounded so familiar. I saw one of his paintings in a museum." She turned to look at Jason, a question in her eyes.

"An ancestor," Jason said. "Prolific but mostly unappreciated."

Leanne studied the largest of the paintings. It depicted a tall man with hair as black as midnight standing alone on a cliff overlooking a turbulent sea. A long black cape billowed out behind him, buffeted by the wind. Dark gray clouds hovered above storm-tossed waves. Just looking at the painting filled her with a sense of loneliness, of emptiness.

"He was very good," she remarked.

Jason shrugged. "For his time, perhaps."

With a nod, Leanne continued her tour, ever conscious that Jason was only a step or two behind her.

The rooms were sparsely furnished, and she noticed he had only a few small table lamps, none of which he had turned on, obviously preferring the softer, more romantic glow of the candles that lit every room, even the bathrooms.

The living room was decorated in earth tones. A brown leather sofa faced the fireplace; there were two matching overstuffed chairs on either side of the hearth. A book about ancient civilizations sat on a carved oak table beside the couch. Heavy beige draperies covered the windows.

The master bedroom was decorated in muted shades of blue, and white. Standing in the doorway, she had the oddest impression that the bed had never been slept in; indeed, she had the feeling that the room had rarely been used at all. Adjoining the master bedroom was a large bathroom with a sunken tub and a skylight. There was an enormous den next to the bedroom. Two of the walls were lined with oak bookshelves that reached from floor to ceiling. She paused in front of one of the bookshelves, her gaze perusing the titles. She saw Shakespeare and Homer, Louis L'Amour and Stephen King, Tom Clancy, a collection of Anne Rice's vampire books, as well as numerous volumes on history and geography, medicine, art, literature, and folklore, many of which were written in foreign languages.

"Have you read all of these?" she asked, amazed by the quantity and variety of books. Judging by their fragile covers, many of the volumes were quite old.

"Not all," Jason replied.

Leanne smiled, thinking it would take a hundred years to read every book on the shelves.

Turning away from the bookshelves, she glanced around the room. A beautiful black marble fireplace took up most of the third wall. The fourth wall contained a large window which was covered with heavy floor-to-ceiling drapes. There was a big comfortable-looking black leather chair and an ottoman in front of the hearth.

Leaving the den, she peered into the kitchen, noting that it was stark and white. Again she was overcome with the impression that, like the bedroom, the kitchen was rarely, if ever, used. But then maybe that wasn't so strange. Jason was a bachelor, after all. Maybe he ate all his meals out.

"So," he said as they returned to the living room, "what do you think?"

"It's very nice." She made a broad gesture with her hand. "I think I like the den the best."

"Yes, it's my favorite, too."

Leanne crossed the floor to the picture window that overlooked the backyard and pulled back the heavy curtains. A full moon hovered low in the sky, bathing the grass and the outbuildings in shimmering silver.

"Is your horse here?"

"Yes."

"Could I see it?"

"If you like."

Taking her hand, he led her out the back door, down a narrow flight of steps. They followed a winding path edged with ferns and willow trees until they reached a large corral.

Jason whistled softly, and a dark shape materialized out of the shadows.

"Hello, Lucifer," he murmured, scratching the big black horse between its ears. "I've brought someone to meet you."

Leanne held out her hand, and the stallion danced away, its nostrils flaring, its eyes showing white.

"I don't think he likes me," she said, disappointment evident in her voice.

"We don't get many visitors here," Jason remarked. Slipping through the rails, he walked up to the horse and stroked its neck.

Like all animals, the stallion had been wary of him in the beginning, but Jason had used his dark power to overcome the animal's instinctive fear.

Now he vaulted lightly onto Lucifer's back and rode around the corral, guiding the stallion with the pressure of his knees.

Leanne clapped her hands in delight. "That's wonderful!" she exclaimed, charmed by the fluid grace of the horse, and the sheer masculine beauty of the man. They looked as if they had been made for each other, the devil-black horse and the raven-haired man.

Jason rode effortlessly, his body in complete harmony with the stallion's. Like a dark angel cast out of the courts of heaven, he rode bareback in the pale light of the moon.

After a few moments, he rode toward the gate and slipped the latch. Riding up to Leanne, he held out his hand.

"Don't you need a bridle or something to control him?" she asked dubiously.

"No. He responds to my voice and the pressure of my legs."

The stallion's ears twitched as Jason lifted Leanne, settling her in front of him, and then they were riding down a sloping path that led to a trail into the hills.

Jason breathed in Leanne's scent as they rode through the quiet night, the only sound that of the horse's muffled hoofbeats and the chirping of crickets.

His thighs cradled her buttocks, his arm circled her

waist, the fall of her hair brushed his cheek. He had only to lean forward to press a kiss to the side of her neck, and as he did so, the longing to sink his fangs into the soft skin behind her ear, to taste the warm rush of her blood over his tongue, rose up within him. One taste, he thought, just one small taste . . .

She leaned against him, her back pressing against his chest, her nearness sparking the embers of hunger and desire that were ever present when she was near.

"Jason?"

He grunted in response, unable to speak past the loathsome need rising hotly within him, the need to drink of her sweetness, to possess her fully.

"Could we stop here for a while?"

He glanced around. They were in a small glade surrounded by tall trees. Wordlessly, he slid over Lucifer's rump, then walked around to help Leanne dismount. His hands lingered at her waist and he drew her up against him, letting her feel the evidence of his desire, afraid she would refuse him, more afraid that she might not.

Leanne took a deep breath. It was all happening so quickly. She felt the pull of his gaze, felt herself falling helplessly in love with a man she hardly knew. A man she wanted to know better.

"Jason, tell me I'm not dreaming. Tell me that the magic between us is real and not just something I've imagined because I want it so badly."

"It's real. Never doubt that."

His eyes were dark, the blue-black before a storm. A lock of hair, as black as ink, fell across his forehead. For a moment, it seemed as if he were a part of the night itself, a dark phantom who had clothed himself in one of her daydreams and stepped out of her imagination.

Compelled by a need she never thought to question, she reached up to brush the hair from his brow, to touch his cheek. To assure herself that he was real.

"Leanne."

He murmured her name, his voice low and husky and filled with such longing, she had no thought to deny him.

She tilted her head back, eager for his kiss, her eyelids fluttering down as he bent his head toward hers.

He hesitated only a moment, battling the ancient urge to drive his fangs into her throat, to drink and drink until his damnable thirst was assuaged. Assuaged, but never quenched. Instead, he kissed her gently, careful not to bruise her tender flesh. As if she were made of fine crystal that might shatter at the slightest touch, he held her in his arms, his body basking in her warmth, in the essence of life that flowed through her.

Holding her close, he was keenly aware of the vast gulf between them. She was light and hope and innocence, children playing in the sun, lovers strolling on the beach on a hot summer day, all the things that were forever lost to him. He was the essence of darkness. It permeated his life and shrouded his soul. He groaned low in his throat, his arms tightening around her, as he sought to draw a part of her goodness into himself.

In the beginning, after he had resigned himself to Jolene's loss, to the fact that he was forever different, forever cursed, he had gloried in being a vampire. His hearing was keen, his eyesight much improved. He discovered he could cover great distances with preternatural speed. He could pass unseen through a crowd, bend another's will to his own. He had thought the taste of blood would disgust him, but it was a part of what he had become and he had learned to accept it, to relish it. What could not be changed must be endured.

In the beginning, he had not realized how long forever was. He had not understood how truly alienated he was from the rest of mankind. With the coming of awareness, he had lost himself in learning. Later, to his amazement, he had discovered that he had an aptitude for painting, and he had spent a century perfecting what talent he had. When he grew bored with painting, he had tried his hand at writing.

It had come easily to him, and he had written scores of novels, many of which he had sold. And when writing lost its appeal, he had turned into a vagabond, traveling from one end of the world to the other, but nowhere had he found a sense of home, of belonging, and so he had come to America, a land where the bizarre was taken for granted, a place where a man who shunned the daylight and lived like a recluse was not considered odd at all.

But now Leanne was here, in his arms, and for the first time in three hundred years he felt a sense of belonging. His hand stroked her hair, traced the curve of her cheek.

"Leanne," he murmured. "Can you save me, I wonder?"

She drew back, a frown furrowing her brow. "Save you?"

Only then did he realize he had spoken the words aloud.

"Save you from what?"

"Nothing." He gazed into her eyes, knowing the hunger was glowing in his own. "We'd better go back."

She didn't argue, only continued to stare up at him, her expression filled with concern and another emotion he could not quite fathom. Not fear. He knew fear when he saw it.

And then, to his surprise, she gently stroked his cheek. "Don't be afraid, Jason," she said quietly. "You're not alone anymore."

Before he could absorb the meaning of her words, a dog came charging through the trees, saliva dripping from its massive jaws.

Instantly, Jason thrust Leanne behind him, putting himself between her and the Rottweiler's slathering jaws. A sharp command kept Lucifer from bolting down the hill.

Summoning his dark power, Jason fixed his gaze on the dog. As though it had slammed into a brick wall, the Rottweiler came to an abrupt halt. Whining softly, it eyed Jason for a moment, then turned and ran down the hill, its tail between its legs.

Leanne blew out the breath she had been holding. Never had she seen anything like that in her life.

"We'd best go," Jason said, and before she had time to argue, before she had time to ask questions, he lifted her onto the back of the horse, then vaulted up effortlessly behind her and kicked the stallion into a canter.

When they reached the house, he dismounted and lifted Leanne from the back of the horse, then put the stallion into the corral and latched the gate. "Jason, that dog—"

"It's getting late." He drew her into his arms and kissed her deeply. "Would you mind if I called a taxi to take you home tonight?"

"I don't mind," she murmured, all thought of the dog forgotten in the sweet afterglow of his kiss.

He yearned to read her mind, to discover what she thought of him, but for the first time in his life, he could not bring himself to steal his way into another's thoughts.

After calling a cab, he walked her down the stairs. "Will I see you tomorrow night?" he asked.

"I'm counting on it."

He took her in his arms and held her, drinking in her nearness, her warmth, basking in her sweetness.

The taxi arrived a short time later.

"Good night, Jason. Sweet dreams."

He kissed her once more, briefly, tenderly, and then, reluctantly, he let her go. Already he could feel the coming of dawn, feel the heavy lassitude stealing over his body, draining his strength, dragging him down, down, into darkness.

His steps were heavy as he made his way down the stairs to the basement. Hollywood might insist that its vampires sleep in silk-lined coffins, but then Hollywood perpetuated a lot of myths that had no basis in fact. He had no need to rest in a coffin; indeed, he found the mere idea macabre.

Instead, he preferred to pass the long, lonely daylight hours resting in a corner of the cellar, his head and shoulders covered by a patchwork quilt similar to the one he had once shared with Jolene.

Jolene . . . he fell asleep with her name on his lips, but it was Leanna's image that carried him to sleep and kept him company until darkness spread her cloak over the land once more.

Chapter Five

He saw her almost every night after that. She arrived at his house shortly after eleven and stayed until the early hours before sunrise.

It was a routine that fit his with remarkable precision. He never had to worry about offering her food because of the lateness of the hour. An occasional cup of coffee or a glass of wine were all she ever asked for.

Often they went riding in the moonlight, sharing the quiet intimacy of the night.

Sometimes, as now, they sat on the sofa watching television. Tonight they were watching an old movie called *Love at First Bite*, which was an affectionate spoof of vampire films. A dashing George Hamilton starred as the infamous Count Dracula. Susan Saint James played the lady of his dreams.

"He's a very romantic night creature," Leanne remarked. " 'With you, never a quickie, always a longie . . .' " She grinned impishly as she quoted a line from the movie.

Jason arched one brow as he watched George Hamilton hurrying down a dark New York street moments before the coming of dawn, his black cape swirling behind him like the devil's breath. Romantic, indeed.

He caressed Leanne's cheek with the tip of his finger. "And would you let the count bite your neck if you had the chance?"

Leanne poked him playfully in the ribs. "Oh, I think I'd let the sexy Mr. Hamilton nibble on anything he liked."

"Have you ever thought of what it would be like to be a vampire?"

"Sure, who hasn't?" Leanne smiled at him, her deep green eyes dancing with laughter. "I mean, except for the blood part, the thought of living forever is very appealing, although I'm not sure I'd want to turn into a bat."

The blood. His gaze moved to the pulse in her neck. He could hear the blood moving through her veins, smell the heat of it, imagine the warmth of it on his tongue. The thought of drinking from her sickened him even as it excited him.

"And do you believe in vampires?" he asked, his voice low and seductive.

Leanne's gaze met his, all humor gone from her expression. "Yes, I do." She lifted one brow. "You look surprised."

"I am. Most people in this day and age don't believe in monsters."

"There are all kinds of monsters."

"Indeed." He glanced at the television, his stomach muscles tightening as George Hamilton enveloped Susan Saint James in the folds of his voluminous black cape to give her the final bite that would change her into a vampire.

He felt Leanne's hand on his thigh, felt his desire stir, his fangs lengthen at the thought of bestowing the Dark Gift upon her, of making her his bride. Forever.

"Is something wrong, Jason?"

He shook his head, and then, unable to keep from touching her, he drew her into his arms and kissed her.

His touch went through her like lightning, igniting every nerve ending, every sense of awareness. His tongue plundered her mouth, stealing her breath away, until she thought she might faint from the sheer pleasure of his touch. He whispered her name, his voice urgent, almost rough, as though he were in pain.

She felt his hands slide under her sweater to settle on her bare back, felt the tremors that coursed through him as his fingertips caressed her quivering flesh. His kiss deepened, taking her to places she had never been, never dreamed of. His intensity frightened her even as it excited her. He seemed to know exactly what she liked, what she wanted. What she needed.

She gasped with pleasure as she felt his teeth nip at the lobe of her ear, then nibble the side of her neck. Desire shot through her, and with it an image of darkness that went beyond black.

"Jason!" Alarmed, she drew back.

The light in his eyes burned brighter than any candle, hotter than any sun. His breathing was erratic, his lips were slightly parted. She watched him draw several deep breaths, felt the effort it cost him to release her.

"I'm sorry," he rasped. "Forgive me."

"It's all right. I'm as much to blame as you are."

"No." He couldn't keep his hands from shaking, couldn't keep his gaze from returning time and again to the pulse beating so rapidly in her throat.

Rising, he extended his hand. "Come, I'll walk you to your car."

She didn't want to go home, she wanted to stay, to spend what was left of the night in his arms, but leaving was definitely the smart thing to do.

Another moment, and she would have lost all control. Another second, and she would have given him whatever he wanted.

Hand in hand, they walked down the stairs to the driveway.

Jason opened the car door for her, kissed her cheek before she slid behind the wheel.

She closed the door, then rolled down the window and leaned out for one more kiss.

He covered her mouth with his, drinking deeply of her innocence. "Don't come here tomorrow night, or any other night," he said, and before she could ask why, he turned away, taking the stairs two at a time.

From the window in the living room, he watched her drive away, wondering if she had any idea of the danger she had been in.

She called him the following day. He had bought an answering machine at her request. The sound of her voice, asking what she had done wrong, tugged at his heart.

She called the next day, and the next, her voice filled with hurt and confusion, and then she stopped calling.

* * *

He sat in his favorite chair in front of the fireplace in the den, his hands clenched into tight fists as he listened to the soundtrack from *The Phantom of the Opera*. The haunting words of the Phantom's plaintive cry as he pleaded for Christine's love filled the room, echoing the need in Jason's heart.

The Phantom's music of the night might be a ballad of love and longing, Jason thought, but his own song was a requiem of blood and death, of darkness as deep and wide as eternity, as bottomless as the bowels of hell.

The Phantom of the Opera had lived in the darkness of life, Jason mused bitterly, but he was trapped in the everlasting darkness of his soul.

He shuddered to think how close he had come to wrapping Leanne in his embrace, to feeding his unholy hunger by stealing the essence of life from a creature who was pure and innocent.

He could not see her again. He loved her too much to put her life in danger, to risk turning her into the kind of monster he had become.

There was no hope for him, but he would not defile Leanne. She was a beautiful young woman, born to walk in the light of the sun, to find love in the arms of a mortal man and bear his children.

A hoarse cry rose in his throat, a cry that became an anguished scream of denial as he imagined her in the arms of another man, a man who could spend the day at her side, who could make love to her when the sun filled the sky, a man who didn't live his life in the shadows.

A man who didn't thirst for that which made him a thief of the worst kind, stealing the very essence of life, and sometimes life itself.

* * *

For the next week, he tormented himself by going to the theater, watching her perform on stage, hearing the sweet magic of her voice.

He listened to the Phantom's anguish with renewed pain. Just once, he thought, just once he would like to see Christine turn her back on the handsome Vicomte de Chagny and give the Phantom of the Opera the love he yearned for, the love only she could give.

When the show was over, he hovered in the deep shadows to make sure Leanne made it safely to her car. It was the worst kind of torture, seeing her from a distance, hungering for her touch, longing to hear the sound of his name on her lips.

Each night, he saw her gaze sweep the crowds waiting at the stage door, the hope in her eyes fading when she didn't see him.

And now he stood in the shadows again, a tall figure dressed all in black. Couples passed him by, never knowing he was there. Frustrated beyond reason, hating what he was because it kept him from the woman he loved, he needed every ounce of self-control he possessed to keep from destroying the innocent creatures who passed him by. He was torn with the desire to lash out, to hurt others as he was hurting.

He watched a young couple pass by, and it was all he could do to keep from sinking his fangs into the man's throat, to turn the man into a monster so that the woman at his side would look at him with loathing instead of desire.

He fought down the growing lust for blood as he saw Leanne coming down the sidewalk. She was late tonight, and he wondered what, or who, had detained her at the theater. Jealousy rose in his throat, as bitter as bile, at the thought of her with another man. A living, breathing, mortal man.

His hands curled into tight fists as he watched her cross the street. More than anything, he wanted to go to her, to take her in his arms and hold her, for just a moment. But he stayed where he was, knowing it would only cause them both pain.

His eyes narrowed as he saw three dark shadows disengage themselves from a doorway and follow her into the parking lot.

He lost sight of her as she turned the corner, and then he heard her scream.

In an instant, he was across the street, his hands closing around the throat of the thug nearest to him. The man's choked cry alerted his companions, and they whirled around to face him. One held a knife; the other a pistol.

Jason heard Leanne scream his name as the gunman fired three times in quick succession. Oblivious to the impact of the bullets, Jason lunged forward, a hand locking around the neck of each of the other two assailants. Slowly, so slowly, his fingers tightened around their throats. He would have killed them, and gladly, if Leanne had not been there. The sound of her sobs penetrated the dark red mist that hovered in front of his eyes. With a muttered curse, he let them go, and they fell in a tangled heap at his feet.

"Jason!" Leanne ran toward him, her face pale, her eyes wide with fright.

"I'm all right." His gaze moved over her in a quick assessing glance. "Did they hurt you?"

"No." She stared at the bullet holes in his coat. Unable to believe her eyes, she touched each one with her fingertips, then looked up at him, her face as pale as the moon.

Hating himself because he had to deceive her, he fixed her with his hypnotic gaze, willing her to forget that the man had fired his gun, to remember only that he had come to her rescue. He left her spellbound while he went to his car, removed his coat, and replaced it with a sweater he had left in the backseat.

Returning to her side, Jason gazed into her eyes once more, releasing her from the power of his mind.

"Come," he said, taking the keys from her hand. "I'll drive you home."

Leanne blinked up at him, then glanced at the three men sprawled on the pavement. "What about them?"

"Leave them."

"Aren't you going to arrest them?"

"No, I'm going to take you home."

"But—"

"Very well. Let's go back to the theater. We can call the police from there."

Twenty minutes later a black-and-white pulled into the parking lot. After the three suspects were handcuffed and tucked into the backseat of the patrol car, Leanne gave the officers her name and address and told them what had happened. Jason corroborated her story.

The police officer who took Jason's statement frowned as he examined the gun. "This weapon's been fired," he remarked, opening the chamber. "Three times."

"I don't remember any gunshots," Leanne said, looking from the police officer to Jason. "Do you?"

Jason shook his head. "No."

The cop scribbled something in his notebook,

thanked Leanne for her time, advised her to be more careful in the future, assured her they would get in touch with her if they had any more questions, and bade them good night.

"Now can I take you home?" Jason asked.

"I've never been so scared," Leanne whispered, and as the knowledge of what could have happened hit her, she began to tremble violently.

"It's over," Jason said, wrapping her in his arms. "Don't think about it."

"I can't help it. I know this kind of thing happens all the time, but I never thought it would happen to me."

"Give me your keys," he said. "You're in no condition to drive home."

"What about your car?" she asked.

"I'll get it tomorrow." Keeping one arm around her shoulders, he unlocked the car door and helped her inside, then went around to the driver's side.

Once he'd pulled out of the parking lot, he took her hand in his and held it tight.

"Where are we going?" Leanne asked as they turned onto the freeway.

"My place."

She didn't argue, merely rested her head against the back of the seat and closed her eyes.

When she opened them again, they were pulling into Jason's driveway.

She was still trembling when she got out of the car. "Nerves, I guess," she murmured, then gasped as Jason swung her into his arms and carried her up the stairs and into the house.

Inside, he placed her on the sofa, poured her a glass of wine, then went into the bathroom to fill the tub with hot water.

"You'll feel better after you've had a bath," he said, taking the glass from her hand.

With a nod, she went into the bathroom and shut the door. A good hot soak was just what she needed. Undressing, she sank into the tub, willing herself to relax, to forget the terror that had engulfed her. Reaching for the soap, she washed vigorously, knowing she would never wash away the fear, or the vile memory of being touched by an unwanted hand. *Thank God for Jason,* she mused, and never thought to question what he had been doing in the parking lot.

Jason stood in the living room, his keen hearing easily picking up the sounds Leanne made as she undressed and then stepped into the bathtub. It was so easy to picture her lying there, the water surrounding her, caressing her, as he so longed to do. . . .

With an oath, he threw the wineglass into the fireplace, feeling a sense of satisfaction as he watched the glass shatter, falling onto the stone hearth in a shower of crystal raindrops. If only he could destroy his accursed need with such ease.

He prowled the room, his fists shoved into the pockets of his jeans, his desire clawing at him with each step. So easy, he thought; so easy to take her, to make her his, to bind her to him forever, body and soul.

The sound of the bathroom door opening echoed in his mind like thunder.

Leanne gasped as he whirled around to face her. The heat in his eyes seemed to engulf her so that she felt suddenly hot all over, as though she were standing in front of a blazing fire.

"Feeling better?" he asked.

"Yes, thank you." She smiled at him, wondering if she had imagined the unnatural red glow in his eyes.

"Would you care for more wine?"

"No. I . . ."

"What is it?"

"Would you mind if I stayed here tonight?"

"Of course not, but you can't sleep in those clothes."

A faint flush brightened her cheeks. "I don't have anything else."

"I'll get you something."

He went into the bedroom, his gaze lingering on the bed. He had lived in this house for twenty years, he mused, and no one had ever slept in the bed. It pleased him to think of Leanne lying there, her hair spread on the pillow, her scent permeating the sheets.

Going to the dresser, he drew out a long nightgown. He had bought it because the color was the same vibrant green as her eyes; because, for one irrational moment, he had wanted to pretend he was an ordinary man buying a gift for the special lady in his life. He had bought it and put it away. Now he held it in his hands, the silkiness of the material reminding him of Leanne's satin-smooth skin.

"Is that for me?"

He turned to see that she had followed him as far as the bedroom doorway.

He lifted one brow. "What do you think?"

"I thought . . ." She lifted her chin, took a deep breath. "When you sent me away, I . . . You stopped coming to the theater; I thought you might have found someone else."

He shook his head. "There will never be anyone else, Leanne."

"Then why? Why did you send me away? Why haven't you come to see me? Did I do something wrong?"

"No." He thrust the gown into her hands, then left the room, firmly closing the door behind him. He never should have brought her here.

He stood in the living room in front of the fireplace, fighting the urge to go to her, to sweep her into his arms and satisfy the awful lust that was roaring through him, the lust to possess her, to drink and drink of her life-sustaining sweetness, and then give it back to her.

He clenched his hands into tight fists, wondering if he had the strength to continue seeing her and not possess her. He knew, at the very core of his being, that their joining would be everything he dreamed of, everything he yearned for.

It would be so easy to take her blood, to bind her to him for all eternity, and end the awful loneliness of his existence, but he recoiled at the very idea of condemning her to the kind of life he led. To do so would be the worst kind of betrayal. Leanne was youth and beauty, a child of the sun. She had brought laughter back into his life, had drawn him out of the depths of despair and given him a reason to rise in the evening. To condemn her to a life in the shadows would be the worst kind of cruelty.

He should send her away now, for her own good, before it became impossible, but even as the thought crossed his mind, he knew he would not do it. Soon, he thought; soon he would send her away, but not now, when he had just found her. He only hoped that he was strong enough to keep his accursed hunger at bay, that there was enough humanity left in him to let her go when the time came.

He felt his whole body tense as the bedroom door opened. Without looking, he knew she was standing there, watching him. He could feel her gaze on his back, feel her confusion.

"Jason?"

"Go to bed, Leanne." He had not meant the words to sound so harsh.

He sensed her hesitation, her hurt, and then, very quietly, she closed the door.

With a sigh, he dropped into his favorite chair and buried his face in his hands, hands that trembled with the need to hold her close, to feel the warmth of her in his arms, to breathe in the scent of her hair and skin. She was so full of life, so vibrant, just holding her made him feel a little alive himself. But it wasn't only her flesh that called to him, and that was why he had to let her go, before it was too late.

He didn't know how long he'd sat there, staring into nothingness, when he heard her cry out.

Chapter Six

Bolting from the chair, Jason ran into the bedroom, ready to do battle with Satan himself if need be. But there was no one in the room except Leanne, tossing restlessly on the bed.

Her hair was spread across the pillow like chocolate silk. She had thrown the covers off, and the gown's full skirt pooled around her thighs, offering him a beguiling glimpse of shapely calves.

Another cry was torn from her throat, and he saw a tear slip down her cheek.

Before he quite realized what he was doing, Jason was at her side, gathering her into his arms. "Hush, love," he murmured. "It was only a dream—a bad dream."

"Jason?"

"I'm here."

She burrowed her face into his shoulder. "It was awful," she said, her voice husky with sleep. "I was dreaming about tonight, but it was worse, much worse." She drew back, her gaze seeking his. "They shot you."

He shook his head. "No."

"Yes!" She put her hand on his chest, over his heart. "I saw it so clearly. It couldn't have been a dream."

"But it was," he said reassuringly. "Look." He lifted his shirt so she could see his chest. "You see? No bullet holes."

"But I saw it, I heard the gunshots. . . ."

He drew her head to his chest and rocked her gently. "Go back to sleep, Leanne. Everything is all right."

"Is it?" She rested her head against his chest and closed her eyes. "You feel so cold."

Unable to help himself, he pressed a kiss to the top of her head, willing her to relax, to sleep, to forget.

"I love you, Jason," she murmured drowsily. "Please don't leave me again."

He closed his eyes, her words pouring over him like hot August sunshine. She loved him.

It was a dream come true.

It was his worst nightmare.

"Promise me," she whispered. "Promise you'll never leave me."

Ah, Leanne, my love, if you only knew what you were asking of me. If you only knew how your nearness torments and tempts me. If you only knew how long forever can be.

She pulled back a little so she could see his face, her eyes searching his. "You don't love me, do you?"

He looked away, unable to bear the sight of the pain that shimmered in the depths of her eyes. Love her, he thought. If only he didn't!

A single tear slipped down her cheek. It was his undoing.

"I do love you, Leanne." The words were wrenched from the depths of his soul. "Please, do not weep. I cannot bear the sight of your tears."

"You mean it?"

"I swear it by all that I hold dear."

"Oh, Jason!" She threw her arms around his neck and kissed him, kissed him until they were both breathless.

She was fire and honey in his arms. All his senses came alive until he was drunk with the taste of her lips, the scent of her flesh, the sound of her whispered endearments. He felt his body grow hard. The need to nourish himself with the very essence of her life burned through him, as potent, as strong, as his desire for her flesh.

He groaned deep in his throat as her body molded itself to his. Her tongue laved the lobe of his ear, his neck; her hands explored the length and breadth of his back and shoulders, then boldly traced the outlines of his thighs.

"Leanne." He caught her hands in his and willed his body to relax, knowing that in another moment his desire and his lust for blood would be impossible to control.

"It's all right," she said, her eyes shining with love and trust. "I want you to make love to me."

"I can't."

"Why?"

Why, why? What possible excuse could he give her? "I don't have any . . . any . . ." Hell's bells, what did they call those things? "Any protection."

"I don't care."

He summoned a tight smile. "I do."

"I don't have any diseases, Jason," she said quietly. "I've never been with a man before."

He felt his self-control hovering on the brink of collapse. "All the more reason why we should wait."

Maybe he was right, she thought, though she couldn't help being disappointed. Her mother had always taught her that good girls didn't "do it" until they were married. Her father, a wise and solemn man blessed with the gift of sight, had warned her that if she let herself be defiled before marriage, her life would be at great risk. When she had asked him to explain, he had taken her in his arms and told her that he'd had a most disturbing vision of her future, a vision in which he had seen her surrounded by darkness and danger, protected only by her innocence. And then he had warned her that if she gave herself to the wrong man, she risked the chance of being forever cursed.

Thinking of that now, she was ashamed of her own weakness and doubly grateful for Jason's self-control.

"If I promise to behave, do you think you could stay with me until I fall asleep?"

With a nod, he drew the covers up to her chin, his expression solemn, and then he sat beside her, her hand cradled in his.

She smiled up at him and then, tucking his free hand under her cheek, she closed her eyes. He sat there, listening to the soft sound of her breathing, aware of her hand in his, of her cheek nestled in the palm of his hand. Her warm, womanly scent filled his nostrils. The steady beat of her heart made sweet music in his ears even as it teased his hunger.

It was both pain and pleasure to sit so close to her. He would have liked to stay until she woke, to be the first thing she saw when she opened her eyes, but all too soon he sensed the approach of a new day. Rising, he brushed a kiss across her lips and then, regretfully, he left the room.

In the kitchen, he wrote her a note, saying he had been called to work early and that he would see her at the theater that night. He invited her to stay as long as she liked, to take Lucifer out for a ride if she was of a mind to. He dropped the keys to her car on top of the note, and then, his steps growing heavier by the moment, he made his way down to the basement.

He closed the door behind him, slipped the bolt into place, then wrapped himself in the quilt and closed his eyes.

Leanne woke with a smile on her face. Jason loved her. She stretched, feeling as contented as a cat. He loved her.

And she couldn't wait to see him. Bounding out of bed, she hurried out of the room. She expected to find him in the kitchen, and when he wasn't there, she checked the other bedroom. It, too, was empty.

Shrugging, she went back into the kitchen. She would fix herself something to eat, shower, and then go home. It was then that she saw the note.

She read it quickly and then, clutching the slip of paper in her hand, she glanced around the kitchen. She had hoped to cook breakfast for Jason. It would have been the first time they'd spent the day together, and she wanted to spend as much time as she could with him before she had to go home and get ready for the theater.

With an effort, she shrugged off her disappointment. If she was going to be in love with a cop, this was the kind of thing she'd have to get used to. Policemen worked irregular hours. They were on call twenty-four hours a day. They missed birthday parties, and Christmas morning, and anniversaries. They worked long hours for little pay. And these days, when law officers were being maligned and criticized more than ever, a cop needed the support of his loved ones.

Crossing the floor, she opened one of the cupboards. It was empty. So was the next one, and the next. Frowning, she opened the refrigerator. Nothing.

Leanne shook her head. She could understand it if he never cooked, but she had expected him to at least have the basics in the house—coffee, sugar, salt and pepper. A loaf of bread. Margarine.

Puzzled, she went into the bedroom and opened the closet. It was reassuring, somehow, to see his clothes hanging there, to see several pairs of shoes and boots in a neat row on the floor.

After getting dressed, she wandered through the house again. There were no personal items to be found; no photos of Jason, no souvenirs or personal mementos. If not for his clothes and the hundreds of books in the den, she would wonder if this was truly his house.

With a shake of her head, she picked up her keys and left the house. He could answer her questions tonight; in the meantime, she had some shopping to do.

He felt her stirring in the house above. Even though he was trapped in the daylight sleep of death, he could feel her presence as she moved from room to room, feel her confusion when she realized there was nothing in the house to eat. He should have thought of that, but then, he hadn't planned to see her again, to bring her here again.

Leanne, Leanne. Her name whispered through the sluggishness of his mind. He yearned to go to her, but his body, held prisoner by the daylight, refused to obey.

Trapped in a web of darkness, he willed the sun to hurry across the sky.

Leanne stood in the wings, peeking out at the audience during intermission. She felt her heart skip a beat when she found him. He was sitting in the fifth row of the orchestra, center section.

How handsome he was! His dark jacket complemented his hair; the dark blue shirt brought out the color of his eyes. Her gaze moved lovingly over his face, the width of his shoulders. He seemed to be in a world apart as he sat there. People milled around, waiting for the second act to begin, laughing and talking, making their way down front to look into the orchestra pit, which really looked like a pit. It was lined in black; the musicians always wore black. She saw several girls talking to Andy, the bassoon player. He was a nice guy, funny and outgoing, and seemed to know everyone.

She took her place backstage as the houselights dimmed and the orchestra began to play the entr'acte. She was glad when the second act began. Soon, she thought; soon she would be with him again.

She was aware of Jason's gaze as she moved onstage during "Masquerade." Of all the scenes she was in, this was her favorite. She loved the costumes and the music; the humor at the beginning; the sudden change in mood as the Phantom appeared in the guise of Red

Death; the way he descended the stairs, each step, each nuance depicting power and mystery. Most of all, she loved the way he disappeared in a flash of smoke.

She never missed hearing Dale Kristien sing "Wishing You Were Somehow Here Again." But of all the songs in the play, her favorite was "Wandering Child." She wasn't sure why; knew only that it touched her deeply.

Jason sat forward, lost in the depths of the Phantom's anguish as he told Christine she must choose between himself and Raoul.

And then Christine's voice, pure and beautiful, filled the auditorium, her words of pity and compassion melting the anger and hatred in the Phantom's heart.

He felt the aching loneliness that engulfed the Phantom as he watched Christine leave the underground lair with Raoul, and Jason wondered what Leanne would do if she knew that the man she loved was truly a creature of darkness. Would she look at him with pity, the way Christine looked at the Phantom, or would she back away from him, the love in her clear green eyes turning to revulsion? Would she flee from his presence, disgusted by the memory of his kisses?

He had felt the lingering sense of her presence when he left the basement earlier that night. Her scent had filled the empty rooms of his house. Her presence had been everywhere. She had placed vases of fresh flowers on the mantel in the living room and on the table in the kitchen. There was food in the refrigerator—food that he couldn't eat, milk and soda he couldn't drink. She was fond of fruit, he noted. Melons and strawberries, apples, oranges, and peaches. He opened the cupboard, curious to see what else she had bought. He found a jar of instant coffee, a box of hot chocolate, three cans of chicken noodle soup, a box of crackers, a jar of boysenberry jam, a jar of peanut butter.

She had left her mark in the bathroom, as well. There was a bar of perfumed soap in the soap dish, a bottle of bubble bath on the sink, a lacy fern on the shelf. She had left a change of clothes on the bed in his bedroom, and a note that said she would fix him a midnight snack after the show.

He had found a rented videotape on top of the television. A mirthless grin had curved his lips when he saw the title: *Dracula* starring Frank Langella. She seemed to have a fondness for vampire movies, he mused ruefully, and, though she didn't know it, for vampires, as well.

Now, sitting in the theater, listening to the applause that thundered through the auditorium as Davis Gaines received a standing ovation, Jason forced himself to admit that, just as the Phantom had let Christine go because he loved her, so he would have to let Leanne go. He could not hide his identity from her forever, and he did not trust himself to go on seeing her without hurting her, without turning her into a creature as wretched as himself.

Just one more night, he thought. Just one more night to hold her and love her, and then he would let her go.

He lifted his gaze to the stage, focusing on her face as she stood with the other chorus members in the background. Her eyes were bright, her lips parted in a smile that was his and his alone.

Just one more night, he thought again; one night to last him for eternity.

Heavy-hearted, he left the theater and went to wait for her at the stage door.

Chapter Seven

Leanne ran up to him, bubbling with excitement. "Wasn't it great tonight?" she exclaimed. "Oh, I know, it's great *every* night, but sometimes it all seems so real, I forget it's just a play and find myself crying when the Phantom sends Christine away."

Jason nodded. He had often felt that way himself.

Leanne threw her arms around Jason and kissed him. "Did you have a good day?"

"The same as always," Jason replied, and then, seeing the expectant look in her eyes, he smiled. "Thank you for the flowers, and everything."

"I hope you don't mind."

"No." He took her hand in his and gave it a squeeze. "Let's go home."

Leanne hummed softly as they drove down the freeway, her hand resting on Jason's thigh, her gaze returning again and again to his profile. She loved the rugged masculine beauty of his face, the finely sculpted nose and lips, the strong, square jaw, dark now with the shadow of a beard. His brows were thick and black above deep blue eyes, his cheekbones pronounced.

How had she fallen in love so quickly, so completely, with this man who was still a stranger in so many ways? She hardly knew him, and yet she felt as if she had always known him, as if her life had begun the night they met.

"Jason?"

He slid a glance in her direction. "What?"

"My folks would like to meet you."

The silence that followed her remark was thick and absolute.

"Jason?"

"One day perhaps."

"How about next Sunday?"

"Leanne—"

"You don't want to, do you? Why not?"

"Surely you must have realized I'm a bit of a recluse when I'm not working."

"I know, but I'd really like for you to meet them. And for them to meet you."

"I'll consider it."

"I'm sorry." She took her hand from his thigh, then looked out the window. "I didn't mean to push you, or make you think I was trying to—"

He muttered an oath as he pulled into the driveway and turned off the ignition. Getting out of the car, he opened the door for her, then drew her into his arms.

"I'm sorry, Leanne, I didn't mean to hurt your feelings. Please, just give me some time." *Just give me to-*

night. "Come," he said, taking her hand. "I have a surprise for you."

Inside, he lit a dozen long blue tapers. "Sit down," he said. "I'll only be a moment."

With a nod, Leanne sank down on the sofa. Kicking off her shoes, she stared at the candles flickering on the mantel.

A few minutes later, Jason returned. Kneeling in front of the fireplace, he lit a fire and then joined her on the sofa.

"Here," he said, handing her a long, slender box. "This is for you."

She opened the box with hands that trembled, uttered a gasp of astonishment as she stared at the contents. "Oh, Jason, it's lovely."

"You like it, then?"

"Oh, yes." She ran her fingertip over the heavy gold chain, then outlined the filigreed heart-shaped locket. "But it must have cost a fortune."

"Only a small one." He lifted the chain from the box and fastened it around her neck. The locket settled in the cleft between her breasts. "I'm glad it pleases you."

"I love it. And I love you."

Her gaze met his, filled with such adoration that it made him want to shout, to sing. To weep. "Leanne, beloved . . ." He cupped her cheek in his hand and gently pressed his lips to hers.

"More," she whispered, and twining her arms around his neck, she kissed him passionately, her body leaning into his, inviting him to come closer.

Her nearness, the wanting he read in her eyes, made his pulse race with desire. Too fast, he thought; they were moving too fast. If he was to have only this one night, he wanted to savor every moment.

Leanne drew back, her eyes aglow. "Tell me," she whispered. "Tell me you love me."

"I love you."

"Have you loved many women?"

"No. Only one other."

"Who?"

"A girl from my childhood. She is dead now."

"Oh, I'm sorry."

"It happened a very long time ago."

He gazed into her eyes, longing to bury his hands in the wealth of her hair, to carry her to bed and sheathe himself deep within the velvet heat of her all the night long, but he dared not. He would make love to her only once, just before dawn, and then he would let her go.

It took every ounce of willpower he possessed to keep from touching her. "Shall we watch your movie?"

"If you like. Have you seen it before?"

"No."

"You'll love it."

Jumping up, she slipped the tape into the VCR, then snuggled up against Jason, her head pillowed on his shoulder.

Langella made a most convincing vampire, Jason thought. Indeed, the movie hit close to home. Too close. He felt his desire for Leanne surge through him, along with a ravening thirst, as he watched Count Dracula seduce his lady love amidst a shimmering crimson backdrop while a bat hovered in the background.

A bat. He had never changed into a bat in all his three hundred years; indeed, he didn't know if he could.

He felt his whole body tense as Dracula made a slit in his chest and offered Lucy a taste of his blood.

"I think he's the most realistic vampire I've ever seen," Leanne remarked. "I almost wish he didn't have to die in the end."

"Good always triumphs over evil, eventually," Jason remarked.

"I suppose, but he doesn't seem evil exactly," she mused. "I mean, I guess he can't help being what he is."

"No," Jason said, his voice strangely thick. "He can't."

"And he does seem to love her."

Jason gazed deeply into Leanne's eyes. "Yes, he does."

"I don't think I want to watch the end." She laughed self-consciously. "I've already seen one sad ending to-night."

"As you wish." Rising, Jason switched off the VCR. "Tell me, how does this Dracula meet his death?"

"On a ship. Dr. Van Helsing catches him on a big hook of some kind and they hoist him into the sun-light." Leanne grimaced. "I think he ages and disinte-grates into ash, but I'm not really sure. I never watch that part. All I remember is seeing his black cape slowly drifting away. It made me want to cry."

"You have a tender heart, my sweet."

"Enough about vampires and unhappy endings," Leanne murmured, reaching for him. "Make love to me, Jason."

"You are weeping now," he exclaimed softly. "Why?"

"I don't know. I feel . . . I don't know . . . as if some-thing awful is going to happen."

He knelt on the floor and drew her down into his arms. "Nothing bad is going to happen, Leanne. You're going to have a long and happy life filled with sunshine and laughter."

"I didn't know you told fortunes," she said with a sniff.

"Only yours." He cupped her face in his hands, his thumbs wiping her tears away. "You're going to marry and have half a dozen children and live happily ever after."

"Am I?"

"I promise."

"And will you be the father of my children, Jason?"

"I should like nothing better," he replied evasively, and then, to stop her from asking any more questions he couldn't answer, he kissed her.

The touch of his lips on hers, the sweet invasion of his tongue, drove all thought from Leanne's mind. She forgot her mother's admonition, forgot her father's dark warning, as Jason's lips feathered across her skin, hotter than the flames that burned in the hearth, engulfing her until she felt as though she, too, were on fire. Perhaps the heat incinerated her clothing, for she was suddenly lying naked beside him while his lips and tongue drifted over her face and neck, exploring the hollow of her throat, her navel, the valley between her breasts, the sensitive skin of her inner thighs.

With a boldness she didn't know she possessed, she stripped him of his clothing, then let her hands wander over his hard-muscled flesh. He was a study in masculine perfection, from his broad shoulders and flat belly to his long, powerful legs. She felt him shudder with pleasure at her touch, heard a low groan that sounded oddly like pain as she rained kisses along his neck and down his chest.

And then he was rising over her, his dark eyes blazing.

"Tell me to stop if you're not sure," he said, his voice low and rough. "Tell me to stop now, before it's too late."

"Don't stop." She wrapped her arms around his neck and drew him closer. "Don't ever stop."

With a strangled cry, he buried himself in her softness. She whimpered softly as he breached her virginity, and he cursed himself for hurting her, but there was no help for it, and it was too late now.

Too late to stop. Too late to think. He was caught up in an inferno of desire and there was no going back.

Leanne clutched at his shoulders, exhilarated by his mastery, frightened by the torrent of emotions that flooded through her. She felt as if she were drowning, being sucked into a swirling vortex from which there was no return. A soft, gentle blackness engulfed her, and then she felt as if she were drowning in a warm red mist.

She moaned as she felt Jason moving deep within her. Her fingernails clawed at his back, drawing blood, and then she was reaching out, reaching for something that shimmered just beyond her grasp, something elusive and beautiful.

She cried Jason's name as he gifted her with that which she sought, cried with the joy of discovery, of wonder, as her body convulsed beneath his.

For a long while, they lay wrapped in each other's arms. She held him tighter when she felt him start to draw away. "No. Don't go."

"I must be heavy."

"You are, but I like it."

He shifted to the side a little so she wasn't bearing

the full burden of his weight. "Did I hurt you?"

"No."

He drew back so he could see her face. How lovely she was, her beautiful green eyes still aglow with passion, her lips pink and swollen from his kisses, her hair spread in wild disarray over the carpet. He felt a ridiculous urge to thank her.

"What are you thinking?" Leanne asked. Reaching up, she brushed a lock of hair from his brow.

"How wonderful you are."

"You are," she replied. "Was it . . . did I please you?"

"Foolish girl, to ask such a question. No one has ever pleased me more."

"I wish you'd never known anyone but me."

He saw the hurt in her eyes, the sudden flare of jealousy, and silently berated himself because the thought of her being jealous pleased him beyond words.

He stroked her cheek with the back of his hand. "After tonight, beloved, there will never be anyone else."

"Truly?"

"Truly." Jason buried his face in her shoulder, knowing he had no wish to go on existing without her.

For three hundred years he had walked the earth, a man separate and apart, and only now, as he contemplated a future without her, did he realize the true meaning of loneliness.

Chapter Eight

He had promised himself he would make love to her only once and then let her go, only to find it was a promise he could not keep.

Selfish monster that he was, he had been helpless to keep from sampling her sweetness again and yet again, and each time he possessed her had only increased his appetite for more.

Holding Leanne in his arms, he wished he could keep the sun from rising in the morning, wished that her face, her beautiful green eyes filled with love, could be the last thing he saw before he slept, the first thing he saw upon rising.

He had made love to her as tenderly as ever a man loved a woman. Each moment he had spent in her arms had brought him the most exquisite pleasure he had ever known, and the most excruciating pain.

The lust to possess her wholly, as only a vampire

could possess a woman, pulsed through him, and only the love he had for her made it possible to keep his accursed bloodlust at bay, to touch the living warmth of her skin, to kiss and caress her, and not bury his fangs in her throat and satisfy the awful hunger that plagued him.

Still buried deep within the warmth of her body, he held her close, listening as her breathing returned to normal. She whispered that she loved him, and then, her eyelids fluttering down, she fell asleep in his arms.

So young, he thought. So trusting.

He felt his fangs lengthen as he gazed at the pulse throbbing in the hollow of her throat. The scent of her blood filled his nostrils, teasing him, tempting him beyond endurance.

One bite. One taste. Just one. Slowly, he bent over her, his tongue stroking her neck, tasting the musky heat of her skin, the salt of her perspiration.

A growl rumbled in his throat. His whole body shook as he fought the need to dip his fangs into her flesh, to swallow a single drop of her blood. Just one small drop. She need never know that a monster had sipped her sweetness.

Hating himself for his lack of self-control, he lowered his head, his teeth gently pricking the tender skin along the side of her neck. Her blood was as warm and sweet as he had so often imagined, and he hovered over her, a dark phantom torn by a driving need to take more, to stop fighting what he was and seize what he wanted, what he so desperately needed. She was his for the taking; she could be his for all eternity. . . .

She moaned softly as he brushed a kiss over the curve of her neck, and then she whispered his name.

Filled with self-loathing for what he had almost done, for what he wanted so desperately, he drew back, surprised to find that he was weeping.

"Sleep, Leanne," he whispered brokenly. "Dream your young girl's dreams. You're safe from the monster tonight."

She dreamed of darkness, a vast, overpowering darkness that shut out the light for all time. And in the heart of that darkness she saw a man with hair as black as ebony and eyes as blue as a midsummer sky. He was dressed all in black. A cloak the color of death billowed out behind him as he walked toward her, as graceful as a panther stalking its prey, but it was his gaze that captured her; mesmerizing, haunting, his deep blue eyes filled with pain and loneliness.

She should have been afraid of him, afraid of the power in his eyes. Instead, she reached out toward him. *Let me help you.*

He shook his head, and she saw that he was weeping, and his tears were the color of blood. *No one can help me*, he said, and the anguish in his voice was more than she could bear.

I'll do anything, she promised. *Anything you ask, only let me ease your sorrow.*

Anything? he asked.

Anything, she replied, and then he was upon her, his arms like steel around her as he gathered her into the enveloping folds of his cloak. His eyes blazed with an unholy light as he lowered his head toward her. She closed her eyes as his mouth covered hers in a searing kiss, and then she felt his teeth at her neck, a sharp pain, a sudden sense of lethargy.

A scream of primal terror rose in her throat, a

scream that brought her awake with a start.

Heart pounding in her breast, she sat up, reaching for Jason, only to find herself alone in the bed with no recollection of how she had gotten there. She gazed wildly around the room, but he was nowhere in sight. Through a crack in the drapes, she saw that it was dawn.

She sat there for a long moment and then, with a hand that trembled, she touched the side of her neck. Was she imagining things, or did she really feel two small puncture wounds?

Slipping out of bed, she started for the bathroom, only to stop when she remembered there was no mirror in the bathroom.

There were no mirrors anywhere in the house.

She shook her head vigorously, refusing even to consider the bizarre possibility that came to mind as she climbed back into bed and drew the covers up to her chin.

She was just letting her imagination run wild.

"Just a dream." She spoke the words aloud as she closed her eyes. "Just a dream."

Leanne stared at the reflection in her bedroom mirror, but all she saw were the two small puncture wounds in her neck. For the fifth time in as many minutes, she touched her fingertips to the tiny holes. As before, heat seemed to flow from the wounds and Jason's image danced before her eyes.

She had looked at those marks in the rearview mirror time and again as she drove home. Looked at them and shuddered. Looked at them and tried to find a logical reason for their existence.

Now, still staring into the mirror above her dresser,

she tried to laugh at the ridiculous image of Jason bending over her, his teeth turning into fangs, biting her neck. She had been watching too many vampire movies, she thought, reading too many books by Rice and Herter and Gideon. She was losing her grip on reality. The marks on her neck were probably nothing more menacing than a couple of mosquito bites.

Leaving the bedroom, she went into the kitchen, grabbed a dust rag, and began dusting the living room furniture. Her apartment had been sadly neglected since she met Jason Blackthorne.

Jason. He had been gone when she woke up. A note informed her that he had been called to court to testify in a case, but promised that he would meet her that night after the show.

She had never seen him in daytime.

She thrust the thought away, plugged in the vacuum cleaner, and ran it over the living room rug. She vacuumed the bedroom, then put the vacuum away and changed the sheets on her bed. She bundled up her laundry, carried it downstairs, and stuffed it into one of the machines, then went back upstairs to fix lunch.

She had never seen him eat.

Sitting at the table, she cradled her head in her hands. It couldn't be. For all her talk to the contrary, in her heart she didn't really believe in vampires. There had to be a logical explanation for the oddities in his life.

There had to be.

She wondered if he was still in court, and then, because she couldn't wait until after the show to see him, she grabbed her car keys and drove to his house, her laundry forgotten.

She had left his house key under a flowerpot on the

front porch. A sudden unease filled her as she unlocked the massive front door. Without thinking, she dropped the heavy brass key into the pocket of her jeans, then stepped into the entry hall. She had never before noticed how still the house was.

"Jason?"

She tossed her car keys on the small table inside the front door and walked through the house, seeing it as if for the first time. The rooms were all dark, the sunlight held at bay by the heavy drapes that covered the windows.

Remembering vampire movies she had seen, she explored every room, every closet, looking for the door that led to the room where Jason slept during the day.

She shuddered at the thought of seeing him lying in a silk-lined casket, sleeping the dreamless sleep of the undead during the hours of daylight. Unbidden, unwanted, came a rush of images as she recalled every vampire book she had ever read, every horror movie she had ever seen. All had vividly portrayed vampires as the embodiment of evil, preying on unsuspecting mortals. She felt a rush of nausea as she imagined Jason stalking some helpless woman, sinking his fangs into his victim's neck. . . .

She pressed her fingers to the marks on her own neck, shuddering as she imagined Jason biting her, drinking her blood. The thought made her gag.

With an effort, she shook the image from her mind. In the den, she paused before one of the paintings signed J. Blackthorne. Jason had told her an ancestor had painted it. She ran her fingers over the distinctive signature, and then she went into the kitchen and picked up the note Jason had left her that morning.

Returning to the den, she compared the handwriting

on the note to the signature on the painting. They were the same.

With growing certainty, she continued her search. There was a laundry room off the kitchen. And a door. A locked door. She stared at it for a long moment, and then she placed her hand against the wood and knew, without a doubt, that Jason was on the other side of the door.

Getting a chair from the kitchen, she sat down to wait.

He felt her presence in the house as soon as he awoke. He had been aware of her nearness all day, aware of the turmoil in her mind. He knew he could use the power of his mind to put her at ease, to make her forget the questions and suspicions that troubled her. But he could not do such a thing. She deserved the truth, and he would give it to her.

He shrugged the quilt off his shoulders and stood up. His feet felt weighted with lead as he climbed the narrow stairway and unlocked the door.

She would know the truth the minute she saw his face.

Leanne's heart climbed into her throat as she watched the doorknob turn and the door swing open.

"Jason."

A faintly mocking grin touched his lips as he met her gaze. "Sorry to keep you waiting so long, my sweet."

"You knew I was here?"

"Of course."

She glanced past him to the darkness beyond the doorway. "What's . . . what's down there?"

"Nothing."

"Nothing?"

"You don't believe me?" He flipped on a light switch. "Perhaps you would care to see for yourself?"

The thought of going down those stairs filled her with dread, but she had to know, had to see for herself.

Summoning every ounce of courage she possessed, she stepped past Jason and walked slowly down the stairs, wondering as she did so if she was making the biggest mistake of her life. What if he followed her? If he was truly a vampire, he wouldn't want anyone to know where he rested during the day.

She paused at the foot of the stars and looked around, but there was nothing to see, only a neatly folded patchwork quilt.

And a small mound of earth. She swallowed hard. Wasn't there some kind of vampire edict that made it mandatory for the undead to rest on the soil of their native homeland?

"What were you doing down there so long?" she asked when she returned to the laundry room.

"Sleeping."

There was no emotion in his voice, no inflection of any kind; it was merely a simple statement of fact.

"I thought—"

"You thought you'd find a coffin." He gave a slight shrug. "I tried sleeping in one once but I found it"—he paused a moment—"distasteful."

"How long have you been . . . been a . . . ?"

"Three hundred years."

It couldn't be true. She glanced around, thinking how bizarre it was to be having such an outlandish conversation in a laundry room. And even as she tried to tell herself she must be dreaming, she knew that everything she had feared was true. She felt it in her heart, saw the truth of it in his eyes.

For the first time, she noticed how pale he was. His skin was drawn tight over the planes of his face; there was a burning intensity in his eyes as he stared at her throat.

Unconsciously, she lifted a hand to her neck. "How could you keep such a secret from me?"

"How could I tell you?"

"But . . . we made love . . ." She stared at him, the horror of what she had done making her sick inside. She had made love to a man who was a . . . a monster.

The revulsion in her eyes sliced through him, and he cursed the hand of fate that had turned him into a vampire, cursed the insatiable hunger that clawed at him even now, urging him to drink from her one more time, to drink and drink until there was nothing left.

For a moment, Jason closed his eyes. Her nearness, her goodness, reached out to him. She shouldn't be here, not now, not when the urge to feed pounded relentlessly through him. The remembered taste of her blood on his lips, warm and sweet, drew a groan from deep in his throat.

She was close. Too close. Needing to put some distance between them, he went into the living room. Standing in front of the fireplace, Jason braced one arm on the mantel and stared at the ashes in the hearth. A blink of his eye brought the cold embers to life.

A sigh rose from deep within him. She knew what he was now, knew where he rested during the day, something no mortal save Jolene had ever known before. With that knowledge, Leanne held the power to destroy him . . . but it didn't matter. Losing her would destroy him as surely as the touch of the sun.

She followed him into the living room, as he had known she would, though she stayed on the far side of the room. Foolish girl, he thought; didn't she realize the danger she was in? He could be at her side between one heartbeat and the next, before she realized he had moved.

Leanne rubbed her fingertips over the two small wounds in her neck. "You did this, didn't you?"

"Yes."

A look of horror filled her eyes. "Am I—?"

"No!" He shoved his hands into his pants pockets, his fists clenching and unclenching as he fought to control the thirst raging through him. "I may be a fiend of the worst kind, but I would never condemn you to a life of darkness."

She touched the wounds in her neck again. "Then why?"

"Last night was to be our last night together." He met her gaze, begging for her understanding, her forgiveness. "I wanted to taste your sweetness just once."

Leanne stared up at him, the thought of never seeing him again suddenly more frightening than the realization that he was, indeed, a vampire. "Our last night?" she repeated tremulously.

"Yes."

His gaze lingered on the pulse throbbing in her throat for a moment before returning to her face. "You'd better go now."

Wordlessly, she continued to stare at him, her eyes filled with anguish and denial.

With preternatural speed, he crossed the floor until he was standing in front of her, his eyes blazing with an unholy light. "Go home, Leanne," he said, his voice harsh and uneven as he fought to control the rapacious hunger clawing at his vitals. "You're not safe here."

"Jason . . ."

A low growl rose in his throat as he bared his fangs. "Go home," he said again, and his voice was filled with pain and tightly leashed fury.

With a strangled cry, she turned and ran out of the room.

And out of his life.

Chapter Nine

He sat in his favorite chair in front of the fireplace in the den, staring unseeing at the flames. In his mind's eye, he saw the horror in Leanne's eyes when she'd thought he might have bequeathed her the Dark Gift and turned her into a loathsome creature such as himself. The sound of her footsteps running away, running away from what he was, echoed like a death knell in his ears.

He stared at his hands. He had not eaten for several days; his skin looked like old parchment. He knew his eyes glowed with hell's own fury, knew that soon he would either have to go to ground and lose himself in sleep or satisfy the awful craving that was eating him up inside.

An unquenchable thirst for blood.

A deep and never-ending hunger for Leanne.

Had it been only two weeks since he had held her

in his arms, tasted her sweetness, heard the sound of her laughter? Only two weeks? It seemed a lifetime.

A lifetime, Jason mused with a bitter smile. He had walked the earth for three hundred years; never had the hours and the minutes passed so slowly.

During the long lonely hours of the night, as he prowled the alleys and dark streets of the city, he seemed to hear the wind taunting him with the sound of her name. Sometimes he paused outside a house, listening to the sounds of life inside: children crying, laughing. He watched people eating, talking, arguing, sleeping. And he thought of Leanne, always Leanne, of how wonderful it would be to be mortal again, to share her life, to sit across the breakfast table from her in the morning, to make love to her in the light of day, to father a child.

He haunted the shadows outside the Ahmanson, torturing himself with glimpses of her face. He read the lingering sadness in her eyes, and he was filled with bitter regret because he knew he was the cause of her sorrow. She didn't smile anymore, and the world was the poorer because of it.

One night, driven by an uncontrollable urge to hear her voice, he had bought a ticket to the evening performance, sitting in the last row of the balcony so there would be no chance of her discovering he was there.

Oblivious to everything else, he had sat with his gaze riveted to her face, silent tears streaming down his cheeks as he listened to her sing. Her voice, while still hauntingly beautiful, lacked the enthusiasm, the *joie de vivre*, that had once set her apart from the others.

Leaving the theater that night, he had told himself she would soon get over him. She was young, so young, and they had spent such a short time together. Soon she would find someone else . . .

Now, staring into the fire's dying embers, he gripped the arms of the chair, his nails gouging long furrows in the wood as he thought of her in the arms of another man.

Rising, he went into the bedroom. Sitting on the edge of the bed, he picked up the pillow she had slept on. Closing his eyes, he took a deep breath, letting her scent engulf him. In his mind, he saw her as she had been the night they made love, her beautiful body lightly sheened with perspiration, her green eyes glowing and alive. He felt again the touch of her hands as she undressed him, recalled the way her fingers had trembled as she caressed him, bold yet innocent. He relived every moment, every touch, embracing the pain of remembering, the shattering sense of loss now that she was gone.

Into his mind came the last soulful cry of the Phantom as he stood alone in his underground lair, bidding a final farewell to the only woman he would ever love.

The urge to kill, to destroy, welled within him, growing until he could think of nothing else. Overcome with rage, he stalked out of the bedroom, his hands clenching and unclenching at his sides. With a strangled cry, he grabbed the fireplace poker, holding it so tightly it bent in his grasp as though it were made of straw.

With an oath, he flung it against the wall, then stormed out of the house, the lust for blood, the need to hurt someone as he was hurting, driving him beyond all reason.

He found his prey in a dark alley. The vagrant struggled in vain, his red-rimmed eyes growing wide as he stared into the remorseless face of death. With a low growl, Jason lowered his head to the man's throat. He smelled the malodorous stench of the drunk's unwashed body, felt the violent tremors that wracked the man as he realized he was about to die.

Unbidden, an image of Leanne rose in Jason's mind and he saw himself as she would see him, his eyes glittering with the insatiable lust for blood, his lips drawn back to expose his fangs as he prepared to drain this hapless creature of its life.

Filled with self-loathing, Jason shoved the man away and disappeared into the shadows of the night.

"Do you want to talk about it?"

Leanne glanced up, meeting Jennifer's face in the mirror. As always, Jennifer looked as if she had just stepped out of the pages of a fashion magazine. Her makeup was flawless. Her long honey blond hair framed her face like a golden halo. Unlike the rest of the cast, who usually arrived at the theater in jeans and a T-shirt, Jennifer invariably looked as if she were about to go to a Hollywood premiere. "Look like a star, be a star," she always said.

Leanne forced a smile. "Talk about what?"

"Whatever's been bothering you for the past two weeks."

"I don't know what you mean," Leanne said, and burst into tears.

Jennifer sat down on the stool beside Leanne and patted her friend's shoulder.

"It has to be man trouble," she murmured with the air of one who spoke from experience.

"Oh, Jen, you don't know the half of it."

"I've got time to listen."

Leanne plucked a tissue from the box on the dressing table and dabbed at her eyes. If only she *could* tell someone, she thought sadly; if only she could pour it all out, all the heartache, the hurt. If only . . .

"There's nothing to tell, Jen. I met a . . . a man, and I thought . . . it doesn't matter what I thought. It's over."

"But you don't want it to be over?"

"No."

"Maybe he'll change his mind."

A rueful smile tugged at Leanne's lips. It wasn't Jason's mind that was keeping them apart. "Maybe."

"Come on," Jennifer said, gaining her feet. "Let's go get a cup of coffee."

It was unusually crowded backstage that night. Some of the cast members were giving friends and family a behind-the-scenes tour, showing them the props: the huge painted elephant that was part of the first act, the boat that ferried Christine and the Phantom across the underground lake, the numerous candelabra that came up through openings in the stage floor to light the Phantom's lair, the enormous winding staircase, the trapdoor that the Phantom used during the "Masquerade" number. Later, they'd see Twin's Gym, where members of the cast and crew sometimes worked out between shows.

Near the stage door, Leanne saw Michael Piontek, who played the Vicomte de Chagny, signing autographs, and Dale Kristen, who had played the part of Christine Daaé for over four years, a role Leanne secretly yearned to play.

When they reached the street, she couldn't help glancing at the corner where she had first seen Jason. There was no one there now, and she experienced anew the pain of their separation, the awful sense of loss that had filled her heart since the night she ran out of his house.

She blinked back the tears that threatened to fall.

"Where shall we go?" Jennifer asked.

"I'm not up to it, Jen," Leanne said. "I think I'll just go home."

"Leanne—"

"Please, Jen. I need to be alone."

Jennifer laid her hand on Leanne's arm. "All right, honey, but you call me if it gets too bad, promise?"

"I promise. And thanks, Jen."

"See you Tuesday."

Leanne groaned softly. Tomorrow was Monday and the theater was dark. What would she do all day, all night, with not even a performance to help fill the lonely hours?

Shoulders sagging, she crossed the street to her car. All the magic had gone out of the play; all the joy had gone out of her singing. Jason was gone from her life, and he had taken her heart and soul with him.

Sliding behind the wheel, she drove out of the parking lot and turned down Temple Street toward the freeway.

At home, she kicked off her shoes and sank down on the sofa. For a time, she stared at nothing, and then, because the silence was too much for her, she switched on the TV.

It took a moment for the black-and-white images to register on her mind, and then she didn't know whether to laugh or cry, for there, clad in funereal black clothes and cape, was Bela Lugosi in his most famous role, that of Count Dracula.

The tears came then, burning her eyes, making her throat ache. She sobbed uncontrollably, wishing she had never gone to Jason's house that day, wishing she could have gone on loving him in blissful ignorance.

For a moment, she considered going to Jason, begging him to do whatever was necessary to change her into what he was so they could be together, but she knew she lacked the courage to face the enormity, the horror, of such a vile transformation. She didn't want to live forever if it meant she would never be able to see the sun again, never be able to jog along the beach on a bright summer day, never experience the joy and wonder of motherhood. And what about matinees? How could she play a matinee if she were a vampire?

How could she live without Jason?

Tears washed down her cheeks as she watched the movie, but it wasn't Bela Lugosi she saw walking down the long stone stairway, a flickering candle in his hand. It was Jason; Jason enveloping Mina in his cloak. How many people had he killed in the last three hundred years? In the last two weeks? Or perhaps he no longer had to kill. She remembered watching *Love at First Bite* and wondered if Jason visited the local blood bank to satisfy his thirst.

A burst of hysterical laughter bubbled to her lips. She must be going insane, she thought, comparing the reality of what Jason was to Hollywood's celluloid illusions.

Jason, Jason. Why couldn't she forget him? Why didn't she hate him? But she couldn't think of him as an evil monster, not when she remembered how tenderly he had made love to her.

Sniffing back her tears, she thought of all the hours they had spent together. Never had he done anything to hurt her; never had he treated her with anything but kindness and affection.

She lifted her hand to her neck. The tiny wounds had all but disappeared. She recalled asking him why he had bitten her, remembered the sadness in his eyes when he told her that that night was to have been their last. She knew now that he had planned to leave her because he was afraid for her, afraid of what he might do.

I wanted to taste your sweetness just once.

Burying her face in her hands, she sobbed, "Jason, help me. I can't go on like this. Please help me."

He paused in his headlong flight to nowhere as Leanne's soulful cry echoed in his ears. He felt her pain as if it were his own, felt her unhappiness, her anguish of spirit.

Closing his eyes, he pressed his forehead against the cool stone wall that ran along the alley.

Ah, Leanne, beloved, he thought, *if it gives you any solace, be assured that your pain is no greater than mine.*

Leanne. The need to see her burned strong and bright within him, and before he quite realized what he was doing, he found himself at her door.

He hesitated for the space of a heartbeat, and then he placed his hand on the latch. It was locked, but nothing as insignificant as a locked door could keep him from his heart's desire.

A wave of his hand, and the door swung open. Quiet as a shadow, he entered the apartment and closed the door behind him.

She was in the front room. Her life force drew him as surely as a beacon.

On silent feet, he followed her scent.

She was curled up in the corner of a high-backed

sofa, her head pillowed on her arms, her cheeks wet with tears.

He watched her for a long moment, and then, unable to help himself, he crossed the room and knelt on the floor in front of the sofa.

"Leanne."

Her eyelids fluttered open, and his breath caught in his throat as he waited—waited to see the horror and the loathing that would be reflected in her eyes when she saw his face.

"Jason?" She reached out to him, her hand trembling. "Tell me you're really here, that I'm not dreaming."

"I'm here if you want me to be."

"I do. Oh, I do!"

Sitting up, she threw her arms around his neck and held him tight.

With a strangled sob, he drew her down into his arms and buried his face in her hair.

For a long while, they simply sat there holding each other close.

Leanne felt the sting of tears behind her eyes. He was here, really here. It didn't matter how or why or for how long, only that he was here, holding her as if he would never let her go.

"I've missed you." She whispered the words, afraid to break the spell between them.

"No more than I've missed you."

"Truly?"

"Truly." He drew back so he could see her face. "I've felt your sadness these past two weeks. I know how unhappy you've been." He brushed her cheek with his knuckles. "I can help you, if you'll let me."

"What do you mean?"

He took a deep breath. "I can make you forget we ever met."

Her eyes grew wide, and then narrowed. "You mean hypnotize me?"

He nodded. "I've done it before."

"When?"

"Do you remember the night those men attacked you in the parking lot?"

"Of course."

"One of them had a gun. He shot me three times."

Leanne shook her head. "That's impossible."

"You saw it all. If I hadn't erased the memory from your mind, you would have started asking questions I couldn't answer." A faint smile curved his lips. "I can show you the bullet holes in my coat if you don't believe me."

She didn't want to believe him, but she knew somehow that it was true. No wonder she'd had that nightmare.

"Do you want me to make you forget that we ever met?"

He would do it if she asked, he thought bleakly, though destroying her memory of their time together would be like destroying a part of himself. And yet, he would do anything she asked of him, anything that would wipe the soul-deep sadness from her eyes.

Slowly, Leanne shook her head. "No, I don't want to forget a single moment. I want . . . I want us to go on as before."

"Leanne, you don't know what you're saying."

"Yes, I do."

Jason shook his head. "No, beloved."

"You don't want me?"

"You know that's not true."

"Then why?"

"Leanne, you think you know what I am, but you don't. There's nothing romantic about being a vampire. It's a life against nature, a life against God. I could never forgive myself if I caused you harm."

"You won't. I know you won't."

"You don't know!" He pushed her away and stood up. "I never should have come here."

"Why did you?"

"Because I needed to see you one last time. Because I heard you call me and I couldn't stay away."

Rising, she wrapped her arms around his waist and pressed her cheek against his chest.

"I love you, Jason. I couldn't bear it if you left me again."

"Leanne, you don't know how hard it is for me to hold you like this and not make you mine. You don't know how many nights I've wanted to take you in my arms and drain you of every drop of life." His gaze seemed to probe the furthest reaches of her heart and soul. "How will you feel about me if one night I can't control what I am? If I take you against your will and make you what I am?"

His words gave her pause. He saw the doubt in her eyes, recognized the fear in the sudden sharp intake of her breath.

"I never should have come here," he said again. "I'm sorry."

"Don't go, please. Stay the night with me. Just one more night."

"Leanne—"

"Please?"

He knew he should leave her, now, before it was too late, but when he opened his mouth to tell her he couldn't stay, the words wouldn't come. Instead, he bent his head and kissed her, kissed her with all the bittersweet longing that had tormented him for the past two weeks.

And when the kiss ended, she took him by the hand and led him into her bedroom. He saw it all in a quick glance: the dresser and nightstand made of burnished oak, the large oval mirror that reflected her image but not his, the double bed covered with a colorful cotton throw, the Broadway posters on the walls, the *Phantom* poster signed by the L.A. cast.

Leanne stood in the middle of the room, her heart pounding wildly in her breast as she waited for Jason to take her in his arms.

Instead, he pressed a kiss to her cheek, and when he looked at her, his eyes were filled with doubt. "Are you sure?"

She nodded, and then she reached under his shirt, letting her hand slide up and down the long line of his back. His skin was firm and cool beneath her fingertips.

With a suddenness that startled her, he swung her into his arms and covered her mouth with his, kissing her until she was breathless, weightless, until she wasn't aware of anything in all the world but the iron-hard arms that held her tight. His face blocked everything else from her vision, and she stared up into his eyes—eyes that burned with a bright blue flame.

"Jason." She whispered his name, just his name, but it conveyed all the loneliness she had felt during their separation, her anguish at the thought of never seeing him again, the deep void his absence had left in her life.

"I know," he said, his voice thick with unshed tears. "I know."

Gently he lowered her onto the bed, his hands moving over her face, lightly tracing the outline of her lips, her brows, the delicate curve of her cheek.

"Leanne, beloved . . ."

He bent to kiss her again, and yet again, knowing he could never get enough of her, knowing that, if he existed for another three hundred years, he would never love like this again.

Leanne stroked his brow. It was so good to touch him again, to know that he still cared. Their separation had not been easy for him either, she thought. There was a dark, haunted look in his eyes that had not been there before, a pain so deep it made her want to weep.

"Jason, let us go on as before."

His expression mirrored his surprise. "You can't mean that?"

"I do. I don't care that you're a . . . a . . . it doesn't matter."

"You say you don't care," he remarked quietly, "yet you cannot even say the word."

"Vampire. *Vampire!* I don't care what you are, only say you won't leave me, that you'll be a part of my life again."

"What kind of life can you have with me?" he asked in a voice filled with self-loathing. "How long will you be content to be with a man, a monster, who can never share the daylight with you, who can come to you only at night, who sometimes feeds on the living because he can't resist the urge to kill, because he can't always control his fiendish hunger, his rage?"

"I'll help you," she replied fervently. "I'll love you so completely you won't have to be angry anymore." She took a deep breath. "And if you need to take someone's blood, you can take mine."

He gazed into the depths of her eyes, eyes filled with trust and hope, and for a moment he let himself believe that such a life was possible.

Knowing it was wrong, knowing that to touch her now would only bring them both pain later on, he kissed her.

Kissed her because he loved her so much, wanted her so much. Needed her so desperately.

He began to undress her then, his hands moving reverently over her as he reacquainted himself with the gentle contours of her body, the softness of her skin.

He closed his eyes, his joy so fierce it was almost agony, as she rid him of his clothes. She explored his hard-muscled body freely, letting her fingertips glide over the width of his shoulders, down his hard, flat belly, along the length of his thighs.

His response to her touch was instant, bringing a smile to her lips and a warm glow of pleasure to her eyes. He groaned softly as he drew her up against him, the lush curves of her body filling the emptiness in his.

His mouth covered hers again in a long, hungry kiss, and he knew that if he held her and kissed her until the end of time, it would not be long enough.

Trembling with the need to merge his flesh with hers, he rose over her, wondering what miracle had brought her into his life. Surely he had done nothing to deserve her love or her trust. He was a creature of the night, a man who had been cursed, but now felt blessed beyond belief.

Her arms wrapped around him as she lifted her hips in invitation, taking him deep within herself, cherishing him, loving him, until he wanted to weep with the wonder of it. She whispered that she adored him, and her words fell on his heart like sunshine, chasing the darkness from his soul, filling him with warmth and light, making him forget, for that moment, that he was more monster than man.

He held her tight as her body convulsed beneath him, felt his self-control begin to slip as he watched the pulse that throbbed in her throat. A red mist veiled his eyes, reminding him that he wasn't a man, but a monster masquerading in human form, a fiend who had no right to love this woman.

He gazed into the depths of her eyes, eyes so like Jolene's, and into his memory came an image of his wife, her beauty fading, her health deteriorating, as time and disease ravaged her face and body while he stayed forever young. He could not endure the agony of watching Leanne grow old, he could not bear the thought that, after a few brief years, she would die and he would be alone again.

Neither could he bear the thought of being parted from her, and yet he knew that if he stayed, it would be only a matter of time before he succumbed to the awful craving for her blood, a need that even now was raging through him, as hot and fierce as his desire for her flesh.

As surely as he knew that he must shun the sunlight or perish, he knew that he would force the Dark Gift on Leanne rather than watch her die. And he knew, just as surely, that she would hate him for it forever.

Painful as it would be, it would be better to leave her now, before he did something they would both regret, before her love turned to loathing.

He held her close, listening to the soft sound of her breathing as she fell asleep in his arms.

He had always feared dying, feared the prospect of an eternity writhing in the flames of hell, but he feared it no longer.

Hell was not a place awaiting his soul, he thought in despair.

Hell would be waiting for him when he kissed her good-bye.

He held her until the last moment, until he could feel the sunrise trembling on the brink of the horizon, feel the promised heat of it.

She murmured sleepily as he drew the covers over her, then bent and kissed her one last time.

And still he lingered, imprinting her image on his mind so that he might carry it with him through all the endless days and nights of eternity.

Tomorrow night he would leave Los Angeles. It was the only way to keep from seeing her, the only way to keep her safe from the monster that dwelled within him.

Chapter Ten

He had left her again. There was no note this time, no written words of farewell.

With grim certainty, she knew he would never come back.

With equal certainty, she knew she would not let him go.

It was Monday, and there were no performances scheduled. She straightened up her apartment, wrote Jennifer a short letter which would account for her absence but explained nothing. Next, she penned a letter to her parents, telling them she loved them, saying she had met a man and they were on their way to Europe for an extended holiday.

She took a long, hot bubble bath, shaved her legs, washed her hair, and then she stood in front of the full-length mirror that hung on the back of the bathroom door, studying her face and figure, knowing that if her plans went as intended, she would never see her face in a mirror again. Wondering, in a distant part of her mind, how a woman applied eye liner and mascara without the benefit of a looking glass.

Before she could lose her courage, she ran down the stairs to the garage, got into her car, and drove to Jason's house.

She lingered on the porch, watching the sun go down in a riotous blaze of pink and lavender, crimson and amber, imprinting the image on her mind.

And then, resolutely, she turned her back on the myriad colors splashed across the sky. Taking a deep breath, she took the big brass key from her pocket and opened the heavy front door.

The inside of the house was as still as death.

Her footsteps made no sound as she made her way to the laundry room, but she was sure that the thudding of her heart could be heard as far away as Catalina.

As she had done once before, she sat down in front of the cellar door and waited for him to rise, wondering as she did so if there was some kind of vampire law that would prohibit them from sleeping together in a bed.

Her heart seemed to jump into her throat when the door swung open, and then she forgot everything else but her love for Jason, and her reason for being there.

So, he thought, he had not imagined her presence, after all.

"Leanne," he said after a lengthy silence. "Why are you here?"

"You know why." She tilted her head back, baring her throat to his gaze. "Do it, Jason. Do it now."

"No!" He turned away from her, his hands knotted into fists.

He recoiled as if in pain when her hand caressed his back.

"I love you, Jason. If you can't, or won't, try to live in my world, then I'll live in yours."

"No. No. No!" He whirled around, his eyes blazing. "How can you even consider it?"

"Because I want to be with you!" She placed her hands on his chest and gazed up at him, her eyes filled with love. "I love you. I don't want to live without you."

He drew in a deep breath and exhaled it slowly, and then he took her hands in his.

"Look at me, Leanne," he said quietly. "Take a good look. Tell me what you see."

"I see the man I love; the man I've waited for my whole life."

"No. I'm not a man, and I can't pretend to be one any longer, not even for you."

He saw the protest rise in her eyes, and he silenced her with a look. "Face it, beloved. I'm a vampire, a monster."

"No."

He lifted her hands to his mouth and kissed her palms, first one, then the other. "Go home, Leanne."

"I won't leave you, Jason. Nothing you can say will make me change my mind."

It was tempting, so tempting. He closed his eyes as he contemplated the ecstasy of bestowing the Dark Gift on her, of knowing that, as a creature of the night, she would be his forever. Never again would he be alone, his existence empty. She would bring him the sunlight he had not seen in three hundred years. He would know love and laughter, the taste of her kisses, the sound of her voice. They could travel the earth together. He could show her the wonders of the ancient world, take her to London, to Paris, to Rome. And perhaps, if he loved her enough, she would never miss the sunlight, never regret forfeiting the opportunity to bear children. . . .

He held the image close, savoring it, even though he knew it would never happen, knew he could never condemn the woman he loved to such a wretched existence. He had cursed Marguerite every night since she had bestowed the Dark Gift upon him, cursed her for his lost mortality, for the life she had stolen from him. He would not selfishly bequeath the same horrible fate to the woman he loved.

Slowly he opened his eyes, drinking in the sight of her beloved face, knowing that, after this night, he would never see her again.

"I love you, Jason." She spoke the words with the simple faith of a child, as if they could make everything all right.

"And I love you," he replied fervently.

"Then you'll stay with me forever?"

Tenderly he brushed his knuckles over her cheek. "Only death will part us, beloved."

At his words, Leanne shivered violently, as if someone had filled her veins with ice water. She knew then what he meant to do, knew it as surely as she knew the sun would rise in the morning.

"No!"

"Yesterday you asked me for one last night. Now I ask the same of you."

"Jason, you can't mean to do it. I won't let you!"

"You cannot stop me."

"I will not live without you!" She pummeled his chest

with her fists. "Do you hear me, Jason Blackthorne? I will not live without you! If you kill yourself, you'll be killing me, too."

She looked up at him, her eyes awash with pain, though only a single tear trickled down her cheek.

He watched it for a moment, and then, compelled by an urge he could neither understand nor deny, he bent down and licked the tiny drop of moisture from her cheek.

For a moment, he gazed into her eyes, and then he reeled back, his whole body on fire.

"Jason, what is it?"

He couldn't answer; he could only stare at her, the warm, salty taste of that single tear incinerating his tongue, burning through every fiber of his being like a shaft of liquid sunlight.

As from a great distance, he heard her voice sobbing his name, but he lacked the power to answer. He dropped to his hands and knees, his head hanging, his breath coming in ragged gasps.

"Go." He forced the word between clenched teeth.

"No, I won't leave you." She knelt beside him and placed her hand on his shoulder, only to jerk it away when the heat radiating from his flesh burned her palm. "What is it? What's happening?"

"Go!" With an effort, he raised his head and met her gaze. "I'm dying."

"No." She shook her head, her eyes filled with denial. "That's impossible."

"It's true." He groaned low in his throat as his body convulsed with agony. His blood was on fire, his skin seemed to be shrinking, melting. "Leave me." He took a deep, shuddering breath. "Please, Leanne, if you love me, go from here."

She was sobbing now, her tears falling to the floor, splashing like liquid fire over his hands. It grieved her to see him in such pain, to know there was nothing she could do to help him.

"Please," he implored her. "I don't want you to see . . ."

He collapsed on the floor, his body writhing in agony, folding in on itself until he lay in a fetal position, his whole body trembling.

Using the chair for support, she stood up. If he wanted her to go, she would go, but only as far as the other room.

"I love you," she whispered as she backed toward the doorway. "I'll always love you. Jason. For as long as I live. Jason."

But he was past hearing.

Chapter Eleven

Numb, she stared down at him, unable to believe he was dead. A distant part of her mind, a morbid part she hadn't even known existed, wondered why his body hadn't aged and dissolved into dust.

And then reality struck home.

Jason was dead.

Slowly she dropped to her knees beside him and cradled his head in her lap, the pain in her heart too deep for tears. Gently she smoothed the long dark hair from his brow. His skin felt warm and alive. Odd, she thought, when it had always felt cool before.

The hours passed unnoticed as she relived every moment she had spent with Jason, remembering how she had found herself looking for him outside the theater long before he had introduced himself, remembering the instant attraction between them, the way she had known, that very first night, that she could trust him.

A faint smile touched her lips as she caressed his cheek. She would have liked to walk along a sunlit beach in Hawaii with Jason at her side, to watch the sun rise over the ocean, to bear his children, to grow old beside him.

She would have liked to make love to him one more time.

With a sigh, she kissed him, and then, very gently, she lowered his head to the floor and stood up.

Feeling empty and alone, she walked out of the house.

She hesitated on the veranda, surprised to see that it was morning. She stood there a moment, her gaze caught by the fiery splendor of the sun as it climbed over the tops of the hills.

"I love you, Jason Blackthorne," she murmured, her fingertips absently stroking the heart-shaped locket he had given her. "I love you and I'll never forget you." Tears welled in her eyes. "Never."

"Never is a long time."

Leanne whirled around, her hand flying to her throat. "Jason! You're alive!"

He held out his arms, turned his hands this way and that, and then flexed his fingers, looking at them as if he had never seen them before. "So it would seem."

"But . . . but how?"

"I don't know." A wry grin tugged at his lips. "The love of a good woman, perhaps?" he mused, his finger catching a tear that hovered at the corner of her eye. "Or perhaps it was the magic of a single tear shed for a monster who yearned to be a man."

They gazed at each other for a long moment, and then Leanne threw herself into his arms and hugged him tight.

"You're alive." She ran her fingertips over his face, then spread one hand over his chest, above his heart. "Alive," she murmured again. "Thank God."

He looked deep into her eyes, and then he smiled, a beautiful smile that went straight to her heart.

Lowering his head, he teased her lips with the tip of his tongue, and then he kissed her as gently as ever a man had kissed a woman, and it seemed he could taste the sunrise on her lips.

"Leanne," he murmured. "Do you think you could love this mortal man as much as you once loved the monster?"

"Oh, yes," she exclaimed softly, and the glow in her eyes was warmer and brighter than the sun he had thought never to see again.

His smile grew wider. "And do you think you could make love to me now, here, in the light of day?"

Happiness bubbled up inside her. "I think so," she replied in a voice trembling with love and joy and excitement.

"And will you spend the rest of your life with me? Bear my children if a merciful God permits? Grow old at my side?"

"Yes," she promised fervently. "Oh, yes."

Jason sighed as he wrapped his arm around Leanne's shoulders and drew her close to his side. Together, they watched as the sun rose above the distant mountains, heralding the birth of a new day, a new beginning.

It was a day of miracles, he thought, and Leanne's love was the greatest miracle of all.

She had been the sun in his sky since the first night he had seen her emerge from the theater.

Now standing beside her, with the sunlight on his face and the warmth of her love shining in the depths of her eyes, he knew he would never dwell in darkness again.

Epilogue

Five years later

Jason leaned forward as his daughter made her entrance on stage. Facing the audience, Kristi Lynn began to sing, her voice pure and clear.

His daughter. Another miracle that Leanne had wrought in his life. And soon they would have a second child. And after that, a dozen more, if God and his wife were willing.

"She's wonderful, isn't she?" Leanne whispered.

"Indeed," he said. "She has her mother's talent."

Leanne grinned at him. "And her father's charm."

Jason took her hand in his and gave it a squeeze. The last five years had been the happiest he had ever known. He had stood beside Leanne and watched the sun rise over the Grand Canyon, sat beside her on a sandy white beach in Hawaii and watched the waves lap at the shore. He grinned at the memory. He had sat there so long he'd gotten one hell of a sunburn. But even that had felt good.

He had watched Leanne's body swell with new life, stood at her side the morning Kristi Lynn had been born, felt his heart swell with awe when the doctor had placed his daughter in his arms. He had been there when she took her first steps, said her first word; ran alongside her the day she had learned to ride a bike.

He had turned to writing again, surprised and pleased when he sold his first book, a novel about a vampire. He had written three others since then, each of which had received rave reviews. His favorite hung on the wall behind his desk. *"Jason Blackthorne's vampires are so real, so vivid, one would think he drew on personal experience."*

He applauded loudly when Kristi Lynn finished her song.

Later that night, standing beside his daughter's bed while Leanne tucked her in, he thanked a generous, forgiving God for granting him a second chance at life.

Dark Dream

Christine Feehan

Prologue

The night was black, the moon and stars blotted out by ominous swirling clouds gathering overhead. Threads of shiny black obsidian spun and whirled in a kind of fury, yet the wind was still. Small animals huddled in their dens, beneath rocks and fallen logs, scenting the mood of the land.

Mists floated eerily out of the forest, clinging to the tree trunks so that they seemed to rise up out the fog. Long, wide bands of shimmering white. Swirling prisms of glittering opaque colors. Gliding across the sky, weaving in and out of the overhead canopy, a large owl circled the great stone house built into the high cliffs. A second owl, then a third appeared, silently making lazy circles above the branches and the rambling house. A lone wolf, quite large, with a shaggy black coat and glittering eyes, loped out of the trees into the clearing.

Out of the darkness, on the balcony of the rock house, a figure glided forward, looking out into the night. He opened his arms wide in a welcoming gesture. At once the wind began to move, a soft, gentle breeze. Insects took up their nightly chorus. Branches swayed and danced. The mist thickened and shimmered, forming many figures in the eerie night. The owls settled, one on the ground, two on the balcony railing, shape-shifting as they did, the feathers melting into skin, wings expanding into arms. The wolf was contorting even as it leaped onto the porch, shifting easily on the run so that a man landed, solid and whole.

"Welcome." The voice was beautiful, melodious, a sorcerer's weapon. Vladimir Dubrinsky, Prince of the Carpathian people, watched in sorrow as his loyal kindred materialized from the mist, from the raptors and wolves, into strong, handsome warriors. Fighters every one. Loyal men. True. Selfless. These were his volunteers. These were the men he was sending to their death. He was sentencing each of them to centuries of unbearable loneliness, of unrelenting bleakness. They would live out their long lives until each moment was beyond endurance. They would be far from home, far from their kin, far from the soothing, healing soil of their homeland. They would know no hope, have nothing but their honor to aid them in the coming centuries.

His heart was so heavy, Vladimir thought it would break in two. Warmth seeped into the cold of his body, and he felt her stirring in his mind. Sarantha. His lifemate. Of course she would share this moment, his darkest hour, as he sent these young men to their horrendous fate.

They gathered around him, silent, their faces serious—good faces, handsome, sensual, strong. The unblinking, steady eyes of confident men, men who were tried and true, men who had seen hundreds of battles. So many of his best. The wrenching in Vladimir's body was physical, a fierce burning in his heart and soul. Deep. Pitiless. These men deserved so much more than the ugly life he must give them. He took a breath, let it out slowly. He had the great and terrible gift of precognition. He saw the desperate plight of his people. He had no real choice and could only trust in God to be merciful as he could not afford to be.

"I thank all of you. You have not been commanded but have come voluntarily, the guardians of our people. Each of you has made the choice to give up your chance at life to ensure that our people are safe, that other species in the world are safe. You humble me with your generosity, and I am honored to call you my brethren, my kin."

There was complete silence. The Prince's sorrow weighed like a stone in his heart, and, sharing his mind, the warriors caught a glimpse of the enormity of his pain. The wind moved gently through the crowd, ruffled hair with the touch of a father's hand, gently, lovingly, brushed a shoulder, an arm.

His voice, when it came again, was achingly beautiful. "I have seen the fall of our people. Our women grow fewer. We do not know why female children are not born to our couples, but fewer are conceived than ever before, and even fewer live. It is becoming much more difficult to keep our children alive, male or female. The scarcity of our women has grown to crisis point. Our males are turning vampire, and the evil is spreading across the land faster than our hunters can keep up. Before, in lands far from us, the lycanthroscope and the Jaguar race were strong enough to keep these monsters under control, but their numbers have dwindled and they cannot stem the tide. Our world is changing, and we must meet the new problems head on."

He stopped, once again looking over their faces. Loyalty and honor ran deep in their blood. He knew each of them by name, knew each of their strengths and weaknesses. They should have been the future of his species, but he was sending them to walk a solitary path of unrelenting hardship.

"All of you must know these things I am about to tell you. Each of you weigh your decision one last time before you are assigned a land to guard. Where you are going there are none of our women. Your lives will consist of hunting and destroying the vampire in the lands where I send you. There will be none of your countrymen to aid you, to be companions, other than those I send with you. There will be no healing Carpathian soil to offer comfort when you are wounded in your battles. Each kill will bring you closer to the edge of the worst possible fate. The demon within will rage and fight you for control. You will be obliged to hang on as long as you are able, and then, before it is too late, before the demon finds and claims you, you must terminate your life. Plagues and hardships will sweep these lands, wars are inevitable, and I have seen my own death and the death of our women and children. The death of mortals and immortals alike."

That brought the first stirring among the men, a protest unspoken but rather of the mind, a collective objection that swept through their linked minds. Vladimir held up his hand. "There will be much sorrow before our time is finished. Those coming after us will be without hope, without the knowledge, even, of what our world has been and what a lifemate is to us. Theirs will be a much more difficult existence. We must do all that we can to ensure that mortals and immortals alike are as safe as possible." His eyes moved over their faces, settled on two that looked alike.

Lucian and Gabriel. Twins. Children of his own second in command. Already they were working tirelessly to remove all that was evil from their world. "I knew that you would volunteer. The danger to our homeland and our people is as great as the danger to the outside world. I must ask that you stay here where the fight will be brother against brother and friend against friend. Without you to guard our people, we will fall. You must stay here, in these lands, and guard our soil until such time as you perceive you are needed elsewhere."

Neither twin attempted to argue with the Prince. His word was law, and it was a measure of his people's respect and love that they obeyed him without question. Lucian and Gabriel exchanged one long look. If they spoke on their private mental path, they didn't share their thoughts with any other. They simply nodded their heads in unison, in agreement with their Prince's decision.

The Prince turned, his black eyes piercing, probing, searching the hearts and minds of his warriors. "In the jungles and forests of far off lands the great Jaguar have begun to decline. The Jaguar are a powerful people with many gifts, great psychic talents, but they are solitary creatures. The men find and mate with the women then leave them and the young to fend for themselves. The Jaguar men are secretive, refusing to come out of the jungles and mingle with humans. They prefer that the superstitious revere them as deities. The women have naturally turned to those who would love them and care for them, see them as the treasures they are. They have, for some time, been mating with human men and living as humans. Their bloodlines have been weakened; fewer and fewer exist in their true form. Within a hundred years, perhaps two hundred, this race will cease to exist. They lose their women because they know not what is precious and important. We have lost ours through nature itself." The black eyes moved over a tall, handsome warrior, one whose father had fought beside the Prince for centuries and had died at the hands of a master vampire.

The warrior was tall and straight with wide shoulders and flowing black hair. A true and relentless hunter, one of so many he would be sentencing to an ugly existence this night. This fighter had been proven many times over in battle, was loyal and unswerving in his duties. He would be one of the few sent out alone, while the others would go in groups or pairs to aid one another. Vlad sighed heavily and forced himself to give the orders. He leaned respectfully toward the warrior he was addressing, but spoke loudly enough for all to hear.

"You will go to this land and rid the world of the monsters our males have chosen to become. You must avoid all confrontation with the Jaguar. Their species, as ours must, will either find a way to join the world or become extinct like so many others before us. You will not engage them in battle. Leave them to their own devices. Avoid the werewolf as best you can. They are, like us, struggling to survive in a changing world. I give you my blessing, the love and thanks of our people, and may God go with you into the night, into your new land. You must embrace this land, make it your own, make it your home.

"After I have gone, my son will take my place. He will be young and inexperienced, and he will find it difficult to rule our people in troubled times. I will not tell him of those I have sent out into the world as guardians. He cannot rely on those much older than he. He must have complete faith in his ability to guide our people on his own. Remember who you are and what you are: guardians of our people. You stand, the last line of defense to keep innocent blood from being spilled."

Vladimir looked directly into the gaze of the young warrior. "Do you take this task of your own free will? You must decide. None will think the less of any who wish to remain. The war here will also be long and difficult."

The warrior's eyes were steady on the Prince. Slowly he nodded acceptance of his fate. In that moment his life was changed for all time. He would live in a foreign land without the hope of love or family. Without emotion or color, without light to illuminate the unrelenting darkness. He would never know a lifemate, but would spend his entire existence hunting and destroying the undead.

Chapter One

Present Day

The streets were filthy and smelled of decay and waste. The dreary drizzle of rain could not possibly dispel the offensive odor. Trash littered the entrances to run-down, crumbling buildings. Ragged shelters of card-board and tin were stacked in every alleyway, every conceivable place, tiny cubicles for bodies with no-where else to go. Rats scurried through the garbage cans and gutters, prowled through the basements and walls. Falcon moved through the shadows silently, watchful, aware of the seething life in the underbelly of the city. This was where the dregs of humanity lived, the homeless, the drunks, the predators who preyed on the helpless and unwary. He knew that eyes were watching him as he made his way along the streets, slipping from shadow to shadow. They couldn't make him out, his body fluid, blending, a part of the night.

It was a scene that had been played out a thousand times, in a thousand places. He was weary of the predictability of human nature.

Falcon was making his way back to his homeland. For far too many centuries he had been utterly alone. He had grown in power, had grown in strength. The beast within him had grown in strength and power also, roaring for release continually, demanding blood. Demanding the kill. Demanding just once, for one moment, to *feel*. He wanted to go home, to feel the soil soak into his pores, to look upon the Prince of his people and know he had fulfilled his word of honor. Know that the sacrifices he had made had counted for something. He had heard the rumors of a new hope for his people.

Falcon accepted that it was too late for him, but he wanted to know, before his life was over, that there was hope for other males, that his life had counted for something. He wanted to see with his own eyes the Prince's lifemate, a human woman who had been successfully converted. He had seen too much death, too much evil. Before ending his existence, he needed to look upon something pure and good and see the reason he had battled for so many long centuries.

His eyes glittered with a strange red flame, shining in the night as he moved silently through the filthy streets. Falcon was uncertain whether he would make it back to his homeland, but he was determined to try. He had waited far too long, was already bordering on madness. He had little time left, for the darkness had nearly consumed his soul. He could feel the danger with every step he took. Not emanating from the dirty streets and shadowed buildings, but from deep within his own body.

He heard a sound, like the soft shuffle of feet. Falcon

continued walking, praying as he did so for the salvation of his own soul. He had need of sustenance and he was at his most vulnerable. The beast was roaring with eagerness, claws barely sheathed. Within his mouth his fangs began to lengthen in anticipation. He was careful now to hunt among the guilty, not wanting innocent blood should he be unable to turn away from the dark call to his soul. The sound alerted him again, this time many soft feet, many whispering voices. A conspiracy of children. They came running toward him from the three-story hulk of a building, a swarm of them, rushing toward him like a plague of bees. They called out for food, for money.

The children surrounded him, a half dozen of them, all sizes, their tiny hands slipping under his cloak and cleverly into his pockets as they patted him, their voices pleading and begging. The young ones. Children. His species rarely could keep their sons and daughters alive beyond the first year. So few made it, and yet these children, as precious as they were, had no one to cherish them. Three were female with enormous, sad eyes. They wore torn, ragged clothing and had dirt smeared across bruised little faces. He could hear the fear in their pounding hearts as they begged for food, for money, for any little scrap. Each expected blows and rebuffs from him and was ready to dodge away at the first sign of aggression.

Falcon patted a head gently and murmured a soft word of regret. He had no need of the wealth he had acquired during his long lifetime. This would have been the place for it, yet he had brought nothing with him. He slept in the ground and hunted live prey. He had no need of money where he was going. The children all seemed to be talking at once, an assault on his ears, when a low whistle stopped them abruptly. There was instant silence. The children whirled around and simply melted into the shadows, into the recesses of the dilapidated and condemned buildings as if they had never been.

The whistle was very low, very soft, yet he heard it clearly through the rain and darkness. It carried on the wind straight to his ears. The sound was intriguing. The tone seemed to be pitched just for him. A warning, perhaps, for the children, but for him it was a temptation, a seduction of his senses. It threw him, that soft little whistle. It intrigued him. It drew his attention as nothing had in the past several hundred years. He could almost see the notes dancing in the rain-wet air. The sound slipped past his guard and found its way into his body, like an arrow aimed straight for his heart.

Another noise intruded. This time it was the tread of boots. He knew what was coming now, the thugs of the street. The bullies who believed they owned the turf, and anyone who dared to walk in their territory had to pay a price. They were looking at the cut of his clothes, the fit of his silk shirt beneath the richly lined cape, and they were drawn into his trap just as he'd known they would be. It was always the same. In every land. Every city. Every decade. There were always the packs who ran together bent on destruction or wanting the right to take what did not belong to them. The incisors in his mouth once more began to lengthen.

His heart was beating faster than normal, a phenomenon that intrigued him. His heart was always the same, rock steady. He controlled it casually, easily, as he controlled every aspect of his body, but the racing of his heart now was unusual, and anything different was welcome. These men, taking their places to surround him, would not die at his hands this night. They would escape from the ultimate predator and his soul would remain intact because of two things: that soft whistle and his accelerated heartbeat.

An odd, misshapen figure emerged from a doorway straight in front of him. "Run for it, mister." The voice was low, husky, the warning clear. The strange, lumpy shape immediately melted back and blended into some hidden cranny. .

Falcon stopped walking. Everything in him went completely, utterly still. He had not seen color in nearly two thousand years, yet he was staring at an appalling shade of red paint peeling from the remnants of a building. It was impossible, not real. Perhaps he was losing his mind as well as his soul. No one had told him that a preliminary to losing his soul was to see in color. The undead would have bragged of such a feat. He took a step toward the building where the owner of that voice had disappeared.

It was too late. The robbers were spreading out in a loose semicircle around him. They were large, many of them displaying weapons to intimidate. He saw the gleam of a knife, a long-handled club. They wanted him scared and ready to hand over his wallet. It wouldn't end there. He had witnessed this same scenario too many times not to know what to expect. Any other time he would have been a beast whirling in their midst, feeding on them until the aching hunger was assuaged. Tonight was different. It was nearly disorienting. Instead of seeing bland gray, Falcon could see them in vivid color, blue and purple shirts, one an atrocious orange.

Everything seemed vivid. His hearing was even more acute than usual. The dazzling raindrops were threads of glittering silver. Falcon inhaled the night, taking in the scents, separating each until he found the one he was looking for. That slight misshapen figure was not a male, but a female. And that woman had already changed his life for all time.

The men were close now, the leader calling out to him, "Throw me your wallet." There was no pretending, no preliminary. They were going to get straight down to the business of robbing, of murdering. Falcon raised his head slowly until his fiery gaze met the leader's cocky stare. The man's smile faltered, then died. He could see the demon rising, the red flames flickering deep in the depths of Falcon's eyes.

Without warning, the misshapen figure was in front of Falcon, reaching for his hand, dragging at him. "Run, you idiot, run now." She was tugging at his hand, attempting to drag him closer to the darkened buildings. Urgency. Fear. The fear was for him, for his safety. His heart turned over.

The voice was melodic, pitched to wrap itself around his heart. Need slammed into his body, into his soul. Deep and hard and urgent. It roared through his bloodstream with the force of a freight train. He couldn't see her face or her body, he had no idea what she looked like, or even her age, but his soul was crying out for hers.

"You again." The leader of the street gang turned his attention away from the stranger and toward the woman. "I told you to stay outa here!" His voice was harsh and filled with threat. He took a menacing step toward her.

The last thing Falcon expected was for the woman to attack. "Run," she hissed again and launched herself at the leader. She went in low and mean, sweeping his legs out from under him so that the man landed on his backside. She kicked him hard, using the edge of her foot to get rid of his knife. The man howled in pain when she connected with his wrist, and the knife went spinning out of his hand. She kicked the knife again, sending it skittering over the sidewalk into the gutter.

Then she was gone, running swiftly into the darkened alleyway, melting into the shadows. Her footfalls were light, almost inaudible even to Falcon's acute hearing. He didn't want to lose sight of her, but the rest of the men were closing in. The leader was swearing loudly, vowing to tear out the woman's heart, screaming at his friends to kill the tourist.

Falcon waited silently for them to approach, swinging bats and lead pipes at him from several directions. He moved with preternatural speed, his hand catching a lead pipe, ripping it out of astonished hands, and deliberately bending it into a circle. It took no effort on his part and no more than a second. He draped it around the pipe wielder's head like a necklace. He shoved the man with casual strength, sent him flying against the wall of a building some ten feet away. The circle of attackers was more wary now, afraid to close in on him. Even the leader had gone silent, still clutching his injured hand.

Falcon was distracted, his mind on the mysterious woman who had risked her life to rescue him. He had no time for battle, and his hunger was gnawing at him. He let it find him, consume him, the beast rising so that the red haze was in his mind and the flames flickered hungrily in the depths of his eyes. He turned his head slowly and smiled, his fangs showing as he sprang. He heard the frenzied screams as if from a distance, felt the flailing of arms as he grabbed the first of his prey. It was almost too much trouble to wave his hand and command silence, to keep the group under control. Hearts were pounding out a frantic rhythm, beating so loudly the threat of heart attack was very real, yet he couldn't find the mercy in him to take the time to shield their minds.

He bent his head and drank deeply. The rush was fast and addictive, the adrenaline-laced blood giving him a kind of false high. He sensed he was in danger, that the darkness was enveloping him, but he couldn't seem to find the discipline to stop himself.

It was a small sound that alerted him, and that alone told him just how far gone he really was. He should have sensed her presence immediately. She had come back for him, come back to aid him. He looked at her, his black eyes moving over her face hungrily. Blazing with urgent need. Red flames flickering. Possession stamped there.

"What are you?" The woman's soft voice brought him back to the reality of what he was doing. She gasped in shock. She stood only feet from him, staring at him with large, haunted eyes. "What are you?" She asked it again, and this time the note of fear registered deep in his heart.

Falcon lifted his head, and a trickle of blood seeped down his prey's neck. He saw himself through her eyes. Fangs, wild hair, only red flames in his otherwise empty eyes. He looked a beast, a monster to her. He held out his hand, needing to touch her, to reassure her, to thank her for stopping him before it was too late.

Sara Marten stepped backward, shaking her head, her eyes on the blood running down Nordov's neck to stain his absurdly orange shirt. Then she whirled around and ran for her life. Ran as if a demon were hunting her. And he was. She knew it. The knowledge was locked deep within her soul. It wasn't the first time she had seen such a monster. Before, she had managed to elude the creature, but this time was very different. She had been inexplicably drawn to this one. She had gone back to be sure he got away from the night gang. She *needed* to see that he was safe. Something inside her demanded that she save him.

Sara raced through the darkened entryway into the abandoned apartment building. The walls were crumbling, the roof caving in. She knew every bolt hole, every escape hatch. She would need them all. Those black eyes had been empty, devoid of all feeling until the . . . thing . . . had looked at her. She recognized possession when she saw it. Desire. His eyes had leaped to life. Burning with an intensity she had never seen before. Burning for her as if he had marked her for himself. As his prey.

The children would be safe now, deep in the bowels of the sewer. Sara had to save herself if she was going to continue to be of any assistance to them. She jumped over a pile of rubble and ducked through a narrow opening that took her to a stairwell. She took the stairs two at a time, going up to the next story. There was a hole in the wall that enabled her to take a shortcut through two apartments, push through a broken door and out onto a balcony where she caught the lowest rung of the ladder and dragged it down.

Sara went up the rungs with the ease of much practice. She had scoped out a hundred escape routes before she had ever started working in the streets, knowing it would be an essential part of her life. Practicing running each route, shaving off seconds, a minute, finding shortcuts through the buildings and alleyways, Sara had learned the secret passageways of the underworld. Now she was up on the roof, running swiftly, not even pausing before launching herself onto the roof of the next building. She moved across that one and skirted around a pile of decaying matter to jump to a third roof.

She landed on her feet, already running for the stairs. She didn't bother with the ladder, but slid down the poles to the first story and ducked inside a broken window. A man lolling on a broken-down couch looked up from his drug-induced fog and stared at her. Sara waved as she hopped over his outstretched legs. She was forced to avoid two other bodies sprawled on the floor. Scrambling over them, she was out the door and running across the hall to the opposite apartment. The door was hanging on its hinges. She went through it fast, avoiding the occupants as she crossed the floor to the window.

Sara had to slow down to climb through the broken glass. The splintered remains caught at her clothes, so that she struggled a moment, her heart pounding and her lungs screaming for air. She was forced to use precious seconds to drag her jacket free. The splinters scraped across her hand, shearing off skin, but she thrust her way outside into the open air and the drizzling rain. She took a deep, calming breath, allowing the rain to run down her face, to cleanse the tiny beads of sweat from her skin.

Suddenly she went very still, every muscle locked, frozen. A terrible shiver went down her spine. He was on the move. Tracking her. She *felt* him moving, fast and unrelenting. She had left no trail through the buildings, she was fast and quiet, yet he wasn't even slowed down by the twists and turns. He was tracking her unerringly. She knew it. Somehow despite the unfamiliar terrain, the crumbling complex of shattered buildings, the small holes and shortcuts, he was on her trail. Unswerving, undeterred, and absolutely certain he would find her.

Sara tasted fear in her mouth. She had always managed to escape. This was no different. She had brains, skills; she knew the area and he didn't. She wiped her forehead grimly with the sleeve of her jacket, suddenly wondering if he could smell her in the midst of the decay and ruin. The thought was horrifying. She had seen what his kind could do. She had seen the broken, drained bodies, white and still, wearing a mask of horror.

Sara pushed the memories away, determined not to give in to fear and panic. That way lay disaster. She set off again, moving quickly, working harder at keeping her footfalls light, her breathing soft and controlled. She ran fast through a narrow corridor between two buildings, ducked around the corner, and slipped through a tear in the chain-link fence. Her jacket was bulky, and it took precious seconds to force her way through the small opening. Her pursuer was large. He'd never be able to make it through that space; he would have to go around the entire complex.

She ran into the street, racing now with long, open strides, arms pumping, heart beating loudly, wildly. Aching. She didn't understand why she should feel such grief welling up, but it was there all the same.

The narrow, ugly streets widened until she was on the fringes of normal society. She was still in the older part of the city. She didn't slow down, but cut through parking lots, ducked around stores, and made her way unerringly uptown. Modern buildings loomed large, stretching into the night sky. Her lungs were burning, forcing her to slow to a jog. She was safe now. The lights of the city were beginning to appear, bright and welcoming. There was more traffic as she neared the residential areas. She continued jogging on her path.

The terrible tension was beginning to leave her body now, so that she could think, could go over the details of what she had seen. Not his face; it had been in the shadows. Everything about him had seemed shadowed and vague. Except his eyes. Those black, flame-filled eyes. He was very dangerous, and he had looked at her. Marked her. Desired her in some way. She could hear her own footsteps beating out a rhythm to match the pounding of her heart as she hurried through the streets, fear beating at her. From somewhere came the impression of a call, a wild yearning, an aching promise, turbulent and primitive so that it seemed to match the frantic drumbeat of her heart. It came, not from outside herself but rather from within; not even from inside her head but welling up from her very soul.

Sara forced her body to continue forward, moving through the streets and parking lots, through the twists and turns of familiar neighborhoods until she reached her own house. It was a small cottage, nestled back away from the rest of the homes, shrouded with large bushes and trees that gave her a semblance of privacy in the populous city. Sara opened her door with shaking hands and staggered inside.

She dropped her soggy jacket on the entryway floor. She had sewn several bulky pillows into the overlarge jacket so that it would be impossible to tell what she looked like. Her hair was pressed tight on her head, hidden beneath her misshapen hat. She flung the hairpins carelessly onto the countertop as she hurried to her bathroom. She was shaking uncontrollably; her legs were nearly unable to hold her up.

Sara tore off her wet, sweaty clothes and turned on the hot water full blast. She sat in the shower stall, hugging herself, trying to wipe away the memories she had blocked from her mind for so many years. She had been a teenager when she had first encountered the monster. She had looked at him, and he had seen her. She had been the one to draw that beast to her family. She was responsible, and she would never be able to absolve herself of the terrible weight of her guilt.

Sara could feel the tears on her face, mingling with the water pouring over her body. It was wrong to cower in the shower like a child. She knew it did no good. Someone had to face the monsters of the world and do something about them. It was a luxury to sit and cry, to wallow in her own self-pity and fear. She owed her family more than that, much more. Back then, she had hidden like the child she was, listening to the screams, the pleas, seeing the blood seeping under the door, and still she hadn't gone out to face the monster. She had hidden herself, pressing her hands to her ears, but she could never block out the sounds. She would hear them for eternity.

Slowly she forced her muscles under control, forced them to work once again, to support her weight as she drew herself reluctantly to her feet. She washed the fear from her body along with the sweat from running. It felt as if she had been running most of her life. She lived in the shadows, knew the darkness well. Sara shampooed her thick hair, running her fingers through the strands in an attempt to untangle them. The hot water was helping her overcome her weakness. She waited until she could breathe again before she stepped out of the stall to wrap a thick towel around herself.

She stared at herself in the mirror. She was all enormous eyes. So dark a blue they were violet as if two vivid pansies had been pressed into her face. Her hand was throbbing, and she looked at it with surprise. The skin was shredded from the top of her hand to her wrist; just looking at it made it sting. She wrapped it in a towel and padded barefoot into her bedroom. Dragging on drawstring pants and a tank top, she made her way to the kitchen and prepared a cup of tea.

The age-old ritual allowed a semblance of peace to seep into her world again and make it right. She was alive. She was breathing. There were still the children who needed her desperately, and the plans she had been making for so long. She was almost through the red tape, almost able to realize her dream. Monsters were everywhere, in every country, every city, every walk of life. She lived among the rich, and she found the monsters there. She walked among the poor, and they were there. She knew that now. She could live with the knowledge, but she was determined to save the ones she could.

Sara raked a hand through her cap of thick chestnut hair, spiking the ends, wanting it to dry. With her teacup in hand, she wandered back outside onto her tiny porch, to sit in the swing, a luxury she couldn't pass up. The sound of the rain was reassuring, the breeze on her face welcome. She sipped the tea cautiously, allowing the stillness in her to overcome the pounding fear, to retake each of her memories, solidly closing the doors on them one by one. She had learned there were some things best left alone, memories that need never be looked at again.

She stared absently out into the dazzling rain. The drops fell softly, melodically onto the leaves of the bushes and shimmered silver in the night air. The sound of water had always been soothing to her. She loved the ocean, lakes, rivers, anywhere there was a body of water. The rain softened the noises of the streets, lessened the harsh sounds of traffic, creating the illusion of being far away from the heart of the city. Illusions like that kept her sane.

Sara sighed and set her teacup on the edge of the porch, rising to pace across its small confines. She would never sleep this night; she knew she would sit in her swing, wrapped in a blanket, and watch the night fade to dawn. Her family was too close, despite the careful closing off of her memories. They were ghosts, haunting her world. She would give them this night and allow them to fade.

Sara stared out into the night, into the darker shadows of the trees. The images captured in those gray spaces always intrigued her. When the shadows merged, what was there? She stared at the wavering shadows and suddenly stiffened. There was someone—no, *something* in those shadows, gray, like the darkness, watching her. Motionless. Completely still. She saw the eyes then. Unblinking. Relentless. Black with bright red flames. Those eyes were fixed on her, marking her.

Sara whirled around, springing for the door, her heart nearly stopping. The thing moved with incredible speed, landing on the porch before she could even touch the door. The distance separating them had been nearly forty feet, but he was that fast, managing to seize her with his strong hands. Sara felt the breath slam out of her as her body impacted with his. Without hesitating, she brought her fist up into his throat, jabbing hard as she stepped back to kick his kneecap. Only she didn't connect. Her fist went harmlessly by his head, and he dragged her against him, easily pinning both of her wrists in one large hand. He smelled wild, dangerous, and his body was as hard as a tree trunk.

Her attacker thrust open the door to her home, her sanctuary, and dragged her inside, kicking the door closed to prevent discovery. Sara fought wildly, kicking and bucking, despite the fact that he held her nearly helpless. He was stronger than anyone she had ever encountered. She had the hopeless feeling that he was barely aware of her struggles. She was losing her strength fast, her breath coming in sobs. It was painful to fight him; her body felt battered and bruised. He made a sound of impatience and simply took her to the floor. His body trapped hers beneath it, holding her still with enormous strength, so that she was left staring up into the face of a devil . . . or an angel.

Chapter Two

Sara went perfectly still beneath him, staring up into that face. For one long moment time stopped. The terror receded slowly, to be replaced by haunted wonder. "I know you," she whispered in amazement.

She twisted her wrist almost absently, gently, asking for release. Falcon allowed her hands to slip free of his grip. She touched his face tentatively with two fingertips. An artist's careful stroke. She moved her fingers over his face as if she were blind and the memory of him was etched into her soul rather than in her sight.

There were tears swimming in her eyes, tangling on her long lashes. Her breath caught in her throat. Her trembling hands went to his hair, tunneled through the dark thickness, lovingly, tenderly. She held the silken strands in her fists, bunching the heavy fall of hair in her hands. "I know you. I do." Her voice was a soft measure of complete wonder.

She did know him, every angle and plane of his features. Those black, haunting eyes, the wealth of blue-black hair falling to his shoulders. He had been her only companion since she was fifteen. Every night she slept with him, every day she carried him with her. His face, his words. She knew his soul as intimately as she knew her own. *She knew him. Dark angel. Her dark dream.* She knew his beautiful, haunting words, which revealed a soul naked and vulnerable, and so achingly alone.

Falcon was completely enthralled, caught by the love in her eyes, the sheer intensity of it. She glowed with happiness she didn't even try to hide from him. Her body had gone from wild struggling to complete stillness. But now there was a subtle difference. She was wholly feminine, soft and inviting. Each stroke of her fingertips over his face sent curling heat straight to his soul.

Just as quickly her expression changed to confusion, to fright. To guilt. Along with sheer terror he could sense determination. Falcon felt the buildup of aggression in her body and caught her hands before she could hurt herself. He leaned close to her, capturing her gaze with his own. "Be calm; we will sort this out. I know I frightened you, and for that I apologize." Deliberately he lowered his voice so that it was a soft, rich tapestry of notes designed to soothe, to lull, to ensnare. "You cannot win a battle of strength between us, so do not waste your energy." His head lowered further so that he rested, for one brief moment, his brow against hers. "Listen to the sound of my heart beating. Let your heart follow the lead of mine."

His voice was one of unparalleled beauty. She found she *wanted* to succumb to his dark power. His grip was extraordinarily gentle, tender even; he held her with exquisite care. Her awareness of his enormous strength, combined with his gentleness, sent strange flames licking along her skin. She was trapped for all time in the fathomless depths of his eyes. There was no end there, just a free fall she couldn't pull out of. Her heart did follow his, slowing until it was beating with the exact same rhythm.

Sara had a will of iron, honed in the fires of trauma, and yet she couldn't pull free of that dark, hypnotic gaze, even though a part of her recognized she was under an unnatural black-magic spell. Her body trembled slightly as he lifted his head, as he brought her hand to his eye level to inspect the shredded skin. "Allow me to heal this for you," he said softly. His accent gave his voice a sensual twist she seemed to feel right down to her toes. "I knew you had injured yourself in your flight." He had smelled the scent of her blood in the night air. It had called to him, beckoned him through the darkness like the brightest of beacons.

His black eyes burning into hers, Falcon slowly brought Sara's hand to the warmth of his mouth. At the first touch of his breath on her skin, Sara's eyes widened in shock. Warmth. Heat. It was sensual intimacy beyond her experience, and all he had done was breathe on her. His tongue stroked a healing, soothing caress along the back of her hand. Black velvet, moist and sensual. Her entire body clenched, went liquid beneath him. Her breath caught in her throat. To her utter astonishment, the stinging disappeared as rough velvet trailed along each laceration to leave a tingling awareness behind. The black eyes drifted over her face, intense, burning. *Intimate.* "Better?" he asked softly.

Sara stared at him helplessly for an eternity, lost in his eyes. She forced air through her lungs and nodded her head slowly. "Please let me up."

Falcon shifted his body almost reluctantly, easing his weight from hers, retaining possession of her wrist so he could pull her to her feet in one smooth, effortless tug as he rose fluidly. Sara had planned out each move in her head, clearly and concisely. Her free hand swept up the knife hidden in the pocket of her sodden jacket, which lay beside her. As he lifted her, she jackknifed, catching his legs between hers in a scissors motion, rolling to bring him down and beneath her. He continued the roll, once more on top. She tried to plunge the knife straight through his heart, but every cell in her body was shrieking a protest and her muscles refused to obey. Sara determinedly closed her eyes. She could not look at his beloved face when she destroyed him. But she would destroy him.

His hand gripped hers, prevented all movement. They were frozen together, his leg carelessly pinning her thighs to the floor. Sara was in a far more precarious position than before, this time with the knife between them. "Open your eyes," he commanded softly.

His voice melted her body so it was soft and yielding like honey. She wanted to cry out a protest. His voice matched his angel face, hiding the demon in him. Stubbornly she shook her head. "I won't see you like that."

"How do you see me?" He asked it curiously. "How do you know my face?" He knew her. Her heart. Her soul. He had known nothing of her face or her body. Not even her mind. He had done her the courtesy of not invading her thoughts, but if she persisted in trying to kill him, he would have no choice.

"You're a monster without equal. I've seen your kind, and I won't be fooled by the face you've chosen to wear. It's an illusion like everything else about you." She kept her eyes squeezed tight. She couldn't bear to be lost in his black gaze again. She couldn't bear to look upon the face she had loved for so long. "If you are going to kill me, just do it; get it over with." There was resignation in her voice.

"Why do you think I would want to harm you?" His fingers moved gently around her hand. "Let go of the knife, *piccola*. I cannot have you hurting yourself in any way. You cannot fight me; there is no way to do so. What is between us is inevitable. Let go of the weapon, be calm, and let us sort this out."

Sara slowly allowed her fingers to open. She didn't want the knife anyway. She already knew she could never plunge it into his heart. Her mind might have been willing but her heart would never allow such an atrocity. Her unwillingness made no sense. She had so carefully prepared for just such a moment, *but the monster wore the face of her dark angel*. How could she *ever* have prepared for such an unlikely event?

"What is your name?" Falcon removed the knife from her trembling fingers, snapped the blade easily with pressure from his thumb, and tossed it across the room. His palm slid over her hand with a gentle stroke to ease the tension from her.

"Sara. Sara Marten." She steeled herself to look into his beautiful face. The face of a man perfectly sculpted by time and honor and integrity. A mask unsurpassed in artistic beauty.

"I am called Falcon."

Her eyes flew open at his revelation. She recognized his name. *I am Falcon and I will never know you, but*

I have left this gift behind for you, a gift of the heart. She shook her head in agitation. "That can't be." Her eyes searched his face, tears glittering in them again. "That can't be," she repeated. "Am I losing my mind?" It was possible, perhaps even inevitable. She hadn't considered such a possibility.

His hands framed her face. "You believe me to be the undead. The vampire. You have seen such a creature." He made it a statement, a raw fact. Of course she had. She would never have attacked him otherwise. He felt the sudden thud of his heart, fear rising to terror. In all his centuries of existence, he had never known such an emotion before. She had been alone, unprotected, and she had met the most evil of all creatures, *nosferatu*.

She nodded slowly, watching him carefully. "I have escaped him many times. I nearly managed to kill him once."

Sara felt his great body tremble at her words. "You tried such a thing? The vampire is one of the most dangerous creatures on the face of this earth." There was a wealth of reprimand in his voice. "Perhaps you should tell me the entire story."

Sara blinked at him. "I want to get up." She felt very vulnerable lying pinned to the floor beneath him, at a great disadvantage looking up into his beloved face.

He sighed softly. "Sara." Just the way he said her name curled her toes. He breathed the syllables. Whispered it between exasperated indulgence and purring warning. Made it sound silky and scented and sexy. Everything that she was not. "I do not want to have to restrain you again. It frightens you, and I do not wish to continue to see such fear in your beautiful eyes when you look upon me." He wanted to see that loving, tender look, that helpless wonder spilling from her bright gaze as it had when she first recognized his face.

"Please, I want to know what's going on. I'm not going to do anything." Sara wished she didn't sound so apologetic. She was lying on the floor of her home with a perfect stranger pinning her down, a stranger she had seen drinking the blood of a human being. A rotten human being, but still . . . *drinking blood.* She had seen the evidence with her own eyes. How could he explain that away?

Falcon stood up, his body poetry in motion. Sara had to admire the smooth, easy way he moved, a casual rippling of muscles. Once again she was standing, her body in the shadow of his, close, so that she could feel his body heat. The air vibrated with his power. His fingers were wrapped loosely, like a bracelet, around her wrist, giving her no opportunity to escape.

Sara moved delicately away from him, needing a small space to herself. To think. To breathe. To be Sara and not part of a Dark Dream. Her Dark Dream.

"Tell me how you met the vampire." He said the words calmly, but the menace in his voice sent a shiver down her spine.

Sara did not want to face those memories. "I don't know if I can tell you," she said truthfully and tilted her head to look into his eyes.

At once his gaze locked with hers, and she felt that curious falling sensation again. Comfort. Security. Protection from the howling ghosts of her past.

His fingers tightened around her wrist, gently, almost a caress, his thumb sliding tenderly over her sensitive skin. He tugged her back to him with the same gentleness that often seemed to accompany his movements. He moved slowly, as if afraid to frighten her.

As if he knew her reluctance, and what he was asking of her. "I do not wish to intrude, but if it will be easier, I can read the memories in your mind without your having to speak of them aloud."

There was only the sound of the rain on the roof. The tears in her mind. The screams of her mother and father and brother echoing in her ears. Sara stood rigid, in shock, her face white and still. Her eyes were larger than ever, two shimmering violet jewels, wide and frightened. She swallowed twice and resolutely pulled her gaze from his to look at his broad chest. "My parents were professors at the university. In the summer, they would always go to some exotic, fantastically named place, to a dig. I was fifteen; it sounded very romantic." Her voice was low, a complete monotone. "I begged to go, and they took my brother Robert and me with them." Guilt. Grief. It swamped her.

She was silent a long time, so long he thought she might not be able to continue. Sara didn't take her gaze from his chest. She recited the words as if she'd memorized them from a textbook, a classic horror story. "I loved it, of course. It was everything I expected it to be and more. My brother and I could explore to our hearts' content and we went everywhere. Even down into the tunnels our parents had forbidden to us. We were determined to find our own treasure." Robert had dreamed of golden chalices. But something else had called to Sara. Called and beckoned, thudded in her heart until she was obsessed.

Falcon felt the fine tremor that ran through her body and instinctively drew her closer to him, so that the heat of his body seeped into the cold of hers. His hand went to the nape of her neck, his fingers soothing the tension in her muscles. "You do not have to continue, Sara. This is too distressing for you."

She shook her head. "I found the box, you see. I knew it was there. A beautiful, hand-carved box wrapped in carefully cured skins. Inside was a diary." She lifted her face then, to lock her eyes with his. To judge his reaction.

His black eyes drifted possessively over her face. Devoured her. *Lifemate*. The word swirled in the air between them. From his mind to hers. It was burned into their minds for all eternity.

"It was yours, wasn't it?" She made it a soft accusation. She continued to stare at him until faint color crept up her neck and flushed her cheeks. "But it can't be. That box, that diary, is at least fifteen hundred years old. More. It was checked out and authenticated. If that was yours, if you wrote the diary, than you would have to be . . ." She trailed off, shaking her head. "It can't be." She rubbed at her throbbing temples. "It can't be," she whispered again.

"Listen to my heartbeat, Sara. Listen to the breath going in and out of my lungs. Your body recognizes mine. You are my true lifemate."

For my beloved lifemate, my heart and my soul. This is my gift to you. She closed her eyes for a moment. How many times had she read those words?

She wouldn't faint. She stood swaying in front of him, his fingers, a bracelet around her wrist, holding them together. "You are telling me you wrote the diary."

He drew her even closer until her body rested against his. She didn't seem to notice he was holding her up. "Tell me about the vampire."

She shook her head, yet she obeyed. "He was there

one night after I found the box. I was translating the diary, the scrolls and scrolls of letters, and I felt him there. I couldn't see anything, but it was there, a presence. Wholly evil. I thought it was the curse. The workmen had been muttering about curses and how so many men died digging up what was best left alone. They had found a man dead in the tunnel the night before, drained of blood. I heard the workers tell my father it had been so for many years. When things were taken from the digs, it would come. In the night. And that night, I knew it was there. I ran into my father's room, but the room was empty, so I went to the tunnels to find him, to warn him. I saw it then. It was killing another worker. And it looked up and saw me."

Sara choked back a sob and pressed her fingertips harder into her temples. "I felt him in my head, telling me to come to him. His voice was terrible, gravelly, and I knew he would hunt me. I didn't know why, but I knew it wasn't over. I ran. I was lucky; workmen began pouring into the tunnels, and I escaped in all the confusion. My father took us into the city. We stayed there for two days before it found us. It came at night. I was in the laundry closet, still trying to translate the diary with a flashlight. I felt him. I felt him and knew he had come for me. I hid. Instead of warning my father, I hid there in a pile of blankets. Then I heard my parents and brother screaming, and I hid with my hands pressed over my ears. He was whispering to me to come to him. I thought if I went he might not kill them. But I couldn't move. I couldn't move, not even when blood ran under the door. It was black in the night, not red."

Falcon's arms folded her close, held her tightly. He could feel the grief radiating from her, a guilt too terrible to be borne. Tears locked forever in her heart and mind. A child witnessing the brutal killing of her family by a monster unsurpassed in evil. His lips brushed a single caress onto her thick cap of sable hair. "I am not vampire, Sara. I am a hunter, a destroyer of the undead. I have spent several lifetimes far from my homeland and my people, seeking just such creatures. I am not the vampire who destroyed your family."

"How do I know what you are or aren't? I saw you take that man's blood." She pulled away from him in a quick, restless movement, wholly feminine.

"I did not kill him," he answered simply. "The vampire kills his prey. I do not."

Sara raked a trembling hand through the short spikes of her silky hair. She felt completely drained. She paced restlessly across the room to her small kitchen and poured herself another cup of tea. Falcon filled her home with his presence. It was difficult to keep from staring at him. She watched him move through her home, touching her things with reverent fingers. He glided silently, almost as if he floated inches above the floor. She knew the moment he discovered it. She padded into the bedroom to lean her hip against the doorway, just watching him as she sipped her tea. It warmed her insides and helped to stop her shivering.

"Do you like it?" There was a sudden shyness in her voice.

Falcon stared at the small table beside the bed where a beautifully sculpted bust of his own face stared at him. Every detail. Every line. His dark, hooded eyes, the long fall of his hair. His strong jaw and patrician nose. It was more than the fact that she had gotten every single detail perfect, it was *how* she saw him. Noble. Old World. Through the eyes of love.

"You did this?" He could barely manage to get the words past the strange lump blocking his throat. *My Dark Angel, lifemate to Sara*. The inscription was in fine calligraphy, each letter a stroke of art, a caress of love, every bit as beautiful as the bust.

"Yes." She continued to watch him closely, pleased with his reaction. "I did it from memory. When I touch things, old things in particular, I can sometimes connect with events or things from the past that linger in the object. It sounds weird." She shrugged her shoulders. "I can't explain how it happens, it just does. When I touched the diary, I knew it was meant for me. Not just anyone, not any other woman. It was written for me. When I translated the words from an ancient language, I could see a face. There was a desk, a small wooden one, and a man sat there and wrote. He turned and looked at me with such loneliness in his eyes, I knew I had to find him. His pain could hardly be borne, that terrible black emptiness. I see that same loneliness in your eyes. It is your face I saw. Your eyes. I understand emptiness."

"Then you know you are my other half." The words were spoken in a low voice, made husky by Falcon's attempt to keep unfamiliar emotions under control. His eyes met hers across the room. One of his hands rested on the top of the bust, his fingers finding the exact groove in a wave of the hair that she had caressed thousands of times.

Once again, Sara had the curious sensation of falling into the depths of his eyes. There was such an intimacy about his touching her familiar things. It had been nearly fifteen years since she had really been close to another person. She was hunted, and she never forgot it for a single moment. Anyone close to her would be in danger. She lived alone, changed her address often, traveled frequently, and continually changed her patterns of behavior. But the monster had followed her. Twice, when she had read of a serial killer stalking a city she was in, she had actively hunted the beast, determined to rid herself of her enemy, but she had never managed to find his lair.

She could talk to no one of her encounter; no one would believe her. It was widely believed that a madman had murdered her family. And the local workers had been convinced it was the curse. Sara had inherited her parents' estate, a considerable fortune, so she had been lucky enough to travel extensively, always staying one step ahead of her pursuer.

"Sara." Falcon said her name softly, bringing her back to him.

The rain pounded on the roof now. The wind slammed into the windows, whistling loudly as if in warning. Sara raised the teacup to her lips and drank, her eyes still locked with his. Carefully she placed the cup in the saucer and set it on a table. "How is it you can exist for so long a time?"

Falcon noticed she was keeping a certain distance from him, noticed her pale skin and trembling mouth. She had a beautiful mouth, but she was at the breaking point and he didn't dare think about her mouth, or the lush curves of her body. She needed him desperately, and he was determined to push aside the clawing, roaring beast and provide her with solace and peace. With protection.

"Our species have existed since the beginning of time, although we grow close to extinction. We have great gifts. We are able to control storms, to shape-shift, to soar as great winged owls and run with our brethren, the wolves. Our longevity is both gift and curse. It is not easy to watch the passing of mortals, of ages. It is a terrible thing to live without hope, in a black endless void."

Sara heard the words and did her best to comprehend what he was saying. Soar as great winged owls. She would love to fly high above the earth and be free of the weight of her guilt. She rubbed her temple again, frowning in concentration. "Why do you take blood if you are not a vampire?"

"You have a headache." He said it as if it were his most important concern. "Allow me to help you."

Sara blinked and he was standing close to her, his body heat immediately sweeping over her cold skin. She could feel the arc of electricity jumping from his body to hers. The chemistry between them was so strong it terrified her. She thought of moving away, but he was already reaching for her. His hands framed her face, his fingers caressing, gentle. Her heart turned over, a funny somersault that left her breathless. His fingertips moved to her temples.

His touch was soothing, yet sent heat curling low and wicked, making butterfly wings flutter in the pit of her stomach. She felt his stillness, his breath moving through his body, through her body. She waited in an agony of suspense, waited while his hands moved over her face, his thumb caressing her full lower lip. She felt him then, his presence in her mind, sharing her brain, her thoughts, the horror of her memories, her guilt. . . . Sara gave a small cry of protest, jerked away from him, not wanting him to see the stains forever blotting her soul.

"Sara, no." He said it softly, his hands refusing to relinquish her. "I am the darkness and you are the light. You did nothing wrong. You could not have saved your family; he would have murdered them in front of you."

"I should have died with them instead of cowering in a closet." She blurted out her confession, the truth of her terrible sin.

"He would not have killed you." He said the words very softly, his voice pitched low so that it moved over her skin like a velvet caress. "Remain quiet for just a moment and allow me to take away your headache."

She stayed very still, curious as to what would happen, afraid for her sanity. She had seen him drink blood, his fangs in the neck of a man, the flames of hell burning in the depths of his eyes, yet when he touched her, she felt as if she belonged to him. She *wanted* to belong to him. Every cell in her body cried out for him. Needed him. *Beloved Dark Angel.* Was he the angel of death coming to claim her? She was ready to go with him, she would go, but she wanted to complete her plans. Leave something good behind, something decent and right.

She heard words, an ancient tongue chanting far away in her mind. Beautiful, lilting words as old as time. Words of power and peace. Inside her head, not from outside herself. His voice was soft and misty like the early morning, and somehow the healing chant made her headache float away on a passing cloud.

Sara reached up to touch his face, his beloved familiar face. "I'm so afraid you aren't real," she confessed. *Falcon. Lifemate to Sara.*

Falcon's heart turned over, melted completely. He pulled her close to his body, gently so as not to frighten her. He trembled with his need of her, as he framed her face with his hands, holding her still while he slowly bent his dark head toward hers. She was lost in the fathomless depths of his eyes. The burning desire. The intensity of need. The aching loneliness.

Sara closed her eyes right before his mouth took possession of hers. And the earth moved beneath her feet. Her heart thudded out a rhythm of fear. She was lost for eternity in that dark embrace.

Chapter Three

Falcon pulled her closer still, until every muscle of his body was imprinted on the softness of hers. His mouth moved over hers, hot silk, while molten lava flowed through her bloodstream. The entire universe shifted and moved, and Sara gave herself up completely to his seeking kiss. Her body melted, soft and pliant, instantly belonging to him.

His mouth was addictive. Sara made her own demands, her arms creeping up around his neck to cradle him close. She wanted to feel him, his body strong and hard pressed tightly to hers. Real, not an elusive dream. She couldn't get enough of his mouth, hot and needy and so hungry for her. Sara didn't think of herself as being a sensual person, but with him she had no inhibitions. She moved her body restlessly against his, wanting him to touch her, *needing* him to touch her.

There was a strange roaring in her ears. She knew no thoughts, only the feel of his hard body against hers, only the sheer pleasure of his mouth taking possession of her so urgently. She gave herself up completely to the sensations of heat and flame. The rush of liquid fire running in her veins, pooling low in her body.

He shifted her closer, his mouth retaining possession, his tongue dueling with hers as his hand cupped her breast, his thumb stroking her nipple through the thin material of her shirt. Sara gasped at the exquisite pleasure. She hadn't expected company and she wore nothing beneath the little tank top. His thumb nudged a strap from her shoulder, a simple thing, but wickedly sexy.

His mouth left hers to blaze a path of fire along her neck. His tongue swirled over her pulse. She heard her own soft cry of need mingle with his groan of pleasure. Teeth scraped gently, erotically, over her pulse, back and forth while her body went up in flames and every cell cried out for his possession. His teeth nipped, his tongue eased the ache. His arms were hard bands, trapping her close so that she could feel the heavy thickness of him, an urgent demand, tight against her.

A shudder shook Falcon's body. Something dark and dangerous raised its head. His needs were swamping him, edging out his implacable control. The beast roared and demanded its lifemate. The scent of her washed away every semblance of civilization so that for one moment he was pure animal, every instinct alive and darkly primitive.

Sara sensed the change in him instantly, sensed the danger as his teeth touched her skin. The sensation was erotic, the need in her nearly as great as the need in him. *Fraternizing with the enemy.* The words came out of nowhere. With a low cry of self-recrimination, Sara dragged herself out of his arms. She had *seen* him take blood, his fangs buried deep in a human neck. It didn't matter how familiar he looked; he wasn't human, and he was very, very dangerous.

Falcon allowed her to move away from him. He watched her carefully as he struggled for control. His fangs receded in his mouth, but his body was a hard, unrelenting ache. "If I planned on harming you, Sara, why would I wait? You are the safest human being on the face of this planet, because you are the one I would give my life to protect."

I am Falcon and I will never know you, but I have left this gift behind for you, a gift of the heart.

Sara closed her eyes tightly, pressed a hand to her trembling mouth. She could taste him, feel him; she *wanted* him. How could she be such a traitor to her family? The ghosts in her mind wailed loudly, condemning her. Their condemnation didn't stop her body from throbbing with need, or stop the heat moving through her blood like molten lava.

"I felt you," she accused, the tremors running through her body a result of his lethal kiss more than fear of his lethal fangs. She had almost wanted him to pierce her. For one moment her heart had been still as if it had waited all eternity for something only he could give her. "You were so close to taking my blood."

"But I am not human, Sara," he replied softly, gently, his dark eyes holding a thousand secrets. His head was unbowed, unshamed by his dark cravings. He was a strong, powerful being, a man of honor. "Taking blood is natural to me, and you are my other half. I am sorry

I frightened you. You would have found it erotic, not distasteful, and you would not have come to any harm."

She hadn't been afraid of him. She had been afraid of herself. Afraid she would want him so much the wails of her family would fade from her mind and she would never find a way to bring their killer to justice. Afraid the monster would find a way to destroy Falcon if she gave in to her own desires. Afraid to reach for something she had no real knowledge of. Afraid it would be sinfully and wonderfully erotic.

For my beloved lifemate, my heart and my soul. This is my gift to you. It was his beautiful words that had captured her heart for all time. Her soul did cry out for his. It didn't matter that she had seen those red flames of madness in his eyes. In spite of the danger, his words bound them together with thousands of tiny threads.

"How is it you came to be here in Romania? You are American, are you not?" She was very nervous, and Falcon wanted to find a safe subject, something that would ease the sexual tension between them. He needed a respite from the urgent demands of his body every bit as much as Sara needed her space. He was touching her mind lightly, could hear the echoes of her family demanding justice.

Sara could have listened to his voice forever. In awe, she touched her mouth, which was still tingling from the pressure of his. He had such a perfect mouth and such a killer kiss. She closed her eyes briefly and savored the taste of him still on her tongue. She knew what he was doing, distracting her from the overwhelming sexual tension, from her own very justified fears. But she was grateful to him for it. "I'm American," she admitted. "I was born in San Francisco, but we moved around a lot. I spent a great deal of time in Boston. Have you ever been there?" Her breath was still fighting to find its way into her lungs and she dragged in air, only to take the scent of him deep within her body.

"I have never traveled to the United States but I hope that we will do so in the future. We can travel to my homeland together and see my Prince and his lifemate before we travel to your country." Falcon deliberately slowed his heart and lungs, taking the lead to get their bodies, both raging for release, back under control.

"A Prince? You want me to go with you to meet your Prince?" In spite of everything, Sara found herself smiling. She couldn't imagine herself meeting a Prince. The entire evening seemed something out of a fantasy, a dark dream she was caught in.

"Mikhail Dubrinsky is our Prince. I knew his father, Vladimir, before him, but I have not had the privilege of meeting Mikhail in many years." Not for over a thousand years. "Tell me how you came to be here, Sara," he prompted softly. The Prince was not entirely a safe subject. If Sara began thinking too much about what he was, she would immediately leap to the correct conclusion that Mikhail, the Prince of his people, was also of Falcon's species. Human, yet not human. It was the last thing he wanted her to dwell on.

"I saw a television special about children in Romania being left in orphanages. It was heartrending. I have a huge trust fund, far more money than I'll ever use. I knew I had to come here and help them if I could. I couldn't get the picture of those poor babies out of my mind. It took great planning to get over to this country and to establish myself here. I was able to find this house and start making connections."

She traced the paths of the raindrops on the window with her fingertip. Something in the way she did it made his body tighten to the point of pain. She was intensely provocative without knowing it. Her voice was soft in the night, a melancholy melody accompanied by the sounds of the storm outside. Every word that emerged from her beautiful mouth, the way her body moved, the way her fingertips traced the raindrops entranced him until he could think of nothing else. Until his body ached and his soul cried out and the demon in him struggled for supremacy.

"I worked for a while in the orphanages, and it seemed an endless task—not enough medical supplies, not enough people to care for and comfort the babies. Some were so sick it was impossible to help them. I thought there was little hope of really helping. I was trying to establish connections to move adoption proceedings along quicker when I met a woman, someone who, like me, had seen the television special and had come here to help. She introduced me to a man who showed me the sewer children." Sara pushed at her gleaming sable hair until it tumbled in spiky curls and waves all over her head. The light glinted off each strand, making Falcon long to touch the silky whorls. There was a terrible pounding in his head, a relentless hammering in his body.

"The children you whistled a warning to tonight." He tried not think about how enticing she looked when she was disheveled. It was all he could do not to tunnel his hands deep in the thick softness and find her mouth again with his. She paced restlessly across the room, her lush curves drawing his dark gaze like a magnet. The thin tank top was ivory, and her nipples were dark and inviting beneath the sheath of silk. The breath seemed to leave his body all at once, and he was hard and hot and uncomfortable with a need bordering on desperation.

"Well, of course those were only a few of them. They are excellent little pickpockets." Sara flashed a grin at him before turning to stare once again out the window into the pouring rain. "I tried to get them to turn in earlier, before dark, because it's even more dangerous on the street at night, but if they don't bring back a certain amount, they can be in terrible trouble." She sighed softly. "They have a minicity underground. It's a dangerous life; the older ones rule the younger and they have to band together to stay safe. It isn't easy winning their confidence or even helping them. Anything you give them could easily get them killed. Someone might murder them for a decent shirt." She turned to look over her shoulder at him. "I can't stay in one place too long, so I knew I could never really help the children the way they needed."

There was a sense of sadness clinging to her, yet she was not looking for pity. Sara accepted her life with quiet dignity. She made her choices and lived with them. She stood there with the window behind her, the rain falling softly, framing her like a picture. Falcon wanted to enfold her in his arms and hold her for eternity.

"Tell me about the children." He glided silently to the narrow table where she kept a row of fragrant candles. He could see clearly in the darkness, but Sara needed the artificial light of her lamps. If they needed lights, he preferred the glow of candlelight. Candlelight had a way of blurring the edges of shadows, blending light into dark. He would be able to talk of necessary things to Sara in the muted light, to talk of their future and what it would mean to each of them.

"I found seven children who have interesting talents. It isn't easy or comfortable to be different, and I realized it was my difference that drew that horrible monster to me. I knew when I touched those children that they would also draw him to them. I know I can't save all the orphans, but I'm determined to save those seven. I've been setting up a system to get money to the woman aiding the children in the sewers, but I want a home for my seven. I know I won't be able to be with them always, at least not until I find a way to get rid of the monster hunting me, but at least I can establish them in a home with money and education and someone trustworthy to see to their needs."

"The vampire will only be interested in the female children with psychic talents. The boys will be expendable; in fact, he will view them as rivals. It will be best to move them as quickly as possible to safety. We can go the mountains of my homeland and establish a home for the children there. They will be cherished and protected by many of our people." Falcon spoke softly, matter-of-factly, wanting her to accept the things he told her without delving too deeply into them yet. He was astonished that she already knew about vampires, and that she could be so calm about what was happening between them. Falcon didn't feel calm. His entire being was in a meltdown.

Her heart pounded out a rhythm of fear at the casual way he acknowledged that her conclusions were correct. The vampire would go after her children, and she had inadvertently placed them directly in his path.

She watched curiously as Falcon stared at the candles. The fingers of his right hand swirled slightly and the entire row of candles leaped to life. Sara laughed softly. "Magic. You really are magic, aren't you?" Her beloved sorcerer, her dark angel of dreams.

He turned to look at her, his black eyes drifting over her face. He moved then, unable to keep from touching her, his hands framing her face. "You are the one who is magic, Sara," he said, his voice a whisper of seduction in the night. "Everything about you is pure magic." Her courage, her compassion. Her sheer determination. Her unexpected laughter in the face of what she was up against. *Monster without equal.* And worse, Falcon was beginning to suspect that her enemy was one of the most feared of the vampires, a true ancient.

"I've told you about me. Tell me about you, about how you can be as old as you are, how you came to write the diary." More than anything else, she wanted the story of the diary. Her book. The words he had written for her, the words that had poured out of his soul into hers and filled her with love and longing and need. She wanted to forget reality and lean into him, taking possession of his perfect mouth.

Sara needed to know how his words could have crossed the barrier of time to find her. Why had she been drawn into the darkness of those ancient tunnels? How had she known precisely where to find the hand-carved box? What was there about Sara Marten that drew creatures like him to her? *What had drawn one of them to her family?*

"Sara." He breathed her name into the room, a whisper of velvet, of temptation. The rain was soft on the rooftop, and his lifemate was only a scant few inches from him, tempting him with her lush curves and beautiful mouth and enormous violet eyes.

Reluctantly he allowed his hands to fall away from her face. He forced his gaze from her mouth when he needed the feel of it again so desperately. "We are very close to the Carpathian Mountains. It is wild still, where we will go, but your plan to establish a house for the children will be best realized there. Few vampires dare to defy the Prince of our people on our own lands." He wanted her to accept his words. To know he meant to be with her and help her with whatever she needed to make her happy. If she wanted a house filled with orphans, he would be at her side and he would love and protect the children with her.

Sara took several steps backward. Afraid. Not so much of the man exuding danger and power, filling her home with his presence, filling her soul with peace and her mind with confusion. She was afraid of herself. Of her reaction to him. Afraid of her terrible aching need of him. He was offering her a life and hope. She had not envisioned either for herself. Not once in the last fifteen years. She pressed her body close to the wall, almost paralyzed with fear.

Falcon remained motionless, recognizing she was fighting her own attraction to him, the fierce chemistry that existed between them. The call of their souls to one another. The beast in him was strong, a hideous thing he was struggling to control. He needed his anchor, his lifemate. He must, for both of their sakes, complete the ritual. She was a strong woman who needed to find her own way to him. He wanted to allow her that freedom, yet they had so little time. He knew the beast was growing stronger, and his new, overwhelming emotions only added to his burden of control.

Sara smiled suddenly, an unexpected humor in her

eyes. "We have this strange thing between us. I can't explain it. I feel your struggle. You need to tell me something but you are very reluctant to do so. The funny thing about it is that there is no real expression on your face and I can't read your body language, either. I just know there's something important you aren't telling me and you're very worried about it. I'm not a shrinking violet. I believe in vampires, for lack of a better word to call such creatures. I don't know what you are, but I believe you aren't human. I haven't made up my mind whether you are one of them; I'm afraid I'm blinded by some fantasy I've woven about you."

Falcon's dark eyes went black with hunger. For a moment he could only stare at her, his desire so strong he couldn't think clearly. It roared through him with the force of a freight train, shaking the foundations of his control.

"I am very close to turning. The males of our race are predators. With the passing of the years, we lose all ability to feel, even to see in color. We have no emotions. We have only our honor and the memories of what we felt to hold us through the long centuries. Those of us who must hunt the vampire and bring him to justice are taking lives. That adds to the burden of our existence. Each kill spreads the darkness on our souls until we are consumed. I have existed for nearly two thousand years, and my time has long since past. I was making my way home to end my existence before I could become the very thing I have hunted so relentlessly." He told her the truth starkly, without embellishment.

Sara touched her mouth, her eyes never leaving his

face. "You feel. You could never fake that kiss." There was a wealth of awe in her voice.

Falcon felt his body relax, the tension draining from him at her tone. "When we find a lifemate, she restores our ability to feel emotion. You are my lifemate, Sara. I feel everything. I see in color. My body needs yours, and my soul needs you desperately. You are my anchor, the one being, the only being who can keep the darkness in me leashed."

She had read his diary; the things he was telling her were not new concepts. She was light to his darkness. His other half. It had been a beautiful fantasy, a dream. Now she was facing the reality, and it was overwhelming. This man standing so vulnerable in front of her was a powerful predator, close to becoming the very thing he hunted.

Sara believed him. She felt the darkness clinging to him. She felt the predator in him with unsheathed claws and waiting fangs. She had glimpsed the fires of hell in his eyes. Her violet eyes met his without flinching.

"Well, Sara." He said it very softly. "Are you going to save me?"

The rain poured onto the roof of her home, the sound a sensual rhythm that beat through her body in time to the drumming of her heart. She couldn't pull her gaze away from his. "Tell me how to save you, Falcon." Because every word he'd spoken was truth. She felt it, *knew* it instinctively.

"Without binding us with the ritual words, I am without hope. Once I speak them to my true lifemate, we are bound together for all eternity. It is much like the human marriage ceremony, yet more."

She knew the ancient words. He had said them to

her, had *whispered* them to her a thousand times in the middle of the night. Beautiful words. *I claim you as my lifemate. I belong to you. I offer my life for you. I give to you my protection, my allegiance, my heart, my soul, and my body. I take into my keeping the same that is yours. Your life, happiness, and welfare will be cherished and placed above my own for all time. You are my lifemate, bound to me for all eternity and always in my care.*

She had stumbled over the translation for a long time, wanting each word perfect in its beauty, with the exact meaning he had intended. The words that had gone from his heart to hers. "And we would be considered married?"

"You are my lifemate; there will never be another. We would be bound, Sara, truly bound. We would need the touch of our minds, the coming together of our bodies often. I could not be without you, nor you without me."

She recognized that there was no compulsion in his voice. He was not trying to influence her, yet she felt the impact of his words deep inside her. Sara lifted her chin, trying to see into his soul. "Without binding us, you would really become like that monster who killed my family?"

"I struggle with the darkness every moment of my existence," he admitted softly. A jagged bolt of lightning lit the night sky and for one moment threw his face into harsh relief. She could see his struggle etched plainly there, a certain cruelty about his sensual mouth, the lines and planes and angles of his face, the black emptiness of his eyes. Then once again the darkness descended, muted by the glow of the candles. Once again he was beautiful, the exact face in her dreams. Her own dark angel. "I have no other choice but to end my life. That was my intention as I made my way to my homeland. I was already dead, but you breathed life back into my shattered soul. Now you are here, a miracle, standing in front of me, and I ask you again: Are you willing to save my life, my soul, Sara? Because once the words are said between us, there is no going back, they cannot be unsaid. You need to know that. I cannot unsay them. And I would not let you go. I know I am not that strong. Are you strong enough to share your life with me?"

She wanted to say no, she didn't know him, a stranger who came to her straight from taking a man's blood. But she did know him. She knew his innermost thoughts. She had read every word of his diary. He was so alone, so completely, utterly alone, and she knew, more than most, what it was like to be alone. She could never walk away from him. He had been there for her all those long, empty nights. All those long, endless nights when the ghosts of her family had wailed for vengeance, for justice. He had been there with her. His words. His face.

Sara put her hand on his arm, her fingers curling around his forearm. "You have to know I will not abandon the children. And there is my enemy. He will come. He always finds me. I never stay in one place too long."

"I am a hunter of the undead, Sara," he reminded, but the words meant little to him. He was only aware of her touch, the scent of her, the way she was looking at him. Her *consent.* He was waiting. His entire being was waiting. Even the wind and rain seemed to hesitate. "Sara." He said it softly, the aching need, the terrible hunger, evident in his voice.

Closing her eyes, wanting the dream, she heard her own voice in the stillness of the room. "Yes."

Falcon felt a surge of elation. He drew her against him, buried his face in the softness of her neck. His body trembled from the sheer relief of her commitment to him. He could hardly believe the enormity of his find, of being united with his lifemate in the last days of his existence. He kissed her soft, trembling mouth, lifted his head to look into her eyes. "I claim you as my lifemate." The words broke out of him, soared from his soul. "I belong to you. I offer my life for you. I give to you my protection, my allegiance, my heart, my soul, and my body. I take into my keeping the same that is yours. Your life, happiness, and welfare will be cherished and placed above my own for all time. You are my lifemate, bound to me for all eternity and always in my care." He buried his face once more against her soft skin, breathed in her scent. Beneath his mouth her pulse beckoned, her life force calling to him, tempting. So very tempting.

She felt the difference at once, a strange wrenching in her body. Her aching heart and soul, so empty before, were suddenly whole, complete. The feeling filled her with elation; it terrified her at the same time. It couldn't be her imagination. She *knew* there was a difference.

Before she could be afraid of the consequences of her commitment, Sara felt his lips, velvet soft, move over her skin. His touch drove out all thought, and she gave herself willingly into his keeping. His arms held her closer still to his heart, within the shelter of his body. His teeth scraped lightly, an erotic touch that sent a shiver down her spine. His tongue swirled lazily, a tiny point of flame she felt raging through her bloodstream. Of their own volition, her arms reached up to cradle his head. She was no young girl afraid of her own sexuality; she was a grown woman who had waited long for her lover. She wanted the feel of his mouth and hands. She wanted everything he was willing to give her.

His hands moved over her, pushing aside the thin barrier of her top to take in her skin. She was softer than anything he had ever imagined. He whispered a powerful command; his teeth sank deep, and whips of lightning lashed through his body to hers. White-hot heat. Blue fire. She was sweet and spicy, a taste of heaven. He wanted her, every inch of her. He needed to bury his body deep within her, to find his safe haven, his refuge. He had fed well, and it was a good thing, or he never would have found the will to curb his strength. It took every ounce of control to stop himself from indulging wildly. He took only enough for an exchange. He would be able to touch her mind, to reassure her. That would be absolutely necessary for their comfort and safety.

He slashed his own chest, pressed her mouth to his ancient, powerful blood, and softly commanded her obedience. She moved sensuously against him, driving him closer and closer to the edge of his control. He wanted her, needed her, and the moment he knew she had taken enough for the exchange, he whispered his command to stop feeding. He closed the wound carefully and took possession of her mouth, sweeping his tongue along hers, dueling and dancing, so that, as she emerged from the enthrallment, there was only the strength of his arms, the heat of his body, and the seduction of his mouth.

Without warning, the storm increased in intensity,

battering at the windowsills. Bolts of lightning slammed into the ground with such force, the ground shook. Sara's little cottage trembled, the walls shaking ominously. Thunder roared so that it filled the spaces in the house, a deafening sound. Sara tore herself out of his arms, clapped her hands over her ears, and stared in horror out into the fury of the squall. She gasped as another bolt of lightning sizzled across the sky in writhing ropes of energy. Thunder crashed directly overhead, wrenching a soft, frightened cry from her throat.

Chapter Four

Before another sound could escape from Sara, Falcon's hand covered her mouth gently in warning. Sara didn't need his caution; she already knew. Her enemy had found her once again. "You have to get out of here," she hissed softly against his palm.

Falcon bent his head so that his mouth was touching her ear. "I am a hunter of the undead, Sara. I do not run from them." The taste of her was still in his mouth, in his mind. She was a part of him, inseparable now.

She tipped her head back to stare up at him, wincing as the wind howled and shrieked with enough force to cause small tornadoes in the street and yard, throwing loose paper, leaves, and twigs into the air in a rush of anger. "Are you any good at killing these things?" She asked it with a hint of disbelief. There was a challenge in her voice. "I need to know the truth."

For the first time that he could remember, Falcon

felt like smiling. It was unexpected in the midst of the vampire's arrival, but the doubt in her voice made him want to laugh. "He is sending out his threat ahead of him. You have angered him. You have a built-in shield, a rare thing. He cannot find you when he scans, so he is looking for an awareness, a surge of fear that will tell him you know who he is. That is how he tracks you. I will send my answer to him so he is aware that you are under my protection."

"No!" She caught his arm with suddenly tense fingers. "This is it, our chance. If he doesn't know about you, then he will come for me. We can lay a trap for him."

"I do not need to use you as bait." His voice was very mild, but there was a hint of some unnamed emotion that made her shiver. Falcon was unfailingly gentle with her, his tone always soft and low, his touch tender. But there was something deep inside him that was terribly dangerous and very dark.

Sara found herself shivering, but she tightened her hold on him, afraid that if he went into the raging storm he would be lost to her. "It's the best way. He'll come for me; he always comes for me." Already her bond with Falcon was so strong, she couldn't bear the thought of something happening to him. She must protect him from the terrible thing that had destroyed her family.

"Not tonight. Tonight I'll go after him." Falcon put her from him gently. He could clearly see her fears and her fierce need to be sure that he was safe. She had no concept of what he was, of the thousands of battles he had fought with these very monsters: Carpathian males who had waited too long, or who had chosen to give up their souls for the fleeting momentary pleasure of the kill. His brethren.

Sara caught his arm. "No, don't go out there." There was a catch in her voice. "I don't want to be alone tonight. I know he's here, and for the first time, I'm not alone."

He leaned down to capture her soft mouth with his. At once there was that melting sensation, the promise of silken heat and ecstasy he had never dared to dream about. "You are worried about my safety and seek ways to keep me with you." He said the words softly against her lips. "I dwell within you now; we are able to share thoughts with one another. This is my life, Sara; this is what I do. I have no choice but to go. I am a male Carpathian sent by the Prince of my people into the world to protect others from these creatures. I am a hunter. It is the only honor I have left."

There was that aching loneliness in his voice. She had been alone for fifteen years. She couldn't imagine what it would be like to be alone for as long as he had been. Watching endless time go by, the changes in the world, without hope or refuge. Sentenced to destroying his own kind, perhaps even friends. *Honor*. That word had been used often in his diary. She saw the implacable resolve in him, the intensity that swirled dangerously close to the surface of his calm. Nothing she could say would stop him.

Sara sighed softly and nodded. "I think there is much more in you to honor than just your abilities as a hunter, but I understand. There are things I must do that I don't always want to, but I know I couldn't live with myself if I didn't do them." She slipped her arms around his neck and pressed her body close to his. For one moment she was no longer alone in the world. He was solid and safe. "Don't let him harm you. He's managed to destroy everyone I care about."

Falcon held her, his arms cradling her body, every cell needing her. It was madness to hunt when he was so close to turning and the ritual had not been completed, but he had no choice. The wind beat at the window, the branches of trees sweeping against the house in a kind of fury. "I will be back soon, Sara," he assured her softly.

"Let me go with you," she said suddenly. "I've faced him before."

Falcon smiled. His soul smiled. She was beautiful to him, nearly unbelievable. Ready to face the monster right beside him. He bent once more and found her mouth with his. A promise. He made it that. A promise of life and happiness. And then he was gone, wrenching open the door while he still could, while his honor was strong enough to overcome the needs of his body. He simply dissolved into mist, mixing with the rain for camouflage, and streamed through the night air, away from the shelter and temptation of her body and heart.

Sara stepped out onto the porch after him, still blinking, unsure where he had gone, it had happened so quickly. "Falcon!" His name was a cry wrenched from her soul. The wind whipped her hair into a frenzy. The rain doused her clothes until the silk was nearly transparent. She was utterly alone again.

You will never be alone again, Sara. I dwell within you as you are within me. Speak to me; use your mind, and I will hear you.

She held her breath. It was impossible. She felt a flood of relief and sagged against the column of her porch for support. She didn't question how his voice could be in her mind, clear and perfect and sexy. She accepted it because she needed it so desperately. She jammed her fist in her mouth to stop herself from calling him back to her, forgetting for a moment that he must be reading her thoughts.

Falcon laughed softly, his voice a drawling caress. *You are an amazing woman, Sara. Even to be able to translate my letters to you. I wrote them in several languages. Greek, Hebrew. The ancient tongue. How did you accomplish such a feat?* He was traveling swiftly across the night sky, scanning carefully, looking for disturbances that would signal the arrival of the undead. Sometimes blank spaces revealed the vampire's lair. Other times it would be a surge of power or an unexpected exodus of bats from a cave. The smallest detail could provide clues to one who knew where to look.

Sara was silent a moment, turning the question over in her mind. She had been obsessed with translating the strange documents wrapped so carefully in oilskin. Perseverance. She had *needed* to translate those words. Sacred words. She remembered the feeling she had each time she touched those scrolled pages. Her heart had beat faster, her body had come to life, her fingers had smoothed over the fibers more times than she wanted to count. She had known that those words were meant for her. And she had seen his face. His eyes, the shape of his jaw, the long flow of his hair. The aching loneliness in him. She had known that only she would find the right translation.

My parents taught me Greek and Hebrew and most of the ancient languages, but I had never seen some of the letters and symbols before. I went to several museums and all the universities, but I didn't want to show the diary to anyone else. I believed it was meant for me.

She had known that the words were intimate, meant only for her eyes. There had been poetry in those words before she had ever translated them. Sara felt tears gathering in her eyes. Falcon. She knew his name now, had looked into his eyes, and she knew he needed her. No one else. Just Sara. *I studied the diary for several months, translated what I could, but I knew it wasn't right, word for word. And then it just came to me. I felt when it was right. I can't explain how, but I knew the moment I hit on the key.*

Falcon felt the curious wrenching in his heart. She could make his soul flood with warmth, overwhelming him with such intense feeling that he was no longer the powerful predator but a man willing to do anything for his lifemate. She humbled him with her generosity and her acceptance of what he was. He had written those words, expressing emotions he could no longer feel. Writing the diary was a compulsion he couldn't ignore. He had never expected anyone to read it, yet he had never destroyed it, unable to do so.

Dawn was a couple of hours away and the vampire would still be lethal. More than likely he was searching for lairs, escape routes, gathering information. Falcon had hunted and successfully battled the vampire for centuries, yet he was growing distinctly uneasy. He should have picked up a trail, yet there were none of the usual signs to indicate the undead had passed over the city. Few of the creatures could achieve such a feat; only a very powerful ancient enemy would have such skills.

You are my heart and soul, Sara. The words I left for you are truth, and only my lifemate would know how to find the key to unlock the code to translate the ancient language. His tone held admiration and an intensity of love that wrapped her in warmth. *I must concentrate on the hunt. This one is no fledgling vampire, but one of power and strength. It requires my full attention. Should you have need of me, reach with your mind and I will hear you.*

Sara crossed her arms across her breasts, moving back onto her porch, watching the sheets of rain falling in silvery threads. She felt Falcon's uneasiness more than heard it in his tone. *If you need me, I will come to you.* She meant it. Meant it with every cell in her body. It felt wrong to have Falcon going alone to fight her battles.

Falcon's heart lightened. She would rush to his aid if he called her. Their tie was already strong, and growing with each passing moment. Sara represented the miracle granted to his species. *Lifemate.*

He was cautious as he moved across the sky, using the storm as his cover. He was adept, able to shield his presence easily. He began surveying the areas most likely to harbor the undead. Within the city, it would be the deserted older buildings with basements. Outside of the city, it would be any cave, any hole in the ground the ancient vampire could protect.

Falcon found no traces of the enemy, but the uneasiness in him began to grow. The vampire would have already attacked Sara if he had known for certain where she was. Obviously, he had vented his rage because he *hadn't* found her, and he had hoped to frighten her into betraying her presence. That left one other avenue open to Falcon. He would have to find the vampire's kill and trace him from there. It would be a painstakingly slow process and he would have to leave Sara alone for some time. He reached for her. *If you feel uneasy, call for me at once. Anything at all, Sara, call for me.*

He felt her smile. *I have been aware of this enemy for half my life. I know when he is close, and I have managed to escape him time after time. You take care of yourself, Falcon, and don't worry about me.* Sara had been alone a long time and was an independent, self-sufficient woman. She was far more worried about Falcon than she was about herself.

The rain was still pouring down, the wind blowing the droplets into dismal heavy sheets. Falcon felt no cold in the form he had taken. Had he been in his natural body, he would have regulated his body temperature with ease. The storm was a deterrent to seeking his enemy by using scent, but he knew the ways of the vampire. He found the kill unerringly.

The body was in an alleyway, not far from where Sara's sewer children had rushed Falcon. His uneasiness grew. The vampire obviously had become adept at finding Sara. There was a pattern to her behavior, and the undead capitalized on it. Once he found the country and the city she had settled in, the vampire would go to the places where Sara would eventually go. The refuges of the lost, the homeless, the unwanted children and battered women. Sara would work in those areas to accomplish what she could before she moved on. Money meant little to her; it was only a means to keep moving and to do what she could to help. She lived frugally and spent little on herself. Just as Falcon had studied vampires to learn their ways, this vampire had studied Sara. Yet she had continued to elude him. Most vampires were not known for their patience, yet this one had followed Sara relentlessly for fifteen years.

It was a miracle that she had managed to avoid capture, a tribute to her courageous and resourceful nature. Falcon's frame shimmered and solidified in the dreary rain beside the dead man. The vampire's victim had died hard. Falcon studied the corpse, careful not to touch anything. He wanted the scent of the undead, the feel of him. The victim was young, a street punk. There was a knife on the ground with blood on the blade. Falcon could see the blade was already corroding. The man had been tortured, most likely for information about Sara. The vampire would want to know if she had been seen in the area. The echoes of violence were all around Falcon.

He couldn't allow the evidence to remain for the police. He sighed softly and began to summon the energy in the sky above him. Bolts of lightning danced brightly, throwing the alley into sharp relief. The whips sizzled and crackled, white-hot. He directed the energy to the body and the knife. It incinerated the victim to fine ashes and cleansed the blade before melting it.

The flare of power was all around him as the lightning burned like an orange flame from the ground back up to the dark, ominous clouds, where it veined out in radiant points of blue-white heat. Falcon suddenly raised his head and looked around him, realizing that the power vibrating in the air was not his alone. He leaped back, away from the ashes as the blackened ruins came to life. An apparition of horror rose up with a misshapen head and pitiless holes for eyes.

Falcon whirled, a fraction of a second too late, to meet the real attack. A claw missed his eye and raked his temple. Razor-sharp tips dug four long furrows into his chest. The pain was excruciating. Hot, fetid breath exploded in his face and he smelled rotting flesh, but the creature was a blur, disappearing as Falcon struck instinctively toward the heart.

His fist brushed thick fur and then empty air. At once, the beast within Falcon rose up, hot and powerful. The strength of it shook him. There was a red haze in front of his eyes, chaos reigning in his mind. Falcon spun around as he took to the sky, barely avoiding slamming bolts of energy that blackened the alley and took out the sides of the already crumbling building. The sound was deafening. The beast welcomed the violence, embraced it. Falcon was fighting himself as well as the vampire, battling the hunger that could never be assuaged.

Falcon? Her voice was a breath of fresh air, pushing aside the call of the kill. *Tell me where you are. I feel danger to you.* It was the naked concern in her voice that allowed him to control the raging demon, to push it aside despite the desire for violence.

Falcon struck fast and hard, a calculated risk, flying toward the bizarre figure made of ash, his fist outstretched before him. The ashes scattered in a whirlwind, rising high like a tower of grotesque charcoal. For an instant a form shimmered in the air as the vampire attempted to throw a barrier between them. Falcon drove through the flimsy structure, again feeling the brush, this time of flesh, but the creature had managed to dissolve again. The vampire was gone, vanishing as swiftly as it had appeared.

There was no trace of the monster, not even the inevitable blankness. Falcon searched the area carefully, thoroughly, looking for the smallest clue. The longer he searched, the more he was certain that Sara was hunted by a true ancient, a master vampire who had managed to elude all hunters throughout the centuries.

Falcon moved through the sky warily. The vampire would not strike at him again now. Falcon had been tested, and the ancient had lost the advantage of surprise. The enemy now knew he was up against an experienced hunter well versed in battle. He would go to ground, avoid contact in the hopes that Falcon would pass him by.

A clap of thunder echoed across the sky. A warning. A dark promise. The vampire was staking his claim, despite the fact that he knew a hunter was in the area. He would not give Sara up. She was his prey.

Sara was waiting for Falcon on the small porch, reaching for him with eager arms. Her gaze moved over him fearfully, assessing him for damage. Falcon wanted to gather her into his arms and hold her against his heart. No one had ever welcomed him, worried about him, had that look on her face. Anxious. Loving. She was even more beautiful than he remembered. Her clothes were soaked with rainwater, her short hair spiky and disheveled, her eyes enormous. He could drown in her eyes. He could melt in the heat of her welcome.

"Come into the house," Sara said, touching his temple with gentle fingers, running her hands over him, needing to feel him. She drew him into her home, out of the night air, out of the rain. "Tell me," she urged.

Falcon looked around him at the neat little room. It was soothing and homey. Comforting. The stark contrast between his ugly, barren existence and this moment was so extreme, it was almost shocking. Sara's smile, her touch, the worry in her eyes—he wouldn't trade those things for any treasure he had ever come across in his centuries on earth.

"What happened to you, Falcon? And I don't mean your wounds." The fear for him she felt deep within her soul had been overwhelming in those moments before their communication.

Falcon shoved a hand through his long hair. He had to tell her the truth. The demon in him was stronger than ever. He had waited too long, been in too many battles, made too many kills. "Sara," he said softly. "We have a few choices, but we must make them swiftly. We do not have the time to wait until you fully understand what is happening. I want you to remain quiet and listen to what I have to say, and then we will have to make our decisions."

Sara nodded gravely, her eyes on his face. He was struggling, she could see that clearly. She knew he feared for her safety. She wanted to smooth the lines etched so deeply into his face. There was blood smeared on his temple, a thin trail that only accented the deep weariness around his mouth. His shirt was tattered and bloody, with four distinct rips. Every cell in her body cried out to hold him, to comfort him, yet she sat very still, waiting for what was to come.

"I have tied us together in life or death. If something were to happen to me, you would find it very difficult to continue without me. We must get to the Carpathian Mountains and my people. This enemy is an ancient and very powerful. He is determined that you are his, and nothing will deter him from hunting you. I believe you are in danger during both the hours of sunlight and darkness."

Sara nodded. She wasn't about to argue with him. The vampire had been relentless in his pursuit of her.

She had been lucky in her escapes, willing to run at the smallest sign that he was near. Had the vampire stalked her silently, he would have had her, she was certain, but he didn't seem to credit her ability to ignore his summons. "He's used creatures during the day before." She looked down at her hands. "I burned one of them." She admitted it in a low voice, ashamed of herself.

Falcon, feeling her guilt like a blow, took her hands, turned them over, and placed a kiss in the center of each palm. "The vampire's ghouls are already dead. They are soulless creatures, living on flesh and the tainted blood of the vampire. You were lucky to escape them. Killing them is a mercy. Believe me, Sara, they cannot be saved."

"Tell me our choices, Falcon. It is nearly morning and I'm feeling very anxious for you. Your wounds are serious. You need to be looked after." She could hardly bear the sight of him. He was smeared with blood and so weary he was drooping. Her fingers smoothed back stray strands of his long black hair.

"My wounds truly are not serious." He shrugged them off with a casual ripple of his shoulders. "When I go to ground, the soil will aid in healing me. While I am locked within the earth, you will be alone and vulnerable. During certain hours of the day I am at my weakest and cannot come to your aid. At least not physically. I would prefer that you remain by my side at all times to know you are safe."

Her eyes widened. "You want me to go beneath the earth with you? How would that be possible?" There were things left undone, things she needed to do in the daylight hours. Business hours. The world didn't accommodate Falcon's people so readily.

"You would have to become fully like me." He said it softly, starkly. "You would have all the gifts of my people, and also the weaknesses. You would be vulnerable during daylight hours, and you would require blood to sustain your life."

She was silent for a moment, turning his words over in her mind. "I presume that if I were like you, that would not be so abhorrent to me. I would crave blood?"

He shrugged. "It is a fact of our lives. We do not kill; we keep our prey calm and unknowing. I would provide for you, and it would not be in such a way that you would find it uncomfortable."

Sara nodded her acceptance of that even as her mind turned over his use of the word *prey*. She had lived in the shadows of the Carpathian world for fifteen years. His words weren't a shock to her. She drew Falcon toward the small bathroom where she had a first aid kit. He went with her because he could feel her need to take care of him. And he liked the feel of her hands on him.

"I can't possibly make a decision like this in one night, Falcon," she said as she ran hot water onto a clean cloth. "I have things I have to finish and I'll need to think about this." She didn't need to think too long or too hard. She wanted him with every fiber of her being. She had already learned in the short time while he was off chasing her enemy what it would be like to be without him.

Sara leaned into him and kissed his throat. "What else?" Her full breasts brushed against his arm, warm, inviting. Very gently she dabbed at the lacerations on his temple, wiping away the blood. The wounds on his chest were deeper. It looked as if an animal had raked claws over his chest, ripping his shirt and scoring four long furrows in the skin.

"I came very close to losing my control this night. I need to complete the ritual so we are one and you are my anchor, Sara. You felt it; you sensed the danger to me and called me back to you. Once the ritual is complete, that danger would no longer exist." He made the confession in a low voice, his overwhelming need evident in his husky tone. He couldn't think straight when she was so close to him, the roar in his head drowning out everything but the needs of his body.

Sara caught his face in her hands. "That's it? That's the big confession?" Her smile was slow and beautiful, lighting her eyes to a deep violet. "I want you more than anything on this earth." She bent her head and took possession of his mouth, pressing her body close to his, her rain-wet silken tank top nearly nonexistent, her breasts thrusting against him, aching with need. A temptation. An enticement. There was hunger in her kiss, acceptance, excitement. Her mouth was hot with her own desire, meeting the demands of his. Raw. Earthy. Real.

She lifted her head, her gaze burning into his. "I have been yours for the last fifteen years. If you want me, Falcon, I'm not afraid. I've never really been afraid of you." Her hands pushed aside his torn shirt, exposing his chest and the four long wounds.

"You have to understand what kind of commitment you are making, Sara," he cautioned. He needed her. Wanted her. *Hungered* for her. But he would not lose his honor with the most important person in his life. "Once the ritual is complete, if you are not with me below the ground while I sleep, you will fight a terrible battle for your sanity. I do not wish this for you."

Chapter Five

Sara blinked, drawing attention to her long lashes. Her gaze was steady. "Neither do I, Falcon"—her voice was a seductive invitation—"but I'd much rather fight my battles briefly than lose you. I'm strong. Believe in me." She bent her head, pressed a kiss into his shoulder, his throat. "You aren't taking anything I'm not willing to give."

How could she tell him, explain to him that he had been her only salvation all those long, endless nights when she'd hated herself, hated that she was alive and her family dead? How could she tell him he had saved her sanity, not once, but over and over? All those long years of holding his words close to her, locked in her heart, her soul. She knew she belonged with Falcon. She knew it in spite of what he was. She didn't care that he was different, that his way of surviving was different. She only cared that he was real, alive, standing in front of her with his soul in his eyes. Sara smiled at him, a sweet, provocative invitation, and simply drew her tank top over her head so that he could see her body, the full, lush curves, the darker peaks. Sara dropped the sodden tank top in a little heap on top of his shirt. She tilted her chin, trying to be brave, but he could see the slight trembling of her body. She had never done such an outrageous thing in her life.

Falcon found the nape of her neck, his fingers curling possessively as he dragged her close to him. His wounds were forgotten, his weariness. In that moment everything was forgotten but that Sara was offering herself to him. Pledging to give her life and her body into his keeping. Generously. Unconditionally.

Falcon thought she was the sexiest thing he had ever seen in all his years of existence. She was looking at him with enormous eyes so vulnerable his insides turned to mush. His breath slammed right out of his lungs. His body was so hot, so hard, so tight, he was afraid he might shatter if he moved. Yet he couldn't stop himself. His hand of its own volition drifted down her throat to cup her breast. Her skin was incredibly soft, softer even than it looked. It was shocking the way he felt about her, the sheer intensity of it. Where he had never wanted or needed, where no one had mattered, now there was Sara to fill every emptiness in him. His fingertips brushed over the curve of her breast, an artist's touch, explored the line of her ribs, the tuck of her waist, returned to cup her lush offering.

His black gaze burned over her possessively, scorching her skin, sending flames licking along the tips of her breasts, her throat, her hips, between her legs. And then he bent his head and drew her breast into the hot, moist cavern of his mouth.

Sara cried out, clutched his head, her fingers tangling in the thick silk of his hair, her body shuddering with pleasure. She felt the strong, erotic pull of his mouth in the very core of her body. Her body clenched tightly, aching, coiled with edgy need.

Falcon skimmed his hand down the sleek line of her back. *Are you certain, Sara? Are you certain you want the complete intimacy of our binding ritual?* He sent her the picture in his head: his mouth on her neck, over her pulse, the intensity of his physical need of her. He was already pulling her closer, devouring her skin, the lush curves so different from the hard planes and angles of his own body.

If Sara had wanted to pull back, it was already far too late. She was lost in the arcing electricity, the dazzling lightning dancing in her bloodstream. The images and the sheer pleasure in his mind, darkly erotic, only added to the firestorm building in her body. She had never experienced anything so elemental, so completely right, so completely primitive. She needed to be closer to him, skin to skin. The need was all-consuming, as hot as the sun itself, a firestorm raging, crowning, until there was nothing else, only Falcon. Only feeling. Only his fierce possession. She cradled his head to her breast, arcing deeper into his mouth while her body went liquid hot.

She wrapped one leg around his hips, pushing her heated center against the hard column of his thigh, a hard friction, moving restlessly, seeking relief. Her hands were tugging at his clothes, trying to get them off him while his mouth left flames on her neck, her breasts, even her ribs. His hands skimmed the curve of her hips, taking the silken pajamas down her thighs so the material pooled on the floor in a heap. He caught her leg and once more wrapped it around his hips so that she was open to him, pressed, hot and wet, tight against him.

Falcon's mouth found hers in a series of long kisses, each inflaming her more than the last. His hands were possessive on her breasts, her belly, sliding to her bottom, the inside of her thigh.

She was hot and wet with her need of him, her scent calling to him. Falcon's body was going up in flames. Sara had no inhibitions about letting him know she wanted him, and it was a powerful aphrodisiac. Her body moved against his, rubbing tightly, open to his exploration. She was pushing at his clothes, trying to get closer, her mouth on his chest, her tongue swirling to taste his skin. He removed the barrier of his clothing in the easy manner of his people, using his mind so that her hands could find him, thick and hard and full and throbbing with need. The moment her fingers stroked him, little firebombs seemed to explode in his bloodstream.

She knew him intimately, his thoughts, his dreams. She knew his mind, what he liked, what he needed and wanted. And he knew her. Every way to please her. They came together in heat and fire, yet for all his enormous strength, his desperate need, his touch was tender, exploring her body with a reverence that nearly brought tears to her eyes. His mouth was everywhere, hot and wild, teasing, enticing, promising things she couldn't conceive of.

Sara clung to him, wrapped her arms around his head, tears glistening like diamonds in her eyes, on her lashes. "I've been so alone, Falcon. Never go away. I don't know if you're real or not. How could anything as beautiful as you be real?"

He lifted his head, his black eyes drifting over her face. "You are my soul, Sara, my existence. I know what being alone is. I have lived centuries without home or family. Without being complete, the best part of me gone. I never wish to be apart from you." He caught her face between his hands. "Look at me, Sara. You are my world. I would not choose to be in this world without you. Believe in me." He bent his head to fasten his mouth to hers, rocking the earth for both of them.

Sara had no idea how they ended up in the bedroom. She was vaguely aware of being pressed against the wall, a wild tango of drugging kisses, of hot skin and exploring hands, of moving through space until the comforter was pressed against her bare body, her skin so sensitive she was gasping with the urgency of her own needs.

His mouth left hers to trace a path over her body, the swell of her breasts, her belly, his tongue trailing fire in its wake. His hands parted her thighs, held her tight as her body exploded, fragmented at the first stroking caress of his tongue.

Sara cried out, her hands fisting in his wealth of thick, long hair. She writhed under him, her body rippling with aftershocks. "Falcon." His name came out a breathy whispered plea.

"I want you ready for me, Sara," he said, his breath warming her, his tongue tasting her again and again, stroking, caressing, teasing until she was crying out again and again, her hips arcing helplessly into him.

His body blanketed hers, skin to skin, his heavier muscles pressed tightly against her softer body so that they fit perfectly. Falcon was careful with her despite the wildness rising within him. He watched her face as he began to push inside her body. She was hot, velvet soft, a tight sheath welcoming him home. The sensation was nothing like he had ever imagined, pure pleasure taking over every cell, every nerve. In the state of heightened awareness that he was in, his body was sensitive to every ripple of hers, every clench of her muscles, every touch of her fingers. Her breath—just her breath gave him pleasure.

He thrust deeper until her breath came in gasps. Until her body coiled tightly around his. Until her nails dug into his back. She was so soft and welcoming. He began to move, surging forward, watching her face, watching the loss of control, feeling the wildness growing in him, reveling in his ability to please her. He thrust harder, deeper, over and over, watching her rise to meet him, stroke for stroke. Her breasts took on a faint sheen, tempting, enticing, a lush invitation.

Falcon bent his head to her, his dark hair sliding over her skin so that she shuddered with pleasure, so that she cried out with unexpected shock at another orgasm, fast and furious.

Sara knew the moment his mouth touched her skin. Scorched her skin. She knew what he would do, and her body tightened in anticipation. She wanted him wild and out of control. His tongue found her nipple, lapped gently. His mouth was hot and greedy, and she heard herself gasp out his name. She held him to her, arcing her body to offer him her breast, her hips moving in perfect rhythm with his.

His mouth moved to the swell of her breast, just over her heart, his teeth scraping gently, nipping, his tongue swirling. Sara thought she might explode into a million fragments. Her body was so hot and tight and aching.

"Falcon . . ." She breathed his name, a plea, needing to fulfill his every desire.

His hands tightened on her hips, and he buried himself deep inside her body and inside her mind, his teeth sinking into her skin so that white-hot lightning lashed through her, through him, until she was consumed by fire. Devoured by it. She cradled his head, but her body was rippling with pleasure, again and again until she thought she might die from it. Endless. On and on, again and again.

His tongue swirled lightly over the small telltale pinpricks. He was trembling, his mind a haze of passion and need. He whispered softly to her, a command as he lifted her head to the temptation of his chest. Falcon felt Sara's mouth move against his skin. His body tightened, a pain-edged pleasure nearly beyond endurance. With Sara firmly caught in his enthrallment, he indulged himself, coaxing her to take enough blood for a true exchange. His body was hard and hot and aching with the need for relief, the need for the ecstasy of total fulfillment. He closed the wound in his chest and took possession of her mouth as he awakened her from the compulsion.

And then he was surging into her, wild and out of control, taking them closer and closer to the edge of a great precipice. Sara clung to him, her softer body rising to meet his with a wild welcome. Falcon lifted his head to look at her, wanting to see the love in her eyes, the welcome, the intense need for him. Only him. No other. It was there, just as when she had first recognized him. It was deep within her soul, shining through her eyes for him to see. Sara belonged to him. And he belonged to her.

Fire rushed through him, through her. A fine sheen

of sweat coated their skin. His hands found hers and they moved together, fast and hard and incredibly tender. She felt him swell within her, saw his eyes glaze, and her own body tightened, muscles clenching and rippling with life. His name caught in her throat, his breath left his lungs as they rushed over the edge together.

They lay for a long while, holding one another, their bodies tangled together, skin to skin, his thigh over hers, in between hers, his mouth and hands still exploring. Sara cradled him to her, tears in her eyes, unbelieving that he was in her arms, in her body, one being. She would never be alone. He filled her heart and her mind the way he filled her body.

"We fit," he murmured softly. "A perfect fit."

"Did you know it would be like this? So wonderful?"

He moved then, rising from the bed and bringing her up with him, taking her to the shower. As the water streamed off them, he licked the water from her throat, followed the path of several beads along her ribs. Sara retaliated by tasting his skin, sipping the water beads as they ran low along his flat, hard belly. Her mouth was hot and tight, so that he had to have her again. And again. He took her there in the shower. They made it as far as the small dresser, where he found the sight of her bottom too perfect to ignore. She was receptive, as hot and as needy as Falcon, never wanting the night to end.

The early morning light filtered through the closed curtains. They lay together on the bed, talking together, holding each other, hands and mouths stroking caresses in between words. Sara couldn't remember laughing so much; Falcon hadn't thought he knew how to laugh. Finally, reluctantly, he leaned over to kiss her.

"You must go if you are going to do this, Sara. I want you high in the Carpathian Mountains before nightfall. I will rise and come straight to you."

Sara slid from the bed to stand beside the bust she had made so many years earlier. She didn't want to leave him. She wanted to remain curled up beside him for the rest of her life.

Falcon didn't need to read her mind to know her thoughts; they were plain on her transparent face. For some reason, her misgivings made it easier for him to allow her to carry out her plans. He stood up, his body crowding close to hers. He needed sleep; he needed to go to ground and fully heal. Mostly he needed to be with Sara.

"I'm afraid that if I leave, I might never get the children. The officials are disturbed because I'm asking for all seven of them and there are no records." Sara's fingers twisted together in agitation.

"Mikhail will be able to get rid of the red tape for us. He has many businesses in this area and is well known." Falcon brought her fingers to the warmth of his mouth to calm her. "I have not been to my homeland in many years, but I am well aware of everything that is happening. He will be able to assist us."

"How do you know so much if you've been away?" Sara wasn't ready to trust a complete stranger with something so important as the children.

He smiled and tangled his fingers in her hair. "The Carpathian people speak on a common mental pathway. I hear when hunters have gone through the land or some trauma has taken place. I heard when our Prince nearly lost his lifemate. Not once, but on two occasions. I heard when he lost his brother and then his brother returned to him. Mikhail will assist you. When you reach the area, he will find you in the evening and you will be under his protection. I will rise as soon as possible and come straight to you. He will assist us in finding a good location for our home. It will be near him and within the protection of all Carpathians. I have marked the trails for you in the mountains." Falcon bent his head to the temptation of her breast, his tongue lapping at the tight, rosy peak. His hair skimmed over her skin like so much silk. "You must be very careful, Sara. You cannot think you are safe because it is daylight. The undead are locked within the earth, but they are able to control their minions. This vampire is an ancient and very powerful."

Her body caught fire, just like that, liquid flames rushing through her bloodstream. "I will be more than careful, Falcon. I've seen what he does. I'm not going to doing anything silly. You don't have to worry. After I contact my friends and get a call through to my lawyer, I'll be going straight to the mountains. I'll find your people," she assured. Her heart was beating a little too fast at that thought, and she knew he heard it. Her own hearing was far more acute than it had been, and the thought of food made her feel slightly sick. Already she was changing, and the idea of being separated from Falcon was frightening. Sara lifted her chin determinedly and flashed him a reassuring smile. "Once I set everything up, I'll get on the road." Her fingers were continually sliding over the bust of Falcon's head, lovingly following the grooves marking the waves in his hair.

Watching her, knowing that statue had been her solace in years past, Falcon felt his heart turn over. He gathered her close to him, his touch possessive, tender, as loving as he could make it. "You will not be alone, Sara. I will heed your call, even in my most vulnerable hour. Should your mind start to play tricks on you, telling you I am dead to you, call me and I will answer."

Sara molded her body against his, clinging to him, holding him close so that he felt real and strong and very solid. "Sometimes I think maybe I dreamed of you for so long I'm hallucinating, that I made you up and any minute you'll disappear," she confessed softly.

His arms tightened until he was nearly crushing her against him, yet there was great tenderness in the way he held her. "I never dared to dream, even to hope. I had accepted my barren existence. It was the only way to survive and do my duty with honor. I am not ever going to leave you, Sara." He didn't tell her he was terrified at the thought of going to ground while she faced danger on the surface. She was a strong woman, and she had survived a long, deadly duel with the vampire completely on her own. He couldn't find it in him to insist she do things his way simply for his comfort.

Sara was touching his mind, could read his thoughts, the intensity of his fear for her safety. A wave of love swept through her. She turned her face up to his, hungrily seeking his mouth, wanting to prolong her time with him. His mouth was hot and dominant, as hungry as hers. As demanding. A fierce claim on her. He kissed her chin, her throat, found her mouth again, devouring her as if he could never get enough. There was an edginess to his kiss now, an ache. A need.

Sara's leg slid up his leg to wrap around his waist. She pressed against the hard column of his thigh, grinding against him, so that he felt her invitation, her own demand, hot and wet and pulsing with urgency.

Falcon simply lifted her in his arms, and she wrapped both legs around his waist. With her hands on his shoulders, her head thrown back, she lowered her body to the thick hardness of his. He pressed against her moist entrance, making her gasp, cry out as he slowly, inch by inch, filled her completely. Sara threw back her head, closed her eyes as she began to ride him, losing herself completely in Falcon's dark passion. They took their time, a long, slow tango of fiery heat that went on and on as long as they dared. They were in perfect unison, reading each other's minds, moving, adjusting, giving themselves completely, one to the other. When they were spent, they leaned against the wall and held one another, their hearts beating the same rhythm, tears in their eyes. Sara's head was on his shoulder and Falcon's head rested on hers.

"You cannot allow anything to happen to yourself, Sara," he cautioned. "I have to go now. I cannot wait much longer. You know I cannot be without you. You will remember everything I have said to you?"

"Everything." Sara tightened her hold on him. "I know it's crazy, Falcon, but I love you. I really do. You've always been with me when I needed you. I love you."

He kissed her, long and tender. Incredibly tender. "You are my love, my life." He whispered it softly and then he was gone. Sara remained leaning against the wall, her fingers pressed against her mouth for a few moments. Then she sprang into action.

She worked quickly, packing a few clothes and tossing them in her backpack, making several calls to ask friends to keep an eye on the children until she could return. She had every intention of coming back for them as soon as she sorted out the extensive paperwork and set up a home for them. She was on the road heading toward the Carpathian Mountains within an hour.

She needed the darkness of sunglasses, although the day was a dreary gray with ominous clouds overhead. Her skin prickled with unease as rays of sunlight pushed through the thick cloud covering to touch her arm as she drove. She tried not to think about Falcon locked deep within the ground. Her body was wonderfully sore. She could feel his touch on her, his possession, and just the thought of him made her hot with renewed desire. She couldn't prevent her mind from continually seeking his. Each time she touched on the void, her heart would contract painfully, and it would take tremendous effort to control her wild grief. Every cell in her body demanded that she go back, find him, make certain he was safe.

Sara tilted her chin and kept driving, hour after hour, leaving the cities for smaller villages until she was finally in a sparsely populated area. She stopped twice to rest and stretch her cramped legs, but continued steadily, always driving up toward the region Falcon had so carefully marked for her. She was concentrating so hard on finding the trail leading into wild territory that she was nearly hit by another vehicle as it overtook her and roared by. It shot past her at breakneck speed, a larger, much heavier truck with a camper. She was forced to veer off the narrow track to keep from being shoved off the trail. The vehicle went by her so quickly she nearly missed seeing the little faces peering out at her from the window of the camper shell. She nearly missed the sounds of screams fading into the forest.

Sara froze, her mind numb with shock, her body nearly paralyzed. The children. Her little ones, the children she had promised safety and a home. They were in the hands of a puppet, a ghoul. The walking dead. The vampire had taken a human, enslaved him, and programmed the creature to take her children as bait. She should have known, should have guessed he would discover them. She gave chase, hurtling along the narrow, rutted trail, clinging to the steering wheel as her truck threatened to break apart.

Two hours later, she was completely and hopelessly lost. The ghoul was obviously aware that she was following and it simply drove where no vehicle should have been able to go, racing dangerously through hairpin turns and smashing his way through vegetation. Sara attempted to follow, driving at breakneck speed through the series of turns, wheels bouncing over the rough pits in the roads. Once a tree was down directly across her path and she had to take her truck deeper into the forest to get around it. She was certain the ghoul had shoved the tree there to block her pursuit, to delay her. The trees were so close together, they scraped the paint from the sides of her truck. She couldn't believe she could possibly have lost the other vehicle; there weren't that many roads to turn onto. She tried twice to look at the map on the seat beside her, but with the terrible jouncing, it was impossible to focus. Branches scraped the windshield; twigs snapped off with an ominous sound.

With her arms aching and her heart pounding, Sara managed to maneuver her truck back onto a faint trail that might pass for a road. It was very narrow and ran along a deep, rocky ravine that looked like a great crack in the earth. In places, the boulders were black and scarred as if a war had taken place. The branches slapped at her truck as it rushed through the trees along the winding road. She would have to pull over and consult the map Falcon had given her.

His name immediately brought a welling of grief, of fear that he was lost to her, but Sara attempted to push the false emotion aside, grateful that he had prepared her for such a possibility. A sob welled up, choking her; tears blurred her vision but she wiped them away, wrenching at the wheel determinedly when her truck nearly bounced off the road from a particularly deep rut.

This couldn't be happening. The children, *her* children in the hands of the vampire's evil puppet. A flesh-eating ghoul. Sara wanted to continue driving as fast as she could, terrified that if she stopped she would never be able to catch them. She was well aware that it was late afternoon and once the ghoul delivered the children to the vampire, she had little hope of saving them.

Sara sighed softly and slowed the truck with great reluctance, pulling to the side of the trail. A steep cliff rose up sharply on her left. It took tremendous discipline to force herself to stop her vehicle and spread the map out in front of her. She needed to look for places where she could have gotten off the track, where the ghoul could have gotten away from her. She found she was nearly choking with grief. She shoved the door open and, leaving the vehicle running, jumped out where she could breathe the cool, crisp, fresh air.

Falcon. She breathed his name. Wanted him. Dashing the tears away, Sara grabbed the map from the seat and stared down at the clearly marked trail. Where had the ghoul turned off? How had she missed it? She had been driving as fast as she dared, yet she had still lost sight of the children.

A terrible sense of failure assailed her. She spread the map out on the hood of the truck and glared at the markings, waiting for inspiration, for some tiny clue. Her fingernails beat out a little tattoo of frustration on the metal hood. All around her was the sound of the wind whipping through the trees and out over the cliffs into empty space. But some sixth sense warned her she was not alone.

Sara turned her head. The creature was lumbering toward her, his blank expression a hideous reminder that he was no longer human. There would be no reasoning with him, no pleading with him. He had been programmed by a master of cunning and evil. She let out her breath slowly, carefully, centering herself for the attack. Sara crouched lower on the balls of her feet, her mind clear and calm as the thing neared her. Its eyes were fixed on her, its fingers clenching and unclenching as it shuffled forward. She didn't dare allow it to get its hands on her. Her world narrowed to the thing approaching her, her mind clear, as she knew it would have to be.

She waited until the creature was nearly on top of her before she moved. She used her speed, whirling in a spin, generating power as her leg lashed out, the edge of her foot catching the ghoul's kneecap in an explosion of violence. She sprang away, out of reach of those clawed hands. The creature howled loudly, spittle spraying into the air, a thick drool oozing from the side of its mouth. The eyes remained dead and fixed on her as its leg buckled with an audible crack. Unbelievably, it lurched toward her, dragging its useless leg but coming at her steadily.

Sara knew its kneecap was broken, yet it continued toward her relentlessly. Sara had faced such a thing before, and she knew it would keep coming even if it had to drag itself on the ground. She angled sideways, circling to the ghoul's left in an attempt to slide past it. It bothered her that she couldn't hear the children, that none of them were crying or yelling for help. With her hearing so acute, Sara was certain she would have been able to hear whimpers coming from the ghoul's truck, but there was an ominous silence.

She stood her ground, shaking her arms to keep them loose. The ghoul swiped at her with its long arm, its huge, hamlike fist missing her face as she ducked and slammed her foot into its groin, then straight up beneath its chin. It howled, the sound loud and hideous, its body jerking under the assault, but it only rocked backward, jolted for a moment. Sara had no choice but to slip out of its reach.

It was a lesson in sheer frustration. No matter how many times she managed to score a kick or hit, the creature refused to go down. It howled, spittle exploding from its mouth, but its eyes were always the same, flat and empty and fixed on her. It was like a relentless machine that never stopped. As a last resort, Sara tried luring it near to the edge of the ravine in the hope that she could push it over, but it stood for a moment, breathing heavily, and then turned unexpectedly and lumbered away from her into heavier brush and trees.

Sara hastily scrambled to her truck, her heart pounding heavily. A thunderous crash made her swing her head around. To her horror, the ghoul's heavier vehicle was mowing down brush and even small trees, roaring out of the forest like a charging elephant, aimed straight at the side of her truck. More out of reflex than rational thought, her foot slammed down hard on the accelerator.

Her truck slewed sideways, fishtailed, the tires spinning in the dirt. Sara's heart nearly stopped as the larger vehicle continued straight at her. She could see the driver's face as it loomed closer. It was masklike, the eyes dead and flat. The ghoul appeared to be drooling. She could hear the screams of the children, frightened and alone in the madness of a world they couldn't hope to understand. At least they were alive. She had been afraid that their former silence meant the ghoul had murdered them.

The truck hit the side of hers, buckling the door in on her and shoving her vehicle closer to the edge of the steep ravine. Sara knew she was going to go over the crumbling cliff. Her small truck slid, metal grinding, children screaming, the noise an assault on her sensitive ears. A strange calmness invaded her, a sense of the inevitable. Her fingers wouldn't let go of the steering wheel, yet she couldn't steer, couldn't prevent the truck from sliding inch by inch, foot by foot toward the edge of the cliff.

Two wheels went over the edge, the truck tilted crazily, and then she was falling, tumbling through the air, slamming into the ravine, sliding and rolling. The seatbelt tightened, a hard jolt, biting into her flesh, adding to the mind-numbing pain. *Falcon*. His name was a soft sigh of regret in her mind. A plea for forgiveness.

Falcon was wrenched from his slumber, his heart pounding, his chest nearly crushed in suffocation. He was far from Sara, unable yet to aid her. He would build a monstrous storm to help protect his eyes so he could rise early, but he still would not reach her in time. *Sara.* His life. His heart and soul. Terror filled him. Took him like a crushing weight. *Sara.* His Sara, with her courage and her capacity for love.

She was already in the Carpathian Mountains, caught in the trap the vampire had laid for her. He had no choice. Everyone of Carpathian blood would hear, and that included the undead. It was a risk, a gamble. Falcon was an ancient presumed dead. He had never declared his allegiance to the new Prince and he might not be believed, but it was Sara's only chance.

Falcon summoned his strength and sent out his call. *Hear me, brethren. My lifemate is under attack in the mountains near you. You must go to her aid swiftly as I am far from her. She is hunted by an ancient enemy and he has sent his puppets to acquire her. Rise and go to her. I warn all within my hearing, I am Falcon, a Carpathian of ancient blood, and I will be watching to protect her.*

Chapter Six

There was a swirling fear in Sara's mind, in his. Falcon burst through the soil and into the sky. Light assailed his sensitive eyes and burned his skin, but it didn't matter. Nothing mattered except that Sara was in danger. One moment he was merged mind to mind with Sara; in the next microsecond of time, there was a blank void. He had an eternity to feel the helpless terror roiling in his gut, the fist clamping his heart like a vise, the emptiness that had been his world, now unbearable, unthinkable, a blasphemy after knowing Sara. Falcon forced his mind to work, reaching relentlessly into that blank void for his very soul. For his life. For love.

Sara. Sara, answer me. Wake now. You must wake. I am on my way to you, but you must awaken. Open your eyes for me. He kept his voice calm, but the compulsion was strong, the need in him raw. *Sara, you must wake.*

The voice was far away, coming from within her throbbing head. Sara heard her own groan, a foreign sound. She was raw and hurting everywhere. She didn't want to obey the soft command, but there was a note she couldn't resist. The voice brought with it awareness, and with awareness came pain. Her heart began to pound in terror.

She had no idea how long she had been unconscious in the wreckage of the truck, but she could feel the metal pressing on her legs and glass cutting her body. She was trapped in the twisted metal, shattered glass all around her, blood running down her face. She didn't want to move, not when she heard movement close to her. She squeezed her eyes shut and willed herself to slip back into oblivion.

Relief washed over Falcon, through him, shook him. For a moment he went perfectly still, nearly falling from the sky, nearly unable to hold the image he needed to stay aloft. His mind was fully merged with Sara's, buried within hers, worshiping, examining, nearly numb with happiness. She was alive. She was still alive! Falcon worked at controlling his body's reaction to the sheer terror of losing her, the unbelievable relief of knowing she was alive. It took discipline to lower his heart rate, to steady his terrible trembling. She was alive, but she was trapped and hurt.

Sara, piccola, do as I ask, open your eyes. Keeping his voice gentle, Falcon gave her no choice, burying a compulsion within the purity of his tone. He felt pain sweeping through her body, a sense of claustrophobia. She was disoriented; her head was pounding. Now his fear was back again in full force, although he kept it hidden from her. Instead, it was trapped in his heart, in his deepest soul, a terror such as he had never known before. He was moving fast, streaking across the sky as quickly as possible, uncaring of the disturbance of power, uncaring that all ancients in the area would know he was racing toward the mountains. She was alone, hurt, trapped, and hunted.

Sara's eyes obeyed his soft command. She looked around her at the crushed glass, the twisted wreckage, and the sheered-off top of her truck. Sara wasn't certain she was still actually inside the vehicle. She couldn't recognize it as a truck any longer. It looked as if she were trapped in a smashed accordion. The sun was falling in the mountains, a shadow spreading across the rocky terrain.

She heard a noise, the scrape of something against what was left of her truck, and then she was looking into the face of a woman. Sara's vision was blurry, and it took a few moments of blinking rapidly to bring the woman into focus. Sara remembered how she had gotten in her predicament, and it frightened her to think of how much time might have past, how close the ghoul might be. She tried to move, to look past the woman. When she moved, her body screamed in protest and a shower of safety glass fell around her. Her dark glasses were missing, and her eyes burned so that they wept continually.

"Lie quietly," the woman said, her voice soothing and gentle. "I am a doctor and I must assess the severity of your injuries." The stranger frowned as she lightly took Sara's wrist.

Sara felt very disoriented, and she could taste blood in her mouth. It was far too much of an effort to lift her head. "You can't stay here. Something was chasing me. Really, leave me here; I'll be fine. I've got a few bruises, nothing else, but you aren't safe." Her tongue felt thick and heavy and her tone shocked her, thin and weak, as if her voice came from far away. "You aren't safe," she repeated, determined to be heard.

The woman was watching her carefully, almost as if she knew what Sara was thinking. She smiled reassuringly. "My name is Shea, Shea Dubrinsky. Whatever is chasing you can be dealt with. My husband is close by and will aid us if necessary. I'm going to run my hands over you and check you for injuries. If you could see your truck, you would know what a miracle it is that you survived."

Sara was feeling desperate. Shea Dubrinsky was a beautiful woman, with pale skin and wine-red hair. She looked very Irish. She was serene despite the circumstances. It was only then that the name registered. "Dubrinsky? Is your husband Mikhail? I've come looking for Mikhail Dubrinsky."

Something flickered in Shea Dubrinsky's eyes behind her smoky sunglasses. There was compassion, but something else, too, something that made Sara shiver. The doctor's hands moved over her impersonally, but thoroughly and gently. Sara knew that this woman, this doctor, was one of *them. The others*. Right now Shea Dubrinsky was communicating with someone else in the same manner Sara did with Falcon. It frightened Sara nearly as much as the encounter with the ghoul. She couldn't tell the difference between friend and foe.

Falcon. She reached for him. Needed him. Wanted him with her. The accident had shaken her so that it was difficult to think clearly. Her head ached appallingly and her body was shaky, trembling beyond her ability to control it. It was humiliating for someone of Sara's strong nature. *She is one of them.*

I am here. Do not fear. No one can harm you. Look directly at her, and I will observe what you see. There was complete confidence in Falcon's voice and he swamped her with waves of reassurance, the feel of strong arms stealing around her, gathering her close, holding her to him. The feeling was very real and gave her confidence.

She speaks to another. She says her name is Dubrinsky and her husband is close. I know she speaks to him. She has called him to us. Sara said it with complete conviction. The woman looked calm and professional, but Sara felt what was happening, knew that Shea Dubrinsky was communicating with some other even though Sara could not see anyone else.

Sara gasped as the woman's hands touched sore places. She tried to smile at the other woman. "I'm really okay, the seat belt saved me, although I hurt like crazy. You have to get away from here." She was feeling a bit desperate searching for signs of the ghoul. Sara tried to move and groaned as every muscle in her body protested. Her head pounded so that even her teeth hurt.

"Stay very quiet for just a moment," Shea said softly, persuasively, and Sara recognized a slight "push" toward obedience. Falcon was there with her, sharing her mind, so she wasn't as afraid as she might have been. She believed in him. She knew he would come, that nothing would stop him from reaching her side. "Mikhail Dubrinsky is my husband's brother. Why are you seeking him?" Shea spoke casually, as if the answer didn't matter, but once again, there was that "push" toward truth.

Sara made an attempt to raise her hand, wanting to remove the broken glass from her hair. Her head was aching so much it made her feel sick. "For some reason, compulsion doesn't work very well on me. If you are going to use it, you have to use it with much more strength." She was struggling to keep her eyes open.

Sara! Focus on her. Stay focused! Falcon's command was sharp. *I sent a call ahead to my people to alert them to find you. Mikhail did have brothers, but you must remain alert. I must see through your eyes. You must stay awake.*

Shea was grinning at her a little ruefully. "You are familiar with us." She said it softly. "If that is the case, I want you to hold very still while I aid you. The sun is falling fast. If you are hunted by a puppet of the undead, the vampire will be close by and waiting for the sun to sink. Please remain very quiet while I do this." Shea was watching Sara's face for a reaction.

There was a movement behind Shea and she turned her head with a loving smile. "Jacques, we have found the one we were seeking. She has a lifemate. He is watching us through her eyes. She is one of us, yet not." Out of courtesy she spoke aloud. There was a wealth of love in her voice, an intimacy that whispered of total commitment. She turned back to Sara. "I will attempt to make you more comfortable, and Jacques will get you out of the truck so we may leave this place and get to safety." There was complete confidence in her gentle tones.

Sara wanted the terrible pounding in her head to go away. She couldn't shift her legs; the wreckage was entombing her as surely as a casket. Falcon's presence in her mind was the only thing that kept her from sliding back into the welcoming black void. She struggled to stay alert, watching Shea's every move. The unknown Jacques had not come into her line of vision, but she felt no immediate threat.

Shea Dubrinsky was graceful and sure. There were no rough edges to her, and she seemed completely professional despite the bizarre way she was healing Sara. Sara actually felt the other woman inside her, a warmth, an energy flowing through her body to soothe the terrible aches, to repair from the inside out. She was amazed that the terrible pounding in her head actually lessened. The nausea disappeared.

Shea leaned over to unfasten the seat belt that was biting into Sara's chest. "Your body has suffered a trauma," she said. "There will be extensive bruising, but you're very lucky. Once we are safe, I can make you much more comfortable." She moved out of the way to allow her lifemate access to the wreckage.

Sara found herself staring up at a man with a singularly beautiful face. His eyes, as he took off his sunglasses, were as old as time, as if he had seen far too much. Suffered far too much. He pushed the glasses onto Sara's face, bringing a measure of relief to her burning eyes. Shea brushed Jacques's hand with hers, the lightest of gestures, but it was more intimate than anything Sara had ever witnessed. She could feel the stillness in Falcon, could feel him gathering his strength should there be need.

"Hold very still," Jacques cautioned softly. His voice held the familiar purity that seemed to be a part of the Carpathian species.

"He has the children. Go after him. If you're like Falcon, you have to go after him and get the children back. He's taking them to the vampire." *Falcon, I'm all right. You must find the children and keep them from the vampire.* She was beginning to panic, thinking much more clearly now that the pain was receding.

Jacques grasped the steering column and gave a wrench, exerting strength so that it bent away from her, giving her more room to breathe. "The ghoul will not reach the vampire. Mikhail has risen and he will stop the puppet from reaching his master." There was complete confidence in Jacques's soft voice. "Your lifemate must be on his way, perhaps already close to us. All heard his warning, although he is not known to us." It was a statement, but Sara heard the question in his words.

She watched his hands push the crumbling wreckage from around her legs so that she could move. The relief was so tremendous she could feel tears gathering in her eyes. Sara turned her head away from the probing gaze of the stranger. At once warmth flooded her mind.

I am with you, Sara. I feel your injuries and your fear for the children, but this man would not lie to you. He is the brother of the Prince. I have heard of him, a man who has endured much pain and hardship, who was buried alive by fanatics. Mikhail will not fail to rescue the children.

You go; don't worry about me. You make certain the children are safe!

She didn't know the Prince. She knew Falcon and she trusted him. If the children could be snatched away from the vampire, he would be the one to do it. And he was closer now, she was certain of it. His presence was much stronger and it took little effort to communicate with him.

"I am going to help you out of there," Jacques warned.

Sara had desperately wanted to be free of the wreckage of her truck, but now, faced with the prospect of actually moving, it didn't seem the best of ideas. "I think I'll just sit here for the rest of my life, if you don't mind," she said.

To her shock, Jacques smiled at her, a flash of white teeth that lit his ravaged eyes. It was the last thing she'd expected of him, and she found herself smiling back. "You do not frighten very easily, do you?" he asked softly. He gave no sign that the light of day hurt his eyes, but she could see they were red and streaming. He endured it stoically.

Sara lifted a trembling hand to eye level and watched it shake. They both laughed softly together. "I'm Sara Marten. Thanks for coming to my rescue."

"We could do no other, with your lifemate filling the skies with his declaration." The white teeth flashed again, this time reminding her of a wolf. "I am Jacques Dubrinsky; Shea is my lifemate."

Sara knew he was watching her closely to see what effect his words had on her. She knew Falcon was watching Jacques through her eyes, catching every nuance, sizing up the other man. And Jacques Dubrinsky was well aware of it, too.

"I am going to lift you out of there, Sara," he said gently. "Let me do the work. I have never dropped Shea, so you do not need to worry," he teased.

Sara turned her head to look at the other woman. She lifted an eyebrow. "I don't think that's much of a reassurance. She's much smaller than I am."

Shea grinned at her, a quick, engaging smile that lit her entire face. "Oh, I think he's up to the task, Sara."

Jacques didn't give her any more time to think about it. He lifted her out of the wreckage and carried her easily to a flat spot in the high grass, where his lifemate bent over her solicitously. The movement took Sara's breath away, sent pain slicing through her body. Shea carefully brushed glass from Sara's hair and clothing. "You have to expect to be a bit shaky. Tell your lifemate we are going to take you to Mikhail's house. You will be safe there, and Raven and I can look after you while Jacques joins the men in the hunt for these lost children."

I want the male to stay near you while I am away.

Sara heard the underlying irony in Falcon's voice and she laughed softly. The thought of any male near Sara was disconcerting to him, but he needed to know she was safe.

Sara's relief that Falcon was close and was searching for the children was enormous. She could breathe again, yet, inexplicably, she wanted to cry.

Shea knelt beside her, took her hand, and looked into her eyes. "It's a natural reaction, Sara," she said softly. "It's all right now, everything is going to be all right." Unashamedly she used her voice as a tool to soothe the other woman. "You are not alone; we really can help."

"Falcon says the vampire is ancient and very powerful," Sara said in warning. She was struggling to appear calm and to control the trembling of her body. It was humiliating to be so weak in front of strangers.

Jacques swung his head around alertly, his eyes black and glittering, his entire demeanor changed. All at once he looked menacing. "Is she able to travel, Shea?"

Shea was straightening slowly, a wary look on her beautiful face. A flutter of nerves in Sara's stomach blossomed into full-scale fear. "He's here, isn't he? The ghoul?" She bit her lip and made a supreme effort to get to her feet. "If he's close to us, then so are the children. He can't have handed them off to the vampire." To her horror, she only managed to get a knee under her before blackness began swirling alarmingly close.

"The ghoul is making his way quickly to his master," Jacques corrected. "The vampire probably has summoned the ghoul to him. The undead is sending his warning, a challenge to any who dare to interfere with his plans."

Shea slipped her arm around Sara to keep her from falling. "Do not try to move yet, Sara. You are not ready to stand." The woman turned to her lifemate. "We can move her, Jacques. I think it best to hurry."

They know something I don't. Sara rubbed her pounding head, frustrated that she was unable to see or hear the things heralding danger. *Something is wrong.*

At once she could feel Falcon's reassurance, his strong arms, warmth flooding her, though he was many miles away. *The vampire is locked within his lair, but he is sending his minions across the land searching for you. The male wishes to take you to safety.*

Do you really want me to go with him? I feel so helpless, Falcon. I don't think I could fight my way out of a paper bag.

Yes, Sara, it is best. I will be with you every moment.

The sky was becoming dark, not because the sun was setting but because the winds had picked up, whirling faster and faster, gathering dust, dirt, and debris together, drawing it into a towering mass. Swarms of insects assembled, masses of them, the noise of their wings rivaling the wind. *The children will be so afraid.* Sara reached out for assurance.

Falcon wanted to gather her close, hold her to him, shelter her from the battles that would surely take place. He sent her warmth, love. *I will find them, Sara. You must stay alert so I can guard you while we are apart.*

For some reason, Falcon's words humbled her. She wanted to be at his side. She needed to be at his side.

Jacques Dubrinsky leaned down to Sara. "I understand how you feel. I dislike to be away from Shea. She is a researcher, very important to our people." He looked at his lifemate as he gathered Sara easily into his arms. His expression was tender, mixed with pride and respect. "She is very single-minded, focused on what she is doing. I find it somewhat uncomfortable." He grinned ruefully, sharing his confession candidly.

"Wait!" Sara knew she sounded panic-stricken. "There's a backpack in the truck, I can't leave it. I can't." Falcon's diary was in the wooden box. She carried it everywhere with her. She was not about to leave it.

Shea hesitated as if she might argue, but obligingly rummaged around in the wreckage until she triumphantly came up with the backpack. Sara had her arms outstretched and Shea handed it to her.

Jacques lifted an eyebrow. "Are you ready now? Close your eyes if traveling swiftly bothers you."

Before she could protest, he was whisking her through space, moving so fast that everything around her blurred into streaks. Sara was happy to be away from the wreckage of her truck, from the fierce wind and the swarms of insects blackening the sky. She should have been afraid, but there was something reassuring about Jacques and Shea Dubrinsky. Solid. Reliable.

She had the impression of a large, rambling house with columns and wrap-around balconies. She had no time to get more than a quick look before Jacques was striding inside. The interior was rich with burnished wood and wide open spaces. It all blended together—art, vases, exquisite tapestries, and beautiful furniture. Sara found herself in a large sitting room, pressed into one of the plush couches. The heavy drapes were pulled, blotting out all light so only soft candles lit the room, a relief to eyes sensitive to the sun.

Sara removed Jacques's sunglasses with a shaky hand. "Thank you. It was thoughtful of you to lend them to me."

He grinned at her, his teeth gleaming white, his dark eyes warm. "I am a very thoughtful kind of man."

Shea groaned and rolled her eyes. "He thinks he's charming, too."

Another woman, short with long black hair, glided into the room, her slender arm circling Jacques's waist with an easy, affectionate manner. "You must be Sara. Shea and Jacques alerted me ahead of time that they were bringing you to my home. Welcome. I've made you some tea. It's herbal. Shea thinks your stomach will tolerate it." She indicated the beautiful teacup sitting in a saucer on the end table. "I'm Raven, Mikhail's lifemate. Shea said you were searching for Mikhail."

Sara glanced at the tea, leaned back into the cushions, and closed her eyes. Her head was throbbing painfully and she felt sick again. She wanted to curl up and go to sleep. Tea and conversation sounded overwhelming.

Sara! Falcon's voice was stronger than ever. *You*

must stay focused until I am at your side to protect you. I do not know these strangers. I believe they do not intend you harm, but I cannot protect you if there be need, unless you stay alert.

Sara made an effort to concentrate. "I have had a vampire hunting me for fifteen years. He killed my entire family and he's stolen children he knows matter a great deal to me. All of you are in great danger."

Jacques's eyebrows shot up. "You eluded a vampire for fifteen years?" There was a wealth of skepticism in his voice.

Sara turned her head to look at Shea. "He isn't nearly as charming when you've been around him awhile, is he?"

Shea and Raven dissolved into laughter. "He grows on you, Sara," Shea assured.

"What?" Jacques managed to look innocent. "It is quite a feat for anyone to escape a vampire for fifteen years, let alone a human. It is perfectly reasonable to think there has been a mistake. And I am charming."

Raven shook her head at him. "Don't count too heavily on it, Jacques. I have it on good authority that the inclination to kick you comes often. And humans are quite capable of extraordinary things." She picked several pieces of glass from Sara's clothes. "It must have been terrifying for you."

"At first," Sara agreed tiredly, "but then it was a way of life. Running, always staying ahead of him. I didn't know why he was so fixated on me."

Shea and Raven were lighting aromatic candles, releasing a soothing scent that seeped into Sara's skin, made its way into her lungs, her body, and lessened the aches. "Sara," Shea said softly, "you have a concussion and a couple of broken ribs. I aligned the ribs earlier, but I need to do some work to ensure that you heal rapidly."

Sara sighed softly. She just wanted to sleep. "The vampire will come if he finds out I'm here, and you'll all be in danger. It's much safer if I keep moving."

"Mikhail will find the vampire," Jacques said with complete confidence.

Allow the woman to heal you, Sara. I have heard rumors of her. She was a human doctor before Jacques claimed her.

Sara frowned as she looked at Shea. "Falcon has heard of you. He says you were a doctor."

"I still am a doctor," Shea reassured gently. "Thank you for your warning and your concern for us. It does you credit, but I can assure you, the vampire will not be allowed to harm us here. Allow me to take care of you until your lifemate arrives." Her hands were very gentle as they moved over Sara, leaving behind a tingling warmth. "Healing you as a Carpathian rather than a human doctor is not really all that different. It is faster, because I heal from the inside out. It won't hurt, but it feels warm."

Raven continued to remove glass from Sara's clothing. "How did you meet Falcon? He is unknown to us." She was using a soft, friendly voice, wanting to calm Sara, to reassure her that she would be safe in their home. She also wanted any information available to be transferred to her own lifemate.

Sara leaned into the cushions, her fingers tight around the strap of her backpack. She could hear the wind, the relentless, hideous wind as it howled and moaned, screamed and whispered. There was a voice in the wind. She couldn't make out the words, but she knew the sound. Rain lashed at the windows and the roof, pounded at the walls as if demanding entrance. Dark shadows moved outside the window—dark enough, evil enough to disturb the heavy draperies. The material could not prevent the shadows from reaching into the room. Sparks arced and crackled, striking something they couldn't see. The howls and moans increased, an assault on their ears.

"Jacques." Shea said the name like a talisman. She slipped her hand into her lifemate's larger one, looking up at him with stark love shining in her eyes.

The man pulled his lifemate closer, gently kissed her palm. "The safeguards will hold." He shifted his stance, gliding to place his body between the window and the plush chair where Sara was sitting. The movement was subtle, but Sara was very aware of it.

The sound of the rain changed, became a hail of something heavier hitting the windows and pelting the structure. Raven swung around to face the large rock fireplace. Hundreds of shiny black bodies rained down from the chimney, landing with ugly plops on the hearth, where bright flames leaped to life, burning the insects as they touched the stones. A noxious odor rose with the black smoke. One particularly large insect rushed straight toward Sara, its round eyes fixed malevolently on her.

Chapter Seven

Falcon, in the form of an owl, peered at the ground far below him. He could see the ghoul's truck through the thick vegetation. It was tilted at an angle, one tire dangling precariously over a precipice. A second owl slipped silently out of the clouds, unconcerned with the wicked wind or lashing rain. Falcon felt a stillness in his mind, then a burst of pleasure, of triumph, a glowing pride in his people. He knew that lazy, confident glide, remembered it well. Mikhail, Vladimir Dubrinsky's son, had his father's flair.

Falcon climbed higher to circle toward the other owl. It had been long since he had spoken to another Carpathian. The joy he felt, even with a battle looming, was indescribable. He shared it with Sara, his lifemate, his other half. She deserved to know what she had done for him; it was she who had enabled him to feel emotion. Falcon went to earth, landing as he shifted into his own form.

Mikhail looked much as his father had before him. The same power clung to him. Falcon bowed low, elegantly. He reached out, clasping Mikhail's forearms in the manner of the old warriors. "I give you my allegiance, Prince. I would have known you anywhere. You are much like your father."

Mikhail's piercing black eyes warmed. "You are familiar to me. I was young then. You were lost to us suddenly, as were so many of our greatest warriors. You are Falcon, and your line was thought to have been lost when you disappeared. How is it you are alive and yet we had no knowledge of you?" His grip was strong as he returned the age-old greeting between warriors of their species. His voice was warm, mellow even, yet the subtle reprimand was not lost on Falcon.

"Your father foresaw much in those days, a dark shadowing of the future of our people." Falcon turned toward the truck teetering so precariously. He began to stride toward the vehicle, with Mikhail in perfect synchronization. They moved together almost like dancers, fluid and graceful, full of power and coordination. "He called us together one night, many of us, and asked for volunteers to go to foreign lands. Vlad did not order us to go, but he was very much respected, and those of us who chose to do as he asked never thought of refusing. He knew you were to be Prince. He knew that you would face the extinction of our species. It was necessary for you to believe in your own abilities, and for *all* our people to believe in you and not rely on those of us who were older. We could not afford a divided people." Falcon's voice was gentle, matter-of-fact.

Mikhail's black eyes moved over Falcon's granite-honed face, the broad shoulders, the easy way he carried himself. "Perhaps advice would have been welcomed."

A faint smile touched Falcon's sculpted mouth, hinted at warmth in the depths of his eyes. "Perhaps our people needed a fresh, new perspective without the clutter of what once was."

"Perhaps," Mikhail murmured softly.

The ghoul had climbed from the truck and moved around the vehicle as if examining it. It didn't look up at the two Carpathian males, or acknowledge their presence in any way. Suddenly it placed its back against the truck, dug its feet into the rocky soil, and began to strain.

The sky erupted with black insects, so many the air seemed to groan with the numbers, raining from the sky with a fury equal to a tempest. From inside the truck, the children began to scream as the metal shrieked. The vehicle was being inched slowly but inevitably over the edge of the cliff.

Falcon put on a burst of preternatural speed, catching the ghoul by the shoulder and whirling it away from the truck. He trusted Mikhail to stop the children from going over. The insects were striking at him, stinging, biting, hitting his body, thousands of them, going for his eyes and nose and ears. Falcon was forced to dissolve into vapor, throwing up a quick barricade around himself as he reappeared behind the ghoul.

The creature swung around awkwardly, dragging one leg as it attempted to turn to face Falcon. Its eyes glowed a demonic red. It was making strange noises, somewhere between growling and snarling. It swiped at Falcon with razor-sharp nails, missed by inches. Falcon stayed just out of reach, watching closely. The ghoul was a mindless puppet to be used by its master. The vampire must have known that Falcon was an ancient, easily able to destroy such a creation, so it made little sense that the creature would attempt to fight him, yet that was exactly what the ghoul did. The macabre puppet grasped Falcon, fumbling to get its hands locked around Falcon's neck.

Falcon easily broke the grip, shattering the thick bones and wrenching the ghoul's head. The crack was audible despite the intensity of the wind and the loud clacking of the insects as they hit the ground. The ghoul seemed to glow for a moment, the eyes lighting an eerie orange in the darkness, the skin sloughing off as if the creature were a snake rather than a man.

"Get those children out of here," Falcon called out gravely, backing away from the creature. The light coming from inside the ghoul was becoming brighter, giving off a peculiar luminescence. "It is a trap."

Mikhail was tossing the children to safer ground. Three little girls and four boys. He leaped out of the way as the truck teetered precariously and then tumbled over the edge. He had shielded the children's minds, knowing they had been terror-stricken for most of the day. The oldest child, a boy, couldn't have been more than eight. Mikhail sensed that each of them was special in some way, each had psychic ability.

Insects were raining from the sky, dropping around them to form thick, grotesque piles of squirming bodies. Although Mikhail had erected a barrier over them and had shielded their minds, the children were staring in wide-eyed horror at the bugs. Mikhail heard Fal-

con's soft warning, glanced at the ghoul, and immediately shifted his shape, becoming a long, winged creature, the fabled dragon. Using his mind to control the children, he forced them to climb onto his back. They clung to him, their bodies trembling, but they accepted what was happening without real comprehension. Mikhail took to the air, laying down a long red-orange flame, incinerating all of the hideous beetles and locusts within his range.

I will transport the children to safety.

Go now! Falcon was alarmed for the Prince, alarmed for the children. The ghoul was spinning, creating a peculiar whirlwind motion reminiscent of a minitornado. The winds were furious, blowing the insects in all directions, even sucking them up into the sky. The glow was bright enough to hurt Falcon's sensitive eyes. *In all my long centuries of battles with the undead and their minions, this is a new phenomenon.*

New to me also. Mikhail was winging quickly through the waning light in the sky, battling the ferocity of the wind and the thick masses of insects attacking from all directions. *The undead is indeed powerful to create this havoc while he still lies within his lair. He is without doubt an ancient.*

I sent word to your brother to wait to fight him, as I am certain this one is as old and as experienced as I am. I hope he listens to Sara.

Mikhail, in the body of the dragon, sighed. He hoped so, too. Immediately he touched Jacques's mind, relayed what had transpired and their conclusions.

Falcon moved carefully away from the ghoul, attempting to put distance between them. *The undead baited a trap, drew us away from Sara using the children and the ghoul. He will go after her.* Each direction Falcon chose, the grotesque creature turned with him in perfect rhythm, matching his flowing motions as if they were dance partners. *Get out of here now, Mikhail. Do not wait for me. This thing has attached itself to me like a shadow. A lethal and difficult spell to break. He is a bomb. Get to Sara.*

I will not be happy if such a despicable creature harms you. There was an edge of humor to Mikhail's soft voice. An edge of worry.

I am an ancient. This one will not defeat me. I am concerned only with the safety of you and the children. And with the delay in reaching Sara. It was the truth. Falcon might not have seen such a thing before, but he had supreme confidence in his own abilities. Already he was working at removing the binding attachment from his cells. It was a deep shadowing, as though the ghoul had managed to embed its molecules into Falcon's. Falcon tried various methods but could not find where the binding was impressed into his body. The ghoul was white-hot, blossoming like a mushroom and emitting a strange low hum. Time was running out.

Falcon ran his hands down his arms, across his chest. At once he felt the strange warmth emanating from his chest. Of course. The four long furrows the vampire had carved into his chest! The undead had left the spell in Falcon's chest, spoor for the ghoul to recognize, to adhere itself to. Falcon transmitted the information immediately to the Prince as he hastily began to detach himself from the monstrous time bomb.

The humming was louder, pitched much higher as the insects clacked with more intensity. The bugs were in a kind of frenzy, flying in all directions, swarming, attempting to scratch their way through the barrier Falcon had erected around himself. He had no time to think about poisonous insects; he had to turn his full attention to removing the hidden shadowing on his body. The vampire's fingerprints were etched deep beneath Falcon's skin.

Falcon glided quickly toward the ravine, drawing the ghoul away from the forest. As he twisted this way and that, taking the vampire's puppet with him at every step, he was examining his body from the inside out. He had missed those tiny prints marring his skin, pressed deeply into the lacerations he had already healed. So small, so lethal. He concentrated on scraping the nearly invisible marks from under his skin. It took tremendous discipline to work as he moved, using only his mind, leading the macabre ghoul right over the edge of the cliff. He was floating over empty space, enticing the unholy creature to take the last step that would send it plummeting to the rocks below. The explosion, when it came, could be contained deep within the ravine. Falcon worked rapidly, knowing that if the ghoul was attached to him, even by such tiny and invisible threads, the explosion would kill him.

The ghoul was in the air with him now, and Falcon began the descent slowly, taking the hideous thing where it could do no harm, even as he continued to find each print in the furrows on his chest. The whirling hot light suddenly shuddered, slipped, as if hanging by only a few precarious threads. The humming was now at fever-pitch, a merciless, unrelenting screaming in his head that made it difficult to think.

Falcon shut out the noise, increasing his speed, knowing he was close to throwing off the ghoul, knowing it was close to the end of its run. The vampire was waiting for sunset, holding Falcon away from Sara as surely as if he had imprisoned him. The ghoul pulsed with red-orange light through the white-hot glow just as Falcon sloughed off the last of the vampire's marks. The puppet began to fall, dropping away as Falcon rose swiftly toward the roiling clouds.

Falcon dissolved into mist as he rushed away from the screeching bomb. The explosion was monumental, a force that blew insect parts in all directions, carved a crater into the side of the ravine, and set the brush on fire. Falcon immediately doused the flames with rain, directing the heavy clouds over the steep ravine as he turned toward Mikhail's home, picking the directions out of the Prince's mind.

When Falcon made contact with Mikhail, he found him engaged in conversation with a human male, cautioning the man to protect the children. He knew he need not worry about the children; Mikhail would never place them in a dangerous situation. *Sara, I am some distance away but I will reach you soon.*

Falcon! Sara pushed herself upright despite her dizziness, staring in horror at the hideous beetle scurrying across the floor toward her. It was staring directly at her, watching her, marking her. And she knew what it was. Just as Falcon could use her eyes to see what was happening around her, the vampire was using the beetle's. The hard shell was on fire, the smell atrocious, but it was moving unerringly toward her, the eyes fixed on her. *He knows where I am. He'll kill all these people.* She was terrified, but Sara couldn't live with more guilt. If this monster wanted her so badly, perhaps the solution was simply to walk out the door and find him.

No! Falcon's voice was strong, commanding. *You will do as I say. Warn the male that this enemy is an ancient, most likely one of the warriors sent out by Mikhail's father who turned vampire. The sun has not yet set, we have a few minutes. The male must use delaying tactics until we arrive to aid him.*

Jacques simply stepped on the large insect, flames and all, crushing the thing beneath his foot, smothering the flames. Sara cleared her throat and looked at Jacques with sorrow in her eyes. "I'm so sorry. I didn't mean to bring this enemy to you. He's an ancient, Falcon says, most likely one of the warriors Mikhail's father sent out."

Raven smoothed back Sara's hair with gentle fingers. Jacques hunkered down so he was level with Sara. His expression was as calm as ever. "Tell me what you know, Sara. It will aid me in battle."

Sara shook her head, had to suppress a groan as her head throbbed and pulsed with pain. "Falcon says to delay the battle, to wait for him, and for Mikhail."

"Heal her, Shea," Jacques ordered gently. "The sun has not set and the vampire is locked deep within the earth. He knows where she is and will come to us, but the safeguards will slow him. We have time. Mikhail will make his way here, and her lifemate will come also. This ancient enemy is a powerful one."

The children, Falcon. What of the children? Sara was finding it difficult to think, with the grotesque remains of the insect on the immaculate shining wood floor.

The children are safe, Sara. Do not worry about them. Mikhail has taken them to a safe house. A man, a human, known to him and our people, is there to watch over them. They will be safe while we are hunting your enemy.

Sara inhaled sharply. Hadn't the others seen what she had? The vampire had penetrated the safeguards and had found her, had watched her through the eyes of its servant. Now the children she wanted to adopt were being taken to a perfect stranger. *Who is this man? How do you know of him, Falcon? Maybe you should go there yourself. They must be so afraid.*

Mikhail trusts this man. His name is Gary Jansen, a friend to our people. He will look after the children until we have destroyed the vampire. We cannot afford to draw the undead to them a second time. Mikhail will not leave them frightened. He is capable of helping them to accept this human and their new situation.

Sara lifted her chin, trying to ignore the terrible pounding in her head. "Do you know someone called Gary? Mikhail is taking the children to him." She knew she sounded anxious but she couldn't help it.

Shea laughed softly. "Gary is a genius, a man very much involved with his work. He flew out here from the States to help me with an important project I'm working on." As she spoke she silently signaled her lifemate to lift Sara and transport her to one of the underground chambers below the house. "I wish I'd been there to see the expression on his face when Mikhail showed up at the inn with several frightened children. Gary is a good man and very dedicated to helping us discover why our children are not surviving, why there are so few female children born, but I can't imagine him attempting to take care of little ones all by himself."

"You are enjoying the thought way too much." Jacques's laughter was low, a pleasant sound in contrast with the loud, frightening noises outside the home. "I cannot wait to tell the human you are pleased with his new role."

"But he *will* take care of them." Sara sought reassurance even as Jacques lifted her high into his arms.

Raven nodded emphatically. "Oh, yes, there's no need to worry. Gary would never abandon the children, and all Carpathians are bound to protect him should he have need. Your children will be very safe, Sara." As they moved through the house, she indicated a framed picture on the wall. "That is my daughter, Savannah. Gary saved her life."

Sara peered at the picture as they went by. The young woman was beautiful, but she looked the same age as Raven. And she looked vaguely familiar. "She's your daughter? She looks your age."

"Savannah has a lifemate." Raven touched the frame in a loving gesture. "When they are small, our children look very young, but their bodies grow at about the same rate as a human child for the first few years. It is only when our people reach sexual maturity that our growth rate slows. That is one reason we have trouble reproducing. It is rare for our women to be able to ovulate for a good hundred years after having a baby. It has happened, but it is rare. Shea believes it is a form of population control, just as most other species have built in controls. Because Carpathians live so long, nature, or God, if you prefer, built in a safeguard. Savannah will be returning home quite soon. They would have returned immediately upon their union, but Gregori, her lifemate, has received word of his lost family and wishes to meet with them first." Raven's voice held an edge of excitement. "Gregori is needed here. He is

Mikhail's second in command, a very powerful man. And, of course, I've missed Savannah."

Sara was suddenly aware that they were going swiftly through a passageway. Raven's chatter had distracted her from her headache and from the danger, but mostly from the fact that they were moving steadily downward, beneath the earth. She felt the leap of her heart and instantly reached out for Falcon. Mind to mind. Heart to heart. *We can only have a child once every hundred years.* She said the first thing she thought of, then was embarrassed that she had whispered a secret dream, now a regret. She longed for a house filled with children. With love and laughter. With all the things she had lost. All the things she had long ago accepted she would never have.

We have seven children, Sara, seven abandoned, half-starved, very frightened children. They will need us to sort out their problems, love them, and aid them with their unexpected gifts. The three girls may or may not be lifemates for Carpathians in sore need, but all will need guidance. We will have many children to love in the coming years. Whatever your dream, it is mine. We will have a home and we will fill it with children and laughter and love.

He was closer, he was on his way to her. Sara wrapped herself in his warmth, in his words. *This is my gift to you.* A dark dream she would embrace. Reach for.

"Where are you taking me?" Sara's anxiety was embarrassing, but she couldn't seem to hold it in check. Falcon had to be able to find her.

She heard the reassurance of his soft laughter. *There is noplace they could take you where I could not find you. I am in you as you are in me, Sara.*

"What you are feeling is normal, Sara," Raven said softly. "Lifemates cannot be apart from one another comfortably."

"And you have a concussion," Shea reminded. "We're taking you where you will be safe," she assured again, calmly, patiently.

The passageway wound deep within the earth. Jacques took Sara through what seemed like a door in the solid rock to a large, beautiful chamber. To Sara's grateful surprise, it looked like a bedroom. The bed was large and inviting. She curled up on it the moment Jacques put her down, closing her eyes and wanting just to go to sleep. She felt that even a few minutes' rest would make her feel better. The comforter was thick and soothing, the designs unusual. Sara found herself tracing the symbols over and over.

The candles leaped to life, flickering and dancing, casting shadows on the walls and filling the room with a wonderful aroma. Sara was barely aware of Shea's healing touch with all the precision of a surgeon. Sara could only think of Falcon. Could only wait for him deep beneath the earth, hoping they would all be safe until he arrived.

Chapter Eight

The attack came immediately after sunset. The sky rained fire, streaks of red and orange dropping straight down toward the house and grounds. Long furrows in the ground appeared, moving quickly, darting toward the estate, tentacles erupting near the massive gates and columns surrounding the property. Bulbs burst through the earth, spewing acid at the wrought-iron fence. Insects fell from the clouds, oozed from the trees. Rats rushed the fence, an army of them, round beady eyes gleaming. There were so many bodies the ground was black with them.

Beneath the earth Jacques lifted his head alertly. His lifemate was performing her healing art. His eyes met Raven's over Sara's head. "The ancient one has sent his army ahead of his arrival. The house is under attack."

"Will the safeguards hold?" Raven asked with her

usual calm. She was already reaching out to Mikhail. They were still separated by many miles, yet his warmth flooded her immediately.

"Against his servants, the safeguards will certainly hold. The ancient one is attempting to weaken the safeguards so that he can more easily penetrate our defenses. He knows that Mikhail and Sara's lifemate are on their way. He thinks to have a quick and easy victory before their arrival." Jacques was calm, his black eyes flat and cold. He was banishing all emotion in preparation for battle. His arms were around Shea's waist, his body pressed close, protectively toward her. He bent his head to kiss her neck, a light, brief caress before moving away.

Raven caught his arm, preventing him from leaving the chamber. "Mikhail and Falcon say this one is dangerous, a true ancient, Jacques. Wait for them, please."

He looked down at her hand. "They are all dangerous, little sister. I will do what is necessary to protect the three of you." Very gently he removed her hand from his wrist, gave her an awkward, reassuring pat, a gesture at odds with his elegance.

Raven smiled at him. "I love you, Jacques. So does Mikhail. We don't tell you nearly enough."

"It is not necessary to say the words, Raven. Shea has taught me much over the years. The bond between us is very strong. I have much to live for, much to look forward to. I have finally convinced my lifemate that a child is worth the risks."

Raven's face lit up, her eyes shiny with tears. "Shea didn't say a word to me. I know she's always wanted to have a baby. I'm happy for you both, I really am."

Shea returned to her body, swaying from the intense effort of healing Sara. She staggered toward Jacques.

He caught her to him, drew her gently into his arms, buried his face in the mass of wine-red hair. "Is Sara going to be all right?" he asked softly. There was a wealth of pride in his voice, a deep respect for his lifemate.

Shea leaned into him, turned up her face to be kissed. "Sara will be fine. She just needs her lifemate." She stared into Jacques's eyes. "As I do."

"Neither you nor Raven seems to have much faith in my abilities. I'm shocked!" Jacques's chagrined look had both women laughing despite the seriousness of the situation. "I have my brother attempting to pull his Prince routine on me, giving me orders not to engage the enemy until His Majesty returns. My own lifemate, brilliant as she is, does not seem to realize I am a warrior without equal. And my lovely sister-kin is deliberately delaying me. What do you think about that, Sara?" He arced one eyebrow at her.

Sara sat up slowly, pushed her hand through her tousled, spiky hair. Her head was no longer pounding and her ribs felt just fine. Even the aches from the bruises were gone. "I don't know about your status as a warrior without equal, but your lifemate is a miracle worker." She had the feeling that Raven and Shea spent a great deal of time laughing when they were together. Neither seemed in the least intimidated by Jacques, despite the gravity of his appearance.

"I cannot argue with you there," Jacques agreed.

Shea grinned at Sara, her face pale. "He has to say that. It is always best to compliment one's lifemate."

"And that is why you and Raven are casting aspersions upon my battle capabilities." Once more Jacques kissed his lifemate. With his acute hearing, he could hear the assault upon the estate.

Sara could hear it, too. She twisted her fingers together anxiously. "He's coming. I know he is."

"Do not fear him, Sara," Shea hastened to assure her. "My lifemate has battled many of the undead and will do so long after this one is gone." She turned her gaze on her husband. "Raven will provide for me while you delay this monster. You will return to me unharmed."

"I hear you, little red hair, and I can do no other than obey." His voice was soft, an intimate caress. He simply dissolved into vapor and streamed from the chamber.

Sara made an effort to close her mouth and not gape in total shock. Raven, one arm wrapped around Shea's waist, laughed softly. "Carpathians take a little getting used to. I ought to know."

"I must feed," Shea said, her gaze steady on Sara's. "Will it alarm you?"

"I don't know," Sara said honestly. For no reason at all, the spot along the swell of her breast began to throb. She found herself blushing. "I suppose I should get used to it. Falcon and I were waiting until I had settled the red tape with the children before we"—she sought the right word—"finalized things." She lifted her chin. "I'm very committed to him." It seemed a pale way of explaining the intensity of her emotions.

"I am amazed he allowed you the time. He must be extraordinarily certain of his abilities to protect you," Raven said. "Feed, Shea. I offer freely that you may be at full strength once again." She casually extended her wrist to Shea. "Carpathian males usually have a difficult time at the first return of their emotions. They have to contend with jealousy and fear, the overwhelming need to protect their lifemate and the terror of losing her. They become domineering and possessive and generally are a pain in the neck." Raven laughed softly, obviously sharing the conversation with her lifemate.

Sara could feel her heart racing as she watched in horrified fascination while Shea accepted nourishment from Raven. Although it was bizarre, she could see no blood. She was almost comforted by the completely unselfish act between the two women. Sara was humbled by Shea's gift of healing. She was humbled by the way she was accepted so completely into their circle, a close family willing immediately to aid her, to place their lives directly in the path of danger for her.

"Are you really planning to have a child?" Raven asked as Shea closed the tiny pinpricks in her wrist with a sweep of her tongue. "Jacques said he has finally convinced you." There was a slight hesitation in Raven's voice.

Sara watched shadows chase across Shea's delicate features. Sara had always wanted children, and she sensed that Shea's answer would be important to her dreams, also.

Shea took a deep breath, let it out slowly. "Jacques wants a child desperately, Raven. I have tried to think like a doctor, because the risks are so high, but it is difficult when everything in me wants a child and when my lifemate feels the same. It was a miracle Savannah survived; you know that, you know how difficult it was. It took both Gregori and me that first year of fighting for her life, along with Mikhail and you. I have improved the formula for infants, since we cannot feed them what was once the perfect nourishment. I do not know why nature has turned on our species, but we are fighting to save every child born to us. Still, knowing all this does not stop me from wanting children. I know now that if something happened to me, Jacques would fulfill my wish and raise our child until he or she has a family. I will choose a time soon and hope we are successful with the pregnancy and keeping the child alive afterward."

Sara stood up carefully, a little gingerly, a frown on her face. She could hear the sizzle of fire meeting water, of insects and other frightening things she had no knowledge of. She could hear clearly, even envision the battle outside, the army of evil seeking to break through the safeguards protecting those within the walls of the house. Yet she felt safe. Deep below the earth, she felt a kinship with the two women. And she knew Falcon was on his way. He would come to her. For her. Nothing would stop him.

It seemed crazy, yet perfectly natural, to be in this chamber talking intimately with Raven and Shea while, just above them, the ancient vampire was seeking entrance. "Will I have problems having a child once I become fully like Falcon?" Sara asked. It had not occurred to her that she would not be able to have a child once she was a Carpathian.

Shea and Raven both held out their hands to her. A gesture of camaraderie, of compassion, of solidarity. "We are working very hard to find the answers. Savannah survived and two male children, but no other females. We have much more research to do, and I have developed several theories. Gary has flown out from the United States to aid me, and Gregori will follow in a few weeks. I believe we can find a way to keep the babies alive. I even believe I'm close to finding the reason why we give birth to so few females, but I am not certain that, even once I know the cause, I can remedy the situation. I do believe that every female who was human at one time has a good chance of having a female child. And that is a priceless gift to our dying race."

Sara paced the length of the room, suddenly needing Falcon. The longer she was away from him, the worse it seemed to be. Need. It crawled through her, twisted her stomach into knots, took her breath away. She accepted it, had known the need long before she had known the reality of Falcon. She had carried his journal everywhere with her, his words imprinted on her mind and in her heart. She had needed him then; now it was as if a part of her were dead without him.

"Touch his mind with yours," Raven advised softly. "He is always there for you. Don't worry, Sara, we will be here for you, too. Our life is wonderful, filled with love and amazing abilities. A lifemate is worth giving up what you had."

Sara pushed a hand through her hair, tousling it further. "I didn't have much of a life. Falcon has allowed me to dare to dream again. Of a family. Of a home. Of belonging with someone. I'm not afraid." She suddenly laughed. "Well . . . maybe I'm nervous. A little nervous."

"Falcon must be an incredible man," Shea said.

Not that incredible. Jacques never quite relinquished his touch on Shea. Over the years he had managed to relearn many things that had once been wiped from his mind, but he needed his lifemate anchoring him at all times. Before, he would have been jealous and edgy; now there was a teasing quality to his voice.

Shea laughed at him. Softly. Intimately. Sent him her touch, erotic pictures of twining her body around his. It was enough. She was his lifemate. His world.

Sara watched the expressions chase across Shea's

delicate features, knowing exactly what was transpiring between Shea and her lifemate. It made Sara feel as if she really were a part of something, part of a family again. And Raven was right, the moment she reached for Falcon, he was there, in her mind, enfolding her in love and warmth, in reassurance. She wrapped her arms around herself to hold him close to her, felt him in her mind, heard him, the soft whispers, the promises, his supreme confidence in his abilities. It was all there in an instant.

"Sara." Raven brought Sara's attention back to the women, determined to keep it centered on them rather than on the coming battle. "Whose children are these that the vampire went to so much trouble to acquire?"

Sara suddenly smiled, her face lighting up. "I guess they are mine now. I found them living in the sewers. They had banded together because of their difference from most. All of them have psychic abilities. Three little girls and four boys. Not all of their talents are the same, but they still knew, as young as they are, that they needed one another. I had great empathy with them because I grew up feeling different, too. I wanted to give them a home where they could feel normal."

"Three little girls?" Shea and Raven exchanged a long, gleeful grin. Shea shook her head in astonishment. "You are truly a treasure. You've brought us an ancient warrior. We may learn much from him. You have seven little ones with psychic talent, and you are a lifemate. Tell me how it is that you accept our world so readily."

Sara shrugged. "Because of the vampire. I saw him killing in the tunnels of a dig my parents were on. Two days later he killed my whole family." She lifted her chin a little as if in preparation for condemnation, but both women only looked sad, their gazes compassionate. "He chased me for years. I always kept moving to stay ahead of him. Vampires have been part of my life for a long time. I just didn't understand the difference between vampires and Carpathians."

"And Falcon?" Raven prompted.

Sara heard a sudden hush outside the house, as if the wind were holding its breath. The night creatures stilled. She shivered, her body trembling. The sun had set. The vampire had risen and was hurtling through space to reach the estate before Falcon and Mikhail had a chance to return.

Sara was positive that both women were aware of the vampire's rising, but they remained calm, although they linked hands. She took a deep breath, wanting to follow their examples of tranquillity. "Falcon has been my salvation for fifteen years. I just didn't know he was real. I found something that belonged to him." *This is my gift to you. Sara, lifemate to Falcon.* She held his words tightly to her. "I saw him clearly, his face, his hair, his every expression. I felt as if I could see into his heart. I knew I belonged with him, yet he was from long ago and I was born too late."

Falcon, winging his way strongly through the falling night felt her sorrow. He reached out to her, flooding her mind with the sheer intensity of his love for her. *You were not born too late, my love. Accept what is and what has been given to us. A great gift, a priceless treasure. I am with you now and for all time.*

I love you with all my heart, with every breath.

Then believe that I will not allow this monster to tear us apart. I have endured centuries of loneliness, a barren existence without your presence. He will not take you from me. I am of ancient lineage and much skilled. Our enemy is indeed powerful, but he will be defeated.

Sara's heart began to ease its frantic racing, slowing to match the steady beat of Falcon's heart. Deliberately he breathed for her, for them, a shadow in her head as much for his own peace of mind as for hers. He was well aware of the vampire moving swiftly toward the house to find Sara. The foul stench was riding on the night wind. The creatures of the evening whispered to him, scurried for cover to avoid the danger. Falcon had no way of communicating with Mikhail and Jacques without the vampire hearing. He could use the standard path of telepathy used by their people, but the vampire would certainly hear. Mikhail and Jacques shared a blood tie and had their own private path of communication the undead could not share. It would make the planning of a battle against an ancient vampire much easier.

Falcon felt heat sizzling through the air as the first real attack was launched by the vampire. The vibrations of violence sent shock waves through the sky, bouncing off the mountain peaks so that wicked veins of lightning rocked the black, roiling clouds. The avian form he was using could not withstand such force. He tumbled through the sky, falling toward earth. Falcon abandoned that form and shifted into vapor. The wind changed abruptly, because a gale force, blowing the droplets of water in the opposite direction from where he wished to go. Falcon took the only avenue safely open to him; he dropped to earth, landing in the form of a wolf, running flat out on four legs toward his lifemate and the Prince's estate.

Despite the miles separating them, Mikhail ran into the same problem. It was no longer safe or expedient to travel through the air. He took to the ground, a large, shaggy wolf running at top speed, easily clearing logs in his path.

Jacques surveyed the sky thick with locusts and beetles, the arrows of flame and the spinning black clouds veined with forks of lightning. Tentacles erupted along the inside of the gates, a small inconvenience announcing the first break in the safeguards. He was calm as he withered the tentacles and protected the structure from the fire and insects. He began to throw barriers up, small, flimsy ones that took little time to build yet would cost the vampire time to destroy. Minutes counted now. Every moment that he managed to delay the ancient vampire gave Mikhail and Falcon a chance to reach them.

I have been in many battles, yet this is the first time I have encountered a vampire so determined to break through obvious safeguards. Jacques sent the information to his brother. *He knows this is the home of the Prince, that the women are protected by more than one male, yet he is persistent. I think we should send the women deep within the earth and you should stay away until this enemy is defeated.*

What of the human woman? The advice didn't slow Mikhail down. The wolf was running flat out, not breathing hard, nature's perfect machine.

I will protect her until her lifemate arrives. We will defeat this vampire together. Mikhail, you have a duty to your people. If Gregori were here—

Gregori is not here, Mikhail interrupted wryly. *He is off with my daughter neglecting his duty to protect the Prince.* There was a hint of laughter in his voice.

Jacques was exasperated. *The undead is unlike anything we have faced. He has not flinched at anything I have thrown at him. His attack has never faltered.*

It seems that this ancient enemy is very sure of his abilities. Mikhail's voice was a soft menace, a weapon of destruction if he cared to use it. There was a note of finality that Jacques recognized immediately. Mikhail was racing through the forest, so quickly his paws barely brushed the ground. He felt the presence of a second wolf close by. Smelled the wild pungent odor of the wolf male. A large animal burst through the heavy brush, rushing at him on a diagonal to cut him off.

Mikhail was forced to check his speed to avoid a collision. The heavier wolf contorted, wavered, took the shape of a man. Mikhail did so also.

Falcon watched the Prince through thoughtful, wary eyes. "I believe it would be prudent on our part to exchange blood. The ability to communicate privately may come in handy in the coming battle."

Mikhail nodded his agreement, took the wrist that Falcon offered as a gesture of commitment to the Prince. Mikhail would always know where Falcon was, what he was doing if he so desired. He took enough for an exchange and calmly offered his own arm in return.

Falcon had not touched the blood of an ancient in many centuries, and it rushed through his system like a fireball, a rush of power and strength. Courteously he closed the pinpricks and surveyed Vladimir's son. "You know you should not place yourself in harm's way. It has occurred to me that you could be the primary target. If you were to be killed by such a creature, our people would be left in chaos. The vampire would have a chance of gaining a stranglehold on the world. It is best if you go to ground as our last line of defense.

Your brother and I will destroy the undead."

Mikhail sighed. "I have had this conversation with Jacques and do not care to repeat it. I have fought countless battles and my lifemate is at risk, as well as the villagers, who are my friends and under my protection." His shape was already wavering.

"Then you leave me no choice but to offer my protection since your second is not present." There was an edge to Falcon's voice. His body contorted, erupted with hair, bent as feet and hands clawed.

"Gregori is in the United States collecting his lifemate." It was enough, a reprimand and a warning.

Falcon wasn't intimidated. He was an ancient, his lineage old and sacred, his loyalties and sense of duty ingrained in him. His duty was to his Prince; honor demanded that he protect the man from all harm no matter what the cost.

They were running again, fast and fluid, leaping over obstacles, rushing through the underbrush, silent and deadly while the skies rained insects and the mist thickened into a fogbank that lay low and ugly along the ground. The wolves relied on their acute sense of smell when it became nearly impossible to see.

They burst into the clearing on the edge of the forest. The ground erupted with masses of tentacles. The writhing appendages reached for them, squirming along the ground seeking prey. The two wolves leaped nearly straight into the air to avoid the grasping tentacles, danced around walls of thorns, and skidded to a halt near the tall, double, wrought-iron gates.

Falcon angled in close to Mikhail, inserting his body between the Prince and a tall, elegant man who appeared before them, his head contorting into a wedge shape with red eyes and scales. The mouth yawned wide, revealing rows of dagger-sharp teeth. The creature roared, expelling a fiery flame that cut through the thick fog straight at them.

Jacques exploded from the house, leaping the distance to the gate, then jumping over to land on the spot where the undead had been. The vampire used its preternatural speed, spinning out of reach. He hissed into the night air, a foul, poisonous blend of sound and venom. Vapor whirled around his solid form, green and then black. A noxious odor was carried on the blast. The vapor simply dissolved into thousands of droplets of water, spreading on the wind, an airborne cloud of depravity.

The hunters pressed forward into the thick muck. Falcon murmured softly, his hands following an intricate pattern. At once the air was filled with a strange phosphorescent milky whiteness. The trail left by the undead was easily seen as dark splotches staining the glowing white. Falcon took to the clouds, a difficult task with the air so thick and noxious. The splotches scattered across the heavens, tiny stains that seemed to spread and grow in all directions, streaking like dark comets across the night sky.

The vampire could only go in one direction, yet the stains were scattering far and wide, east and south, north and west, toward the village, high over the forest, along the mountain ridge, straight up, blowing like a foul tower and falling to earth as dark acid rain.

On the ground the rats and insects retreated, the walls of thorn wavered and fell, the tentacles retreated beneath the earth. Near the corner of the gate, a large rat stared malevolently at the house for several moments. Teeth bared, the rodent spat on the gate before it whirled around and scurried away. The wrought iron sizzled and smoked, the saliva corroding the metal and leaving behind a small blackened hole.

Mikhail sent out a call to all Carpathians in the area to watch over the villagers. They would attempt to cut off the vampire's source of sustenance. With the entire region on alert, he hoped to find the vampire's lair quickly. He signaled the other two hunters to return to the house. Chasing the vampire when there was no clear trail was a fool's errand. They would regroup and form a plan of attack.

"This one is indeed an ancient," Jacques said as they took back their true forms at the veranda of the Prince's home. "He is more powerful than any other I have come across."

"Your father sent out many warriors. Some are still alive, some have chosen the dawn, and a few have turned vampire," Falcon agreed. "And there is no doubt that this one has learned much over the years. But he had fifteen years to find Sara, yet she escaped. A human, a child. He can and will be defeated." He glanced toward the gate. "He left behind his poisonous mark. I spotted it as we came in. And, Jacques, thank you for finding Sara so quickly and getting her to safety. I am in your debt."

"We have much to learn of one another," Mikhail said, "and the unpleasant duty of destroying the evil one, but Sara must be able to go to ground. She is beneath the earth in one of the chambers. For her protection, it is best that you convert her immediately."

Falcon's dark eyes met his Prince's. "And you know this can be safely done? In my time such a thing was never tried by any but the undead. The results were frightening."

Mikhail nodded. "If she is your true lifemate, she

must have psychic abilities. She can be converted without danger, but it is not without pain. You will know instinctively what to do for her. You will need to supply her with blood. You must use mine, as you have no time to go out hunting prey."

"And mine," Jacques volunteered generously. "We will have need of the connection in the coming battle."

Chapter Nine

Sara was waiting for Falcon in the large, beautiful chamber. Candles were everywhere, flames flickering so that the glowing lights cast shadows on the wall. She was alone, sitting on the edge of the bed. The other women had been summoned by their lifemates. Sara jumped up when Falcon walked in. She wore only a man's silken shirt, the tails reaching nearly to her knees. A single button held the edges together over her generous breasts. She was the most beautiful thing he had ever seen in all his centuries of existence. He closed the door quietly and leaned against it, just drinking her in. She was alive. And she was real.

Sara stared up at him, her heart in her eyes. "It seems like forever."

Her voice was soft but it washed over him with the strength of a hurricane, making his pulses pound and his senses reel. She was there waiting for him with that same welcome on her face. Real. It was real, and it was just for him.

Falcon held out his hand to her, needing to touch her, to see that she was alive and well, that the healer had worked her miracle. "I never want to experience such terror again. Locked within the earth, I felt helpless to aid you."

Sara crossed to his side without hesitation. She touched his face with trembling fingertips, traced every beloved line—the curve of his mouth, his dark eyebrows—and rubbed a caress along his shadowed jaw. "But you did come to my aid. You sent the others to me, and you were always with me. I wasn't alone. More than that, I knew you would save the children." There was a wealth of love in her voice that stole his heart.

He bent his head to take possession of her tempting mouth. She was soft satin and a dark dream of the future. He took his time, kissing her again and again, savoring the way she melted into him, the way she was so much a part of him. *Are you ready to be as I am? To be Carpathian and walk beside me for all time?* He couldn't say it aloud but whispered it intimately in her mind while his heart stood still and his breath caught in his lungs. Waiting. Just waiting for her answer.

You are my world. I don't think I could bear to be without you. She answered him in the way of his people, wanting to reassure him.

"Is this what you want, Sara? Am I what you want? Be certain of this—it is no easy thing. Conversion is painful." Falcon tightened his hold on her possessively, but he had to tell her the truth.

"Being without you is more painful." Her arms crept around his neck. She leaned her body against his, her soft breasts pushing against his chest, her body molding to his. "I want this, Falcon. I have no reservations. I may be nervous, but I am unafraid. I want a life with you." Her mouth found his, tiny kisses teasing the corners of his smile, her teeth nibbling at his lower lip. Her body was hot and restless and aching for his. Her kiss was fire and passion, hot and filled with promises. She gave herself into his keeping without reservation.

He melted inside. It was an instant and complete meltdown, his insides going soft and his body growing hard. She tore him up inside as nothing had ever done. No one had ever penetrated the armor surrounding his heart. It had been cold. Dead. Now it was wildly alive. His heart pounded madly at the love in her eyes, the touch of her fingertips, the generous welcome of her body, the total trust she gave him when her life had been one of such mistrust.

His kiss was possessive, demanding. Hot and urgent, the way his body felt. His hands went to her waist in a soft caress, slid upward to cup the weight of her breasts in his hands. But his mouth was pure fire, wild and hot even when his hands were so tender. He slipped the single button open, his breath catching in his throat, and he stepped back to view the lush temptation of her breasts. "You are so beautiful, Sara. Everything about you. I love you more than anything. I hope you know that. I hope you are reading my mind and you know that you are my life." His finger trailed slowly down the valley between her breasts to her navel. His body reacted, that painful ache of urgent demand. And he let it happen.

Sara watched his eyes change, watched the way his body changed, and she smiled, unafraid of the wildness she glimpsed in him. Wanting it. Wanting him crazy for her. She unbuttoned his shirt, slipped it from his shoulders. Leaning forward, she pressed a row of kisses along his muscles, her tongue sliding around his nipple. She smiled up at him as she rubbed her hand over the bulging material of his trousers, her fingers deftly freeing him from the tight confines. Her hand wrapped around the thick length of him, simply held him for a moment, enjoying the freedom of being able to explore. Then she hooked her thumbs into the waistband of the trousers to remove them. "I think you're beautiful, Falcon," she admitted. "And I know that I love you."

He wrapped his arm around her waist, dragged her to him, his mouth fusing with hers, all at once aggressive, demanding, a little primitive. Sara met him kiss for kiss. His hands were everywhere; so were hers. He slid his palm over her stomach, wanting to feel a child, his child, growing there, wanting everything at once—her, a child, a family, everything he had never had. Everything he'd believed he never could have. His fingers dipped lower into the thatch of tight curls, cupped her welcoming heat even as his mouth devoured hers. "I know I should slow down," he managed to get out.

"There's no need," she answered, feeling the exact same sense of wild urgency. She needed him. Wanted him. Every inch of him buried deep within her merging their two halves into one whole.

Shadows danced on the wall from the flickering candlelight, threw a soft glow over Sara's face. He lifted his head as he slowly, carefully, pushed two fingers deep inside her. He wanted to watch the pleasure in her eyes. She held nothing back from him, not her thoughts, her desires, or her passion. She gasped, her body tightening, clamping around his fingers, hot and needy. She moved against his hand, a slow, sexy ride, her head thrown back to expose her throat, her breasts a gleaming enticement in the candlelight.

He pushed deeper into her, felt the instant answering wash of hot moisture. Very slowly he bent his head to her throat. His tongue swirled lazily. His teeth nipped. He hid nothing from her, his mind thrusting into hers, sharing the perfect ecstasy of the moment with her, his body's reaction and the frenzy of heated passion. His fingers penetrated deep into her feminine channel as he buried his teeth in her throat. The lightning lanced both of them, hot and white, a pain that gave way to an erotic fire. She was hot and sweet and just as wild as he was. Falcon was careful to keep his appetite under control, taking only enough blood for an exchange. His mouth left her throat with a soothing swirl of his tongue; he lifted her with only one arm wrapped around her waist and took her to the bed. All the time, his fingers were sliding in and out of her, his mouth was fused to hers, the pleasure blossoming and spreading like wildfire through both of them.

She expected to find the taking of her blood disgusting, but it was erotic and dreamy, almost as if he had drawn a veil over her mind, ensnaring her in his dark passion. Yet she shared his mind and knew he had not. She also shared the intensity of his pleasure in the act, and it gave her courage.

"It isn't enough, Falcon. I want more, I want you in my body, I want us together." Her voice was breathless against his lips, her hands sliding over him eagerly, tracing each defined muscle, urging his hips toward hers.

He kissed her throat, her breasts, swirling his tongue over her nipples, along her ribs, around her belly button. Then she was gasping, rising up off the bed, her hands clutching fistfuls of his hair as he tasted her. She was shattering with the sheer intensity of her pleasure. Falcon could transport her to other worlds, places of beauty, emotion, and physical rapture.

He rose above her, a dark, handsome man with long, wild hair and black, mesmerizing eyes. There was a heartbeat while he was poised there, and then he surged forward, locking them together as they were meant to be, penetrating deeply, sweeping her away with him. He began to move, each stroke taking him deeper, filling her with a rush of heat and fire. She rose to meet him, craving the contact, wanting him deep inside, all the time her body winding tighter and tighter, rushing toward that elusive perfection.

Sara gasped as he thrust deeper still, the fiery friction clenching every muscle in her body, flooding every cell with a wild ecstasy. Then he was merging their minds, thrusting deep as his body took hers. She felt his pleasure, he felt hers, body and mind and heart, a timeless dance of joy and love. They soared together, exploding, fragmenting, waves of release rocking the earth so that they clung together with hearts pounding and shared smiles.

Falcon held her tightly, buried his face in her neck, whispered soft words of love, of encouragement before reluctantly untangling their bodies.

They lay on the bed together . . . waiting. Her heart was pounding, her breath coming too fast, but she tried valiantly to pretend that everything was perfectly normal. That her entire world was not about to be changed for all eternity.

Falcon held her in his strong arms, wanting to reassure her, needing the closeness as much as she did.

"Do you know why I wrote the journal?" He kissed her temple, breathed in her scent. "A thousand years ago, the words welled up inside me when I could feel nothing, see nothing but gray images. The emotions and words were burned into my soul. I felt I needed to write them down so I would always remember the intensity of my feelings for my lifemate. For you, Sara, because even then, a thousand years before you were born, more even, I felt your presence in my soul. A tiny flicker and I needed to light the way." He kissed her gently, tenderly. "I guess that doesn't make much sense. But I felt you inside of me and I had to tell you how much you mattered."

"Those words saved my life, Falcon. I wouldn't have survived without your journal." She leaned into him. She would survive this, as well. She was strong and she would see it through.

"I shudder to think what trouble the children are giving this poor stranger who has been called into service," Falcon teased, wanting to see her smile.

Sara nibbled at his throat. "How long will it take us to get the children in a real home? Our home?"

"I think that can be arranged very fast," Falcon assured, his fingers sliding through her thick, silken hair, loving the feel of the sable strands. "The one wonderful thing about our people is that they are very willing to share what they have. I have jewels and gold stashed away. I was going to turn it over to Mikhail to aid our people in any way possible, but we can ask for a house."

"A large house. Seven children require a large house."

"And a large staff. We will have to find someone we trust to watch over the children during the day," Falcon pointed out. "I am certain Raven and Shea will know the best person to contact. The children have very special needs. We will have to aid them . . ."

She turned her head, frowning at him. "You mean manipulate them."

He shrugged his powerful shoulders, unperturbed by her irritation. "It is our way of life in this world. We must shield those who provide sustenance for us, or they would live in terror. Officials who do not want to hand us these children are easily persuaded otherwise. To keep the children from being afraid and allow them to become more used to their environment and more accepting of a new lifestyle, it will be necessary. It is a useful gift, Sara, and one we depend on to keep our species from discovery."

"The children want to live with me. We have discussed it on many occasions. I would have taken them to my home immediately but I knew that eventually the vampire would come. I was attempting to set up a safe house for them, a refuge where I could see them without endangering them. But the officials continually put roadblocks in my way, mostly to charge more money. But the children knew I was trying. They believed in me, and they won't be afraid of a new life."

"You will not be with them during the day, Sara. We must ensure that they trust the humans we will have to rely on to guard them during those hours."

Just then a ripple of fire moved through Sara's body. She put her hand over her stomach and turned her head, meeting his shadowed gaze. He put his hand over hers.

He bent to kiss her, a kiss of sorrow, of apology. "I would spare you this pain if I could." He whispered it against her skin. His body trembled against hers.

She caught his hand, twining their fingers together. Her insides were burning alarmingly. "It's all right, Falcon. We knew it was going to be like this." She wanted to reassure him even though every muscle was cramping and her body was shuddering with pain. "I can do this. I want to do this." She allowed nothing else to enter her mind. Not fear. Not growing terror. It had no place, only her complete belief in him, in them. In her decision. A convulsion lifted her body, slammed it back down. Sara tried to crawl away from him, wanting to spare him.

Falcon caught at her, his mind firmly entrenched in hers. *Together, piccola. We are in this together.* He could feel the pain ripping through her body and he breathed deeply, evenly, determined to breathe for both of them, protecting her as best he could. He wanted, *needed*, to take the pain from her, but even with his great strength and all of his powers, he could not alleviate the terrible burning as her organs were reshaped. He could only shoulder part of the terrible pain and share her suffering. He held her as her body rid itself of toxins. Never once did he detect a single moment when she blamed him or wavered in her choice to join him.

For Falcon, time inched by slowly, an eternity, but he forced serenity into his mind, determined to be as accepting as Sara. Determined to be everything she needed, even if all he could do was believe that everything would turn out perfectly. In the centuries of his existence, he had mingled with humans and had seen extraordinary moments of bravery, but her steadfast courage astounded him. He shared his admiration of her, his belief in her ability to ride above the waves of pain and the convulsions possessing her body. She took each moment separately, seeking to reassure him when each wave ebbed, leaving her spent and exhausted.

Once, she smiled and whispered to him. He couldn't hear her, even with his phenomenal hearing. *Having a baby is going to be a piece of cake after this.* There was a wry humor in her soft voice brushing at the walls of his mind. Falcon turned his head away to keep her from seeing the tears in his eyes at the evidence of her deep commitment to him.

The moment he knew it was safe to send her to sleep, Falcon commanded it, opening the earth to allow the healing properties to aid her. Carpathian soil, more than any other, rejuvenated and healed its people, yet they could use whatever was available, as he had been doing for centuries. He had forgotten the soothing richness of his homeland. Falcon carefully cleaned the bedchamber, removing every trace of illness and evidence of Sara's conversion. He took his time, relying on the other two Carpathian males to hold a watchful vigil against further assaults by the ancient vampire. It had been far too long since he had been home, since he had known the comfort of being with his own people, the luxury of being able to depend on others.

Falcon took the sustenance offered to him by Jacques, again grateful for the powerful blood supplied by an ancient of great lineage. He rested for an hour, deep within the earth, his arms wrapped tightly around Sara.

When Falcon was certain that Sara was completely healed, he brought her to the surface, laying her carefully on the bed, her naked body stretched out, clean and fresh, the lit candles releasing a soothing, healing fragrance. His heart was pounding, his mouth dry. *Sara. My life. My heart and soul. Awake and come to me.* He bent his head to capture her first breath as a Carpathian. His other half.

Sara woke to a different world. The vivid details, the smells and sounds, were almost too much to take in. She clung to Falcon, fitting her body trustingly into his. They both could hear her heart pounding loudly, frantically.

He kissed the top of her head, rubbed his chin over the silken strands of her hair. "Ssh, my love, it is done now. Breathe with me. Let your heart follow the rhythm of mine."

Sara could hear everything. *Everything*. Insects. The murmur of voices in the night. The soft, hushed flight of an owl. The rustle of rodents in nearby brush. Yet she was far beneath the earth in a chamber constructed of thick walls and rock. If she could hear everything, so could all people of this species.

Falcon smiled, his teeth immaculately white. "It is true, Sara," he agreed, easily monitoring her thoughts. "We learn discretion at a very young age. We learn to tune out what is not our business. It becomes second nature. You and I have been alone far too long; we are now a part of something again. The adjustment will take some time, but life is an exciting journey now, with you by my side."

Against his shoulder she laughed softly. "Even before I ever underwent conversion, I could read you like a book. Stop being afraid for me. I am strong, Falcon. I made the decision fifteen years ago that you were my life. My everything. You were with me in my dreams, my dark lover, my friend and confidant. You were with me in my darkest hours when everything was bleak and hopeless and I had no one. All my days, all my nights, you were in my heart and mind. I know you. I lived only because of your words. I would never have survived without your journal. Really, Falcon. You know my mind, you know I am telling the truth. I am not afraid of my life with you. I want it. I want to be with you."

He felt humbled by her tremendous generosity, her gift to him. He answered her the only way he could, his kiss tender and loving, expressing with his body the deep emotion that could not be described by words. "I still cannot believe I found you," he whispered softly.

Her arms circled his neck, her soft breasts pressed tightly against his chest. She shifted her legs in invitation, wanting his body buried deep in hers. Wanting the safe anchor of his strength. "I still can't believe you're real and not my fantasy, the dream lover I made up from a vision."

Falcon knew what she needed. He needed the same reassurance. Sara. His Sara. Never afraid of appearing vulnerable to him. Never afraid of showing her desires. His mouth found hers, shifting the heavens for both of them. Her body was warm and welcoming, his haven, a refuge, a place of intimacy and ecstasy. The world fell away from them. There was only the flickering candlelight and the silk sheets. Only their bodies and long, leisurely explorations. There was gasping pleasure as they indulged their every fantasy.

Much, much later, Falcon lay across the bed, his head in her lap, enjoying the feel of the cool air on his body, the way her fingers played through his hair. "I cannot move."

She laughed softly. "You don't have to move. I like

where you are." Her breath tightened, caught in her throat as he blew warm air gently, teasingly, across her thighs. Her entire body clenched in reaction, so sensitized by their continual lovemaking that Sara didn't think she would ever recover.

"Ahh, but I do, my love. I have our enemy to hunt. No doubt he is close and very anxious to finish his work and leave these mountains. He cannot afford to bide his time here." Falcon sighed. "There are too many hunters in this area. He will want to leave as soon as possible. As long as he is alive, the children and you will never be safe." He turned his head slightly to swirl a small caress along her inner thigh with his tongue. His hair slid over her skin so that she throbbed and burned in reaction.

"Stop trying to distract me," she said. His arm was around her, his palm cupping her buttocks, massaging gently, insistently. It was very distracting, rendering her nearly incapable of rational thought.

"And all this time I thought you were distracting me." His voice was melodic with amusement. Deliberately he slid his finger along her moist core. "You are incredibly hot, Sara. Did you stay in my mind while we made love? Did you feel how tightly you wrapped around me? The way your body feels to me when I'm surrounded by your heat? Your fire?" He pushed two fingers into her, a long, slow stroke. "The way your muscles clamp around me?" He let out his breath slowly. "Yes. Just like this. There is nothing else like it in this world. I love everything about your body. The way you look." He withdrew his fingers, brought them to his mouth. "The way you taste."

Her body rippled to life as she watched him insert his fingers into his mouth as if he were devouring her all over again. He smiled, knowing exactly what he was doing to her. Sara laughed softly, happily, the sound carefree. "If we make love again, I'm certain I'll shatter into a million pieces. And you, crazy man, will not be in any shape to go chasing after vampires if you touch me one more time. So if you're determined to do this, behave yourself."

He kissed the inside of her thigh. "I thought I was behaving just fine."

She caught a fistful of his hair. "What I think is that you need me to bag the vampire. To bring him right to you."

He sat up, his black gaze wary all at once. "You just stay right here where I know you are perfectly safe."

"I'm not the safe type, Falcon, I thought you knew that by now. I expect a partnership and I'm not willing to settle for less," she said firmly.

He studied her face for a long moment, reached out to trace the shape of her breast, sending a shiver through her body at his feather-light touch. "I would not want less than a partnership, Sara," he answered honestly. "But you do not fully comprehend what would happen if something should harm you."

She laughed at him, her eyes suddenly sparkling like jewels. "I don't think you fully comprehend what would happen if something should harm *you*."

"I am a hunter, Sara. Please trust my judgment in this."

"More than anything I do trust your judgment, but it is very biased at the moment, isn't it? It makes no sense not to use the one person he would come out into the open to find. You know that if he chased me for fifteen years, he isn't going to stop. Falcon"—she placed a hand on his chest, leaned forward to kiss his chin—

"he will show himself if he thinks he has a serious chance of getting to me. If you don't use me as bait, everyone will continue to be in danger. Our children are frightened and in the care of a total stranger. These people have been good to us; we don't want to bring them and the surrounding villagers trouble." She pushed a hand through her short sable hair. "I know I can bring him out into the open. I have to try. I can't be responsible for any more deaths. Every time he follows me to a city and I read about a serial killer in the papers, I feel as if I had brought him there. Let me do this, Falcon. Don't look so stubborn and intimidating. I know you understand why I have to do this."

Falcon's hard features slowly softened. His perfectly sculpted mouth curved into a smile. He framed her face between his hands and bent his head to kiss her. "Sara, you are a genius." He kissed her again. Slowly. Thoroughly. "That is exactly what we will do. We will use you as bait and trap ourselves a master vampire."

She raised an eyebrow, not trusting the sudden grin on his face.

Chapter Ten

Sara sat on a boulder, dipped her hand into the small pool of water, and looked up at the night sky. The clouds were heavy and dark, blotting out the stars, but the moon was still valiantly attempting to shine. White wisps of fog curled here and there along the forest floor, lending an eerie appearance to the night. An owl sat in the high branches of the tree to her left, completely still and very aware of every movement in the forest. Several bats wheeled this way and that overhead, darting to catch the plethora of insects flying through the air. A rodent scurried through the leaves, foraging for food, drawing the attention of the owl.

Sara had been out for some time, simply inhaling the night. Her favorite perfume mingled with her natural scent and drifted through the forest so that the wildlife were very aware of her presence. Sara stood up slowly and wandered back toward the house. Rare night blossoms caught her attention and she stopped to examine one. Her fresh scent mingled with the fragrant flower and was carried on the breeze, wafting through the forest and high into the trees. A fox sniffed the air and shivered, crouching in the heavy underbrush near the boulder where the human had been.

There was a soft sound in the vegetation near her feet. Sara froze in place, watching the large rat as it foraged in the bushes quite close to her. Too close to her. Between her and the house. She backed away from the rodent, back toward the interior of the forest. She glanced toward the boulder, judging its height. Vampires were one thing, rats quite another. She was a bit squeamish when it came to rats.

When Sara turned back, a man stood watching her. Tall. Gaunt. With gray skin and long white hair. The vampire stared at her through red-rimmed eyes. Eyes filled with hatred and rage. There was no false pretense of friendship. His bitter enmity showed in every deep line of his ravaged face. "After all those wasted years. At last I have you. You have cost me more than you will ever know. Stupid, pitiful woman. How ridiculous that a nothing such as you should be a thorn in my side. It disgusts me."

Sara retreated from him, backing the way she had come until her legs bumped against rock. With great dignity she simply seated herself on the boulder and watched him in silence; her fingers twisting together were the only sign of fear. This was the monster who had murdered her family, taken everyone she had loved, virtually taken her life from her. This tall, gaunt man with hollow cheeks and venomous eyes.

"I have nearly limitless power, yet I need a little worm like you to complete my studies. Now Falcon's stench is all over you. How that sickens me." The vampire laughed softly, tauntingly, spittle flying into the air, fouling the wind. "You did not think I knew who he was, but I knew him well in the old time. A stooge to do the Prince's bidding. Vladimir lived long with Sarantha, yet he sent us out to live alone. His sons stayed behind, protected by him, yet we were sent to die alone. I did not choose death but embraced life, and I have studied much. There are others like me, but I will be the one to rule. Now that I have you, I will be a god and nothing will touch me. The Prince will bow to me. All hunters will tremble before me."

Sara lifted her head. "I see now. Although you think yourself all-powerful, a god, you still have need of me. You have followed me for fifteen years, a puny human woman, a child when you found me, yet you could not catch up to me."

He hissed, an ugly, frightening sound, a promise of brutal retaliation.

Sara frowned at him, sudden knowledge in her eyes. "You need me to find something for you. Something you can't do yourself. You killed everybody I loved, yet you think I will help you. I don't think so. Instead I intend to destroy you."

"You do not have any idea of the pain I can inflict on you. The things I can make you do. I will derive great pleasure in bending you to my will. You have no idea how powerful I am." The vampire's parody of a smile exposed stained, jagged teeth. "I will enjoy seeing you suffer as you have been a plague to me for so long. Do not worry, my dear, I will keep you alive a very long time. You will find the tomb of the master wizard and the book of knowledge that will give me untold power. I have acquired several of his belongings, and you will know where the book is when you hold these items. Humans never know the true treasures for what they are. They lock them up in museums few people ever visit, and none see what is truly valuable. They believe that wizards and magic are mere fairy tales, and they live in ignorance. Humans deserve to be ruled with an iron fist. They are cattle, nothing more. Prey only, food for the gods."

"Perhaps that is your impression of humans, but it is a false one. Otherwise how could I have evaded you for fifteen years?" Sara asked mildly. "I am not quite so insignificant as you would like me to believe."

"How dare you mock me!" The vampire hissed, his features contorting with hatred as he suddenly looked around warily. "How is it you are alone? Are your keepers so inept they would allow you to walk around unprotected?"

"Why would you think they are not guarding me? They are all around me." She sounded truthful, sincere.

His eyes narrowed and he pointed one daggerlike fingernail at her. Had she denied it, he would have been far more wary, but she was too quick to give the hunters away. "Do not try my patience. No Carpathian hunter would use his lifemate to bait a trap. He would hide you deep in the earth, coward that he is, knowing I am too powerful to stop." He laughed softly, the sound a hideous screech. "It is your own arrogance that has caused your downfall. You ignored his orders and came out into the night without his knowledge or consent. That is a weakness of women. They do not think logically, always whining and wanting their way." His dagger-sharp finger beckoned her. "Come to me now." He used his mind, a sharp, hard compulsion designed to hurt, to put tremendous pressure on the brain even as it demanded obedience.

Sara continued to sit serenely, a slight frown on her soft mouth. She sighed and shook her head. "That has never worked on me before. Why should it now?"

Cursing, the vampire raised his arm, then changed his mind. The vibration of power would have given him away immediately to the Carpathian hunters. He stalked toward her, covering the short distance between them, his strides purposeful, his face a mask of rage at her impertinence.

Sara sat perfectly still and watched him come to her. The vampire bent his tall frame, extending his dagger-tipped bony fingers toward her. Sara exploded into action, only it was Falcon's fist slamming hard into the chest cavity of the undead, as he returned to his true form. As Falcon did so, the vampire, with a look of sheer disbelief, stumbled back so that the fist barely penetrated his chest plate. Overhead, Jacques, in the shape of the owl, launched himself from the branches and flew straight at the undead, talons outstretched. The small fox grew in stature, shape-shifting into the tall, elegant frame of a male hunter, and Mikhail's hands were already weaving a binding spell to prevent the vampire from shifting or vanishing.

Pressed from the air, caught between the hunters and unable to flee, the vampire launched his own attack, risking everything in the hopes of defeating the one Carpathian whose death might force the other two to pause. Calling on every ounce of power and knowledge he possessed, he slammed his fist into Falcon's elbow, shattering bone. Then he whirled away, his body replicating itself over and over until there were a hundred clones of the undead. Half the clones initiated attacks using stakes or sharp-pointed spears; the others fled in various directions.

Jacques, in the owl form, drove talons straight through the head of a clone, going through empty air so that he was forced to pull up swiftly before hitting the ground. The air vibrated with power, with violence and hatred.

Each of the clones on the attack was weaving a different spell, and sprays of blood washed the surrounding air a toxic crimson. Falcon's mind shut off the pain of his shattered elbow as he assessed the situation in that one heartbeat of time. It was all he had. All he would ever have. In that blink of an eye the centuries of his life passed, bleak and barren, stretching endlessly until Sara. *This is my gift to you*. She was his life. His soul. His future. But there was honor. There was what and who he was, what he stood for. He was guardian of his people.

She was there with him. His Sara. She understood that he had no other choice. It was everything he was. Without regret, Falcon flung his body between his Prince and the vampire moving in for the kill. A multitude of razor-sharp spears pierced Falcon's body, taking his breath, spilling his life force onto the ground in dark rivers. As he toppled to earth, he reached out, slamming both open hands into the scarlet fountain on the vampire's chest, leaving his prints like a neon sign for the other hunters to target.

Sara, sharing Falcon's mind, reacted calmly, already knowing what to do. She had made good use of Falcon's knowledge and she shut down his heart and lungs instantly, so that he lay as still as death on the battlefield. She concentrated, holding him to her, a flickering, dim light that wanted to retreat from pain.

She had no time for sorrow. No time for emotion. She held him to her with the same fierce determination of the Carpathian people's finest warrior as the battle raged on around him.

Mikhail saw the ancient warrior fall, his body riddled with holes. The Prince was already in motion, snapping the spears like matchsticks as he drove forward, directing Jacques with his mind. The clones tried to regroup to throw the hunters off the scent, but it was too late. The vampire had revealed himself in his attack, and Mikhail locked onto Falcon's marks, as certain as fingerprints.

The undead snarled his hatred, shrieked his fury, but the holding spell bound him. He could not shift his shape and it was already too late. The Prince buried his fist deep, following the twisted path the ancient warrior had mapped out. Jacques took the head, slicing cleanly, a delaying tactic to give his brother time to extract the black, pulsating heart. The sky rained insects, great stinging bugs, and pellets of ice and rain.

Mikhail calmly built the charge of energy in the roiling clouds. All the while, the black heart jumped and crawled blindly, seeking its master. Blisters rose on the ground and on their arms as the scarlet spray embedded itself in their skin. The fury of the wind whipped them, moaning and hissing a dark promise of retaliation. Mikhail grimly continued, calling upon nature, directing a fiery orange ball from the sky to the pulsing heart. The thing was incinerated with a noxious odor and a cloud of black smoke.

The body of the vampire jerked, the head rolled, the eyes staring at Falcon's still form with a hatred beyond anything the hunters had ever witnessed. A hand moved, the dagger-tipped claws reaching for the fallen warrior as if to take him along on the path to death. The orange ball of energy slammed into the body, incinerating it immediately, then leaping to the head to reduce it to a fine powder of ashes.

Jacques took over the cleansing of the earth, and then their own skin, erasing the evidence of the foul creature which had gone against nature itself.

Raven met her lifemate at the door, touching his arm, sharing his deep sorrow, offering him comfort and warmth. "Shea has gone ahead to the cave of healing, opening the earth and taking the candles we will need. Jacques has brought Falcon there. The soil is rich and will aid her work. I have summoned our people to join with us in the healing chant." She turned to look at Sara.

Sara stood up slowly. She could see compassion, even sorrow, on Raven's face. Tears streaked Raven's cheeks and she held out both hands. "Sara, they have brought him to the best place possible, a place of power. Shea says . . ." She choked back a sob and pressed a fist to her mouth even as she caught Sara's hand in hers. "You must come with us quickly to the cave of healing."

Mikhail stepped back, avoided her eyes, his features a mask of granite, but Sara knew what he was thinking. She touched his arm briefly to gain his attention. "I was sharing his mind when he made the decision. It was a conscious decision, one he didn't hesitate to make. Don't lessen his sacrifice by feeling guilty. Falcon believes you're a great man, that the loss of your life would be intolerable to him, to your people. He knew exactly what he was doing and what the cost might be. I am proud of him, proud of who he is. He is an honorable man and always has been. I completely supported his decision."

Mikhail nodded. "You are a fitting lifemate for an ancient as honorable as Falcon. Thank you for your kindness in such a bleak hour, Sara. It is a privilege to count you among our people. We must go to him rapidly. You have not had time to become used to our ways, so I ask that you allow me to take your blood. Falcon's blood runs in my veins. I must aid you in shape-shifting to get to this place of healing."

She met his black gaze steadily. "You honor me, sir."

Raven's fingers tightened around Sara's as if holding her close, but Sara could barely feel the contact. Her mind was firmly entrenched in Falcon's, holding him to her, refusing to allow him to slip away despite the gravity of his injuries. She felt the prick of Mikhail's teeth on her wrist, felt the reassuring squeeze of Raven's hand. Nothing mattered to Sara but that flickering light so dim and far away.

Mikhail placed the image of an owl in her mind, and she actually felt the wrenching of her bones, the contorting of her body, and the sudden rush of air as she took flight. But there was only Falcon, and she didn't dare let go of that fading light to look at the world falling away from her as she winged her way to the cave of healing.

Deep beneath the earth, the air was heavy and thick with the aroma of hundreds of scented candles. Sara went to Falcon, shocked at the terrible wounds in his body, at his white, nearly translucent skin. Shea's body was an empty shell. Sara was vividly aware of her in Falcon's body, valiantly repairing the extensive damage. The sound of chanting—ancient, beautiful words in a language she recognized yet didn't know—filled the chamber. The ancient language of the Carpathians. Those not present were there nonetheless, joined mind to mind, sending their powers of healing, their energy, to their fallen warrior.

Sara watched the Prince giving his blood, far more than he could afford, yet he waved the others off and gave until he was weak and pale, until his own brother forced him to replenish what he had given. She watched each of the Carpathians, strangers to her, giving generously to her lifemate, reverently, paying a kind of homage to him. Sara took Falcon's hand in hers and watched as Shea returned to her own body.

Shea, swaying with weariness, signaled to the others to pack Falcon's terrible wounds with saliva and the deep rich earth. She fed briefly from her lifemate and returned to the monumental task of closing and repairing the wounds.

It took hours. Outside the cave the sun was climbing, but not one of the people faltered in their task. Sara held Falcon to her through sheer will, and when Shea emerged, they stared at one another across his body, both weary, both with tears shimmering in their eyes.

"We must put him to ground and hope that the earth works its magic. I have done all I can do," Shea said softly. "It's up to you now, Sara."

Sara nodded. "Thank you. We owe you so much. Your efforts won't be wasted. He'll live. I won't allow anything else." She leaned close to her lifemate. "You will not die, do you hear me, Falcon?" Sara demanded, tears running down her face. "You will hold on and you will live for me. For us. For our children. I am demanding this of you." She said it fiercely, meaning it. She said it with her heart and her mind and her soul.

Gently she touched his beloved face, traced his worn features. *Do you hear me?*

She felt the faintest of stirrings in her mind. A warmth. Soft, weary laughter. *Who could not hear you, my love? I can do no other than comply.*

The house was large, a huge, rambling home built of stone and columns. The veranda wrapped around the entire structure on the lower story. A similar balcony wrapped around the upper story. Stained-glass windows greeted the moon, beautiful unique pieces that soothed the soul. Sara loved every single thing about the estate. The overgrown bushes and thick stands of trees. The jumbles of flowers that seemed to spring up everywhere. She would never tire of sitting on the swing on her porch and looking out into the surrounding forest.

It was still difficult to believe, even after all these months, that the vampire was truly out of her life. She had been firmly in Falcon's mind when he assumed her shape. Her thoughts and emotions had guided his disguised body. Falcon buried deep, so that the vampire would fail to detect him. The plan had worked, the vampire was destroyed, but it would take a long while before she would wake without being afraid. She could only hope that the book the vampire had been searching for would remain hidden, lost to mortals and immortals alike. The fact that the undead had gone to such lengths to find the book could only mean that its power was tremendous. In the wrong hands, that book could mean disaster for both mortals and immortals.

Falcon had told Sara he'd known the vampire as a young boy growing up. Vladimir had sent him to Egypt while Falcon had gone to Italy. Somewhere along the way, Falcon had chosen honor, while his boyhood friend had wanted ultimate power. Sara rocked back and forth in the swing, allowing the peace of the evening to push the unpleasant thoughts from her mind.

She could hear the housekeepers in the kitchen talking quietly together, their voices reassuring. She could hear the children, upstairs in their bedrooms, laughing and murmuring as they began to get ready for bed. Falcon's voice was gentle as he teased the children. A pillow fight erupted as if often did, almost on a nightly basis.

You are such a little boy yourself. The words appeared in Falcon's mind, surrounded by a deep love that always took his breath away. Sara loved him to have fun, to enjoy all the simple things he had missed in his long life. And she was well aware Falcon loved her for that and for the way she enjoyed every moment of their existence, as if each hour were shiny and new.

They attacked me, the little rascals. Sara could see the image of him laughing, tossing pillows as fast as they were thrown at him.

Yes, well, when you are finished with your war, your lifemate has other duties for you. Sara leaned back in her swing, tapped her foot impatiently as a small smile tugged at her soft mouth. Deliberately she thought of her latest fantasy. The pool of water she had discovered by the waterfall in the secluded cliffside. Tossing her clothes aside. Standing naked on the boulder stretching her arms up in invitation to the moon. Turning her head to smile at Falcon as he came up to her. Leaning forward to chase a small bead of water across his chest, down his belly, then lower, lower.

The air shimmered for a moment and he was standing in front of her, his hand out, a grin on his face. Sara stared up at him, taking in his long silken hair and his mesmerizing dark eyes. He looked fit and handsome, yet she knew there were still faint scars on his body. They were etched in her mind more deeply than in his skin. Sara went to him, flowed to him, melted into him, lifting her face for his kiss, knowing he could move the earth for her.

"I want to check out this pool you have discovered," he whispered wickedly against her lips. His hands moved over her body gently, possessively.

She laughed softly. "I had every confidence you would."

Midnight Serenade

Ronda Thompson

Chapter One

The hunters were close. The wolf caught the scent of their sweat, smelled the liquor on their breath, knew which man had been with a woman the night before, and who had eaten meat for dinner. The crunch of boots against the pebbled ground and the sound of labored breathing made him pause. His strange abilities confused him. How could he identify what should be beyond his animal comprehension? He glanced skyward and understood. A full moon hung suspended over the valley, flanked by rugged mountain peaks. He was trapped. Caught in a time of in-between.

Soon, darkness would give way to light. He would stumble from one world into another. His fur would become skin. His paws would become hands and feet. He would rise from the mist as a man, the night fading away into a jumble of blurred images—visions of bloodlust and killing.

God have mercy, he prayed, while the man struggled to emerge from the beast. *Ease my suffering. End the nightmare. End it tonight.*

A bullet kicked up dust at his hind legs. The man inside of him tried to slow his pace, wanting the hunters to end his suffering, but the animal's instinct for survival remained strong. He hated this time the most. When both worlds fought to claim him. When he could think like a man one second, and react like a beast the next.

Another sound exploded. Pain ripped through his back leg. The wolf tumbled, rolled, then tried to get up. His body would not cooperate. The scent of his blood mingled with the smell of humans, closer now. Very close.

"Hey, I think we got him!"

A short, plump man stumbled through the brush. To the wolf, he was merely the enemy. But his human half identified the hunter. The man inside knew all of them, had talked to them in the bright light of day, helped them, been their friend, deceived them.

"Holy moly, look at the size of him!"

Another hunter, taller and more solidly built, held his rifle aimed and ready. "Biggest damn wolf I've ever seen, Gus."

The wolf growled, part of him warning them to stay back, the other part goading them to finish what they had started.

"Look at those fangs," the shorter one whispered.

"Yeah, make a nice necklace and a set of earrings for Rita—"

"Hell, Gus, Larry, one of you shoot him," a third man ordered, stepping from the brush. A shiny object the man wore on his shirt caught the moonlight and glittered in the dark. "Go ahead and put him out of his misery."

"Darn, Hugh, we want him to suffer," the short man argued. "He's part of the pack that's been killing our sheep, stealing our livelihood."

The man wearing the shiny object frowned. "He's just an animal. He doesn't know any better. We've been chasing him half the night, and my feet hurt. Kill him and get it over with."

"Can I have the pelt, Hugh?" the short man asked.

"We're not taking souvenirs. We can't leave any evidence behind, either. We'll have to bury it."

"Crap," the taller man muttered. "I wanted those teeth."

"What you don't want is the trouble hunting these wolves will cost us," the shiny man said. "I'll take care of it." He lifted his rifle.

The wolf bared his fangs, his thoughts focused on survival, until another scent distracted him. A softer scent than that of a man. The crunch of boots he heard was also different. Lighter.

"Hold it right there!" A figure holding a weapon stepped up behind the men.

"Who the hell are you?" the short man asked.

"I'm Stephanie Shane. It's illegal to hunt wolves in the wild. They're still an endangered species, and under the protection of the United States Fish and Wildlife Service."

"Hell, we know that," the tall man grumbled. "What are you doing here?"

"I work for a privately funded wildlife research and rescue organization," she answered. "We received a report that wolves have migrated to this area. I'm here to verify the rumors, possibly pave the way for a documentary. I just finished setting up my campsite when I heard the shooting."

"Documentary?" The man scratched his head. "We don't know anything about a movie—"

"A documentary is not the same thing as a movie," the woman interrupted. "And if you don't lower your weapons and leave right now, I'll call in the authorities."

Chuckling, the tall man said, "Report away. Hugh here is the sheriff."

The woman's eyes widened. She turned toward the man wearing the shiny object on his shirt. "You're Hugh Fielding? Didn't you get my fax a couple of months ago? I told you I'd be coming to the area for research—"

"I got it," the man interrupted. "And if you'll recall, I didn't send you one back giving you permission to intrude on our area."

She straightened. "I don't need your permission, Sheriff. The fax was merely a courtesy."

The wolf tried to rise. Fresh pain stabbed through his back leg. He knew that the change drew nearer—felt a sense of urgency to escape. The animal feared death, but the man inside of him feared a greater danger: exposure.

"Lower your weapons and leave," the woman instructed. "Otherwise, you leave me no choice but to report your actions."

The shiny man sighed. "The wolves are killing livestock. They've become a menace to the community."

"And as a law enforcement officer, you should know the proper procedure to follow when wolves are killing livestock," the woman countered.

"Hell, by the time Hugh wades through all that red

tape, half our sheep herds could be wiped out," the short man complained.

"So you've taken the matter into your own hands?"

"That's about the short and long of it, ma'am."

"Well, the short and long of it right now, Sheriff, is that you're not killing this wolf, or any other wolf while I'm here. Back off or I'll have this place crawling with wildlife defendants in a matter of hours."

The wolf watched the exchange curiously. The female was smaller than the men, weaker, yet he sensed hesitation from the men to confront her.

"All right," the shiny man said. "We won't shoot the wolf. But I can't leave you alone out here with an injured animal. That wolf would just as soon tear your throat out as look at you."

Lifting her weapon, the woman said, "I have this. I know how to use it, and how to conduct myself in the company of wolves. Leave so I can take a look at him. See what kind of damage you and your friends have done."

"She's freakin' nuts," the tall man muttered.

The man with the shiny star swore, but said, "Okay, it's your neck, lady. It'll be daylight soon. If you turn up dead, anyone I should contact? Friends? Family?"

For a moment, the wolf sensed a shift in the woman's tough demeanor. A sadness oozed from her and licked at his own festering wounds.

"No," she whispered. "There's no one." She straightened again. "Even if there were, you'd have no reason to contact them. I'm a big girl, Sheriff. Good night."

After casting the woman a skeptical glance, the shiny man and the others stomped off into the brush. The wolf knew his odds had just improved. He could take the woman down, easily rip her throat out, but the man in him fought the battle. Which would win out, he had no way of knowing. Nor would he remember what unforgivable deeds he had committed beneath the cover of darkness when the sun rose. If morning dawned for him.

Stephanie Shane lowered the gun. She breathed a small sigh of relief when the men disappeared. Turning back to the wolf, she realized she'd never seen one as large, or as beautiful. Wounded and frightened, he would be dangerous. In order to examine him, she'd have to tranquilize the animal. First, she'd try to soothe him with the sound of her voice, convince him she was not a threat.

"Easy, big boy. I'm not going to hurt you."

The wolf growled, his fangs flashing white in the fading darkness. She steadied her aim. The weapon she held didn't shoot bullets, but tranquilizer darts.

"This is going to sting, but it won't harm you."

For a moment, the wolf stared at the gun, then raised his glowing eyes to her face, as if he understood the contradiction between her words and the weapon in her hand.

"I'm going to put you to sleep so I can determine the seriousness of your injury." She stepped closer. "That's it. Sit still so I can get a good shot."

Stephanie fired, then cussed because she had the gun on safety. In the time it took her to glance down, pull the safety back and glance up, the wolf attacked. The force knocked her to the ground. She tried to raise the gun, but the animal's teeth clamped around her wrist.

Pain registered before she yanked her hand away and fired. The dart hit him in the shoulder. The animal stared down into her eyes. His hot breath fanned her face. Saliva dripped from his sharp fangs. Stephanie had been filming wolves for three years, but she'd never gotten this close and personal with one. She was terrified, but she was fascinated at the same time.

The only thing she could do was remain motionless, hope the animal wouldn't rip her throat out, and pray the drugs took effect quickly. The beast snorted, then sniffed at her neck. She closed her eyes, waiting for the pain of his teeth to follow. A wet tongue touched her throat. The animal licked her neck. She opened her eyes.

The night was quickly fading, but she saw him more clearly. More clearly than she wanted to see him at this close range. He was as black as midnight. But his eyes—she swore they were blue. She blinked, and in an instant he was gone.

Lying perfectly still, she tried to control the racing of her heart, the ragged sound of her breathing. For all she knew, the animal hadn't gone. He could be watching. Waiting to pounce. It seemed as if an eternity passed, although Stephanie imagined it hadn't been long.

Slowly she rolled to her side and sat up. She glanced around the area. Nothing. How had the animal managed to run away, injured as he was? He wouldn't get far, that much she knew. The drugs would take him down. When she tried to rise, pain shot through her wrist. She stood and tried to look at her injury. The light wasn't strong enough. Her campsite wasn't far. Stephanie planned to return, disinfect and bandage the wound, then gather the supplies needed to nurse the wolf.

She followed a trail she'd created with a package of tissues back to camp. It was dark inside her tent. Without wasting time to light the lantern, she fumbled through her supplies, disinfected her wrist, then wrapped a bandage around the wound. It stung like hell. After gathering the supplies she needed, Stephanie hurried out. She retrieved a flashlight from her Jeep, annoyed she hadn't thought of snatching it after she'd heard the gunshots, and before she'd run unthinking into the night. Poaching was a serious problem all over the world. Her response earlier had been automatic. She'd assumed that whatever was being hunted, it was probably illegal. She'd been right.

The trail of tissues she'd marked had been easy to follow. Locating a trail of bloodstains from the wounded wolf was not as simple. Once she did, Stephanie expected to find the sedated animal quickly. The sun had completely risen by the time the trail led her to a small clearing, and to a house—a cabinlike structure with animal pens in the back and the front door standing wide open.

A sign outside the cabin read "Rick Donavon, DVM." She followed the bloodstains up the creaky steps. Pulling her gun from her jacket pocket, she stepped inside the cabin.

Nothing looked out of the ordinary. There were no immediate signs of human life, or of the animal. On the floor she saw bloodstains leading to a hallway, where she heard the sound of running water.

She found two rooms off the hallway, an unoccupied bedroom and a bathroom. The bathroom door stood cracked an inch. She pushed it open, stepping inside. Hot steam curled around her. Through the haze, she spotted another bloodstain, on the floor in front of the shower door.

The shower door suddenly burst open. A man

stepped out, reached inside and shut off the water. He turned. His gaze locked with hers. His eyes widened a fraction, then lowered to the weapon trained on him. Stephanie stood stunned, unable to form complete sentences in her head, much less speak them.

It wasn't as if she'd expected the big bad wolf to climb out of the shower. But she hadn't seen a man as finely put together as this one in a long time. He stood at least six foot three, and his hair was darker than pitch. His eyes were blue in contrast to his thick dark lashes. Her gaze lowered of its own accord. She swallowed loudly. He was magnificent. All muscle and smooth, tawny flesh.

"Can I help you?"

Her gaze shot up to his face. "Oh yeah," she breathed, then realized she'd been staring at parts of him she had no business seeing. "I—I mean, I'm looking for a wolf."

His brows rose. "Four-legged or two?"

Real cute, she thought. The sarcastic remark and the man. Stephanie tugged at her jacket collar. The bathroom felt hotter than before, which didn't make sense since the open doorway had allowed most of the steam to escape.

"Four," she answered dryly. "I've been tracking an injured wolf all morning. A trail of bloodstains led me inside your cabin."

"You don't plan to shoot me, do you?"

Realizing she still held the gun trained on him, she lowered the weapon. "Sorry. Your front door was open. The wolf must have come inside. There's a bloodstain on the floor in front of the shower."

The man looked down. Stephanie used his distraction to run her gaze over him again.

"Excuse me?"

She glanced up. "I—I thought the blood might be yours. That you might have hurt yourself."

"Do I look injured?"

He'd as good as invited her to examine him to her heart's content. The man obviously had no issues with modesty. "Shouldn't you get a towel or something?" she asked, tugging at her jacket collar again.

He smiled. "Shouldn't you wait in the other room while I do?"

"Oh, right." Stephanie turned and left the bathroom. Even flustered by the sight of a sinfully gorgeous naked man, she maintained the clarity of thought to move slowly into the living area. The kitchen was part of the room, separated by a long bar. Dart gun trained, she moved around the bar. She didn't see a wolf, but she spotted a coffeepot. Digging inside the cabinets, she found a can of coffee and some filters. The coffee had just started to brew when she heard the front door close.

Stephanie moved around the bar. The man from the shower now stood at the door. He wore a pair of faded jeans and a flannel shirt, unbuttoned, which called attention to his broad, masculine chest. He leaned against the closed door, staring at her.

The hairs at the back of her neck bristled. She supposed he had every right to close his own door, but the sight of him leaning casually against it made her feel nervous. Trapped.

"I—I made some coffee," she said. "I hope you don't mind."

"You don't have trouble barging into a man's lair and making yourself at home, do you?" His voice was low, deep, and sensual despite the slight irritation she read in his tone.

To the contrary of what he'd said, Stephanie usually felt ill at ease in someone else's home. She had a problem with walls, which was what had led her into wildlife research. Lots of wide-open spaces. Had he said lair?

"I'm sorry. I didn't get any sleep last night. Coffee seemed like a good idea."

He sighed and pushed away from the door. "I'm sorry, too. I don't get much company. A farmer with a sick animal once in a while. I've forgotten how to be hospitable."

She recalled the sign out front. "You must be Dr. Donavon."

The man stopped before her. "Any woman who has seen me naked should call me by my first name. I'm Rick."

Her face flushed. "I apologize for that, too."

He moved past her into the kitchen. "The part where you barged in on my shower? Or the part where you held a tranquilizer gun aimed at me?"

"Both." She followed him into the kitchen, then drew up short. "How did you know the gun wasn't a real one?"

Reaching into the cabinet to remove two coffee cups, he answered. "I'm a vet, remember? I've seen dart guns before."

That made sense. "Well, anyway, I'm sorry for doing both. Like I told you, I was tracking an injured wolf."

When he handed her a cup, his hand shook. His skin had an unhealthy sheen, as well. Maybe he hadn't dried off, she thought. His hair was still wet and slicked back from his face. And it was a very handsome face.

"It's fortunate your wife isn't home," she found herself saying. "She might have barged in on a scene that didn't look very innocent."

A smile that really wasn't one hovered around his mouth. Stephanie wanted to snatch the ridiculous words back. She wasn't the type to worm out information concerning a man's marital status. Regardless of how good he looked naked.

"I don't have a wife," he said, brushing against her sleeve while reaching for the coffeepot. His glance toward her left ring finger didn't go unnoticed. She held out the cup. He tried to pour, but his hands shook badly.

"Maybe you'd better get your own. I'm not feeling well this morning."

She stared into his eyes. A sense of déjà vu washed over her, as if she'd looked into those eyes before, another time besides this morning. "You don't *look* well, either." She lifted a hand to his forehead.

He flinched. "Are you a doctor?"

She was beginning to wonder if she hadn't managed to tranquilize herself. "No. I just thought you might have a fever. You look hot."

Deliberately, his gaze moved over her. "Likewise."

His statement and the warmth of his eyes couldn't be mistaken, but she wasn't in the mood to play games with him. "It does feel warm in here," she said, purposely misinterpreting his compliment. "I should be going." She set her cup down and walked toward the door. Rick Donavon moved quicker than any animal she had seen. He blocked her exit.

"You didn't tell me what you're doing here."

The fight-or-flee instinct gripped her again. "I did tell you. I was—"

"I didn't mean what you're doing in my cabin. What are you doing in a sleepy little Montana mountain community?"

She kept willing him to move from the door. He didn't. "I'm researching a lead. The organization I work for heard rumors that a pack of Yellowstone wolves had migrated to this area. I'm supposed to uncover the truth, which I have obviously done. Now I'm going to take some pictures and do some filming so we can identify the group. I need to find out how many are in the pack. How or if they're adjusting to the terrain. Things like that."

"There are twelve in the pack. And what they're doing is killing livestock."

"I don't see how you can be sure of that," she said. "There are also grizzlies and mountain lions in this area."

"It's the wolves. I'm very sure."

Escape momentarily forgotten, she placed her hands on her hips. "Are you aware that the wolves are being illegally hunted?"

He swayed. "We had a bad winter. Not much game in the area. The wolves have been forced to feed on livestock. The farmers are tired of losing sheep to them. No one will blame the men for protecting their herds."

Her opinion greatly differed. "There's a large group of wildlife defendants who would love to argue that matter. Where do you stand on the issue? I'd think being a veterinarian, you wouldn't condone—"

"I don't condone the senseless slaughter of animals," he interrupted. "But this is different. It's survival of the fittest. The way of the wild. You should pack up and leave. You don't want to get caught between the wolves and the sheep farmers."

"I'm already caught in the middle," she said. "If I hadn't intruded on a hunt last night, the wolf I'm tracking would be dead!"

His gaze narrowed. "He might not be all that appreciative that you spared his life."

As if an animal could think in such a way, she thought. "I need to find him before the drugs wear off. He's wounded. I want to see how seriously."

Thinking to force him from his position in front of the door, she reached for the knob. He grabbed her shoulders.

"Leave the wolf alone. If he's injured and drugged, he'll also be dangerous. I'm warning you now. Get away from this place. Leave before . . ."

"Before what?" she demanded.

His eyes were still glazed, and a little wild looking. He seemed to notice that he'd taken hold of her shoulders, and relaxed his grip. "Before it's too late."

Stephanie waited for him to explain, but he stumbled forward, nearly knocking her over in the process. She caught him, slinging his arm around her neck. "You are ill," she said. "I'm taking you to bed."

He made an odd noise. A deep sound that sounded very much like a growl.

"Don't argue with me," she warned. "I won't take no for an answer." She helped him to the bedroom, allowing him to fall on the bed. The bedsprings creaked in protest. "Can you take aspirin? Should I get you to a doctor?"

"No drugs," he mumbled, then closed his eyes. "And no doctor. Just go. I'll be all right."

She had serious doubts that he'd be all right when

his teeth started clicking against one another. His body shivered uncontrollably. Chills and fever? That sounded like a dangerous combination to her. She wondered if he'd refused drugs because he couldn't take them, or simply because he'd wanted to get rid of her. His medicine chest should tell her what he could or could not tolerate.

The medicine cabinet was empty. A toothbrush, obviously recently used, and a bottle of mouthwash sat on the counter. She opened a drawer. Toothpaste, floss, but no drugs. Not even Band-Aids. Another cabinet held towels and washcloths. She snatched a washcloth and ran it under cold water.

Rushing back into the bedroom, she sat next to him. He moaned. Her worry increased. Should she contact someone? She hadn't noticed a phone, and she'd left her cell phone in her Jeep. If worse came to worst, she could run back to camp and get her vehicle. The small town she'd driven through last night wasn't far. Surely they had a doctor or a clinic of some kind. She placed the cool cloth against his forehead. He grabbed her wrist.

"Easy," she said, wondering why she used her animal-soothing tone with him. "I'm only trying to help you."

His eyes opened, his brilliant blue gaze locking with hers. In a voice that sounded perfectly lucid, he said, "Then kill me."

Chapter Two

His hand fell away and his eyes closed. She sat frozen in place. It was probably the fever talking, not him. Still, she couldn't dismiss the look in his eyes when he'd whispered the plea. She'd seen it before. Suffering. The look of an animal in pain; the same look in her father's eyes the last year of his life.

She shuddered, rubbing her arms although she wore her jacket and the room felt uncomfortably warm. It was a nice room, she noticed. Nothing fancy, but the antique furniture and the homemade quilt on the bed gave it a cozy, lived-in look. There were no pictures on the walls. A mirror hung over an old dresser, and a rosary lay on the nightstand next to the bed.

Donavon. Irish Catholic. That made sense. The feather-soft feel of the mattress beneath her sang a siren's song. It would beat a sleeping bag on the hard ground, and she'd gotten very little sleep the previous night. But she couldn't sleep, anyway. Not until she knew if Rick Donavon would be all right, or if she needed to get him to a doctor. She glanced down at him.

He looked at peace despite the unnatural sheen of his skin. His lashes were dark, thick, and enviably long. His every feature looked as if it had been specially designed to fit his face. Puzzle pieces that made up a striking picture. Stephanie glanced away. She shouldn't gawk at him while he lay helpless.

She'd obviously been on her own for too long. Cut off from civilization. Once, she'd thought this was the life she wanted—the life she needed. But three years of solitude had taken its toll. She missed her parents—missed being part of a family. And then there was the matter of men, or the lack of them in her life. Studying her patient, she had to admit that her first reaction to seeing him naked had surprised her. Immediate lust was not an emotion that she'd ever experienced before.

As if he sensed her appraisal of him, Rick tossed, mumbling incoherently. Stephanie placed a hand against his forehead, more careful this time. He still felt too warm, but not so hot that she thought desperate measures should be taken. She'd give him a while longer. If his fever broke, chances were he'd be all right. If it didn't, she'd have to figure out how to haul him to her Jeep. All six feet three inches, probably close to two hundred pounds of him. The other side of the bed tempted her. She moved around him and climbed onto the soft mattress. Weary, she closed her eyes. She just wanted to rest them for a moment.

* * *

The hunters chased him again. Only this time, the men had hair on their faces and long fangs like the werewolves Rick had once laughed about in old black-and-white movies. They growled and snapped, their mouths flecked with foam, their eyes glowing red.

Ahead of him, a woman stepped out of the trees. An angel with blond flowing hair and eyes the color of the forest in early spring. She held out her arms, beckoning him to safety. Rick went willingly into her embrace. It had been too long since he'd held a woman, kissed one, made love to one. Those were human pleasures, and not for the likes of him.

Her hair smelled like wildflowers, felt silky beneath his fingertips. The full contours of her breasts pressed against him. She smelled good, felt good, and he wanted to taste her lips. They were petal-soft beneath his. After a moment of no response, she opened to him. He kissed her deeply, his hunger for her building, his senses so much stronger now.

Her body heat rose, fanning the flames of his passion. It was hell, wanting her, but it was heaven, too. Glorious to experience so human an emotion, and agony to know he had no right. The dream shifted. He suddenly sensed her withdrawal—the moment her mind rejected him.

He clung to the fantasy, unwilling to give it up, to surrender either the pleasure he felt with her or the wonder of being merely mortal. He moved on top of her, pressing her down. His fingers clamped around her wrists, forcing them up over her head. The scent of fear mingled with her intoxicating natural fragrance. He hesitated, the man in him understanding that her reaction was not one of compliance, the animal urging him to continue regardless of her wishes.

A moment later, pain ripped through his groin. He moaned and rolled off her. The soft, sensuous ripples of the dream gave way to a whirlpool of emotions. He opened his eyes, the brightness of day cutting into his skull. A woman stood above him, her green eyes narrowed, lips swollen and shirt gaping open. He remembered her, the angel in his dream, the woman who'd barged in on him in the shower—the same one who'd spared his worthless life.

"I thought I was dreaming," he said.

Her labored breathing caused her breasts to strain against the gaping shirt, affording him a tantalizing view.

"Well, you weren't," she huffed. "If you're well enough to do that, you're well enough for me to leave."

And she did. She stormed from the room. Rick groaned and rolled off the bed. He swayed but caught himself. The tranquilizer drugs that had done a number on his system earlier were beginning to wear off. His head still felt a little fuzzy, but he recalled a couple things all too clearly: his hunger for the woman, and the fact that he'd behaved like a rutting beast instead of a man. She was out the door by the time he reached the living area.

The smell of coffee hung heavy on the air. He rushed outside, cursing when a splinter from the wooden porch sliced into his toe. The woman had already made it down the steps.

"Hey!" he shouted. When she didn't respond, he called, "Stephanie, would you stand still long enough for me to apologize?"

She stopped. Slowly she turned to face him. He noticed that her shirt had been rebuttoned—all the way to her neck.

"How did you know my name? I don't remember introducing myself."

Seldom did Rick recall the nights he ran wild with the wolves. But he remembered the scene just before dawn, the meeting between the men and this woman, Stephanie Shane. He recalled her bravery, pieces of conversation, and how she'd stood up to the men. The rest blurred, he supposed because his mind had shifted between man and beast.

"You must have told me at some point, or I wouldn't know."

"I suppose," she admitted, then lifted a brow. "You were saying something about an apology?"

Rick wasn't sorry he'd kissed her. If given half a chance, he'd kiss her again. "I'm sorry if I did anything you didn't want me to do."

"That little introduction between my knee and your crotch should have been a clear indication that I didn't want you to do anything to me. And I don't count that as an apology. Good-bye, Dr. Donavon, and good riddance."

She wheeled away and stomped off. He had to admire her sass. His gaze lowered and he admired the way she looked walking away, too. Rick started to call out, but thought better of it. Let her dislike him, consider him a beast, believe the worst, because it was the truth. She should steer clear of him. He closed his eyes and inhaled deeply. The fading scent of her fragrance clung to his clothes.

His head still pounded. He turned and walked back inside the cabin. He'd experimented with drugs before, hoping he could knock himself out before the change claimed him. It hadn't worked. Nothing had. For three years he'd suffered his curse. Been trapped in a nightmare—had awakened during the stages of the full moon with the taste of blood in his mouth, the stench of death clinging to his skin. Stephanie Shane's intrusion into his life only made the nightmare worse. She was a reminder of all he could not have.

Rick moved into the bedroom. Her jacket lay draped over an old rocker that had belonged to his grandmother. He collapsed on the bed. The drugs, along with his need for sleep, caused him to drift off. He awoke abruptly, his heart pounding. He glanced toward the window and the darkness beyond. Lifting a hand, he stared at the thick hair that hadn't been there earlier. Pain ripped through him. He doubled up, clutching his gut.

Sounds of bones popping, changing, rearranging themselves made his stomach churn. That along with the intolerable pain. He fought the change just as he always did, knowing that, as always, he would lose in the end. Pain shot through his gums. He knew without looking into a mirror that his teeth were growing, becoming canine. He howled at the injustice of it all and tore at his clothing. Usually, he stripped before the change took place. Tonight, he supposed he'd hoped that because he'd felt a man's needs, a man's desires earlier, it would be different. He'd hoped that Stephanie Shane might save him again. Save him from himself. But hope waned, and without it, he gave in to the inevitable.

Stephanie awoke with an immediate sense of danger. Cold air drifted through the flap she'd left open on her tent. Darkness had fallen. She sat up and came face to face with a wolf. Her breath caught in her throat. A pair of glowing eyes stared directly into hers. The saliva dried up in her mouth. She sensed that to move or to make a sound would instigate an attack.

Her dart gun was in the pocket of the jacket she'd left at Rick Donavon's cabin. She didn't have a weapon, not even a stick to beat the animal off should it attack. There was nothing she could do but stare helplessly back at the wolf. That and silently beg for it to leave. The animal leaned forward, sniffing her hair. It sneezed, and she nearly jumped out of her skin.

What did it want? She had no food in her tent. Stephanie had learned long ago that anything edible should be kept in storage containers inside her Jeep when camping. Of course, *she* was edible. Rick Donavon had said the wolves were hungry and that was the reason they attacked sheep.

A flash of teeth showed in the darkness. The animal yawned, shook his head, then sauntered out. Even though the animal had left, she was afraid to move, afraid to breathe.

A distant howl raised the hackles on the back of her neck. Would this one answer the call? Invite others to join him? She scrambled to the tent flap and tried to zip it closed. Her hands shook badly. Once she accomplished the act, Stephanie searched the floor for her flashlight.

The sudden presence of light calmed her. She crept to the flap and unzipped it enough to shine her flashlight around the area. The wolf stood close by. The light helped her see him better, and she swore it was the same wolf she'd tracked before dawn. He was as big and as black, but when he moved, she dismissed the possibility. This wolf did not limp, showed no signs of injury.

She followed his movements until he disappeared; then she sat back and took in deep gulps of air. What a strange place. She'd never had such close encounters with wolves before. Usually, they were timid, and she had to chase after them or hide cameras in order to observe the animals. In less than twenty-four hours, she'd gotten a close glimpse of not just one, but two wolves. Too close.

Stephanie crawled to her sleeping bag and climbed inside. The adrenaline rushing through her veins would make sleep impossible, at least until she calmed down. What she needed was a distraction from her recent encounter with the wolf.

Rick's handsome face immediately surfaced, offering a solution. She didn't want to think about that wolf, either. Not his ruggedly handsome features, or his magnificent body. She certainly didn't want to think about that kiss, or the fact that she had responded to him before she'd realized what she was doing—what he was doing. She really had been on her own for too long, and thoughts of Rick Donavon weren't helping her to relax one bit.

Other thoughts drifted to her. Remembrances of her childhood. The happy days before too much sadness had entered her life. Gradually, she drifted off to sleep. She dreamt of wolves, and of Rick Donavon, but the dream became jumbled, and somewhere along the way, she had trouble distinguishing between the two. The wolves and the man.

Chapter Three

The night had been a long one. Stephanie rose at the crack of dawn and placed her cameras in strategic places around the area. She scrambled eggs in a sturdy cast iron skillet over a fire, feeling as if she hadn't rested at all. She glanced at the bandage around her wrist.

The bite needed further attention. She berated herself for not making it a priority. Oddly enough, she felt no discomfort beneath the bandage, which she supposed was the reason she'd been lax in giving the injury proper care. She planned to examine the bite as soon as she finished breakfast.

After stirring the eggs again, she rose and stretched. Closing her eyes, she breathed deeply of the crisp, pine-scented air. When she opened them, movement directly ahead caused her to stiffen. An animal had darted from behind one tree to another. One too large to be a squirrel or a rabbit. Stephanie eased back down and grabbed a sturdy stick she'd used to poke the fire.

A twig snapped. A larger shape came into view. She dropped the stick, but on second thought, moved it within easy reach. Rick Donavon strolled into her campsite, her jacket draped over one arm, a thermos tucked under the other.

"I brought coffee," he said, lifting the thermos. "A peace offering."

His dark good looks nearly took her breath away. She had to remind herself to breathe . . . and not to stare. "I could have used that jacket earlier," she grumbled, stirring the eggs.

He walked over and sat beside her. "I see your mood hasn't improved since we parted company. Still mad about that little kiss?"

Her face heated. It had not been a little kiss. Tongues and groping had been involved. "I've already forgotten about that," she lied.

From the corner of her eye, she saw him frown. His expression almost made her smile. His next words kept her from giving in.

"Then you're just naturally cranky in the mornings?"

She looked at him. "I am not."

"Unsociable?"

"Not as a rule." She leaned down, dug two tin cups from one of her packs, and shoved them at him. "Make yourself useful and pour."

Rather than take the containers, he took her wrist. "What happened here?"

The warmth of his touch penetrated the flimsy bandage. She was unnaturally aware of him. The deep sound of his voice. The gentleness of his touch. The clean soap-and-water smell of him. "Guess I got too close to the wolf I was tracking yesterday."

His gaze snapped to her face. "Did it bite you?"

She laughed over the sudden concern mirrored on his face. "Probably barely broke the skin. It doesn't hurt."

"Let me see it," he demanded.

Stephanie snatched her wrist away. "You're not a doctor. Not an M.D., anyway."

"Humor me."

Since she had planned on tending the bite, she unwound the bandage. Light bloodstains marked the inner gauze, but when she looked at her wrist, she had trouble believing her eyes. There was no wound. No teeth marks. Nothing.

"That's strange," she whispered. "I could have sworn he bit me."

"You're certain?"

She glanced up and found the vet's face too close for comfort. His eyes were intense, searching. Stephanie shrugged. "Obviously not. I must have been mistaken."

"Did you examine your wrist after it happened?"

His questions wore on her nerves. She still felt confused by her lack of an injury. It didn't make sense. She had felt the animal's teeth sink into her flesh.

"There was no time, and it was dark inside my tent. I just poured disinfectant over my wrist and wrapped a bandage around it."

"Did the disinfectant sting? Like the skin had been broken?"

Sighing, she answered, "The skin wasn't broken or I'd have teeth marks, or at least scratches. Even a scratch or two couldn't have healed this quickly. It isn't possible. Could I have a cup of coffee now?"

For a moment, he looked as if he wouldn't drop the matter. He finally turned his attention to pouring the coffee, but she noticed that his hands shook.

"Are you feeling better?" she asked, noting that his eyes looked clear. Still, she was concerned about the shaking.

He shoved a coffee cup toward her. "I bounce back quickly."

Lifting the cup, Stephanie breathed in the scent before she took a sip. "What was wrong with you yesterday?"

Rick shrugged. "Twenty-four-hour bug, or maybe too many beers with the guys the night before."

"You should learn to dodge those silver bullets," she said, giving her eggs another stir.

His head turned toward her. "What?"

"Isn't there a brand of beer called a silver bullet?"

He ran a hand through his thick dark hair. "Oh, yeah, *those* silver bullets."

Something he'd said yesterday still bothered her. The words he'd spoken and the suffering she'd seen in his eyes. Stephanie moved the eggs from the fire and turned to him. "When you were ill, you asked me to kill you."

The cup he held stopped halfway to his mouth. His face flushed slightly. "You know how hangovers are. Sometimes you just want to be put out of your misery."

She couldn't so easily dismiss his plea, whether he was out of his head with fever or not. "I've never seen anyone react that way to alcohol. Food poisoning has been known to bring on fever and chills, but—"

"That was probably the culprit," he interrupted. "I tend to eat my meat too raw."

Stephanie shuddered. "You shouldn't eat meat at all. I'm a vegetarian."

For some reason, he found her declaration funny. When he laughed, she noticed how straight and white his teeth were.

"You find that amusing?" she asked.

Still smiling, he said, "A vegetarian veterinarian. Try saying that three times fast."

She laughed, too, breaking a little of the tension. The smell of cooked eggs made her stomach rumble. She felt starved but didn't want to eat in front of him. That left only one alternative. "Would you care for breakfast?"

His smile faded. "I don't think that would be a good idea. You know what they say? Feed a stray and it'll just keep hanging around."

Stephanie thought it would be best if he didn't hang around. She had trouble keeping her eyes off him. Although he claimed to feel better, she thought he looked tired. Which reminded her of why she felt exhausted.

"I had a late night visitor," she said.

A dark brow rose.

"A wolf," she continued. "It was very strange. I woke up and he was inside my tent, staring at me."

The cup in his hand shook again. He set it down. "Are you sure you weren't dreaming? Wolves don't usually—"

"I know," she interrupted. "They usually avoid people. But I wasn't dreaming, and I could have sworn it was the same wolf the hunters had wounded. But when I followed him outside, I noticed he wasn't limping, showed no sign of injury at all, so it couldn't have been the same animal."

"You should leave," he said. "It could be dangerous here for you."

She dug in her pack and removed a tin plate. "For me, or for the hunters if I decide to turn them in to the authorities?"

Rising, he stretched his long legs. "Don't get between the farmers and the wolves. Mostly, they're just good old boys looking out for their own interests."

While scooping eggs onto her plate, she muttered, "What are they going to do? Shoot me?"

"Not on purpose, but these men are farmers, not expert marksmen. You don't want to get caught in the middle."

Stephanie glanced up at him, suspicion causing her gaze to narrow. "That's what this visit is about, isn't it? You came to scare me off?"

"I came to talk some sense into you," he corrected. "What's going on here isn't any of your business."

She set her plate aside and rose, meeting him on his level. "Wolves are being illegally hunted and that's none of my business? I'm making it my business, and I'm also calling the Fish and Wildlife Service on your crooked sheriff and his hillbilly friends. What do you think of that?"

"I think you're poking your nose into something dangerous," he shot back. "The farmers are good men, and the sheriff is a good man, too. He's protecting the community. Today the wolves are only killing sheep. Tomorrow it may be a child who's wandered too far into the woods, or a woman camping alone."

She snorted disdainfully. "I'm not that easily frightened. And for your information, there's no proof that a healthy wild wolf has attacked a human in North America for the past decade."

* * *

Rick felt tempted to shake her silly. She had no idea they were not discussing "normal" wolves. At least one of them wasn't normal. He couldn't believe he'd come here last night. Crept into her tent and stared at her. Thank God that was all he'd done. He must have picked up her scent from her jacket draped over the rocker in his room.

He'd hoped his strong attraction to her the day before might be a result of the drugs in his system. Not so. He fought himself not to kiss her again. She was beautiful, and tempting, and forbidden.

"You're stubborn," he added out loud.

"I'm dedicated," she corrected. "And I won't be bullied around or frightened away. The last man I let tell me what to do was my father, and that only lasted until I was old enough to talk back."

He could imagine her as a child. Small angelic face surrounded by blond curls; twisting men around her finger even then. "I don't want to be your father," he assured her, not bothering to add that he wouldn't mind being her lover. He'd made that clear enough yesterday. "I thought you might listen to reason."

"But you're not being rational," she pointed out. "If I leave, who will save these wolves?"

She was right. He wasn't being rational. Leaving was no longer an option for her. Not until he was certain he hadn't bitten her. To his knowledge, Rick had never attacked a human. Research he'd read insisted a person couldn't become a werewolf by being bitten by one, but he knew that was a lie. To assure himself that he hadn't passed his curse to Stephanie Shane, Rick had to keep her nearby until the next full moon cycle.

"If you call the authorities about the hunters, you

won't get your research or your documentary. The place will be crawling with people. Wolves don't particularly like people, remember? They'll go into hiding."

Her teeth worried her bottom lip. "That's true. But what am I supposed to do, just let them continue to kill wolves?"

It was hard for him to concentrate when she stood close to him. Harder still to keep from sampling her lips again. Rick returned to the stump she'd been sitting on. He sat and lifted his coffee. "I could talk to Hugh. Ask him to forgo any more hunting until you're finished here."

Stephanie joined him, retrieving her unfinished breakfast. "And I suppose in exchange, I have to agree not to report his actions?"

He smiled. "You're smart, too."

"Too smart to agree to that. I won't spend time and emotion on these wolves only to hear reports at a later date that they've all been killed."

"But your work could launch a campaign to have them relocated rather than destroyed," he said. "I can placate the sheriff and the farmers if you agree to film the wolves killing livestock. They would have their proof that something needs to be done."

"And what if my cameras prove the wolves are not responsible, but some other predator?"

He shrugged. "It won't, but then you'll have proof that the wolves should be left alone."

"Why are you so sure the wolves are responsible?" she asked, then shoved a bite of eggs into her mouth.

"I've seen the remains. These are pack killings. More than one animal. The thing is, the sheep being killed are most likely animals that are diseased or weak, and might not survive anyway. That's how survival of the fittest works."

"Sounds to me as if the wolves are only doing their job," she commented. "Can you prove that the sheep being killed are sick?"

Rick shook his head. "Not enough left of the remains to perform an autopsy."

Stephanie set her plate aside. "So much for my appetite. And I have work to do." She rose, affording him a view of her long legs wrapped in tight denim. "I'm hoping to find one of the dens today. I thought I could set up a camera close by to catch them coming and going."

Her long legs were so distracting, he almost didn't hear her words. When they sank in, he tensed. "That wouldn't be a smart move. The females are probably ready to whelp or already have. Get too close to the dens, and the wolves will become aggressive."

"But getting close is my job." She scraped the remains of her plate back into the skillet, gathered her dishes, and moved off toward a stream beside her campsite. Rick went after her.

"I'm serious," he insisted. Now that the moon's cycle had ended, he didn't have to worry about stumbling from a den naked come daylight and being caught on film in the process. But he knew for a fact that there were pups in the dens, and the animals would be protective.

"I'll be careful," she assured him, bending next to the stream to wash her dishes.

Rick bent beside her. "Like you were the other night? You've already been bitten once—"

"No, that was a mistake," she interrupted. "I only thought the animal bit me. And I plan to be more careful from here on out. Don't you have something to do besides bother me?"

He leaned in, smelling her hair. He loved her scent. "Am I bothering you?"

When she turned her head, they were eye to eye. Her gaze lowered to his mouth. "Yes," she answered.

She bothered him, too. And in a big way. He had visited her campsite with the intention of scaring her off, but now, she had to stay. Now he had to keep a close eye on her and, at the same time, keep his raging hormones at bay. Not an easy task for a werewolf.

Backing off when she sat so close, her eyes still locked with his, took a great amount of willpower. She glanced away, gathered her dishes, and stood up.

"Good-bye, Dr. Donavon."

He rose, watching the sway of her hips as she walked away. The sunshine bounced off her hair. She stopped, and he waited for her to turn and say something else to him. When she continued to stand perfectly still, he moved up behind her. Blocking the path to her campsite stood a large gray wolf. The animal curled back its lips and growled.

Chapter Four

Stephanie's heart was in her throat. The wolf wasn't the same one that had crept into her tent the night before, and he wasn't as large, but he looked as if he could hurt someone if the mood struck him.

"Stand very still."

The warmth of Rick's breath brushed her ear. She hadn't heard him approach. He stepped around her, shielding her body with his. The wolf immediately ceased his growling. Stephanie raised herself on tiptoes to look over Rick's shoulder. It appeared to her as if the wolf and the country vet were having a staredown. When the animal finally whimpered and scurried off, she breathed a sigh of relief.

"How did you do that?"

He turned around, and for a moment, she thought his eyes were glowing. He blinked, and they appeared normal again.

"Do what?"

"S-scare him off that way?" she stammered. "It was almost as if he recognized you as the Alpha male."

"He did recognize me. The wolves are used to seeing me in these woods. You're the one they consider an intruder."

She supposed he had a point. "I guess I need to stay on my guard. These particular wolves seem to be more aggressive than the ones I've studied in the past."

"I told you why," he reminded. "They have pups, or females in the pack getting ready to whelp. They'll be more protective of their territory than usual. Maybe you should stay in town."

Stephanie laughed off his suggestion. "I don't remember seeing a hotel when I passed through yesterday, and I can't very well research wildlife from town. I'll be fine."

They stood there for a moment, the silence between them awkward. She felt the heat rolling off his body, thought she even heard his heart beating. The longer he stared at her, the more uncomfortable she became. But she couldn't look away. It seemed he held some strange power over her. Even though the morning chill had faded, goose bumps rose on her arms.

A vision flashed through her mind. Cool sheets and sweat-soaked skin. Seeking mouths and roaming hands. Pleasure so intense it forced a soft moan from her lips. Rick blinked, and the spell was broken.

He turned and walked away, leaving her shaken and unsure of what had just happened between them. She watched him move through the trees. Shapes crept from the shadows to follow him. Wolves. Stephanie shuddered and returned to her campsite. She lifted her jacket from the stump where it lay draped, spotted the thermos, and sighed irritably.

He'd forgotten to take it with him, which meant he'd be back, or that she would have to return the item. She had work to do, and he'd already proven to be too much of a distraction. He had said he would try to dissuade the hunters, however, and she would rather gather her research information without getting the authorities involved.

Stephanie picked up the coffee and poured herself a fresh cup. She would not use the thermos as an excuse to visit the handsome country vet. In fact, she didn't plan on giving him another thought for the rest of the day.

She recalled her strong reaction to him earlier, the visions that had flashed through her mind. She remembered her momentary belief that his eyes had been glowing. It seemed ridiculous to her now. The sun must have reflected in his gaze a certain way. Rick Donavon was very handsome, maybe a little strange, but he wasn't some kind of monster.

Rick slept for two days straight. He stood at the kitchen sink; splashed cold water on his face, then stuck a glass beneath the faucet. He'd dreamed of the woman again. Hot, forbidden dreams. A monster such as himself had no right even to dream about her. She seemed innocent to him, and he was cursed. His fingers tightened around the glass he held.

The irresistible Miss Shane was only a reminder of all that been lost to him. Maybe this was his punishment for the life he'd lived when he'd been normal. He'd never had time for anyone else, not even a wife. His own desires and needs had always come first.

Women had called him a loner, and much worse. He used them for pleasure, had given pleasure in return, but he'd never given his heart.

It was ironic, all the things he'd taken for granted—companionship, a woman to share his life, bear his children, love him for better or for worse—would never be his. Not now. He laughed harshly, then hurled the glass at the wall. It shattered, just as his life had shattered three years ago.

Rick walked to the mess and bent. He lifted a piece of glass, allowing the sharp edge to slice his finger open. Blood seeped from the cut. He stuck the injured finger into his mouth. By morning, the cut would heal itself. Just like the bullet wound he'd taken in his leg. There was only one way to kill him, or so he'd read. A wound to the head, or to the heart. Those were the only organs that couldn't heal themselves.

Ripping open his shirt, he held the glass to his chest. If he plunged it in deep enough, he could end the nightmare, here, now, today. He'd been raised to believe that taking one's life was the greatest sin. That doing so would condemn his soul to eternal hell. Hell was the reason he hadn't done it before now. Hell had become a familiar place to him, and Rick longed for peace and salvation.

If someone else did the job for him, it couldn't be counted against his soul. Thanks to Stephanie, he probably couldn't rely on the hunters to handle the task. In all good conscience, he couldn't plunge the glass deep into his chest, as he wanted to do. Not yet. He had to stick around long enough to be certain she hadn't been bitten. Rick had also promised to speak to the sheriff on her behalf—ask him and the hunters to give her free rein to study the wolves.

A knock on his door made him jump. He threw the glass shard on the floor and rose. Rick was surprised to see the woman who'd been occupying his thoughts standing on the porch. She shoved his thermos at him.

"You forgot this the other day," she said.

"I would have been back for it," he assured her.

"I know. That's why I decided to return it."

He smiled. "Would you like some more?"

Her gaze lowered to his mouth. "More?"

"Coffee," he specified.

"No, thank you."

When she continued to stand there, he asked, "Would you like to come inside?"

She moistened her lips with her tongue. "No, I should probably get going."

Yes, she should leave, Rick thought. But no amount of reasoning seemed to work when she stood within touching distance. He was painfully aware of her. Her gaze lowered to his open shirt. She sucked in her breath and reached out.

"You're bleeding."

The feel of her fingers on his skin nearly drove him wild. He fought the urge to yank her inside the cabin and into his arms. "I broke a glass in the kitchen. It's just a scratch."

"It looks fairly deep." She pushed past him. "We should get that cleaned up and see if you need stitches."

Rick followed her inside. He smiled and closed the door behind him. "You should be more careful," he called.

Stephanie turned, raising a brow.

"The glass," he reminded her. "Watch where you step. It could slice through your shoes."

She nodded and hurried into the kitchen. Rick pushed away from the door. He moved toward the kitchen, realized his actions were furtive like those of a stalking animal, and approached more directly. Stephanie already held a paper towel under the faucet.

"Come here," she ordered.

Like a well-trained dog, he obeyed. She squeezed water from the paper towel and turned toward him, wiping the blood from his chest. Her knock on the door had startled him. His hand must have slipped. Her scent curled around him. He'd thought she smelled good the other day, but her fragrance seemed stronger to him now. He closed his eyes and breathed deeply.

"I don't think you need stitches," she said. "But you'll have a nasty scratch for a while."

It would be gone by tomorrow. He felt the flesh already healing, just as the cut on his thumb would also disappear.

"Be sure you keep it clean so it doesn't get infected."

Rick opened his eyes and glanced down. Her features were perfect. Small oval face, high cheekbones, delicate nose, inviting lips. "I do know a little about that," he said dryly.

Her cheeks turned a pretty shade of pink. "Of course you do. Sorry, I forgot for a moment." Her brow furrowed. "Why aren't there any animals in the pens outside?"

He shrugged and walked away. "The wolves are doing a good job of separating the weak from the strong. Mostly all I get is sheep." Rick grabbed a broom and a dustpan. "A sick calf once in a while. I only practice on large animals. I prefer to make house calls rather than have owners leave animals here."

"Because they wouldn't be safe," she said.

He didn't look at her. "Exactly."

She walked over and took the dustpan from his hand. "Too many wolves roaming this area."

"Right," he agreed, his tone dry.

Stephanie bent, holding the dustpan while he swept up the broken glass. He would have preferred that she take the broom. Having a beautiful woman kneeling before him didn't help his raging hormones. Once he'd swept all the broken glass into the dustpan, Stephanie rose.

"Where's your trash?"

He nodded toward the sink. "Cabinet under the sink."

Replacing the broom, he watched her open the cabinet door and empty the dustpan. His gaze roamed her backside. Her natural instincts were not very good, he decided, or she'd sense what he was thinking and make a hasty retreat. Instead, she straightened, walked back toward him, and held out the dustpan. He replaced it beside the broom.

"I'd wear shoes in here for a few days," she mumbled. "We might have missed some of the smaller pieces."

"I'll be careful," he assured her, wishing cuts and scrapes were something he had to worry about. That would mean he was normal.

She glanced around. "I'll just wash my hands and be on my way."

Rick didn't want her to go, but he really didn't want her to stay, either. His attraction to her became stronger every second she remained. For his sake as well as hers, parting company would be for the best.

Even as he told himself that, he moved up behind her while she washed her hands.

She smelled of wildflowers and sunshine. That, and something else. Some unidentifiable scent he couldn't resist. She turned and nearly bumped into him.

"W-were you sniffing me?" she stammered.

"I like your shampoo."

He should step back and let her pass, but Rick's feet felt glued to the floor. He kept staring into her eyes, thinking how green they were. His gaze lowered to her neck. He'd tasted her there. But he couldn't recall if he'd been a man or an animal when he'd done so. Her hand crept up, pulled her collar closer around her neck.

"Why do I get the feeling when I'm around you that you'd like to gobble me up like a snack?"

He smiled. "I'd never rush anything with you. I'd eat you nice and slow. Savor you."

Her mouth trembled slightly. She pushed past him. "That reminds me. I'm starving. I thought I'd try the café in town for lunch."

Berating himself for what he'd just said, Rick took off after her. "Can you give me a ride?"

She didn't answer until she'd opened the door and placed herself safely upon the porch. "Don't you have a vehicle?"

Rick nodded. "I have a truck, but it's not running at the moment. I haven't had time to work on it. I thought I should speak to the sheriff about what we discussed."

"I planned on shopping. I need more film and a few other items."

The pretty wildlife photographer felt uncomfortable with him. That was obvious. Rick couldn't blame her. He shouldn't have made that crack. But it had been the truth. He would savor her. Every inch of her. "I'll go another time."

Stephanie started to turn away, stopped, and sighed. "You should speak to the sheriff as soon as possible. I would do it myself, but he'd probably listen to you before he would a stranger. I'll get my Jeep and come back for you." She looked him up and down, then grinned. "You are going to change that shirt, right? In case you haven't noticed, the buttons are missing."

He grinned back. "Any other instructions?"

She cocked her head to the side and studied him. "A haircut wouldn't hurt," she said, then turned and walked away.

He watched her walk down the steps and toward the trees, still smiling to himself over her instructions. They sounded so ordinary. Like something a woman would say to a normal flesh-and-blood man. Like something a wife might say to her husband.

His smile faded. He was not ordinary. And she should never become too comfortable in his company. Wild animals couldn't be trusted. They turned on people.

Chapter Five

Stephanie had wondered what type of reception she'd get from the townspeople. It was a chilly one at best. The café looked like something out of a black-and-white movie. Even the people inside appeared as if they'd stepped from the screen of an old *Twilight Zone* episode. The waitress still wore her hair in beehive fashion. Her name was Betty, and she nearly melted on the spot when she caught sight of Rick, but frosted up when she realized he wasn't alone.

"So what will you have, miss?" she asked, without looking at Stephanie and drooling over Rick.

"What's good?" Stephanie asked.

"The lamb chops are always fresh."

With a shudder, Stephanie studied the menu again. "I'll have a salad."

Betty's gaze finally swung toward her. She snorted. "Figures." She turned a stunning smile on Rick. "No wonder she doesn't have any meat on her bones."

He smiled back. "Miss Shane doesn't eat meat. She's a vegetarian."

The waitress lifted a brow, snorted again, then asked, "Will you have your usual?"

"Burger and fries. You know me. I'm a meat and potatoes man."

"Rare?" Betty asked.

"The redder the better," he answered.

Stephanie's stomach rolled. She didn't know if it was due to the bloody meat reference or a result of the way Betty kept eyeballing Rick. It shouldn't have surprised her. He was a handsome single man in a town where probably few could be found. She imagined he could have his pick of the single women. Maybe even the married ones. The waitress took their menus and sashayed off, her ample hips swinging.

"Why is everyone staring at me?" Stephanie asked through tight lips.

Rick glanced around. "They're just curious. We don't get many strangers here." His gaze swung back to her. "I'm curious, too. Tell me about yourself."

Stephanie wasn't comfortable discussing her past with anyone, much less a man she didn't know. She shrugged. "Not much to tell."

"Why aren't you married?"

"Why aren't you?" she countered.

He smiled, and she tried not to melt. "Never got around to it. I used to travel a lot."

"You said used to. Don't you enjoy traveling?"

Rick tugged at his shirt collar and shifted against his seat. "No. I've become a homebody of sorts."

"I love to travel," Stephanie admitted. "It's one of the

things I like most about my job. That and being outdoors."

"And the animals," he added. "You do like animals, don't you?"

She laughed. "Of course I like animals. I'm naturally suspicious of anyone who doesn't."

"And you like wolves in particular?"

His line of questioning seemed strange to her. "Yes," she answered. "Wolves in particular."

Lifting a salt shaker to examine, he continued, "Why wolves in particular?"

Stephanie had never given her attraction to the species much thought. "I suppose because they're beautiful. And they have values. The pack is like a family. They love and protect one another."

"What about your family?"

He'd hit upon a sore subject. It had been three years since her father's death, and she still felt an empty place inside. "My parents were in a car accident. My mother was killed instantly. Dad held on for another year, but he was in bad shape. An invalid." She lowered her gaze because she felt the tears gathering. "I don't think he even knew who I was in the end."

The gentle touch of his hand startled her. "I'm sorry for your loss."

His touch felt comforting; his expression held sincerity. Stephanie managed to get her emotions under control. "What about you? Are your parents still living?"

"Yes," he answered.

"Do you see them much?"

"No." He glanced away from her. "Not in a while."

"Why not?"

He removed his hand from hers. "Too busy, I guess. They live in Texas."

"You should visit them as often as you can. You won't have them forever." They sat silently for a moment. "What about brothers and sisters?" Stephanie asked.

"I have a brother," he responded. "Or I did. We were together on a hunting expedition in Canada a few years back. He . . . he was killed."

"How horrible," she breathed. "What happened?"

Rick glanced around as if looking for someone. "I'd rather not talk about it."

She supposed she was getting too personal and tried to change the subject. "You don't strike me as the hunting type."

"I'm not," he admitted. "I went because Jason wanted us to spend time together." Betty appeared, and he looked relieved. "Great, here's our food. I'm starving."

And he evidently was, because he attacked his food only moments after the waitress set his plate in front of him. Stephanie had to glance away. She was surprised the burger wasn't still mooing. She tried to concentrate on her salad.

"You should have children."

"What?"

"Children," he repeated, taking a bite of his bloody hamburger. "You'll make a good mother."

She loved children. Once, she'd pictured herself with a husband and babies of her own. She didn't know if she could stand to love someone that much again, because she felt certain she couldn't stand to lose anyone else she loved.

"And you have arrived at this conclusion based upon . . . ?"

"You have a nurturing nature," he answered. "You like to take care of people."

Stephanie laughed. "For a man who hardly knows me, you assume a lot."

He lifted a brow. "You don't want children?"

A hot flush spread up her neck. She could imagine having his children. And what beautiful offspring he would produce. "Most women want children. That was an easy assumption." She moved her fork around in her salad, not looking at him. "Would you like to have children?"

When he remained silent, she glanced up. He mumbled, "I can't," then looked away.

"Oh, I'm sorry," she said, realizing she'd gotten too personal again.

Rick wiped his mouth with a napkin. "Hugh's here. Do you mind if I talk to him?"

She glanced behind her and saw the sheriff conversing with Betty. "No. Go ahead. I'll wash my hands and freshen up, then meet you at the door."

He grabbed the bill, slid across the seat, and waited for her to rise. Conversation stopped at each booth or table they passed. Stephanie felt self-conscious. She nodded at the sheriff when they reached the man, then proceeded to the restroom. Once inside, she washed her hands and splashed her face with cool water.

She found herself primping before the mirror, which wasn't at all like her. Stephanie knew she was pretty, in a natural, no-fuss sort of way. Her job didn't allow her to waste time with makeup or hot rollers. That was the bad thing about camping out. No electricity. Of course, it had never bothered her much before. But then, she'd never had a single, handsome man living near her campsite before, either.

Frowning over her silly primping, she threw the paper towel in the wastebasket and left the restroom. Rick stood at the register talking to Betty.

"Sure you can't stop by later tonight and look at my Sugar, Rick? Her appetite hasn't been at all good lately."

"You know I don't practice on small animals. You'll have to take her—"

"But Sugar doesn't like that old vet," Betty interrupted, her plump red lips forming a pout. "And it's so far over there."

He dug in his back pocket for his wallet. "Sugar doesn't like me either, remember?"

Stephanie stepped up to the register. "Who's Sugar?"

"My poodle," Betty answered, frowning over the interruption. "I wanted Rick to come over tonight and have a look at her, but I forgot, she pitches a fit anytime she comes within sniffing distance of him. He's the reason we've all had to take to penning up our pets."

"You should keep them penned up anyway," Rick said. "Confinement stops the spread of disease and keeps them from getting run over."

"I suppose you're right about that," she admitted. "Well, don't be such a stranger."

"Keep the change," he said, ushering Stephanie outside.

"Why don't dogs like you?" she immediately asked, finding that strange since Rick was a veterinarian.

He looked a little embarrassed. "They just don't."

"But that's odd, isn't it? Haven't you ever had to practice on small animals?"

He nodded. "There's the drugstore. You can get film and anything else you need. I'm going for a haircut."

Although it pleased her that he'd taken her suggestion to heart, Stephanie wouldn't be put off. "Well, haven't you?"

Rick sighed. "I used to practice on small animals when I lived in the city. I can only assume that dogs no longer like me because they smell wolf on me."

She drew up short. "What?"

"My shoes," he specified. "Tromp around a forest inhabited by wolves and you're bound to pick up their scent on your shoes. Spoor and things."

"Oh." She wrinkled her nose. "I suppose you're right. I hadn't thought of that. How'd it go with the sheriff?"

He shrugged. "Okay. He said he'd speak to the farmers, but he also said to tell you to be careful. Some might listen and some might not."

"I guess it's a start," she said.

"Do you mind shopping alone while I get a haircut?"

The idea wasn't too pleasing since she was a stranger in town and evidently not highly regarded, but Stephanie answered, "No problem."

"I'll meet you back at your Jeep."

With a nod, Stephanie veered off toward the drugstore. She received a chilly reception from the owner after she entered, but ignored the balding older man. Stephanie picked up a few rolls of film, strolled the aisles until something caught her eye. She smiled and plucked a bottle of her favorite shampoo from the shelves. Since she didn't know how long it would take Rick to get a haircut, she lingered over the magazine section and chose a mystery novel from the limited selection of books.

The man running the cash register didn't thaw a fraction toward her, even though she'd spent more money than she intended, maybe unconsciously trying to win him over. She took her sack and headed back outside. The barbershop was just up the street, but Stephanie decided to wait at her Jeep. She headed toward the vehicle. A woman stepped from the alley beside the drugstore.

The woman's appearance startled Stephanie. She had long, tangled hair and wore ragged clothing. Her face was a mask of wrinkles. She lifted a bony finger and pointed.

"Beware of the wolf," she croaked.

Stephanie glanced behind her, unsure if the woman was speaking to her, and also to make certain there wasn't anything frightening standing behind her. There was no wolf. Only Rick walking toward her. She turned back. The woman had disappeared. Stephanie scanned the streets, searching for the woman. When she didn't find her, she stepped into the alleyway. It was deserted.

Rick held the shampoo bottle beneath his nose. He took a deep breath, then sighed with pleasure. He smiled, recalling how Stephanie had pulled it from the sack once she'd brought him home. A gift, she had teased, so he wouldn't have to sniff her. He wouldn't use the shampoo on his now shorter hair, but he liked having her scent floating around the room.

His smile faded when he recalled something he hadn't liked. Stephanie had said an old woman stepped from the alley and warned her to beware of the wolf. He'd thought she might be seeing things until they spotted the old woman later, hobbling down the road.

He hadn't seen her before, but she'd stopped as they passed, staring at him with eyes too knowing. Rick had turned his head to look at her, and she'd lifted a bony finger, pointing at him accusingly. Did she know? How could she? And who was she? His immediate feelings on the matter were that she'd come from a county fair in one of the neighboring towns. She looked like a gypsy, a fortune-teller. The road she'd been traveling only veered off to one place—a broken-down shack up in the mountains that had long been abandoned.

If this woman knew what lurked beneath the facade of his human flesh, she was dangerous. He didn't want his curse exposed to the world. His parents had suffered enough; he wouldn't bring this down on their heads, as well.

He didn't like to recall the turn of events that had forever changed their lives, and his. He'd gone to Canada on a hunting trip with his older brother, Jason. Rick wasn't a hunter, but Jason had laid a guilt trip on him about how little time they spent together. Rick wished the trip had been an instance when he'd remained self-absorbed, instead of giving in. Then he and Jason would not have fallen into the nightmare.

They were drinking beer and bragging about women that night in front of the campfire. Jason had excused himself, muttering he had to see a man about a dog. Rick sat quietly for a moment, enjoying the silence of the wilderness and the popping of the fire. A short time later, he'd heard his brother's calls for help.

He'd grabbed his rifle and charged through the foliage. Rick stumbled upon a scene he would never forget. A huge wolf had his brother down, its powerful jaws wrapped around his throat. Rick lifted the rifle and shot at the animal, missing because he was no marksman.

Then the animal had come at him. Rick barely managed to lift the rifle when the wolf sunk its teeth into the flesh of his thigh. He'd shot the animal in the back at close range. The wolf yelped and fell to the ground. Dragging his injured leg, Rick rushed to his brother's side. It had been too late. Jason was dead. Even though he knew, Rick removed his jacket and wrapped it around Jason's throat, hoping he was wrong.

He'd carried him to their vehicle, thrown him in the backseat, and raced for the nearest town. The rest seemed like a blur. Because he'd lost a lot of blood from the gaping wound in his leg, he passed out at the hospital. He'd awakened in a room, tubes running from his arms, with the recollection that something had gone horribly wrong tugging at his conscience.

His brother had, in fact, been dead upon arrival at the hospital, he learned later. He'd taken him home in a casket. Or at least he thought he had. The loss of his brother had blunted his emotions. He hadn't even noticed that the wound in his leg healed at an impossible rate. Then the changes started. The restlessness. The sleepless nights. His infatuation with the moon. A need for raw meat. He'd never believed that werewolves truly existed.

Not until he realized he had become one. He'd wake in the morning to find dirt beneath his fingernails, sometimes blood on his hands and the taste of it in his mouth. The newspaper had started reporting accounts of a wolf roaming the streets of the city. He tried to convince himself it was impossible—a man could not assume the shape of an animal—but deep down, he knew it was possible, and that he was such a man.

Rick brought trembling hands to his head, burying his face. He didn't want to think about when he had come to accept the curse that fate had dealt him—the day his dead brother had paid him a visit. Rick had almost died of shock. He'd thought he might be hallucinating, had prayed he was dreaming, even though he was overjoyed to see his only brother again. But he hadn't been dreaming. It took seeing Jason to convince him that what he suffered was also real.

Jason was a werewolf. He wasn't in the casket Rick had flown home with. Confused and delirious, his brother had escaped the hospital. Rick later figured the hospital didn't want to admit they'd lost a body, so they'd played along with a hoax. But Jason soon learned what he'd become, and convinced Rick that he shared the same curse. His brother told him he would return to Canada, find the wolf that had bitten them, and kill it. Only then would they both be free. That had been three years ago. Jason had obviously not found the wolf.

He wondered if his brother had lost sight of the human within him, and now ran wild in the Canadian wilderness. Rick had a lot of questions he wanted answered. He'd done research, of course, but one claim disputed another, and he didn't know what to believe. If the curse could truly only be broken by killing the werewolf that had bitten him, he feared it would haunt him for the rest of his life. Finding that one particular wolf in the wilds of Canada would be like searching for a needle in a haystack.

An ad for a country vet had caught his attention one

day. A secluded mountain town nestled against the rugged mountains of Montana sounded like a good place for him.

The wolves came shortly after he arrived. For all he knew, he had called them in the lonely hours when the moon hung full in the sky. They were his companions, the only ones who didn't judge him. He'd awoken many times among them. Rising naked in the cold light of dawn in his glaring human form. But they accepted him, either way, man or beast, which was more than his own kind would do.

They would kill him if they knew. He would be talked about, publicized, and crucified. His parents would suffer even more than they already had. Rick wouldn't allow that to happen. They'd lost two sons to that hunting expedition. At least the two they knew and loved.

Once, he wouldn't have given the strange woman he'd seen in town a second thought; now the beast within him said he must. He would wait awhile, see if she disappeared as mysteriously as she had appeared; if she didn't, he'd be forced to do something about her.

Chapter Six

Stephanie stared up at the moon. Although it was no longer full, she thought it had never shone more brightly, or been more mesmerizing. In the distance, a mournful howl floated to her on the wind. The sound tugged at her heart—made loneliness bubble up inside her.

She hadn't seen Rick in two days, but he'd crept into her thoughts often. Mostly during the darkest hours of night. The time when she felt lost. Cut off from the world. The time when she longed for companionship, for the feel of strong arms wrapped around her—the touch of flesh against flesh, and the sound of another heart pounding in unison with her own.

Her attraction to the man was purely physical. At least she had believed so in the beginning. But in the past two days, the attraction had transformed itself into something else. Something beyond her comprehension. When she thought of him, desire, the hot pulsating kind, rose up inside her.

He came to her in dreams, his eyes aglow with passion. She tossed and turned in her sleeping bag, only to wake clutching air and moaning his name. In those moments of midnight madness, Stephanie fought the urge to go to him. She wanted to creep into the night, into his house, and into his bed.

A twig snapped and she glanced toward the sound, hoping that thinking of the man had conjured him before her. But it wasn't Rick who stood staring at her from the bushes, the dying embers of the campfire casting his face in an eerie glow. It was the woman she'd seen in town.

"You must kill him," she croaked. "Take his life to save your own."

Stephanie jumped up, more frightened by the woman's instructions than by her hideous appearance. "What do you want?" she whispered. "Who are you?"

"A seer," she answered, moving from the bushes. "A saver of souls. You are in danger. I see what you cannot see. What he cannot hide behind a handsome face." The hag pointed at her again. "You must send him to hell where he belongs!"

The woman was obviously crazy, and she had the kind of face that nightmares were made of. Stephanie wouldn't hang around to find out if the woman was dangerous. She took off into the woods.

"Do not run to him! He is not what you think he is! Come back and listen to me!" the woman shouted after her, but Stephanie wasn't about to take instructions from a crazy person.

She raced into the night, running faster than she'd

ever been able to run, her heart pounding in her chest. She leaped over fallen logs, ducked beneath low branches, and ran smack into a tree. Or she thought it was a tree until a pair of arms closed around her. A scream rose in her throat.

"Stephanie? What are you doing?"

Her scream turned into a relieved sob. "Rick. I was frightened. That old woman, she came to my campsite."

"The one from town?"

She nodded, pressing closer to him. The steady beat of his heart beneath her ear comforted her, and the solid strength of his arms made her feel safe.

"What did she want?" Rick asked.

Shivering from the aftereffects of her scare, she answered, "I'm not sure. She didn't make any sense. She said I have to kill someone to save myself. She said she could see beneath his face or something. It was horrible."

His arms tightened around her. His heartbeat increased a measure. "Whom did she say you have to kill? Whose face can she see beneath?"

"I don't know," she answered, a little of her fear subsiding now that Rick held her. "And I didn't stick around to find out."

The tenseness she felt in him faded. He sighed. "She probably is crazy. Probably harmless, too. Maybe she just wanted something to eat."

"She could have just asked. She didn't have to scare me half to death."

His hand moved up and down her back. "I'll see if she's still there. Go to the cabin and wait."

"Don't leave me." She didn't want to be left alone, and she didn't want to worry about him while he was gone. "Let's wait awhile. I'm sure she'll move on or raid my food supply."

"I don't mind," he assured her.

"I do," she responded.

They stood, arms wrapped around one another in the night. Stephanie glanced up at him. His face was close; his lips within touching distance were he to bend a little and she to rise up to meet him. Suddenly, she became very aware of his body, the way they fit against one another perfectly.

The sensible thing to do would be to break away from him, return to his cabin, and make silly small talk while they waited. She didn't feel like talking. The nights she'd spent dreaming of him, longing for his touch, caught up with her.

"We should go inside. You're trembling."

It wasn't the cold that made her tremble, but a fight with her own morality. She wasn't the type who believed in casual sex with a stranger. In fact, she didn't believe in having sex for the sole purpose of pleasure. Emotions should be involved—respect, mutual caring, most importantly, love.

She didn't know Rick well enough to feel any of those things for him, but she felt desire. This man, this stranger, had awakened her on a level beyond normal consciousness. He had slipped into the darkest recesses of her mind. A place where there was no right or wrong, but only need—a burning hunger that must be fed.

Maintaining reason was like clutching air. She had no control over her limbs, felt as if an invisible force propelled her mouth toward his. His lips felt warm, firm . . . and unresponsive. She pulled back to look at him.

"You don't know me," he said, his voice low and husky.

"I know I want you," she countered, surprising herself.

He glanced away as if he couldn't stand to look at her. "You're not making this any easier."

"No. I'm not," she agreed, then turned his face toward hers and kissed him again. With a groan of defeat, he surrendered. He claimed her lips without a hint of gentleness. Rather than being frightened by the intensity of his ardor, she reveled in the taste, smell, and feel of him. Her fingers clutched his thick hair.

His hands slid down her back, pulled her hips up firmly against him. Her breath caught in her throat at the solid proof of his desire for her, but again, she felt no fear of him, or shame over her own behavior, only a desperate need to feed the hunger he stirred within.

When he pulled away again, she moaned in frustration. He took her hand and led her toward the cabin. She went willingly, running to keep up with his long strides. As soon as they were inside, he slammed the door and pinned her against the sturdy wooden frame, his body pressing into hers. He kissed her like a man starved for human contact, making love to her with his mouth, teasing and nipping at her lips, probing inside with his tongue.

She couldn't breathe, felt as if she were on fire, consumed by a passion beyond her control. Her breasts ached with a need to be held, and lower, she throbbed with another need, one stronger than common sense, one that eclipsed the deeply embedded morals she'd once possessed.

Rick led her into the bedroom. A small lamp burned, casting a soft glow over the cozy room. He immediately drew her into his arms, his kisses slower, deeper. His hand strayed to the buttons on her shirt. He unfastened them with maddening slowness, the tips of his fingers brushing sensually against her burning skin.

She moaned when he cupped her breasts, his thumbs dipping inside her bra to tease her nipples. He slid her shirt over her shoulders and unclasped her bra, removing both articles in one sweep.

"You are so beautiful," he whispered, molding her breasts in the palms of his hands. "So perfect."

His husky words and the feel of his fingers stroking her flesh fueled her passion and erased what few inhibitions she had left. Stephanie unbuttoned his shirt. She kissed his throat, then ran her tongue down his smooth chest. She liked the taste of him, the feel and heat of him. That was when a strange realization struck her. She stumbled back.

"What's the matter?"

"Your chest," she whispered.

Rick glanced down. "What about it?"

"T-the cut from the glass," she stammered. "It's gone."

Almost in an unconscious gesture, his hand lifted to his chest. He looked like a child trying to hide a secret. "I'm a fast healer."

Confused, she said, "That cut was fairly deep. It would take at least a couple of weeks to heal."

He took another step toward her. "It obviously wasn't as deep as you thought. Come here."

His command was difficult to ignore. With effort, Stephanie took another step back. Whatever force had driven her moments before weakened. She suddenly felt very much in control of her emotions, and totally embarrassed by her behavior. Cool air clashed with her hot skin. She crossed her arms over her bare breasts.

"There should be a nasty scratch there, even if the cut wasn't as deep as it looked," she insisted.

Rick ran a hand through his hair, bent, and scooped up her discarded clothing. "Would it make you feel better if I put one there?"

She wondered if he meant to hand her the clothes, or keep her from getting back into them. "We shouldn't have started this."

He lifted a brow. "You're the one who started it. Now you want to end it because I'm not mortally wounded?"

Reaching for her shirt, she answered, "I want to end it because it isn't right."

The lack of a cut on Rick's chest unnerved her. It was creepy. No normal person could heal that quickly. Her own behavior totally confused her. It was as if she'd become an animal. Rick stared at the hand she held extended toward him. For a moment, she thought he might not comply with her wishes. He sighed and handed her the clothing. Stephanie turned her back and quickly slipped into the shirt, wadding the undergarment into a ball before stuffing it in her pocket. She felt that she owed him some type of explanation.

"I'm not normally like this," she said.

His hands settled upon her shoulders. "You mean you don't normally work a man into a frenzied pitch and then leave him in agony?"

The warmth of his hands soaked through her shirt. She almost relented. So what if he should have a nasty gash in his chest and he didn't? So what if she hardly knew him? They both wanted the same thing. Men and women of her generation had sex together all the time without any emotional commitments. But Stephanie wasn't that type of person. She never had been. Not until tonight.

"I'm not acting like myself."

He turned her around. She expected his expression to be angry, but instead, he looked concerned. "What do you mean, you're not acting like yourself?"

She had trouble looking at him. "The old woman frightened me . . . and then I don't know what happened. I'm not into casual sex."

He smiled slightly. "I didn't plan on being casual about it."

Her resistance wavered. "Normally, I would never . . . I mean, we don't know each other that well. I really have no idea what got into me."

"You said you wanted me," he reminded.

"I wanted . . . something," she agreed. "But I'm not certain what exactly."

"Did you feel driven to mate with me?"

Her gaze shot up. His question made what she'd felt sound animalistic, dirty. "I'm leaving, and I think it would be best if we just stayed away from one another."

His hands tightened on her shoulders. "Why did you feel driven? Physical attraction alone? Because I'm strong? Because deep down, you feel I can provide for you?"

Stephanie struggled, pulling away from him. His suggestions sickened her. She had no dark motives for desiring him.

Humiliated, she shoved past him and left the bedroom. She only made it to the door before she remembered that her campsite didn't seem like the safest place to be tonight. Neither was his cabin.

"I'll go with you," he said. "Unless you trust me enough to stay the night."

She wasn't certain she could trust him, and wasn't at all sure she could trust herself.

"I'm not letting some crazy old woman scare me away from my campsite. Besides, for all I know, she's stolen my camera equipment and everything else. I need to check on things."

When he joined her, he'd buttoned his shirt back up. "Then let's go."

She worried her bottom lip with her teeth. "Shouldn't we take something for protection? Maybe a gun?"

"I don't need a weapon." His voice held a chill. "If she's still there, I can handle her."

Glancing down, she noticed the unconscious flexing of his large hands. He could snap the old woman in two if he wanted, she imagined. The thought did not comfort her, nor did the walk to her site help relax her. She felt like a tease. What had possessed her to act so out of character?

Lust. The word wasn't a soft one. That was what she had felt for him. Lust was what she had responded to, that and his touch, his kisses—her own loneliness. She wondered if she would have responded to any other man the way she had to Rick, but she didn't think so. There was something about him she had trouble resisting. Something she sensed beneath his skin. She waited while he searched the area and checked inside her tent.

"No sign of her."

She breathed a sigh of relief. "Does it look as if anything's been stolen?"

He shook his head. "Nothing seems out of place."

The news bothered her more than if the old woman had stolen her blind. Then there would at least be a logical explanation for the woman's appearance, and for her frightening behavior.

"Nothing makes sense tonight," she said quietly. "Thank you for walking me back."

"Are you sure you want to stay out here alone?"

Of course she didn't want to be alone. Tempting visions of Rick sharing a sleeping bag with her made her profess bravery she didn't feel at the moment.

"I'll be fine," she assured him. "I plan to drag my sleeping bag in the Jeep and lock all the doors."

His gaze met hers, and for an instant, she thought his eyes glowed again. A trick of the moon. "If you need me, you know where to find me."

That was the problem. Rick Donavon was a little too convenient. "I won't need you," she said, vowing to make good her claim. "Good night."

He didn't respond, but turned and walked away. The moment he disappeared, loss and loneliness welcomed Stephanie home. She could have been in his arms, in his bed, but she'd chosen to be rational. The absence of a cut on his chest still bothered her. Maybe the cut wasn't as deep as it had looked. Maybe he was just one of those people who healed quickly. What other explanation could there be?

She couldn't think of a single one. And suddenly, she had trouble coming up with a single reason why she should have left. Morals? Fear? What were those compared to the thrill of his kisses, the sensuous trail of fingers across flesh? She shook her head, worried she'd developed the morals of a cat in heat. Her morals were important, had always been, and she needed to get a grip.

Stephanie wouldn't throw herself at him again. Next time, she might get exactly what she asked for. She shivered, a result of worry that the old woman might come back, she told herself. But deep down, she knew that her response had been anticipation. Excitement to see him again.

Chapter Seven

For three days Stephanie followed the wolf pack. She tried to put Rick out of her mind and concentrate on her research. It worked sometimes, but mostly during the daylight hours. The old woman had not returned. She'd gotten many good shots of the pack members, and had come to identify certain animals. One individual was missing—the huge black wolf she'd saved the night she'd arrived. The same one she later suspected had crept into her tent to stare at her.

His loss saddened her. He'd obviously died of his wounds, or had fallen victim to another menace. She'd noticed there seemed to be a shortage of females hunting, which probably meant Rick was right, and a few were in dens tending pups.

Being able to film the pups would help her cause considerably. All baby animals were cute and people softened toward them. If she could keep up with the pack, she might be able to discover their dens. Rick's warning to avoid the dens resurfaced in her mind. Not only his warning, but the man himself. The sensuous feel of his hands gliding over her body, the huskiness of his voice, the way he kissed a woman completely, nothing held back.

A fly buzzed around her face and she shooed it away, along with her thoughts. She felt hot and sweaty after a morning trying to keep up with the pack. She'd taken to bathing in the stream next to her site in the early morning hours. The water was usually freezing. What she wouldn't give for a nice hot shower. She knew where she could get a shower.

Stephanie mentally cursed her inability to put Rick out of her head and lifted her camera. She took several still shots of the wolves in the distance. They were on the move, so she perched a video camera on her shoulder and followed. The camera around her neck and the one on her shoulder weren't heavy. Not unless a person had been lugging them around for three days.

She'd already traveled a good distance from her campsite, but she continued to follow the wolves until she came upon a scene that made her draw up short. In the valley below, a large herd of sheep grazed. Sheep being stalked by wolves.

In all fairness to the farmers, she knew she had to film the scene. She lifted the video camera to her eye. Keeping the pack in focus proved difficult. The wolves moved in, the sheep scattered, and the task became more taxing.

A loud snap, then a yelp of pain echoed off the mountains. Stephanie swung her camera toward the sound. A wolf was caught in a steel trap and struggled to get out. The rest of the pack lost interest in the chase and crept to where the wolf fought to free itself. They sniffed the steel, circled the trapped animal as if confused as to what they should do.

Stephanie knew what to do. She placed her cameras on the ground and ran from the scene. The trail was rocky and she slipped several times, got up and continued on. She ran until she felt sweat soaking her shirt. By the time she reached her destination, she was totally out of breath.

She stopped, her gaze darting around the area. The door to an outbuilding stood open. She heard banging noises. Racing to the shed, she glanced inside. The shed housed an old truck. The hood was up; the lower half of a man's body stuck out from beneath.

"Rick," she panted.

He jerked, hit his head on the hood and swore. With a scowl, he turned to her. His gaze flitted over her for a moment before he moved toward her.

"What's wrong?"

"A wolf," she huffed. "The farmers are setting traps."

Rick swore again. "Where?"

"I'll show you," she managed.

She still couldn't catch a normal breath, but she set out again. Not long into the race, her legs felt like rubber. Rick pulled ahead of her. He seemed to know where he was going, so she lagged back, trying to pace herself. She stumbled again, her legs folding beneath her. With a jar, she landed on the ground. She sat for a moment, took deep breaths, and struggled up.

When she came over the rise where her cameras lay in a heap, she spotted Rick nearly upon the scene below. He slowed before reaching the trapped animal. The other wolves still circled the wounded pack member nervously. Her heart started to pound wildly in her chest. He'd walked into a dangerous situation. She wondered what the wolves would do when they noticed a man approaching.

Stephanie didn't have the dart gun with her. No weapon of any kind. She searched the ground, found a thick stick, and picked it up. Luckily, the uninjured wolves melted away as Rick neared the trapped animal. Stephanie assumed he'd proceed with caution. He didn't. He marched right up to the wolf and bent, grasping the trap. She wanted to scream at him to stay back. The animal would surely attack him!

Without thought of her own safety, she hurried down the hill, the stick still clutched tightly in her hand. She was terrified for Rick and lifted the stick, ready to defend him if the need arose, and she felt certain it would.

"It's all right," she heard him say to the wolf. "I'll have you out of there in a minute."

"Rick?" she whispered.

He glanced over his shoulder, noticed the stick and said, "Put that down and help me spring this trap."

The stick fell from her hand. "Are you crazy?"

"It'll take both of us to pry it open."

"But—"

"Hurry, Stephanie," he called. "She's suffering."

She stumbled forward. The wolf stared curiously at her, but the animal didn't bare its fangs or seem aggressive. Cautiously, Stephanie bent, her gaze locked with the wolf's golden stare.

"Take hold of that end and pry the teeth open while I pull on this end," Rick instructed. "Watch your hands. We only have to get it part way open so she can get her foot free."

Never breaking eye contact with the wolf, Stephanie

did as he instructed. The trap was sturdy steel. She pulled with all her strength. Rick's muscles bulged beneath the sleeves of his light work shirt. Sweat beaded his forehead. Together, they opened the trap enough for the wolf to free itself. The trap snapped back a second later. The animal tried to limp away.

"No, you don't." Rick rose and snatched the animal up in his arms. "Not until I look at that foot."

He walked away, carrying the wolf. Stephanie supposed her mouth dropped open. The man was crazy. She'd been foolish enough to mess with an injured wolf, but at least she'd planned on tranquilizing the animal first. Dazed, she stumbled after Rick. The animal snuggled its head on his shoulder. Stephanie had never seen anything like this—a wild wolf allowing itself to be carried by a man without being drugged or muzzled? It seemed unreal, and so did the quick journey back to Rick's cabin.

He didn't enter the cabin, but moved toward another shed around the back. "Get the door, please," he said.

Stephanie stepped in front of him and opened the door.

"And the light. It's there next to the door."

She switched on the light. Bright fluorescent light lit up the room. The place looked sterile. Shelves along the walls were lined with medicines, syringes, and bandages. Rick laid the wolf on a stainless steel table.

"You want to play assistant?"

"D-don't you think you should sedate her?" Stephanie stammered.

"You obviously didn't notice her milk supply," he answered. "She has pups and needs to get back to them."

Stephanie hadn't noticed. "Why isn't she fighting you, or trying to bite you?"

He slid his hand down the female's back, stroking her fur gently. "She knows me. She trusts me."

"What is it with you and these animals?" she asked. "I've never seen wild wolves interact with a human the way they do with you."

"I fed them most of last winter," he admitted. "It was a hard one, and I knew the game in the area weren't surviving some of the bigger storms. There was a shortage of food supply for the wolves. Then and now."

Walking to the other side of the table, Stephanie allowed plenty of distance between her and the injured wolf. "You *do* care about them."

He glanced up, the light blue of his eyes a startling contrast to his dark lashes and brows. "Of course I do. It gets lonely out here. They're like my family. They accept me for what . . . who I am."

"Yet you allow the farmers to hunt them," she reminded.

Rick ran his hand over the wolf's muzzle. He smiled. "I'll tell you a secret. These wolves are a lot smarter than those farmers."

She smiled in return, then sobered, looking at the proof that such wasn't always the case. "What are we going to do about this?"

"Clean the wound, stitch her up, and send her on her way."

"You know that's not what I meant. What are we going to do about the traps?"

Instead of answering, he nodded toward the shelves. "Grab that disinfectant in the green bottle and some cotton balls for me. I'm afraid she'll try to jump off the table if I walk away."

Fully intending to bring up the matter again, Stephanie left to retrieve the requested items. She watched him clean the wound, soothing the animal with the soft tone of his voice. The animal even bent its head and licked his hand once. She couldn't believe what she was seeing.

"My cameras," she groaned. "I left them behind."

"I'll get them for you. I'm going back to snap all the traps I find after I've finished here."

"I'll go with you," Stephanie decided.

He glanced up again, his gaze roaming her in a way that made her cheeks burn. "I thought you might prefer to stay here and have a nice long shower while I'm gone."

She'd been longing for a hot shower earlier, and wondered if Rick read minds as a sideline. Glancing down at her dirty clothes, Stephanie realized it wouldn't take a rocket scientist to figure out she needed a shower. "You've found another of my weaknesses. Hot showers and hot coffee."

Rick pulled open a drawer beneath the table and removed some instruments. He didn't glance up when he said, "I plan to find all of them."

"What?" she asked breathlessly.

"The traps," he answered, but that almost smile of his hovered over his mouth.

"Oh," she said. "Do you want me to do anything else for you?"

He paused long enough to make her think he was considering his options. "No," he finally answered. "I'll be done here in a minute. Go on in and have your shower. None of my jeans will fit you, but feel free to borrow a shirt if you'd like."

"Thanks." She hurried out, needing a cold shower

instead of a hot one. His gentleness with the wolf, and his admission of loneliness reached her on a level beyond the physical. But there was something very strange about him. She still became upset when she remembered his smooth bare chest, not a hint of a cut or a scratch on him.

The lighting hadn't been good, she reasoned. The scratch was probably there, she just hadn't noticed. She supposed she could rip his shirt open when he came in and have a nice long look. Now, there was an appealing idea. A better one occurred to her a while later when she stepped beneath the soothing hot spray of Rick's shower. If he joined her, she could hunt for all types of imperfections on his tall, muscled body. Stephanie sighed and adjusted the faucet to cold.

Rick finished attending to the wolf. He'd stitched her up and now took her outside. She rewarded him with a wet lick on his face. "You're welcome," he said softly. "Now go home. Your pups will be wanting supper."

The female trotted off into the woods, favoring the injured leg, but he'd given her a good dose of antibiotics and he felt certain she'd heal without incident. His gaze swung toward the cabin. He imagined Stephanie would be in the shower by now. Naked.

What would she do if he stripped down and joined her? The desire to find out was almost more than he could resist. But he needed to resist. If he had any conscience left, he wouldn't encourage further intimacy between them. He'd already made that mistake once. And Stephanie Shane wasn't the type of woman a man used for sex, then walked away from.

She expected more, and she deserved more. The appearance of the old woman at her campsite still bothered him. Rick's immediate instinct had been to hunt the old woman down, to make sure she never told anyone else what she suspected about him. He'd fought those dark urges. They were part of the wolf, not of the man. Since he'd been standing guard at night over Stephanie's campsite, unbeknownst to her, he hadn't felt compelled to act concerning the woman. He hoped she'd disappeared, gone back to wherever she came from, and had the sense to know he wasn't anyone she should threaten.

Stephanie's behavior the other night also worried him. He hoped it had just been an instance where loneliness had overcome good judgment. He hoped so, because he didn't like the implications of her responding to nothing more than the call of the wild. Animalistic need.

If she wanted him for no other reason than the fact she was a female and he was a male, he'd have to worry about her. So far, he hadn't noticed anything different about her. Only time would tell. And the days between the full moon cycles, he knew from experience, were all too short.

Casting a longing glance toward the cabin, he set off toward Larry Anderson's place. His was the property where the wolf had been trapped. He imagined if Larry had set traps, so had some of the others. Rick planned another visit to Hugh. The farmers might have the right to set traps on their own property, but if Stephanie continued to follow the wolves and film them, she could get hurt.

The trek didn't take him long. He was in good shape. Rick retrieved Stephanie's cameras and moved down the hill where they'd discovered the first trap. He found a long stick and used it to snap any traps he came across. Several more were located around the area. He took his time, hoping Stephanie might be gone when he returned.

Of course, he had her cameras, so the possibility seemed slim. The sun was sinking. It would soon be dark. He had enough trouble battling his attraction to her when he wasn't under the night's influence. Darkness made him more vulnerable to his baser needs. Stephanie was definitely a baser need.

The cabin was dark as he approached. Surely if she'd stayed, lights would be burning inside. He breathed a small sigh of relief. She did have some common sense where he was concerned. Rick trudged up the steps of the porch and went inside. He had great night vision and felt no need to switch on a light. After setting Stephanie's cameras on the kitchen bar, he moved toward his favorite chair. He plopped down. A scream had him jumping back up.

"Stephanie?"

"Rick," she breathed. "You scared me to death."

"I didn't know you were there." He walked over and switched on a lamp.

"I must have dozed off."

He turned in time to see her stretch. She wore one of his shirts, which swallowed her, but her legs were bare. And they were incredibly long.

"I hope you don't mind, but I used your washer and dryer. I can't stand to put on dirty clothes after I've had a shower."

Did that mean she had nothing on beneath his shirt? The mere thought was enough to make him hard. Rick tugged his shirttail from his jeans to cover the problem.

"I could use a shower, too." He nodded toward the kitchen bar. "I brought your cameras back."

"Thank goodness." She rose and walked to the counter. His shirt hit her at the knees, and by the slight bouncing motion of her breasts as she moved, he thought it safe to assume she'd washed all of her clothing, underwear included. His problem worsened.

"Did you find more traps?"

"Yeah," he answered, thinking she had a trap he wouldn't mind getting snared in.

"Should we talk to the sheriff again?"

She leaned over the bar, studying her camera, probably checking to see how many pictures she had left. The position made the shirt hike up in the back, teasing him with possibilities. It would be simple for him to walk over, yank that shirt up all the way, bend her over the bar, and do what he'd been foaming at the mouth to do since the first time he saw her. He took a step toward her. She straightened and turned around.

"Did you hear me?"

He glanced up. "What?"

"The sheriff. We should tell him about the traps."

Rick nodded. "I'll talk to him tomorrow. That is, if I can get a ride into town."

She frowned. "Why don't you have a phone?"

"Too far from town. They haven't run the lines out this far yet."

Stephanie replaced her camera and moved toward the couch. She sat and drew her legs up beneath her. "I'd think that wouldn't be too good for your business."

The woman was killing him. If she moved a fraction, he might catch a glimpse of something he didn't need to see at the moment. "Most everyone just brings an animal in if it's sick and leaves it in the pens, or they come get me. It really hasn't been a problem, since everyone else out this far doesn't have a phone, either."

"How about a cell phone?" she suggested. "In fact, you can use mine if you'd rather call the sheriff."

Rick shook his head. "Poor reception out here because of the mountains. If you'd tried to make a call since you arrived, you would have already realized that."

"Oh. I haven't tried to contact anyone."

She shifted. He groaned.

"I'm going to take a shower." Rick marched toward the bathroom.

"My clothes are probably dry. I'll get dressed."

"Good idea," he muttered.

"Ah, I used your razor, too," she called. "I don't know how I got so hairy so fast, but my legs looked like Christmas trees."

He paused. Since he didn't shave his legs, he didn't know if unusual hair growth was anything that should concern him. He'd always had a heavy beard, so he'd never paid much attention. "That's fine," he said, forcing himself to move on. He walked into the bathroom and unbuttoned his shirt. A timid knock sounded a second later.

"Can I grab my shoes before you get undressed?"

Rick opened the door. She scooted inside, brushing up against him. Contact with her was like having volts of electricity pumped into his body. Her gaze lifted, and he knew she felt it, too, the undeniable attraction that stood between them.

"Thanks for your help today," she said, her gaze still glued to his mouth. "You're very good with the wolves. You just marched right up to the female without the least bit of concern for your own safety. I think you might be the bravest person I've ever met."

The compliment pleased him, and sickened him. "Maybe just the stupidest." Rick glanced around and spotted her small hiking boots. He bent and swept them up, handing them to her. "You should get dressed."

She took the boots. "Yes, and I should be returning to my campsite. It's already dark outside."

"Wait for me and I'll walk you back," he said, although it would be better if she were gone when he finished his shower. The temptation to seduce her became stronger with every second that passed. Still, he wasn't comfortable about her roaming in the night with a crazy woman on the loose. A crazy woman who wasn't so crazy.

"That won't be necessary. I feel confident that I won't be bothered by that woman again, and besides, I'm starving. I need to get back and scrounge up something to eat."

"I would offer to fix you dinner, but I don't imagine I have anything you'd want."

Her gaze drifted over him. Although Rick hadn't been intimate with a woman in three years, he knew when he was being assessed. She continued to study him, moistening her tempting lips with the tip of her tongue. He clenched his hands at his sides, battling the urge to pull her into his arms.

"That's all right," she finally said. She seemed to mentally shake herself. "I really do need to be going. Thank you for your help today." Turning toward the door, she added, "I'll pick you up around noon tomorrow. We can have lunch at the café again and talk to the sheriff afterward."

"That will be fine," he said curtly.

"Good night then."

If she didn't get the hell away from him, he would lose what little control he maintained. "Good night."

He thought she might say something else, but he nudged her from the bathroom. His hand shook on the knob, and he quickly locked the door. Not locking her out, but locking himself in. Of course, the problem with that was that the lock should be on the other side. Rick hurried to the shower and turned on the water. He stripped down and climbed beneath the chilly spray.

Chapter Eight

Stephanie hurried through the woods. Her behavior with Rick embarrassed her. That feeling had come over her again. An irresistible urge to make love with him. He must have sensed her desire, because he'd hurried her out of the bathroom and locked the door. He'd rejected her.

He'd shut her out, made it clear he didn't want her. Humiliation had washed over her, and all she could think of was escape. She'd grabbed her clothes from the dryer, hurried into them, and run from the cabin—run from her own shame.

She didn't understand the things she felt for him. Stephanie wasn't completely innocent. She'd had a lover before. A boy she'd known in college. One she'd planned to marry until the accident happened. Afterward, he'd stopped calling, stopped coming to see her because she couldn't leave her father, couldn't even leave the house most of the time.

So much for true love. True love was when one person stood beside another no matter the circumstances. Through sickness and in health, for better or for worse. True love was what her parents had had, what she wanted. Certainly not a wild physical attraction to a man who seemed strange in some way she couldn't put her finger on.

But there were things she liked about Rick besides his face and body. He'd shown tenderness and compassion to the injured wolf that afternoon. She knew he could be gentle, caring, and certainly brave. He could even be funny. So what if he seemed to be a tortured soul at times?

His brother's death had surely affected him as much as the loss of her parents had affected her. He was lonely—he'd admitted that to her today. She was lonely, too. It only made sense they would be drawn to one another. What suddenly didn't make sense was the fact that as Stephanie hurried along in the dark woods, she realized she could see quite well.

She stopped and looked around. The shapes of trees, bushes, and even the rocks strewn along her path were easily distinguishable. Glancing up, she noted that the moon wasn't particularly bright.

"This is odd," she whispered, unsettled by her strange ability. She quickly tried to come up with a logical reason. She'd been camping for some time now; perhaps she had simply become used to the dark.

What other reason would there be for suddenly developing wonderful night vision? Maybe she'd always been able to see this well in the dark, she reasoned. She probably hadn't noticed before because she was usually so wrapped up in her work.

She lifted her face to the wind and caught a scent. One she immediately identified with the old woman. A chill raced up her spine. Somehow she knew the woman wasn't gone. She was somewhere nearby . . . waiting.

The next day, Rick stared at Stephanie across the café table. Although she grew more beautiful to him every day, she had dark circles beneath her eyes and she'd been quiet during the trip to town. She'd ordered a salad with about as much enthusiasm as she would have ordered a plate of worms.

"What's the matter with you?" he finally asked.

She glanced up from fiddling with her car keys. "I didn't say anything was wrong."

"You didn't have to." He studied her face. "Have you been sleeping all right?"

Her lashes drifted downward, merging with the dark circles beneath her eyes. "I can't seem to settle down and get comfortable," she admitted. "And the noise . . ."

"The noise?" he repeated with a laugh. "What noise?"

Running a hand through her long hair, she said, "Owls hooting, branches snapping, leaves rustling. I never realized the great outdoors was so noisy."

"Most people wouldn't notice," he said, then frowned. His own hearing had become sharper after the incident that had forever changed him. It had taken him a while to notice, but he'd lived in the city then.

The sirens blaring on the expressway in the distance had always sounded annoyingly loud when he'd been trying to sleep. But later, they had sounded as if they were right outside the house.

"Maybe you should stay with me," he suggested, thinking he should keep a closer eye on her. She was starting to worry him.

She lifted a brow. "Stay with you?"

"You could have the bedroom, and I'd sleep on the couch," he assured her, but considering what had already gone on between them, he had as much trouble believing that as she probably did.

"I don't think that would be a good idea. You don't have locks on all the doors to keep me out."

Her last comment startled him. Was that what she'd thought? That he'd been locking her out rather than locking himself in? "I was trying to be a gentleman," he said.

"You succeeded." She sighed. "I'm sorry I made that crack about locked doors. I'm tired and I got up on the wrong side of the ground this morning."

"I offered you my bed," he reminded. She looked exhausted and embarrassed. "Feather down mattress, hot showers, coffee in the morning."

"Don't tempt me." She laughed, but her gaze drifted over him in lazy inspection before she seemed to realize her actions. "I'm perfectly fine where I am. I'm not on vacation, I'm on assignment." She glanced around the small café. "I don't see the sheriff here today. I guess we'll have to go to his office once we finish."

Rick nodded, then dug into his meal. He hated cooking for one and, as a result, seldom ate a hot meal. He couldn't tolerate meat if it was cooked too long, either. He liked it almost raw, nice and juicy. The french fries that came with his burger weren't that appealing to him, but he didn't suppose he could order a whole plate of raw hamburger meat.

"Do you think the sheriff can do anything about the sheep farmers setting traps?"

"I doubt if he can legally do much about it, or that he'd want to," he answered. "We'll bring up the matter of your safety, but you were trespassing on private property yesterday, so it won't do much good."

She reached across the table and snatched a fry from his plate. "I have to trespass if they want me to capture footage of the wolves attacking their livestock. I assumed being allowed on their property was part of the deal."

"That's the argument we'll present." Rick grabbed for napkins from the container, found it empty, and glanced around. "I'll be right back."

The container at the next booth was also empty. He looked for Betty but didn't see her anywhere. Spotting a full container on another nearby table, he bent and tried to wrest a handful of napkins from the overstuffed receptacle. He felt a little embarrassed that he couldn't get the wadded napkins out and glanced over his shoulder at Stephanie.

She didn't look amused by his struggle, but was staring thoughtfully at what could only be his ass, given her eye level. The hair on the back on his neck prickled. He wasn't offended, by any means. If she'd been bent over in front of him, he'd be assessing her, too. What caused his reaction was the fact that while she stared, she greedily munched away on his hamburger.

He turned toward her. "Stephanie?"

Her gaze shot up. "I—I didn't mean to stare—"

"I thought you were a vegetarian," he interrupted.

She blinked up at him. "I am," she responded, her mouth full.

"Then why are you eating my burger?"

Stephanie's gaze lowered. A piece of red meat stared back at her from a sesame seed bun. Unconcerned with manners, she spit the contents in her mouth out onto her salad plate. The taste of blood lingered on her tongue. Sweet, delicious. The thought sickened her.

She clamped a hand over her mouth and jumped up from the table. The restroom might be occupied. She couldn't take that chance. Racing outside, she stumbled into the alley and lost the contents of her stomach. A pair of strong hands settled upon her shoulders.

"Stephanie?" Rick asked. "Are you all right?"

No, she was not all right. Something was terribly wrong with her. Wiping the sleeve of her shirt across her mouth, her eyes filled with tears. She glanced up at him.

"What's happening to me? Last night I could see in the dark. I ate your hamburger . . . and I liked it. The blood tasted sweet to me. I—"

"I think I'd better get you to my place," he interrupted. Rick helped her up and shoved a wad of napkins into her hand. "I left some money on the table for the bill and grabbed your keys. I'll drive."

Although she seldom let anyone drive her vehicle, she nodded, allowing him to help her to the Jeep. She climbed into the passenger side and rested her head against the back of the seat. Rick jumped in and started the engine.

"What about talking to the sheriff?" she asked weakly.

"That will have to wait. I'm taking you to bed."

Her pulse leaped. Even though she felt ill, she smiled, recalling that she'd said the same thing to him the morning they met. The same morning she'd tracked a wolf into his cabin and caught him climbing from the shower. A vision of him, muscled body slick and shiny, dark hair dripping wet, blue eyes bright with fever, floated through her mind.

"What?"

She glanced at him. "I didn't say anything."

A moment later, she realized she *had* responded. The noise she'd made sounded suspiciously like a growl.

Chapter Nine

Once at the cabin, Rick handed Stephanie a flannel shirt. "Change into this and climb into bed. Can I get you anything?"

She placed her hands on her hips. "This is silly. I told you, I feel better now. This isn't necessary."

He wouldn't take any arguments from her. "Would you like me to help you undress?"

A thoughtful pause followed. She sighed and snatched the shirt from him. "I should go back to my campsite and take a nap. I'm tired, that's all. That's why I became emotional earlier."

"You can nap here," he insisted. "In a real bed."

They had a stare-down. Rick wasn't giving in. Her recent behavior had upset him, but he didn't want to frighten her when he wasn't certain whether there was any real cause for concern.

"You know I don't like to be bullied," she finally said.

He touched her cheek gently. "I'm not bullying you. I'm concerned. You need rest, and I'm going to make sure you get it."

Her expression softened. "Okay. But only because you're right in this case."

Rick smiled at her. "I'm always right."

She rolled her eyes and turned away from him. "Don't let the door hit you on your way out."

Rick laughed and left the room. As soon as he closed the door, his smile faded. Stephanie was suffering all the symptoms he had suffered before he became a werewolf. Were all the things happening to her simply a coincidence? Could they all have a logical explanation? He didn't think so.

There weren't many explanations for people suddenly developing keen night vision. For a vegetarian to suddenly develop a taste for raw meat. Or for a woman who might not normally give him the time of day to fight primitive instincts to mate with him whenever she got within sniffing distance.

If he was responsible for changing Stephanie, changing her life forever, Rick didn't think he could deal with the guilt. She was a young, vibrant, beautiful woman. He couldn't stand to think of her as a monster. An animal like himself. A virtual recluse who had shut himself off from those he loved most. A man denied normal life in both worlds that claimed him.

Rick ran a hand through his hair, angry with her for intruding upon his territory, angry with himself for allowing even minimum contact with humans. Because of his own selfishness, he had not ruled out the possibility that he might bite someone.

"Rick?"

Stephanie's voice floated to him from behind the closed door. He walked over and eased it open. She'd slipped beneath the covers. The sight of her in his bed had the animal in him creeping to the surface. He fought it back and moved into the room.

"Do you need anything? A glass of water or—"

"No, I'm fine. I may borrow your shower again after I've rested, if that's all right."

He nodded, trying to ignore the steamy image of her naked and soapy. "Would you like me to wash your . . . clothes?"

She smiled. "Somehow, I never would have pictured you offering maid service. No." She glanced toward her clothing draped over the old rocker. "They were clean this morning."

"Fine." He needed to get away from her. That scent, the one that hovered just below the surface of her sweet natural fragrance, was about to drive him crazy. "I'll let you get some sleep then."

"Rick?" She stopped him, patting a place on the bed next to her. "Can we talk for a minute?"

He bit back a groan and walked to the bed. With more than a little trepidation, he sat beside her. "What's on your mind?"

She glanced up into his eyes. "I know you're not a medical doctor, but what do you think could be wrong with me? Fatigue might be responsible for my not noticing that I was eating your meal earlier, but what about last night? My vision has always been good, but I could see in the dark. I mean really see. And there was something else."

Rick started to feel sick to his stomach. "Something else?"

Despite her earlier claim of feeling better, tears filled her eyes. "I—I know this is going to sound crazy, but I thought I smelled that old woman. I had a sense that she was still close by, waiting for something to happen."

He squeezed his eyes closed for a moment, then opened them again, hoping she didn't see the panic rising inside him. "You're just tired. You need rest. We'll talk more about it later, all right?" He eased her down on the bed. She didn't argue.

"All right. I am tired," she mumbled, closing her eyes.

He settled the covers around her and stared down at her beautiful face. His excuses for Stephanie's increasingly strange behavior were wearing thin. He didn't want to face facts. He'd obviously bitten her the night she saved his life. His curse had now become her own. He had to save her. Do something—find a way to spare her from the same hell his own life had become. He thought he knew how, but he wanted to be certain.

He also thought he knew who could tell him the answer. After assuring himself that Stephanie slept soundly, he grabbed a jacket and left the cabin. He didn't get far before the wolves joined him. They moved in single file, as if on a hunt. He had a keen sense of smell, just as Stephanie had developed. He followed the old woman's trail easily. It led him to the abandoned shack on the road where he'd first spotted the old woman. He was surprised to see her sitting in front of the shack, as if she were waiting for him.

"Have you come to kill me?" she asked calmly.

A stab of guilt cut through him. Not long ago, his answer might have been different. "No. I've come to ask how to save her."

Her glassy eyes widened. She rose and walked toward him. "Today, I see more man than wolf in you.

You have met a woman who has made you see the light. Understand that with love comes sacrifice."

"What do I have to do?" he demanded.

She eyed him sadly. "You already know the answer."

He glanced away from her. "I thought so. I wanted to make certain."

"Are you afraid?"

Oddly enough, he wasn't. "Only for her."

The touch of her leathery hand against his face startled him. "When I first saw you, I saw only the wolf hiding beneath your face. Now I look into your heart, into your soul, and I see they are both good."

Another fear plagued him. "Is there hope for my soul?"

"If you do what must be done, you can save your soul. For your sacrifice, you can be reborn."

"What does that mean?" he asked, confused.

She turned away from him. "Go home, wolf. Do what you must; then you will see."

"Who are you?"

The old woman paused, glancing over one humped shoulder. "No one of importance. An old gypsy who makes my living telling fortunes at county fairs. A wanderer who, at times, runs across an unnatural such as yourself."

"Then you've seen others like me?"

With a heavy sigh, she answered, "Yes. And some even more unnatural than you. I do what I can, and sometimes what I must to ease their suffering. But now I trust in you to see to your own fate, and to that of the woman you love. She has been your destiny from the beginning, and you hers."

Rick didn't know if he believed in destiny, but then there was little he couldn't believe in since he'd become a monster. He'd come to get verification of what he'd known he must do all along. He turned and walked away, feeling remarkably calm, almost at peace with himself. The answer was simple. All he had to do to save Stephanie was kill himself.

Darkness fell. Stephanie paced the small cabin. Where was Rick? She'd begun to worry about him—worry over the strange feelings the darkness brought with it of late. She felt restless, not quite herself beneath the skin. The walls were closing in on her. She needed to go out.

Wearing only Rick's oversized shirt, she walked outside. Stephanie drew in deep breaths of fresh air. She glanced up at the moon, surrounded by twinkling stars so close it seemed as if she might reach up and touch them. The moon wasn't full, but it was bright, and again she marveled at how well she saw the surrounding area.

Close by, a wolf howled. Did he call to a mate? She felt tempted to throw back her head and answer him. Instead, she rubbed her arms, the chill penetrating her body as well as her heart. There was nothing worse than being alone. Feeling empty inside because she had no family. No mate. No children. No one to turn to in times of sorrow, or in times of joy. She'd thought her heart couldn't withstand the pain of loving again. The truth she'd come to realize was that her heart needed to love again in order to heal.

Lifting her face to the wind, she caught Rick's scent. A moment later, she heard sounds of his approach. The slight snap of a stick, the fluttering of a leaf as he passed. Her pulse quickened. Other emotions gripped her. Need, hunger, desire.

Drawn to him, Stephanie walked out into the woods. His soft footsteps halted. He had caught her scent, as well. She sensed these things—also knew he battled his need for her. Would he fight or flee? Retreat or surrender?

She found him in a clearing a few feet away. He stood straight, rigid in the night. The moon bathed him in a soft glow. His hands were balled at his sides, his jaw clenched.

"You don't know what I am."

"I know that I want you," she said, then moved toward him. "That's enough for me. Enough for tonight."

As if her words, the very sight of her, caused him pain, he glanced away. She ached to be held by him, to feel his arms around her. Reaching out, she touched his face, forcing him to look at her.

"Don't you want me? Can't you give me one night?"

The light dancing in his eyes flared. "You deserve more than one night."

"I deserve you," she whispered. "We deserve each other."

Standing on her tiptoes, she pressed her lips against his. He didn't respond for a moment; then it was as if she'd opened the floodgates to his passion. He clutched her shoulders and pulled her close, his mouth moving over hers possessively. His tongue danced with hers, teasing, then delving deep. The chill faded—the night sounds drifted away. All she heard was the sound of their breathing. All she felt was his hands moving over her, down to the bottom of the shirt where he bunched it up around her waist.

She wore her bikini underwear beneath the shirt, but hadn't slipped on her bra. His hands moved higher, cupping her breasts, his thumbs brushing her sensitive nipples.

"I want to see you," he said. "All of you."

He unbuttoned her shirt and slipped it off her shoulders. Stephanie realized she should be freezing, considering the temperature, but she wasn't. She stood before him wearing only the moonlight and her silky panties. He bent, placing soft kisses against her stomach before he eased her panties over her hips, kissing every inch of flesh he exposed.

Her fingernails bit into his shoulders. Despite his skillful attentions, she wanted to see him—touch him the way he touched her. She twisted her fingers in his hair and forced him up, their mouths meeting again while she unbuttoned his shirt. His skin felt smooth and warm beneath her touch. She shoved his shirt along with his jacket off his shoulders, allowing both to fall to the ground.

The sensation of skin against skin sharpened her desire for him. She wanted to feel all of him. Fumbling with his belt, she undid the buckle. His jeans were tighter than usual in the area of the zipper, but she managed to free him. His size impressed her. She wrapped her fingers around his sex. He sucked in his breath sharply, then rid himself of boots, socks, and all clothing that remained. When he stood before her naked, she could only stare, marvel at his perfection.

He was sleek, muscled, tall, and dark. She would have been content to stare at him longer, but he pulled her back into the warmth of his arms. His mouth sought hers, his hands roaming, teasing, pleasing. He found her greatest weaknesses, her most private secrets. His fingers stroked her gently, but her response was not tender. She wanted him to claim her—wanted to claim him in return. With that intention in mind, she wrapped her arms around his neck and pulled him down to the dew-damp ground.

* * *

Rick wanted to love her gently, slowly, completely, but she drove him beyond rational thought. He allowed her to pull him down, then covered her beautiful body with his. Her long legs parted, inviting him inside. He went eagerly, gasping at the tight, hot feel of her as their bodies joined. She gasped, as well, and he realized he might be hurting her.

Man overcame beast, and for her, he gentled the wolf. He eased back, dipped his head to her full breasts, tracing the circles of her nipples with his tongue before taking them in turn inside his mouth. She moaned, her fingers twisting in his hair. He slid his hand between them, stroking her into readiness. Her hips arched and she took him deeper inside her, forcing a moan from his lips.

The sounds of their labored breathing echoed around them, and then the song began. A serenade from the wolves gathered on the distant bluffs. A song of celebration. The song they sang when one mate found another. Louder and louder the cries echoed around them, and harder and harder he strained, pumped, fighting for the control to wait for her. She was heaven, inside and out, perfectly made for him and him alone. Even as he felt the tremors of her approaching climax, saw her eyes glowing up at him, he realized that his surrender had been a mistake. Leaving was much easier when loving wasn't involved. But he did love her, had loved her from the beginning.

Her back arched, she cried out, sucking him down into the deep vortex of his own release. It was heaven, loving her, and it was hell, because he knew he had to let her go. Her arms crept around his neck; her mouth found his and drained the fight from him. As he surrendered to her again, dark whispers floated through his head. The selfish side of him suggested he could keep her. Could make her his and his alone. His mate. His lover. His monster.

Chapter Ten

Stephanie ran her hands over Rick's soap-slick skin. They had spent the night making love. Only once outside; then they'd gathered their clothes and moved their activities inside. Virile was definitely a word she'd use to describe him. The man had a hearty appetite for more than food. He'd put the coffee on while she started her shower; then he'd climbed inside the steamy enclosure with her.

She could get used to this, she admitted, tracing lazy soap designs on his back. He turned and pulled her into his arms, kissing her deeply. Her pulse jumped. She has thought she'd be too sore from a night of vigorous lovemaking to want him again this morning, but she'd awoken feeling wonderful. Finding herself wrapped within the arms of a handsome man hadn't hurt.

The soap slipped from her fingers. She kissed him.

sliding her tongue inside his mouth. He groaned and pulled back.

"You dropped the soap," he said, then smiled wickedly. "I'll get it."

He took his sweet time about retrieving the soap. Stephanie didn't complain. He kissed her knees, the inside of her thighs, and moved higher. She braced her hands on each side of the shower wall to keep her legs from buckling. He was very good with his mouth, with his hands, his whole body, for that matter. She closed her eyes and let sensation take over.

Her body, long starved for affection, responded quickly to his tender explorations. She felt the tightening in her stomach, the gathering ecstasy with each steady stroke of his tongue. When she could stand no more, she urged him up. He lifted her onto his straining sex. She wrapped her arms and legs around him, felt her back pressed against the slick shower wall.

He filled her completely, gave unselfishly, and sent her plummeting over the edge into madness. His own release exploded inside her. She loved the deep animal sound he made when he surrendered to pleasure. The gentle nip of his teeth against her neck. The husky words he whispered in her ear.

In his arms, she felt complete, whole, and happy for the first time in a long while. But happy for how long? She pushed the thought away, not ready to deal with it. She'd bravely told him that one night would be enough for her, which had been easy to believe until morning found them still together. What now? She must have said the words out loud, because he nuzzled her ear and answered, "Coffee and breakfast."

Rick turned out to be an excellent cook as well as an exceptional lover. Stephanie sat at his small kitchen table, attacking the scrambled eggs and toast as if she hadn't eaten for days. He watched her over the rim of his coffee cup, smiling at her enthusiasm.

"I have a surprise for you today," he said.

Since her mouth was stuffed with eggs, she lifted her brows to indicate he should continue.

"You wanted to see a den, remember? I know where one is."

"Are there pups?" she asked despite her full mouth.

"A litter of four about five weeks old."

"Can I film them?"

"I think I can convince the mother to allow you close enough."

Excited, Stephanie jumped up from the table. "I need to go back to my campsite and get my camera equipment." She moved around the table and hugged his neck. "I'll meet you back here in thirty minutes." She left humming a happy tune.

Rick wished he felt as carefree. The night he'd spent with Stephanie had been incredible. And not because it had been so long since he'd made love to a woman. With her, it wasn't just sex, but something deeper. A commitment because his heart had been included in the exchange. He loved her. Maybe he had from the moment he glanced up and saw her green eyes shooting sparks at him because he'd taken advantage of her. He'd taken advantage again last night. Knowing what he must do, he should have walked away from her. But he hadn't . . . couldn't, in fact.

He couldn't be honest with her, either. She wouldn't believe him if he told her the truth. She'd think he should be locked up in a mental hospital. So he'd taken that one night with her. Told himself it was his last chance to give and receive love. His last time to feel human again. But last night had been a mistake, because now that he loved her, he wasn't sure he could let it end with one night.

Rick rose from the table and gathered the dishes. He glanced at the calendar and cringed. Only three days until the full moon. Three more days of loving her; then he must end the nightmare. Why? the dark whispers began again. Why couldn't he continue his life, but with a mate by his side? He'd no longer be alone. He could help Stephanie adjust to her new life.

He shook his head, denying the tempting thoughts. Forcing Stephanie to share his cursed existence would be a selfish act. A cruel one. His plan was to help her finish her research and get her the hell gone. He only had three days. They'd have to hurry. He'd promised to contact the Fish and Wildlife Service himself as soon as she left. She could scurry back and get her project up and running.

Then he'd be called to do what he must. On the first night of the full moon, he'd take his life and save hers. He'd do it before the changes began. He'd have to or she'd suffer. Her scent still hung in the air. Rick closed his eyes and breathed deeply. Visions of tangled limbs and smooth, damp skin filled his head. He could happily spend the rest of his life with her, and he guessed he would.

Trusting or not, the female wolf hadn't been all that compliant about allowing them to stick their heads in her den. Just in case, Rick had brought along a mild sedative. The female had let him give her the drug; then they'd waited until she grew calm. Stephanie had both camera and video recorder. She took several shots of the frisky pups. Now she sat among them, cooing and lifting them, kissing each one on the head.

Despite the dark clouds gathering overhead, Rick smiled at her antics. She glanced up and smiled back at him. His heart warmed at the sight of her, wolf pups climbing all over her lap. She looked so beautiful to him in that instant, so innocent and trusting. She deserved a special man. Deserved a normal home and children of her own. She deserved all he could not give her.

"Come play with us," she urged.

Rick walked over and sat beside her. "That sedative will be wearing off soon," he warned her. He glanced up. "And it looks as if we're in for a storm tonight."

She turned her gaze on him. "I may have to take refuge at your place. I'm scared of storms."

He laughed. "You're not afraid of anything."

"We could pretend I am," she said, smiling seductively. A moment later, she sobered. "I mean, if you want me to stay."

What he wanted was forever, but he'd settle for another night with her. "Or we can pretend that storms frighten me."

It was her turn to laugh. "Okay," she agreed. "I like that better."

Thunder rumbled overhead. The female wolf resting inside the den growled.

"Time to go." Rick rose and offered Stephanie a hand up. "Come on, we'll have to run to make it back before the storm breaks."

After placing the pups inside the den with their mother, Stephanie took his hand. Rick shoved her video camera beneath his shirt and watched as she did likewise with the camera hanging around her neck.

Another loud rumble of thunder had him tugging her away from the den. They scrambled down a bluff and ran full out across the meadow where they had made love the previous evening. Large drops of rain fell from the sky. Stephanie squealed and pulled ahead of him. She ran inside the cabin, leaving the door open.

When he entered, he saw her stomping around and rubbing her arms. "That rain is freezing cold."

"Maybe I can warm you up," he said.

In answer, she quickly removed her camera from her neck, set it on the bar and began stripping. She dropped her wet shirt on the floor on her way to the bedroom. Rick growled low in his throat and followed.

Later, while the rain made drumming noises on the roof, and lightning flashed outside the windows, he held her naked and content in his arms.

"Rick?" she asked. "Do you ever think about leaving this place?"

Of course he'd thought about it. But where could he go except another remote place just like this one? A place where he could run wild during the full moon with those of his kind. "No," he answered.

"Would you consider it?" she asked after a hesitant pause.

"I can't leave, Stephanie," he said point-blank.

"It's not as if your business is thriving. And a good vet along on an expedition is always a plus."

There was nothing he could say to spare her feelings. He'd love to get out of this place, back to civilization, or to follow her around on her expeditions doing whatever he could. Anywhere she was would be fine with him. But that wasn't possible.

"I might consider leaving," he amended his earlier answer. "I'd have to get some things in order first."

"Well, of course," she said. "I didn't mean tomorrow. I meant . . . someday."

He kissed the top of her head, wishing he didn't have to lie to her. There was no future for them. "I'd like for you to meet my parents," he said, then realized he'd expressed the thought out loud.

Stephanie shifted so that she could see him. "I'd love to meet them."

His mother, he felt certain, would be very pleased with Stephanie. She had once complained that the women he dated seemed plastic and shallow. She'd insisted that he meet a sweet down-to-earth girl and get married. He had the perfect woman lying in his arms, and no right to hold on to her. Rather than lie to Stephanie further, he kissed her into silence.

A kiss led to a touch, a touch to another kiss; then nature took its course. He made slow love to her while the storm outside raged. Rick felt grateful for one more night of being human. One more night to love her, hold her, and wish it could last forever. But even lost in the feel and taste of her, he couldn't block out the clock ticking in his head. Time would soon run out for them.

Chapter Eleven

"Leave? What do you mean, leave?" Stephanie asked. She and Rick sat at his kitchen table again, having coffee and toast. She'd spent the previous day getting some great coverage of the wolves. With him by her side, she'd even managed to get coverage of the pack attacking a sheep herd.

She'd tried to hide the strange things happening to her from Rick. There was no way she'd tell him she felt the urge to run wild with the wolves. To take down prey and feast on blood. He'd think she'd gone bonkers. And maybe she had. But his kisses chased away her fears. In his arms, she forgot the weird way she felt at times: her keen night vision, her hunger for raw meat, her desire to howl at the moon.

"I think you should get things started on the other end," he answered. "I told you I'd call the authorities later today. You need to get a rescue started, use your pictures and research to make a case for our wolves."

"But why can't I just wait for the authorities to show up here with you? I could tell them—"

"I'll tell them," he assured her. "Your job is to show them."

He had a point. She needed to get her pictures and material back to the organization as soon as possible. It would take the proper authorities a while to arrive on the scene anyway. The truth was, she didn't want to leave him. She'd felt uneasy all morning, as if something were about to happen. Something bad.

"And you think I should leave right away?" she asked, hoping he'd say he didn't want her to go at all.

"The sooner the better," he answered.

His response hurt her feelings. She tried to hide it by lowering her gaze. "It won't take me long to pack up. I can be gone by this afternoon."

Rick rose from the table. "If I help, you'll be on the road faster."

All right, she wasn't imagining his haste to get rid of her. She shouldn't have expected anything more. All she'd asked for was one night, and she'd received more than that. Still, he didn't have to act so cold about it. He didn't have to shove her out as quickly as possible so he could get on with his life.

She rose. "No need. I'm used to doing for myself. I'll be out of your hair in no time."

Snatching up her cameras, Stephanie headed for the door. As fast as a predator, Rick blocked her exit.

"I—I don't know what to say," he stammered.

She glanced up. "You could say 'don't go.' You could say you'll come with me. You could at least say you'll miss me while I'm gone."

"I will miss you." He placed his hands on her shoulders, and she thought he'd pull her close, but he released her almost as quickly as he'd taken hold of her. "Take care of yourself."

Tears threatened. Stephanie blinked them back. "Of course I will," she said, her words clipped. "Good-bye, Rick."

Before she made a fool of herself, she brushed past him and out the door. She didn't look back, either. Her heart felt as if it were breaking, but she wouldn't give him the satisfaction of knowing how deeply he'd hurt her. How much she had foolishly come to care for him.

Real love took time. Rick had simply been an infatuation. Her hormones had been on the rampage. He'd used her for sex, and she'd allowed him to do so. Had, in fact, encouraged him. And it was great sex, so she shouldn't complain. She'd stopped believing in fairy tales years ago. Men and women seldom lived happily ever after in today's world. She was on her own, had been for the past three years, and probably would be for the rest of her life.

"No problem," she said to bolster her spirits. But it was no good. She did believe in fairy tales. She wanted true love. She wanted a husband and children. She wanted Rick. The tears gathered again, and she allowed them to fill her eyes. Even allowed them to flow down her cheeks. A good cry never hurt anyone.

"I love you, Stephanie."

She stopped and wheeled around. No one stood behind her. Her gaze frantically searched the area, hoping against hope that she hadn't imagined his voice in her head. Hadn't wanted him to love her so much that she'd conjured up his voice in her mind. But he was not there.

He was back at the cabin, had already dismissed her. Not a care in the world. He probably felt relieved that she'd left. Happy that he could continue with his boring little life. Thankful that she hadn't cried or made a scene so he wouldn't have to feel guilty.

"Typical man," she muttered, turning to resume her trek to the campsite. He wanted her gone, fine. She would leave, and she'd concentrate on the task at hand. When she returned to the area with the documentary team, she would not melt on the spot the minute she saw him, or hope like a silly schoolgirl that he'd have a change of heart—rush to her, go down on one knee, and beg her to be his wife. The thought was so pleasing she almost forgot how angry she was with him. But not for long. She was out of here, and Rick Donavon be damned.

"Dammit," Rick swore, fumbling through his closet like a madman. Thanks to an unexpected visit from Hugh Fielding, the hour had grown later than he'd realized. Rick had told him about the traps, and the sheriff had agreed to dissuade the farmers from setting them again.

Hugh had also agreed to contact both the Fish and Wildlife Service and the United States Department of Agriculture concerning the problem. Stephanie, and other wildlife defenders like her, would see that the animals were not destroyed, but relocated to another area where wild game was more abundant, and livestock less likely to be threatened.

He'd taken care of everything he'd wanted to tie up today—making certain that Stephanie left, his concern over the wolves, and the letter to his parents. It was the longest letter he'd ever written, telling them he missed them and would come for a visit soon; then he'd casually mentioned that he planned on doing some hunting in the next few days.

A glance out his bedroom window confirmed that it would soon be dark. His hand closed around what he'd been searching for, his gun-cleaning kit. He wanted his death to look like an accident. He'd retrieved the rifle he purchased before his hunting trip with Jason. His parents would believe the rifle had accidentally discharged while he was cleaning it. No guilt for them. No wondering what they had done wrong or if they could have done something to make him change his mind.

He wanted Stephanie to believe his death had been an accident, as well. His one regret was that he hadn't told her that he loved her. He'd crept into the woods and hidden, making certain she packed up her campsite. Watching her drive away was the hardest thing he'd ever done. But she was safe now, would soon be safe forever. At least from the curse that plagued him.

Rick grabbed his rifle, a box of ammunition, and the gun-cleaning kit and moved into the living area. He glanced at his favorite chair, frowned at the idea of messing up the place, and went outside. He propped the rifle against the cabin, placed the cleaning kit and the ammunition on the steps, then went back inside. There was something he'd forgotten. He walked into the bedroom. With shaking hands, he picked up the rosary resting on his nightstand. He fingered the beads, then closed his eyes and prayed.

He prayed for courage, prayed for his eternal soul, and prayed for those he loved to be watched over and protected. His hand shook harder, and he knew it had nothing to do with fear. The change was coming. It lurked just beneath the surface of his humanity. The beast wanted to be free. Rick replaced the beads and hurried through the cabin.

Once outside, he sat on the steps and fumbled with the box of ammunition. He'd managed to get two shells loaded when he spotted headlights on the road moving toward him. "What now?" he growled in frustration.

The closer the vehicle came, the harder his heart pounded. Stephanie's Jeep pulled up in front of him. He groaned, his hands clamping tightly around the barrel of the rifle. She opened the door and climbed out.

"I couldn't leave," she said, walking up to the porch. "I had a feeling. A feeling that something bad was about to happen."

What she felt was the wolf beneath her skin. Her body preparing for the change. "There's nothing wrong, Stephanie," he said, trying to keep the panic from his voice. "If you leave right now, you should be able to reach a hotel before it gets too late."

"I had planned on driving through the night." She took a step closer and glanced at the rifle in his hands. "What are you doing?"

"Cleaning my gun," he answered. "Just passing time."

"You told me once that you're not the hunting type. Why do you need a gun?"

"I don't need it," he answered. "I'm just cleaning it!"

She looked a little taken aback by his impatient explanation. Rick immediately regretted losing his temper, but dammit, she was supposed to be gone. Safely away from him and the nasty business he must conclude.

"You should be careful," she said. "People get killed every day messing around with guns. Is that what happened to your brother?"

"No," he answered, but didn't bother to elaborate. He didn't see any way for this situation to end but badly. Sparing her feelings wasn't anything he could do at the moment. "I told you to leave earlier," he reminded. "I've already taken care of everything with Hugh. You're no longer needed here."

Her bottom lip trembled. He wanted to jump up and take her in his arms. Rick forced himself to remain seated, his expression blank.

"Or wanted," she said, lifting her chin. "I thought you cared about me."

The expression of hurt on her face was almost his undoing. He wanted to tell her she hadn't been wrong about him, or what he felt for her, but then she wouldn't leave. In order to be kind, he had to be cruel. That was nature's way.

"I cared about having a good time," he said. "And now the good time is over. Get in your Jeep and leave."

Rifle in hand, he rose and walked into the cabin, shutting the door. He closed his eyes and waited—silently begged her to obey him. His skin had started to itch. His gums hurt. The sound of her vehicle starting nearly made his knees buckle. She would probably hate him from this day forward, but that was just as well, too. She'd be more willing to find someone else and get on with her life.

Worried that time had run out, Rick lifted the rifle, placing the barrel against his heart. His finger found the trigger. He said another short prayer and started to squeeze. The cabin door burst open.

"Rick?" Stephanie whispered. "Look at my eyes. I

glanced in the rearview mirror and caught a glimpse of myself. My eyes are glowing!"

And they were, as he suspected his were. She suddenly took a step back. Her glittering gaze moved from the rifle to his eyes.

"W-what's going on, Rick? What's happening to me . . . to you?"

"I don't have time to explain," he said. "Just go. Get away as fast as you can. I promise, you'll be fine soon."

Her hand flew to her mouth. "Why do my teeth hurt? I feel strange. My skin itches."

"Go!" he shouted.

When she just stood there, staring at him, he swore. Rick lifted the rifle to his chest.

"Rick?" Her voice shook. "What are you doing?"

"I'm saving you. I love you, Stephanie."

She moved faster than any animal he'd ever seen—practically flew across the room. The slight force of her weight was enough to knock him off balance.

"No!" she screamed, wrestling the rifle from him with superhuman strength. "I won't let you do this! I love you, Rick."

"Then kill me," he ordered. "It's the only way to save yourself. Don't you see what I am?" He reached out, showing her the hair forming on his arms. "I'm a monster! I'm a werewolf!"

She backed away from him, still clutching the rifle. "T-there's no such thing as werewolves. You're just sick. I'm sick. We're hallucinating."

He opened his mouth, showing her his canine fangs. "Does this look like a dream? It's a nightmare, Stephanie. A living hell I have to save you from. I bit you, remember? That first night? It was me you saved. I'm the black wolf!"

She shook her head. "No. This can't be happening. It's not possible. People can't turn into wolves."

"Look at your hands!" he shouted.

Her gaze lowered to her hands, clutched around the rifle in a death grip. He saw the fur there, blond, but thick. Her gaze widened. A whimper of alarm escaped her throat.

"If you kill me, the hair will disappear, Stephanie. It's the only way to break the curse. The only way to spare yourself the hell I've gone through during the past three years."

She lifted her terrified gaze. But more than horror showed in her eyes. "But what will happen to you?"

Pain ripped through him, made him double over. "I can die in peace," he bit out. "Do it, Stephanie!"

"No!" She threw the rifle down. "I've lost everyone I ever loved. I don't want to lose you, too."

Even through the pain, her words settled over him like a healing balm. She loved him despite the monster he was—regardless that her own soul lay in jeopardy. Her heart was truly pure. She loved unconditionally. And so did he. With a growl of pain tinged with joy, he sprang on the rifle she'd dropped to the floor. Rick had the weapon in his hands, pointed at his heart before she could react. He squeezed the trigger, and the explosion echoed off the wall along with her scream.

Stephanie fell to the floor beside him. He lay very still, his eyes staring up at the ceiling. The glow began to fade from them.

"No!" she screamed. Grabbing his collar, she tried to make him sit up. He was a dead weight. A dead man. Before her eyes, the thick fur that covered her hands disappeared. She felt her teeth retract, become normal. But nothing could stop her heart from breaking.

She buried her face against his neck. "I would have loved you anyway," she whispered. "I would have become an animal if it meant staying by your side. I love you, Rick. Please don't leave me. I don't want to be alone again."

Tears ran down her cheeks. She threw the rifle aside and snuggled her body on top of him, hoping her warmth would penetrate the coldness she felt creeping into his limbs. This man, monster or saint, had sacrificed himself for her. He'd done so to save her soul. To spare her the same pain he had endured. His love was true. The everlasting kind. The kind she'd been searching for all her life.

She held him tighter, wishing she felt the beat of his heart against her own, wishing for all the tomorrows they would never share together.

"Come back to me," she whispered. "Come back to me, Rick."

A strong current of heat raced through her, almost as if she'd exploded inside. She tried to rise, but felt merged with Rick's body. She felt dizzy. A loud ringing noise started in her ears. She groaned. . . . no, *he* groaned.

Stephanie's head shot up. She glanced down at him. He gasped. His eyes fluttered open. They were blue. And they were not glowing.

"Stephanie?" he whispered. "What happened?"

"Rick," she sobbed his name. "You came back to me."

His brows furrowed, and then he tensed. "It didn't work. Get away from me." He struggled, pushing her away from him. He reached for the rifle, but Stephanie grabbed it first.

"It's all right, Rick. Look at me! Look at yourself!"

He stared at her, glanced down at the smooth skin on her hands, then lifted his own. There was no thick fur there. He rose, moving to the bedroom. Stephanie scrambled up and followed him. He stared into the mirror at his image.

"Is it really over?" he whispered. "Did you save me?"

Stephanie stepped up behind him. "I don't think I saved you. I think you saved yourself. One selfless act of love made your heart pure again, made you reborn."

"The old woman." He turned to her. "She said saving you would save me."

"Y-you spoke to her?" Stephanie stammered.

He clasped her shoulders. "Don't you understand now? It was me she warned you about. I thought she might know for certain how to break the curse, so I hunted her down."

"Then she never meant to hurt me," Stephanie said. "She only wanted to help."

He stared deep into her eyes. "People aren't always what they appear to be on the surface. Surely you've learned that tonight."

She leaned forward and kissed him. "I learned something more important tonight. I learned the true meaning of sacrifice. You gave your life for me."

"I love you. I couldn't let what happened to me happen to you."

"I love you, too," she whispered. "And I would have withstood anything to stay with you." Stephanie took his hand and led him through the house, outside where the moon hung full in the sky. As if awestruck, he stared up at the heavens.

"This is the first time in three years I've seen a full moon and known it was just a celestial body in the distance."

Since he looked as if he might fall, she made him sit on one of the porch steps, then sat beside him.

"What will you do now?" she asked.

He shook his head. "I'm not sure. I need to find my brother."

She turned to him, surprised. "I thought he was killed in a hunting accident."

"Attacked by a wolf," he explained. "The same one that bit me. He's a werewolf, too. If I can find him, I can tell him how to break the curse. All he has to do is find true love."

Her heart melted. "Where is he?"

"Canada."

Smiling at him, she said, "Canada has great wildlife. Lots to film."

He took her hand in his. "Will you come with me?"

"Anywhere," she promised. "As long as we're together."

His mouth moved toward hers; then he paused. "I just had an idea. We'll take the old woman with us. She has the sight and can use her abilities to make finding Jason easier."

Stephanie wasn't listening. She'd become lost in the depths of his eyes, in the wonderful sense that she'd finally come home again. She leaned closer to him. Their lips met in a promise neither time nor curses would ever threaten again. They were mates, would be for life, and they had work ahead of them. Wolves to save, and lost souls to rescue. And somewhere along the way, a life of their own to begin.